Praise for Emma Wildes

"Of all the authors I've read, I believe Emma Wildes to be my hands-down favorite. . . . Ms. Wildes has once again shown her ability to present new variations of romance in all of its infinite forms. Be prepared to feel your passions grow as you read the beautifully written love scenes."
—Just Erotic Romance Reviews

"Emma Wildes has an amazing flair for taking what could be considered controversial subject matter and turning it into a beautiful love story that has the reader cheering for the characters . . . it is a truly rare and remarkable talent."
—Euro-Reviews

"Unique, masterfully written, and engaging story lines coupled with fascinating characters are what every reader can expect from Emma Wildes. For fans of historical and Regency romance, look no further. Ms. Wildes possesses a beautiful, flowing writing style that t̶⋯⋯⋯rts her readers to another time as the si̶g̶h̶⋯⋯⋯⋯⋯e to life around them. My e̶⋯⋯⋯⋯⋯⋯⋯⋯ime I read one of her b̶⋯⋯⋯⋯⋯⋯⋯oLips Reviews

"Chock-f̶⋯⋯⋯⋯⋯⋯⋯⋯⋯unforgettable characters⋯⋯⋯⋯⋯⋯⋯⋯
—Romance Junkies

" 'Sexy and enchanting' aptly describes Wildes's latest . . . this is delightful reading from beginning to end."
—*Romantic Times* (4 stars)

"Erotic romance at its finest. Emma Wildes skillfully combines an intriguing plot, vibrant characters, and toe-curling sex. . . . Perfection."
—Fallen Angel Reviews

An Indecent Proposition

Emma Wildes

A SIGNET ECLIPSE BOOK

SIGNET ECLIPSE
Published by New American Library, a division of
Penguin Group (USA) Inc., 375 Hudson Street,
New York, New York 10014, USA
Penguin Group (Canada), 90 Eglinton Avenue East, Suite 700, Toronto,
Ontario M4P 2Y3, Canada (a division of Pearson Penguin Canada Inc.)
Penguin Books Ltd., 80 Strand, London WC2R 0RL, England
Penguin Ireland, 25 St. Stephen's Green, Dublin 2,
Ireland (a division of Penguin Books Ltd.)
Penguin Group (Australia), 250 Camberwell Road, Camberwell, Victoria 3124,
Australia (a division of Pearson Australia Group Pty. Ltd.)
Penguin Books India Pvt. Ltd., 11 Community Centre, Panchsheel Park,
New Delhi - 110 017, India
Penguin Group (NZ), 67 Apollo Drive, Rosedale, North Shore 0632,
New Zealand (a division of Pearson New Zealand Ltd.)
Penguin Books (South Africa) (Pty.) Ltd., 24 Sturdee Avenue,
Rosebank, Johannesburg 2196, South Africa

Penguin Books Ltd., Registered Offices:
80 Strand, London WC2R 0RL, England

First published by Signet Eclipse, an imprint of New American Library,
a division of Penguin Group (USA) Inc.

First Printing, April 2009
10 9 8 7 6 5 4 3 2

Printed in the United States of America

For Chris, for all the times you have taken the trouble to not disturb me at my desk. Flowers are romantic, a bottle of wine is nice, but *that* is the definition of thoughtful. So, you see, I did notice.

ACKNOWLEDGMENTS

I'd like to extend my heartfelt thanks to Barbara Poelle. You are fantastic in every way possible. Thanks also to Becky Vinter for being such a gracious and talented editor. You two fabulous ladies made this process a joy.

Prologue

The horses thundered down the stretch amid the roars of the crowd and moments later Nicholas Manning, the sixth Duke of Rothay, won again with his spectacular black. His stable of racers, in fact, had swept the day so far.

Not much of a surprise.

There was no doubt about it; the man had a magic touch when it came to horses, and, rumors were, even more skill when it came to women.

It was easy to believe. Caroline Wynn watched him head through the stands toward his private box, his legendary smile flashing at the well wishes from friends. The duke had a particular brand of flagrant handsomeness that coupled stark masculinity with splendid classical bone structure and dramatic dark coloring. He was also tall and athletically built, and moved with natural ease as he went up the stairs, no doubt looking forward to celebrating his victories. He was dressed with casual elegance in a navy tailored coat, buff breeches, and polished boots, the ebony silk of his hair contrasting with the dazzling white of his perfectly tied cravat.

"Rothay certainly looks pleased with himself," Melinda Cassat murmured, fanning herself vigorously against the late-afternoon heat. Small dark brown curls moved around her face with each flick of her wrist. Where they sat was shaded by a small striped awning, but there wasn't so much as a breeze. The cloudless sky was a clear, deep cobalt blue.

"He won, so why shouldn't he be pleased?" Caroline watched his tall form disappear into the box with a faint quiver in the pit of her stomach.

What am I doing?

"It isn't like he needs the money. The man is rich as Croesus." Melinda pushed a tendril of wayward hair off her neck and pursed her mouth. "Of course, betting on a horse race is far less scandalous than the latest rumor of his escapades. Have you heard about it?"

Glad the warmth of the sun could account for the flush in her cheeks, Caroline lied outright. "No. Whatever are you talking about?"

An avid gossip, Melinda looked delighted at the question. She leaned forward, her brown eyes narrowed conspiratorially. Her plump bosom heaved as she took a quick breath. "Well, it seems . . . or so they say, you know . . . that the bonny duke and his close friend Lord Manderville, who, as you've heard, is heir to his father's reputation as a rake of the first order, have made some outrageous bet on which one of them is the best lover."

"Really?" Caroline wore what she hoped was a very bland expression.

Her friend's face was alight with excitement and intrigue. "Can you believe it?"

"Are you certain it is true? I mean, my dear, this is London, and this is the *haut ton*. Not every rumor is gospel. You know as well as I that most of them are patent falsehoods or at least exaggerations."

"Yes, but I understand they aren't denying it. The wager is duly recorded in the books at White's and the bets on who will win are now piling up in record quantity. They're ever treading the edge of scandal, but the two of them have truly outdone themselves this time."

Caroline watched the jockeys mount up for the last race. "How on earth could anyone prove such an absurd thing? At the very least the outcome must be subjective. After all, if they are placing a bet on which one of them is the best lover, who is the judge in all this?"

"Well, my dear, that's the truly scandalous part. They need an impartial critic. All of fashionable society is speculating on who she will be."

"That's a bit barbaric, isn't it? She would have to agree to be intimate with . . . well, both of them, I suppose. Good heavens."

Melinda looked at her in open amusement. "I would expect you to say that, since you are so prudish. I don't know if it is barbaric precisely, but it is certainly beyond the pale, even for such celebrated rogues. However, even more bets are being made over how quickly they can find someone suitable to consent to sample what each one has to offer. It's madly wicked, but two of the most handsome men in England would do their utmost to pleasure the chosen party. Imagine what's in store for the lady who agrees."

Well, she was quite aware of her cool and standoffish reputation, but still, being called prudish made Caroline feel defensive. "I am not exactly some withered-up old matron. I can understand why a woman would succumb to a handsome, charming man capable of effortless seduction. Certainly those two would qualify, as they have reputedly practiced enough."

"Indeed they have, and I have never implied you are old or withered—quite the opposite." Her friend sighed with dramatic emphasis. "But you are not very approachable, Caroline. I know you have put up shields since your marriage and Edward's death, but quite honestly, you need to let yourself live again. If you wanted, half of London would be prostrate at your feet, darling. You are young and beautiful."

"Thank you."

"It's true. Men would be lining up with flowers and sonnets. There's no reason for you to languish in unwedded solitude."

"I don't *wish* to marry again." It was completely true. Once had been quite enough. Once had been more than enough.

"Not every man is like Edward."

Abstractly Caroline watched the horses line up and heard the pistol retort before they lunged forward. She certainly hoped not every man was like her late husband, she thought as the magnificent animals instinctively shot forward, for soon the rakish duke would be reading her note.

Chapter One

"This is interesting." Nicholas muttered the words and reached for the brandy decanter, dashing a large measure in the crystal snifter at his elbow. He plunked down the bottle and scanned the piece of vellum in his hand again. A return to London after an exacting but triumphant day of the sport of kings had him in a fine mood, mellowed by both victory and the resulting celebration. A retreat to his study seemed to be in order. It was in many ways his sanctuary, even if he did spend an inordinate amount of time working there.

It reminded him of his father, and perhaps it was because of a maudlin side of him he wouldn't admit to anyone, but he hadn't changed a thing. The same rug covered the polished floor, faded on one side from the sun slanting through the mullioned window, and the desk was just as cluttered. Books in the oak cases set next to the fireplace produced the familiar musty odor of gently decaying leather and yellowing paper.

"What's interesting? Something to do with the races?" Across from him, Derek Drake, the Earl of Manderville, lifted a dark blond brow and settled lower in his seat in a comfortable sprawl. As usual, Derek was dressed in the latest fashion, the tailored clothes fitting his lean body to perfection, polished Hessians crossed as he lounged in his chair. His fine-boned face reflected only mild curiosity. "Nick, your horses outdid themselves today. Surely that isn't a damned surprise. Not that I mind. I made a tidy sum on that last race on your word Satan was fit. Thanks for the tip."

"You're welcome, but it isn't that." The dismissive attitude wasn't because Nicholas didn't care about the races—his horses were his passion and he was competitive to the point of it being a personal flaw—but the neat script on the note in front of him had him intrigued. He glanced up and extended the piece of vellum with two fingers. "Look at this, Derek."

His companion took the folded piece of paper, his interest obviously sharpening as he read the words. Like Nicholas, Derek read the neat script twice and glanced up. "Well now, this sounds promising, doesn't it?"

"It isn't our first offer." Nicholas took a drink, the French brandy like warmed silk in his mouth. He'd paid a small fortune for it, but unless smuggled in, it was impossible to find, and he voted the cost worth it. "But I admit I like this lady's direct approach."

"A challenge to a challenge. Yes, inventive. I admire her already. It would be nice, though, to know who she is." Derek's mouth quirked and he read out loud, " 'If you promise complete discretion and wish an impartial judge for your ridiculous bet, I will assist you. Be forewarned, my experience so far in the matters between men and women has not impressed me. If you are interested in a meeting to discuss this matter, I am amiable to pursuing it.' "

It was clever, Nicholas thought, to use a taunt of previous sexual disappointment to pique their interest. The lady was correct, if he allowed himself to admit it; the wager *was* ridiculous, made when they were both more than a little foxed.

"A little jab of an insult in there, I notice," Nicholas commented with amusement. "A proposition with an edge. Our mystery lady has some spunk. That appeals to me."

"Does it?" Derek sent him a speculative look.

They tended to view females with the same carnal interest tempered by a decided tendency for emotional detachment. Sexual conquest was a game, and they were both seasoned players.

Nicholas didn't elaborate. He was feeling increasing pressure to marry, from both society and his family. It was expected—he'd always known it was expected—but admitting his reluctance to find a wife meant acknowledging some truths about himself he wasn't yet ready to face.

All men made mistakes. His memorable one was catastrophic in nature, but then again, the catastrophe was his alone, caused by youth and inexperience, and he had made up for it since in every way possible. That apparently included wild wagers of the most outré sort. He remarked with studied casualness, "Of course. An adventurous woman is always appealing in the bedroom, don't you agree?"

"I agree that if we go through with this, our reputations will hardly suffer any more than they have already, so why not?"

The word *embarrassed* didn't exist in Nicholas's vocabulary. He had realized long ago that gossip was an inevitable part of London society and staying out of scandal took entirely too much effort for little gain. However, he and Derek both agreed they would have done better to not actually write down the contest and make such a large bet on the outcome. Now all the *haut ton* was atwitter.

He gave Manderville a lazy smile. "There is no way we can possibly not rise to the bait, is there? So far, the offers to jump into the bet—and our beds—have been made mostly by ladies of questionable reputations, who wish to share in our notoriety. This one sounds a little different. She wants anonymity, it seems."

"I have no objection to an experienced woman, but I agree, the secrecy she requests is a unique angle." Derek tapped the piece of paper with a finger, his long legs outstretched. "She might be perfect as long as she isn't unattractive or some unmarried young miss angling for a fortune and title."

"Amen to that." The very thought of a young ingenue becoming involved in the bet was out of the question. The wager had been merely an amusing diversion; it had just gotten a little out of hand. In retrospect, the third bottle of claret had been a bad idea that night, but Derek especially had seemed bent on drinking himself into oblivion.

Now that Nicholas considered it, that was a bit out of character. He couldn't put his finger on it, but he had a feeling something was wrong. Derek's usual good humor had seemed forced lately. His easygoing, effortless charm was one of the reasons women found him so attractive, but he'd been both subdued and distracted for the past several months at least.

"We don't have to do this, you know," Nicholas reminded his companion, watching his face to gauge his reaction, the glow of the brandy making him feel mellow and introspective. "It was an impulsive jest between two friends and we tend to be a bit competitive with each other, which is no secret."

"Backing out, are we, Nick?" Derek asked in sardonic reproof. Blond, tall, with eyes the color of an azure sky and almost angelic good looks, he bore the antithesis of Nicholas's own dark coloring. "Who could blame you, since you are going to lose?"

There it was again, the uncharacteristic restive dig.

It worked. Nicholas snorted at the smug look on his friend's face. "What makes you think so? The bevy of insipid ladies constantly in your bed? Let me remind you that quantity does not substitute for quality, Manderville."

"If you are trying to pretend to be less promiscuous, Rothay, sell it to someone else."

He wasn't, actually, and he had to stifle an irritated response. Promiscuous, that is, no matter what the rumors were about his private life. Nicholas did enjoy women—but despite his reputation, he was selective and tried to be discreet. For that matter, he knew Derek wasn't as bad as the backhanded whispers painted him either, and his inclinations were much the same. Lately, he hadn't even heard about Derek pursuing anyone. If he wasn't celibate, he was certainly keeping a low profile over the matter.

Maybe that's where the impulsive wager had come from.

Derek's challenge and his own response, both due to mutual restlessness caused by . . . well, he wasn't sure. Too much inner searching wasn't good for the soul.

Not a tarnished one like his.

In their defense, at least most casual affairs were a pleasant understanding between two parties that did not involve deeper feeling. Though Nicholas doubted society would believe it, he thought marriage should be based on more than a female's bloodlines and her ability to bear a child of the appropriate lineage. The fact he was a romantic at heart was something he kept to himself. Not because it was an unfashionable attitude—though it was—but because it was private. God knew he'd had little enough of privacy in his life due to his aristocratic upbringing and the prominence of his family and title.

Then he'd just made matters worse by accepting this outlandish wager and making himself the focus of more public attention.

Nicholas rubbed his jaw. "I must be more bored than I thought," he admitted, "to even consider bedding a woman with a scorecard in her hand."

"We both suffer the malaise, then." Manderville shot him a cynical look. "But we did embark on this. Let's look at it this way: if the note is correct, we can do this woman a favor by changing her mind about sexual pleasure."

"Like some charitable act? That's an interesting way to justify the situation."

"Keep in mind, we didn't contact her. She came to us."

Well, *that* was true.

"So I take it you think we should reply in the affirmative and arrange the meeting she wants?" He waved his empty glass.

Derek nodded. "I cannot wait to meet the young lady."

"What makes you think she's young? For that matter, maybe we need to decide just what we're going to say if neither of us finds her attractive. That could be a sticky point. Desire is a necessary component of being a competent lover, after all."

"True enough. I doubt I would acquit myself well with a homely old hag. There is one thing a male cannot fake and that's sexual arousal."

Nicholas had to agree on that point. Though he didn't believe a woman had to be a dazzling beauty to catch his interest, part of sexual chemistry was mutual attraction.

The evening had settled into a pattern of brilliant stars and a few high-flying clouds, the dim moonlight visible outside the window. In a lazy movement, he replenished his drink and set the decanter down close enough for his guest to do the same. Slowly, he said, "I think our worries on that score are unfounded. I speculate she's beautiful, for the tone of her note shows a certain confidence that we'll approve."

Derek picked up the missive once more and glanced over it again. "I think you're right." Blue eyes showed a tinge of his usual teasing humor, but his mouth looked a little tight. "Now I truly cannot wait to meet her. Will you write the response, or shall I? We also need to figure out an appropriate place to meet, since she demands utter secrecy."

"Let's let the lady decide. She is the one who wants to keep her identity from being known."

"Fair enough," Derek agreed with a lazy smile.

"We ought to have rules, if she proves to be the right person."

"I suppose we should, though we are adding a whole new dimension to the term *notorious*, you realize, Nick."

Yes, he did. What *were* they doing? Both of them posturing, pretending the bet was serious in any way. In his heart, immune to sentiment or not as it might be rumored, he didn't believe either of them really was vain or shallow enough to enter such a ludicrous contest. But for whatever reason, Derek was most determinedly lighthearted about it, and on his own part, he approached seduction as he approached estate matters, political issues, and social situations: with cool, calculating assessment.

Emotion had no place in business, politics, or a man's sexual affairs. A certain part of him wished it did, but that part had been scalded once already by harsh reality.

Charm, well, of course. He was Rothay. He liked women. Liked the soft yielding of their entrancing bodies, the music of female laughter, the whispered heated words exchanged in bed during a passionate interlude, the lazy aftermath of carnal culmination. In his estimation, there was nothing like that particular breathy sigh a woman gave when you were deep inside her, and the bite of her nails, just so, on your bare shoulders.

But love, no. Satisfying his body was one thing, his heart another.

He just wasn't a man to make that mistake twice. Sexual prowess, now, that was not a problem. Especially since the death of his father when he was seventeen, he'd courted notoriety and found it. Without thinking, he murmured, "'All is ephemeral—fame and the famous as well.'"

Derek gave him a measured look. "Quoting Marcus Aurelius, are we? May I inquire as to the introspective mood?"

"No." The answer was too clipped and his old friend knew him too well. The last thing he wanted was to dredge up ghosts from the past. He took a long leisurely sip from his glass, reclining in his chair, and amended, "I'm looking forward to this, whatever our motives."

Chapter Two

"I repeat the question: why were you there, madam?"

The query, said so coldly, made Caroline's mouth tighten in annoyance. To her dismay, her dead husband's cousin the current Lord Wynn had called, and though she had avoided seeing him for weeks, there hadn't seemed much choice but to finally receive him. Since the family resemblance was strong, it was always a small shock to come face-to-face with Franklin, as if a ghost were materializing in front of her.

A most unwelcome specter at that.

They sat in her formal drawing room, the tall windows open to the warm late-morning air, the elegant combination of cream and gold furnishings reflecting her own taste, the redecoration something she had done after Edward's death. Brocade settees, two graceful chairs by the fireplace imported from Italy, several picturesque watercolor paintings on the silk-covered walls. A precious and very expensive urn she'd commissioned held a bouquet of various flowers from the back garden, the scent a wash of floral delight, especially on such a lovely day. Eradicating anything that reminded her of Edward's presence was a pleasure. He would have loathed the femininity of the small, delicate personal touches, but as far as she could tell, he had loathed quite a lot of things that were not his specific idea.

Franklin had taken in the new decor with a twist of his mouth and a cold glitter in his pale eyes. *The town house*

should have been mine, that look said, and the cost of the re-
furbishment came from the fortune he thought to inherit.
Not that Caroline cared, for it was her money and if she
wished to wipe her husband's taste from the house room by
room, she would do so.

"I went to see the horses run, naturally, my lord. Luckily
it was a lovely day, so I very much enjoyed it." Caroline
kept her tone cool and detached, trying to deflect his interest in her social activities. "I'm sorry I was out when you
called last week. I fear I have been rather busy lately."

"Last week, the week before that . . . yes, I've noticed. I
do hope you realize that going unescorted to a place such as
the races is not advisable. It is, as always, a very male-
dominated crowd. Proper ladies do not roam around without
a chaperone. The next time you wish to attend such a public
function, contact me and I will make the arrangements to attend at your side."

*Dear God, he looks so like Edward with those same cold
blue eyes. . . .*

He had a face like a hawk, all sharp angles and a slightly
hooked nose, and his hair was thick and dark. His cheekbones slashed down to a thin-lipped mouth that rarely
smiled. In his mid-thirties and now titled, Franklin was considered very eligible. She supposed he was handsome, but
his resemblance to Edward, both physically and in his demeanor, was too unsettling. Heavy-lidded eyes regarded her
with his usual chilly appraisal.

It was like being ogled by a bird of prey, she thought in
distaste. No, a vulture, ready to pick the flesh from her
bones if she didn't protect herself.

She stiffened at his tone and the presumption he could
dictate anything about her life, much less lecture her on propriety. "I went with Melinda Cassat and her husband, so I
was hardly alone. You needn't worry about my welfare in
any case."

Franklin leaned forward a fraction, dapper in clothes
more suited to a courtier than a gentleman making a morning call. Lace bunched at his throat and the edges of his

sleeves. "Ah, but let's not forget you are my widowed cousin, so worry I must."

"Pray, do not concern yourself." She wanted nothing more than to put any association with the Wynn family firmly behind her, and Franklin always made her uneasy. If she had to guess, his interest in her welfare had little to do with her person and everything to do with how much money Edward had left her. Luckily the will had been able to stand up to his protests. The entire affair had been yet another lesson in how hard-won independence could be.

"Your reentry into society is of infinite concern to me." His emotionless gaze seemed to bore right through her.

"I cannot think why it would be. I live a quiet life for the most part. I am gradually beginning to accept some invitations, but—"

"Perhaps I should be consulted on what events you attend."

Annoyance deepened into something more. "I'm a widow," she reminded him in stiff reproof. Then, since he was the one who had called and he was the one who insisted on making presumptions, she added unwisely, "With my own fortune."

It was his turn to be irritated, the subject a sore one. It took him a moment, but he visibly conquered the flare of anger. "I realize full well, my dear, the state of your finances. I also know you are young and still very marriageable. Unscrupulous gentlemen do exist and it is my duty to protect you."

Whatever Caroline might have said next probably would have been rash and ill-advised, but luckily she was able to bite her tongue. She glanced around at the pale walls and luxuriant fabrics, which she felt were indicative of her independence. She did wish the return note from Rothay wasn't currently clutched in her rather damp hand. She could have maintained more self-possession in Franklin's company if the damning piece of vellum hadn't been burning a hole in her palm. Her butler had brought it in at the same time as announcing her unwanted visitor, and Caroline was desperately curious to get rid of Franklin and read Rothay's response. It felt like a glowing-hot coal she should throw as far away from her person as possible.

If Franklin knew what it was, he'd smear her name, and with great pleasure. She had no illusions about what he was capable of doing if given the chance.

"Melinda and her husband were quite adequate chaperones and no one approached me. Not having attended the races before, I wasn't sure what to expect. I thought it all quite exciting."

It had been, from the well-dressed crowd, the exuberant cheers, the thundering glory of the sleek horses, to the moment she'd taken a deep breath as she'd seen the Duke of Rothay and Lord Manderville, a contrast of dark male satanic beauty and golden Apollonian good looks. Alike, yet so very different physically, both so at ease with their notoriety, so comfortably above the whispers and furtive looks, as if they were laws unto themselves and just didn't notice the swivel of heads or the furtive whispers behind gloved hands.

What would Melinda do if she knew the return note from Rothay sat—unread at this time—in her possession? Or worse, what would she think if she realized that Caroline, of all people, had approached the infamous duke and his equally renowned friend?

It was an easy question to answer. Melinda wouldn't believe it. No one would.

She wasn't sure she believed it herself.

"I am delighted you enjoyed yourself, my dear, but you know I am always at your disposal." Franklin settled back in his chair as if he intended to stay a while, crossing his elegantly clad legs at the ankle.

The slight suggestive tone to his voice made her stifle a shiver. Disposal. Hardly a sexual word, but something in the way he enunciated it gave it a lewd insinuation. It was hard not to wonder if he wasn't like Edward in more ways than just his physical appearance. Not that he would ever bother to court her—she had no illusions in that quarter. He wanted control of the inheritance he thought should be rightfully his, and she stood between him and his goal, hence his solicitous interest.

Caroline nodded, but it was a dubious inclination of her head to cover her revulsion. In her bitter experience, the Wynn family had a tenacious edge that was hard to disregard, so a direct confrontation was not a good idea. "I thank you for the offer."

"I still look forward to a sojourn in the country so we can discuss matters like this at our leisure. My mother will chaperone, naturally."

Though Franklin had told her she could use the house if she wished, she'd declined to accept anything from him, even hospitality.

"Perhaps someday." She was acutely aware of the missive sitting next to her on the fabric of her chair, her hand settled over it in a casual manner to cover it as much as possible.

What does it say?

How difficult it was to sit there, composed, with the complete cool serenity that made her seem so unapproachable to most importunate gentlemen.

The outward image was fine.

The inner truth a bit harder to face.

Franklin persisted, "As for London, I can modestly say that I can advise you on what invitations to accept or decline. After all, I have more experience."

Was the room too warm or was it just her? Caroline fought the urge to fan herself and smiled instead. "I so admire your ability to move through society with such utter ease, my lord."

"Another advantageous marriage would help you along as well." He lifted a heavy brow, the arrogance of his implication like the jab of a needle.

He wanted her money. She had a disgusted feeling he coveted her body as well, but on the pain of death, she'd never, *ever* agree to that idea.

He didn't need to know the reticence she felt in public, and in private actually, was something she was trying to overcome. With the help of one very handsome duke and one equally attractive young earl.

Maybe.

It felt like an eternity before he glanced at the ormolu clock on the mantel and got to his feet. "My apologies, but I have an appointment. I'll call for you next week. If the weather is pleasant, perhaps we can plan a small outing."

She'd rather be run over by a herd of stampeding elephants, but she somehow managed a banal smile. "Perhaps."

Caroline waited until she heard the rattle of the departing carriage before she carefully lifted the envelope that had been delivered.

Even the duke's handwriting was arrogant, she thought, staring at the missive for a moment before taking a deep breath and opening it. She removed the single sheet of paper inside with fingers that shook in a betraying manner as she held it and read the answer to her imprudent proposal.

He was probably going to lose the infamous wager, but the best way to conceal a broken heart was with foolish male bravado, or at least that's how *he* was dealing with it.

The carriage rumbled along Upper Brook Street and Derek Drake stared out the window, not seeing the view, but instead absorbed in his thoughts.

They weren't the most pleasant, unfortunately. Mostly they involved visions of Annabel—no, a correction was necessary: soon-to-be Lady Hyatt—in the arms of her new husband. Naked, in his embrace, his mouth on hers, her golden hair gleaming across the bed linens as they moved together in an age-old rhythm, her slim legs spread wide as her lover thrust inside her willing body . . .

Well, it was certainly productive to picture *that*, he chided himself morosely, sinking lower against the squabs and letting out a frustrated breath. Torturing himself was not helping matters. It was what landed him into his current predicament. The fact he'd gotten so deep in his cups the night he and Rothay had started their adolescent debate didn't surprise him, and maybe even the public bet had been a way to strike back at Annie for the announcement that had appeared in the paper.

> *The Honourable Thomas Drake wishes to announce the formal engagement of Miss Annabel Reid to Lord Alfred Hyatt. The nuptials will take place four months hence. . . .*

Derek hadn't been able to read any further.

It had hurt. Bloody hell, seeing it there in stark print had *hurt*. More than even he expected, though his uncle Thomas had already told him of the offer for her hand and her acceptance along with his own opinion it was a suitable match.

Yet the slice of the pain as Derek sat there and stared at the bold lettering of the public announcement and felt the implications settle into his soul had opened a raw, bleeding wound.

So to improve things, he thought with an inner wince, he'd gotten thoroughly foxed and decided to worsen the reputation Annabel already found repugnant by making a challenge that now had London buzzing with speculation. It didn't help that he and Nicholas had a past history of competition in everything from academics to athletics to—of course—women. Part of it was just an innate aspect to both their personalities, part of it the result of similar backgrounds. They'd inherited their wealth and titles young, and along with them both the freedom and constraints that came with the legacies. Their friendship had been immediate and natural, like two brothers meeting face-to-face for the first time and recognizing each other.

It had spurred on the nonsensical debate of the other evening. Nicholas had his own demons he held close. Derek was well aware his friend had a less-than-happy experience that kept him guarded, no matter how charming he might seem on the outside. Nick didn't talk about it, and Derek didn't ask questions about the near-disastrous brush with romance that revealed itself as calculated avarice rather than deep feeling on the part of the woman Nicholas thought he would marry. It was an unspoken agreement between them not to discuss the matter, not violated for the ten years of their acquaintance.

They were, after all, very alike.

Now it seemed to be Derek's turn to burn in hell.

No doubt Annabel was even less fond of him than ever. *If* that was even possible. Why was it he'd never realized he was in love with her until it was too late?

Because he was a damned fool, of course. She loved someone else. Lord Alfred Hyatt was a decent sort as far as he could tell, which only made matters worse. If she were marrying a cad, he could reasonably voice an objection, but she wasn't, so he couldn't, and she would never listen to his advice anyway.

Why should she? He was an expert on impermanence, not marriage.

"My lord?"

The voice roused him from his abstraction and he realized the vehicle had come to a halt and his driver stood there waiting, the door ajar. The young man gave a discreet cough.

"Sorry." Derek clambered out, a rueful smile on his face. "Drank a bit this afternoon," he said unnecessarily, wondering why he was offering an explanation to a servant. Probably because he had no idea how long he might have been sitting there in morose contemplation. He went up the steps to his town house, nodded his thanks to the footman who opened the door, and headed straight for his study.

Unlike the cluttered room at the sprawling Mayfair mansion the dukes of Rothay had called home for several centuries, Derek's sanctuary was neat and organized. All his papers were stacked on one corner of his desk, the new correspondence in the middle of the blotter, his favorite whiskey in a decanter on a tray to the side. The room smelled like beeswax and faintly of tobacco, and usually he found comfort in the paneled walls, and the oil painting of the Berkshire countryside above the fireplace was one of his favorites. In his current state of emotional unrest, even the bucolic impression of the rolling downs did nothing for his restless spirit.

He sank into the chair behind his desk and eyed his unopened letters with a jaded look. On top sat a plain envelope with no seal, only his name written in neat script on the front. Curious, he plucked it off the pile and opened it.

> *My Lord Manderville:*
> *Meet me at the Flower and Swine in Holborn at ten o'clock this evening. The private parlor will be reserved for our discussion.*

Ah yes, the damned bet.

No signature, but he recognized the writing from the note he'd read earlier. Well, the lady was prompt, he'd give her that. It was an easy assumption to guess Nicholas had gotten a similar missive.

He picked up the letter opener with his family crest emblazoned on the metal handle, and twirled it idly between his fingers.

Fine, he thought with fierce resignation. Why not attend? Why not do his best to prove his sexual prowess? At the least, he'd have a distraction from his current state of apathetic self-pity, plus be able to entertain himself with a warm, willing woman.

If he closed his eyes, maybe he could even pretend he was making love to Annabel. With that strategy he might win after all.

Chapter Three

The inn was small, tucked into an East End neighborhood Caroline hadn't visited before. The disreputable exterior had given her pause, but it was perfect for her purposes, as the few bleary patrons in the smoky, dank taproom paid her little attention. The innkeeper had shown her to a sitting room that was at least a step up from the sticky floor and wobbly tables of the main area, and brought a bottle of wine that was doubtless not at all what the lofty Duke of Rothay and Lord Manderville were used to drinking, but it would have to do.

Discretion was the order of the day.

Her palms were damp underneath her gloves as she sank into a chair, and the veil felt as if it was going to suffocate her. Caroline arrived early, for she had no intention of making a grand entrance with both men already there, and she tried to ignore some definite inner trembles.

Some sultry seductress you are, she mocked herself, not at all certain, even if she'd come this far, she didn't want to bolt out of the room. The blackened beams in the low ceiling seemed too close, and a raucous laugh from some drunken patron drifted in with jarring clarity. The odor of stale spilled ale hung like a pall.

I should leave now.

No. She stiffened her spine and lifted her veil to take a quick sip from her glass. The life she'd lived so far was the stifling existence of a woman who never took a risk. She hadn't had the opportunity to do so—until now. A wicked, scandalous chance to do something so daring and utterly out of character that she just couldn't pass it by. An opportunity to change the damage done to her life, if things worked out as she hoped.

That is, unless the duke and the earl declined once they realized just who she was. She supposed it was possible, but quite frankly, she thought she was the perfect person to settle their absurd male dispute. Time and again she'd gone over it.

She was a widow, so it wasn't like they'd be despoiling an innocent.

She wanted nothing from them except the sensual promise implied in the very nature of their wager, which she intended to make clear.

She was the last person society would guess would aid them, so surely that might intrigue them a little bit. Her icy reputation alone should make them curious about her and enhance their desire to prove their supercilious point about sexual competency. Shouldn't it?

There. Those points would be her argument.

Would she even have to argue? With two such seasoned libertines, at a guess, her willingness was probably all they required. Their reputations were all but set in stone.

"My lady, you have a guest." The obsequious innkeeper appeared in the uneven doorway and then scurried away, to be replaced by a tall dark figure, a man who paused for a second before strolling in with his usual predatory grace.

Rothay.

The legendary duke wore dark evening clothes, obviously intent on going somewhere much more elegant after this assignation, probably the same ball she was going to attend later. Nicholas Manning looked, as usual, urbane, sophisticated, and a touch arrogant. Glossy raven hair with just a hint of wave emphasized the sculpted handsomeness of his features: downy arched brows, a straight nose, the line of jaw and chin clean and just a little square. His mouth—infamous for that signature wicked smile—curved slightly at the sight of her veiled face. Dark eyes surveyed her attire in open assessment, and she could see the gleam of curiosity there.

He was as beautiful as ever, as imposing as everyone whispered, and the seductive lift of his mouth was just part of his celebrated persona. His gaze inspected her décolletage and the smile widened slowly.

Good, he was intrigued. As long as she didn't lose her nerve and got the assurances she needed, this bargain would be sealed soon. Caroline said with cool deliberate intonation, "Good evening, Your Grace."

Something flickered in his eyes, maybe a realization that he recognized her voice. He bowed politely, the movement fluid and practiced. When he straightened, it looked like his head was a just a foot or so below the sagging ceiling. "Good evening."

"Shall we wait for Lord Manderville? I took the liberty of ordering some wine. Please help yourself. I requested we be left without a servant. It seemed . . . prudent."

What an ironic word choice. Nothing about what she was doing was prudent.

"Of course. Whatever you wish." He gave the small, plain room a cursory glance and chose a chair, settling into it in a smooth muscular movement and extending his long legs. "This is an excellent choice for our little meeting, to be sure. I don't think anyone we know would stumble across us in this place. Please tell me you did not come here unescorted."

He was perfectly right. The neighborhood was questionable, but her driver was a burly young man, pure Welsh, grateful to have escaped the fate of working in the mines like generations of his family, and therefore staunchly loyal. Huw had seen her safely inside, and would see her back home with the same care. She shook her head, the veil moving slightly, his solicitude for her safety a bit unexpected. "I am not foolish, Your Grace."

"I would never imply such a thing. But I admit freely to being most curious about you. What prompted you to contact us, if I am permitted to ask?" The bottle of wine sat on the table along with glasses, and he reached for it casually to pour himself a drink, but she had a feeling he was intensely interested in her answer, despite the apparent nonchalance of his gesture.

What did he think? That she was a desperate, lonely woman so starved for male attention she'd lie with two men just to have a little affection? Well, it was probably logical, she supposed, but not the case. If she wanted male company, she could find it easily enough. Even with her reputation for standoffishness, she grew weary of fending off potential suitors. As for the loneliness, she most certainly preferred being a widow to being a wife, so everything came with a price.

She'd paid enough and it was why she was there. Was she dissatisfied? Yes, because there was something missing in her life, like a glaring part of an unfinished puzzle that ruined the picture. To find that piece and fit it neatly into a slot was important to her. It affected her whole future in every conceivable way.

Physical passion was an elusive mystery. She saw no way to stay respectable and solve it.

Except this one.

She'd been cheated by the inadequacy of a marriage she hadn't wanted in the first place, and her husband's insensitivity in the bedroom was only part of it. Now that he was gone, there was nothing she could do about his neglect in other ways, but she *could* find out if it had been her fault she didn't enjoy conjugal relations, as Edward claimed.

It was a logical assumption that if she didn't like it in the arms of London's two most celebrated lovers, then it *was* her fault. Until she knew, she was unlikely to ever become involved with any man again. Being a bitter disappointment to a husband once was more than enough. She wasn't sure she even wished an intimate relationship with any male again, but she did want the chance to make the choice without the stranglehold of her past intruding on her present.

"I suppose it is natural for you to wonder over my motivation in offering to give my opinion for your unconventional competition," she said without inflection, gazing at the man across from her through the gauzy veil. "I think it is implied in my initial communication."

Arched ebony brows lifted a fraction. "Ah yes, the implication that the lovers you have had so far have disappointed you. What a pity any woman should feel such a way."

The caress of his rich voice was tangible, as if he'd really reached over and touched her. There was something in the way he held himself also. He couldn't be unaware of how his looks affected women, but it wasn't the weapon he used to win them over.

No wonder women fell for him as if tossing themselves off cliffs, she thought, gazing at him across the worn, chipped table. If he personified sin, it was of the most delicious kind. Somehow the framing of the tasteless surroundings showcased his potent power. Being superimposed on the display of grooved floors, stained walls, and a chair ill suited to his impressive height emphasized how male and aristocratic he was in every way.

"Lover," she corrected. "There is no plural." And what had happened in her marriage bed had certainly not seemed to have anything to do with love, so she wasn't sure the term applied. His pity didn't interest her. His assistance did.

"Only one man? I see."

Only one. Surely a foreign concept to a man like the rakish duke, who counted scores of lovers in his profligate past.

He continued with that same accomplished and devastating smile. "Don't judge us all too harshly from the failures of a single example of our gender."

"Shouldn't I?" It would be nice if she could sound flirtatious, but she feared she didn't quite pull it off.

"Indeed not." His gaze once more drifted to the swell of pale flesh above her bodice. "Just as every woman is unique, I imagine we are also all different. By nature, I think, men are more selfish on the whole. I am sorry for your previous experience, but once again, not all of us are the same."

She felt the tantalizing heat of that perusal as if he'd run a finger along her skin.

Then again, his charisma wasn't in question. They were very unevenly matched, but she had no intention of letting him know it. With chill poise, she said, "Perhaps you will get a chance to prove your point, Your Grace."

"I have the distinct feeling I will have no objection to doing so, my mysterious lady."

Drinking her wine was impossible without lifting the veil, so she uncertainly fingered the stem of her glass instead, watching the man across the table with wary contemplation.

"Sorry, I am a bit late." Lord Manderville's arrival stopped her from having to say more. She didn't want to give too many clues as to her identity until they both offered her their word as gentlemen they would never reveal it.

The earl came into the room and gave her much the same assessment as his friend had done, a sweeping glance that lingered just a moment on the neckline of her fashionable gown, then ended on the draping cloth that concealed her face. An impish smile revealed white straight teeth. "I see we are truly playing a game of intrigue here. It is a pleasure to meet you."

"You have met me before," Caroline said, as calmly as possible. Having them both in the room was a bit disconcerting, she found. For one thing, they were both very tall, and had that formidable air of male self-confidence that seemed to fill the small space. Derek Drake's golden good looks had earned him the epithet "the Angel." Rothay, in contrast, was christened in a tongue-in-cheek manner "the Devilish Duke."

They made a potent—if disparate—pair, the Angel and the Devil, and she felt her stomach knot with nervous tension.

That would hardly do. Here she was, boldly offering them a sexual proposition. Women who traveled to obscure inns to meet with libertines of the order of the two men with her now should not succumb to an attack of nerves.

Her spine stiffened as resolve resurfaced.

"*Have* I met you?" Manderville accepted a glass of wine from the duke with a nod of thanks, his gaze still fastened on her face, and sat down in a rickety chair. It gave a protesting squeak.

"You both have."

"Ah, I thought your voice seemed cultured and perhaps familiar. We can't be close acquaintances, though, or I would have recognized it with more certainty. I have an ear for that sort of thing." His smile was as angelic as the duke's was wickedly enticing.

Whereas Nicholas Manning exuded an almost dangerous air of intensity, the earl was all lazy, insouciant male grace.

So different, yet the same in the offer of a supposed paradise in their arms.

Next came the tricky part. Caroline couldn't blame them for wanting to know just who she was—and take a look at her—before they agreed, but neither was she going to remove the veil before she had their assurance of silence. If it wasn't forthcoming, she was going to leave at once. Even the couriers she'd hired to deliver the notes back and forth had to go through a convoluted process to make sure there was no direct connection between her and them.

This was supposed to save her, not destroy her life.

They might have reputations for dalliance and departure, sleeping their way through bevies of society beauties, but she had never heard one word against their honor as far as anything else went, so she was prepared to accept their word. With his vast wealth, surely Rothay had to manage large financial holdings efficiently, and Manderville was also a rich man with the same responsibilities. They held seats in the House of Lords, and were active, if what she read in the paper was true. It was almost comical to see the efforts of all the scheming mothers trying to bring their eligible daughters to their attention, but both reputedly avoided unmarried young ladies as if they carried a dread disease.

In short, they were honorable in their own way, or she certainly hoped so. She was about to risk her reputation on that assumption. The veil had been insurance in case, for whatever reason, they refused.

Caroline said firmly, "Before we even discuss this unusual

situation, I need your solemn word my name is never to be tied to this in any way. Even if we do not reach an agreement this evening, I want no one to know I ever even considered it." Without thinking she quoted softly, "'At every word a reputation dies.'"

"Alexander Pope, I believe," the duke said, looking amused, those downy brows elevated. "I am too curious now to refuse. I will tell no one."

"My word on it also." Derek Drake nodded his blond head, his eyes narrowed just a fraction as he gazed at her shielded face. "Your secret is safe here."

"Very well." Caroline lifted off her hat and veil and set them aside, smoothing her hair with fingers that trembled only slightly. She was the amused one when she saw the shock on both their faces. The room was silent.

It was a testament to her reputation. She was supposed to be icily formal and unattainable, not a woman who arranged meetings in disreputable taverns.

How often, she wondered, was either of them at a loss for words?

Rarely, if she had to guess.

"Lady Wynn." It was Rothay who recovered first, but still he stared at her, his wineglass dangling from long fingers. "I admit I am surprised."

She felt a small nervous smile twitch her lips. "In a good way, Your Grace, or in an unpleasant one?"

Chapter Four

Now, this was an unexpected development indeed.

Of all the faces he'd thought he might see behind that veil, Caroline Wynn's was not one of them. Nicholas had considered at length which of the ladies of his acquaintance might contemplate participation in their outrageous little rivalry, but the woman sitting across the table never occurred to him.

Yet there she was, with a slight lift to one of her auburn brows at his astounded expression, just a hint of amusement in those much talked about, magnificent silver eyes. The seedy little inn indicated her serious approach to the matter, but he still found it hard to believe *she* was the one who'd sent that provocative note.

The beautiful young widow of the late Lord Wynn had a reputation for being aloof to the point of discouraging even the most determined of suitors. He knew her only in passing, but yes, she was right, both he and Derek had been introduced to her at some point. Her cool, withdrawn exterior sent an obvious message to any predatory male that she was hardly interested in an entanglement, so he had merely admired her undeniable loveliness and dismissed any idea of further acquaintance. Besides, she was younger than the sophisticated ladies he usually took to bed, and still very marriageable. If he could recall correctly, she'd been wedded to the viscount for several years before he suddenly died, and then in mourning for even longer than necessary, but still she was probably at most twenty-three, if not a bit younger.

Definitely still marriageable. Lushly attractive—it went without saying—but dangerous to any man who valued his independence.

Which he did. Maybe *independence* was the wrong choice of word. What he valued was slightly more complex.

Nicholas felt a flicker of alarm. He sought something diplomatic to say. "My lady, you are very lovely, of course, so the surprise is hardly a bad one, but this does seem a bit reckless in your situation."

Derek had a bemused expression on his face. Nicholas could only imagine the same thoughts were running through his friend's mind at an equally swift pace. Derek said, "Er . . . I agree. I have no objection, believe me, but you shouldn't—"

"Squander my virtue?" she interrupted, demurely lowering her long lashes. Her eyes were truly a remarkable color, not pale blue but actually a pure gray. Auburn hair, rich and glossy, glowed against her pale flawless skin. Her striking beauty made the squalid room look even more drab, more deplorable. Slender fingers held the stem of a wineglass. "Please remember, gentlemen, I am a widow. My virtue has already been squandered."

An interesting way of describing one's marriage, Nicholas couldn't help but think. He took a drink from his own glass and tried to analyze how he felt about this twist to the situation. "You're very young. You will most likely marry again. I doubt your future husband would approve of your involvement in this little wager."

"Your Grace, I have no intention of ever marrying again. I don't *have* to wed, as I am self-sufficient financially, and if I ever *should* remarry, it would be none of his business what I did or whom I did it with anyway." She gave them both a challenging look.

Like hell it wouldn't be, Nicholas thought, but he admired the way she lifted her chin and dared them to say otherwise. It was a double standard—he knew that—but it existed. Men liked promiscuous women; they just rarely married them.

She went on in a reasonable tone, as if they weren't sitting in a tawdry inn somewhere discussing a planned illicit rendezvous based on a drunken bet. "Since I am a widow, I am allowed a great deal more freedom. No one would ever think I would do such a thing anyway."

"I wouldn't have," Nicholas agreed wryly, speculating on just how ineffectual her deceased husband must have been in performance of his husbandly duty. He'd known the former Lord Wynn only in passing, and he'd seemed pleasant enough as an acquaintance. But then again, how males treated their casual friends and how they regarded their wives were often two different matters.

"Maybe you really know nothing about me, Your Grace."

She might have the delectable appearance of Venus incarnate, but it had never occurred to him the sensuality to match might simmer under that tempting exterior. The Northern ice cap was rumored to be warmer than Lady Wynn.

"I concede I don't." His gaze held hers.

Her unique eyes reflected a flicker of uncertainty as they looked at each other and the moment held for a long heartbeat. And then another.

Oh yes, he was intrigued.

"Thank you for acknowledging it," she said without any inflection at all.

But those expressive eyes were something else altogether. He knew when he affected a woman and this seemed to be one of those situations.

With the standoffish Lady Wynn? How damned interesting.

Derek interjected, "If we are to never reveal your identity, my lady, explain to me how you are ever going to settle the contest."

She gave a small nod, as if she'd expected the question. "I have it all thought out. With your endorsement, I'll publish the results in the society column of the paper, under the cloak of anonymity, of course. Since my name will be left out of it, I will be comfortable writing down my frank thoughts."

That statement was alone enough to evoke the same spirit

of combativeness that had gotten them into trouble in the
first place, but since Derek didn't blink an eye, Nicholas
also contrived to look bland.

"Fine," they said in unison, and then glanced at each other
with mutual male annoyance.

She laughed with delightful spontaneity, lighting up her
already very lovely face and adding animation to those
haunting eyes.

Damn, she was a very tempting prospect. If they really
were going to go through with this, Lady Wynn was a captivating candidate. It was common opinion that she was a
true beauty, her heavy, lustrous hair framing a delicate face
with high cheekbones, a straight small nose, and a soft pink
mouth, her unusual eyes long-lashed and large. The fact she
was built with willowy grace, her body curvaceous yet slender, was something plenty of men had noticed and commented on. The fullness of her breasts under the bodice of
her fashionable gown drew Nicholas's eye.

Derek apparently wasn't blind either. His friend murmured, "You sound as if you have made up your mind, Lady
Wynn."

"That depends." She adjusted a fold in her dark emerald
silk skirt, the hue of her gown a complement to her vivid
coloring. "How would we work this exactly? We will have
to be extremely discreet."

She truly was sincere, Nicholas decided, his initial resis-
tance to the idea gone.

And he was damned interested.

It had been a while since that had happened. Lady Wynn
was a fascinating young woman. Since her persona had always been distant and cold, not at all what he sought in a
lover, he'd never considered her in any context, especially
the one they were currently discussing. He spoke without
thinking. "Give us each a week of your time."

Derek turned to look at him, a glimmer of open surprise
in his eyes at the time period suggested.

A week?

Where the impulsive suggestion had come from, Nicholas

wasn't sure, but he did feel one night with the beautiful woman sitting across from them would not be enough. The mystery of why she'd do something so unexpected both jolted him and drew him in. Nicholas shrugged and smiled. "I'm sure you'll agree lovemaking is a varied world. Getting to know your partner is also beneficial. A week in each other's company, in and out of bed, seems logical for a fair conclusion."

Whatever Lady Wynn expected, it obviously wasn't that. She seemed nonplussed for a moment, but then she nodded slowly. One loose ringlet of coppery hair brushed the ivory column of her neck and he watched it slide along her smooth skin with almost unwilling fascination. She said, "I suppose if I have come this far, I can agree to that. I'll come up with some excuse to be gone that amount of time."

Excellent.

An outburst from a small quarrel between some of the extremely questionable patrons in the taproom echoed around the room, along with a few rough words not meant for a lady's ears, but she didn't blink an eye.

Yes, her poise was remarkable.

"I have a small country estate in Essex." Nicholas tried to remember the last time he'd been there, and failed. When he retired to the country, he went to the much larger family seat in Kent. The smaller holding had been part of his inheritance, and it sat empty except for the minimal staff there to maintain it. "It's tucked into the countryside not near any towns in particular, but rather pretty and quiet if I recall, and close enough to London we wouldn't have to travel for days. It should be perfect for a quiet, discreet retreat."

A week with a woman he didn't even know was more than impulsive; it was downright irrational. Usually a night here and there was plenty, his detachment legendary because his transitory relationships did not demand anything but passing amusement. He didn't keep a mistress, because he just didn't need one. Any number of ladies would oblige him on very short notice and he took for granted that if he wanted female companionship, he could have it whenever he wished.

However, an insidious voice whispered in his head, Lady Wynn's untried status in the art of sexual enjoyment made her more captivating than most. He wasn't interested in deflowering some virgin, but she wasn't one, and her dazzling beauty and delicate femininity overrode his sense of caution over the knowledge she was still young and very desirable on the marriage mart.

She'd stated clearly she didn't wish to marry again, and he believed her; the conviction in her tone unmistakable.

A week of initiating her into the pleasures of the flesh sounded like quite a pleasant distraction from his busy schedule. Parliament was out right now and he could let his steward know how to reach him. . . .

Yes, he thought, studying the sensual fullness of her lower lip, the swell of ivory flesh above the bodice of her low-cut evening gown, the faint color in her cheeks as she blushed at his overt appraisal. A week would probably be easy enough to endure in her company.

She blushed. How remarkable. Coarse words didn't do what one look could.

"Are we agreed?" He set aside his wineglass and lifted a brow in question.

"I suppose I can find a similar place." Derek nodded. He lounged in his chair, also gazing at their beautiful companion as if he approved in full measure. "As long as Lady Wynn understands the implications of what would happen to her reputation should we be discovered. Neither of us will ever breathe a word, but attempted discretion is not infallible."

Caroline Wynn glanced away for a moment, and her mouth tightened. Then she looked back and squared her slender shoulders. "Naturally, I am not anxious for a scandal, but if it happens, it will be of my own making and I hope the risk proves . . . well, to be worth it."

Now, there was a challenge if he'd ever heard one.

Nicholas smiled lazily. "It will be, my lady."

She didn't smile back but simply looked at him with those

remarkable eyes, the only betrayal of any emotion in the slight tremble of her lips. "You sound very confident, Your Grace."

Was he? Perhaps, but it was tempered by how little he knew of her. Maybe that was why he suggested a full week. She was an enigma in a world he often found all too predictable. "We both are, I'm sure, or we wouldn't have made the wager in the first place, now, would we?"

"I believe this is settled, then," she said, getting to her feet. "Feel free to contact me with the specifics of the arrangements. We can communicate in the same way as before. Send it to the same address and they will bring it to me."

He and Derek both rose politely.

"My driver is in the taproom, waiting. He'll see me out."

Nicholas felt a protective protest rise, the rough crowd in the other room a concern. "I'll walk you to the carriage."

"No, thank you, Your Grace. Even here, I prefer to not be seen with you."

That calm, collected declaration rendered him silent. For most of his adult life he'd been besieged by women who were more than eager to be seen on his arm. This was new. The sting of it surprised him a little. Why would he care one way or the other?

She picked up her hat and put it on, adjusted the veil over her face, and left in a swirl of emerald green and a delicate hint of floral perfume.

Chapter Five

"Such a lovely party. Don't you agree, my lord?"

Absently Derek Drake glanced down at the woman in his arms. Good God, for a moment he couldn't remember her name. How unsettling.

Amelia. Yes, sister to a friend, which was why he was dancing with her in the first place. Horace had foisted her on him and he'd agreed to take her out on the floor, mostly because if one attends a ball, one should at least make the pretense of enjoying oneself.

Derek wasn't, but then again, he hadn't expected to.

What he'd come for had nothing to do with entertainment. His motives were more akin to self-flagellation.

Very productive, that, he thought in self-mockery as he waltzed across the floor. His partner was very short, and Derek was a tall man, and he expected they looked a bit absurd together. Out loud, he said, "Yes, lovely."

That type of banal conversation would certainly win him dazzling titles as a superlative lover, wouldn't it? Lucky for him, Amelia seemed to find his reply gratifying, for she beamed up at him as if he'd said something clever.

"Quite."

What would he say to that? Nothing seemed best. His reputed silver tongue was lead coated this evening. He felt immense gratitude when the music dwindled to the end and he led her off the floor, bowed over her plump hand, and fled.

The ball was a predictable crush and Derek edged through the crowd. The room was crammed with people, the open windows providing not much relief from the heat, and the murmur of voices vied with the orchestra for prominence. Luckily his height made it possible to keep his objective in sight. Finally, he reached Nicholas. His friend was propped against a Grecian-style pillar and sipping champagne.

Without preamble, Derek said, "A week? Are you insane, Nick?"

They were surrounded by people, but between the music and the resonance of hundreds of voices, their conversation was relatively private, as if they were sequestered somewhere. The Duke of Rothay gave him one of his undecipherable looks for which he was so well-known. "It seems reasonable."

Derek snorted with inelegant derision. "You have never consistently spent that amount of time with one female in your life, aside from, perhaps, your mother."

The dowager duchess was a formidable figure despite the fact she barely came up to her son's shoulder. A renowned beauty in her day, she still wielded a great deal of social power in all the right circles. Her disapproval of her son's detached approach to any marriageable young woman was public knowledge.

Nicholas laughed, openly amused at the reference. "And not even her once I was old enough to avoid it. I'm fond of my mother, but the thought of a week of her constant advice makes me shudder."

"Hence my surprise at your suggestion. You don't know Lady Wynn." It was so much easier to concentrate on the frivolous bet than Derek's own state of misery.

"Are you telling me you'd object to having someone so lovely in your bed for that long?"

"She's very beautiful." Derek obliquely didn't answer the question, gazing over to where Caroline Wynn sat in a corner with several older ladies, as usual looking remote and unapproachable. She rarely accepted an invitation to dance, but men still tried. Even from a distance the pale perfection of her skin against the lustrous color of her auburn hair was striking. She was all opulent female beauty and he should be looking forward eagerly to the prospect of bedding her.

Why wasn't he?

"I am not prone to long entanglements any more than you are," Derek remarked in an offhand tone.

Except one. He could be prone to *one* long entanglement, but he'd ruined everything.

It was a lesson in idiocy, but he scanned the room with a restless, searching gaze.

And found her.

Of course Annabel would be there, damn all. Derek caught a glimpse among the well-dressed throng of hair a certain shade of gold, a flash of porcelain profile he knew as well as he knew his own face, and his chest tightened.

Well, he reminded himself with as much pragmatic detachment as possible, *you expected to see her*. That his uncle's ward was in attendance was no surprise. Half of London was crammed into this ballroom. It was natural Annabel would attend, and it wasn't much of a leap to assume she was on the arm of her fiancé.

Damn the man to hell.

"How shall we decide who has the privilege of whisking her away first?"

Nicholas's question brought his attention back to the topic at hand and Derek forced himself to look away. Since it amounted to torture at the moment to even see Annabel, concentrating on something else had merit. Like a nice passionate interlude with the luscious Lady Wynn. Annabel was lost. Need he turn into a monk?

No, of course not.

Yet he hedged. "I suppose it depends on how fast the lady can get away. My schedule this next week includes several appointments I can't miss, and besides, I need to come up with a similar secluded spot."

"I think I can clear things so I can leave in a day or two. Shall we say it's settled?"

They had been friends a long time. A decade, since they'd met at Cambridge in their first year at university, and there was an unfamiliar note in Nick's voice. Derek recalled the younger version of the Duke of Rothay, still stinging from his ill-fated first foray into what he perceived as love, determined in a way only Nicholas could be to shrug off the experience. Derek signaled a passing footman, plucked a glass off the tray, and gave his companion an amused look. "She intrigues you."

"A little."

It was about time, with all the women who had come and gone in Nicholas's life, that someone did.

Derek chuckled. "A lot. Maybe you could fool someone else, but not me."

"She's very attractive."

"That's true enough, but all your entanglements involve gorgeous women."

"I wish you wouldn't use the term *entanglement*. It makes me think of a poacher's trap and a wounded animal."

In Derek's estimation, that was an apt description. God alone knew he felt painfully backed against some proverbial wall with little recourse. With neutral inflection, he replied, "Fair enough. Tell me what you'd call them."

"Lustful escapades." Nicholas supplied the phrase with a grin that mitigated the facetious correction.

"I suppose that fits. But since our lovely judge is obviously not trying to trap you, at least you can relax and indulge your interest."

"Perhaps." Rothay sipped from his glass and looked bland. "Doesn't she interest you?"

The devil take it, Annabel and Hyatt were on the floor now, swirling among the dancers to one of the newest popular tunes. Her face was flushed to a becoming pink, the light gleamed off her pale hair, and in a gown of rose-colored silk she looked . . .

Ravishing. Captivating. So beautiful his chest hurt. Hyatt also looked happy and unfortunately—though he wasn't

particularly good at judging the looks of other men—
Derek knew the man was considered appealing to women.

Hardly an encouraging thought, but he really couldn't remember ever being so discouraged in his life anyway.

"Derek?"

Oh hell, he'd been asked a question, hadn't he? Startled
out of his abstraction, Derek turned. "I'm sorry."

Nicholas must have noticed something odd in his manner,
but thankfully he didn't mention it. "I just inquired if our unexpected volunteer intrigued you."

"Of course." Derek answered too quickly and took a gulp
of champagne to cover the blunder.

Nicholas, he had to remind himself, was not easily fooled.
Dark eyes narrowed slightly as they regarded him.

The only solace was that they had an unwritten but inviolate rule between them. No intrusive questions. A gentleman's bargain between two men who respected each other's
privacy.

It held. After a moment, Nicholas merely said, "Then you
don't mind my taking her first."

Taking her. How appropriate. A laugh stuck in his throat.

Derek really needed to regain his composure. The champagne might be too warm, but it worked, for he took another
sip and then managed what he hoped was an easy grin. "No.
I'm sure you'll do it very well, too. But keep in mind, it's me
she'll remember."

"Feel free to think so, Manderville. I plan on making an
indelible impression now that the three of us have an agreement. I doubt I would have selected the lady in question, but
now that she has stepped forward, I'm . . . eager."

Curious that, for the Duke of Rothay was always the
epitome of careless seduction. Impatience was most out of
character.

"The situation certainly took a turn we didn't expect,
didn't it?" Derek asked, but since he knew his own eagerness was tempered by his current personal unhappiness, it
was hard to say whether Nicholas was more interested than

expected in Lady Wynn's unusual offer to participate, or Derek was just so off-balance that he couldn't judge.

As someone who had so dismally failed to discern his own feelings, maybe he shouldn't presume to understand anyone else's.

If Nicholas was so enthusiastic to escort the lady to seclusion in the country, let him take her there at once and exert his infamous charm and seduce her. At the moment, Derek's heart just wasn't in it.

He said in an idle tone, "Let me know when the two of you return to town."

Mrs. Haroldson leaned forward with a definite conspiratorial air, her considerable bosom making it look as if she might topple to the floor. "It isn't," she said in a sibilant whisper, "something a person should be surprised over, I suppose."

Caroline strove to look reserved and cool when, in truth, the crowded ballroom was unbearably stuffy. A trickle of sweat ran in an inelegant way between her breasts. "Surprised over what?"

"The way His Grace and the earl stand there chatting about it, bold as brass, the two of them."

Were they discussing the wager? They did seem engrossed in conversation. Since it hadn't been more than an hour or two since all three of them had left the inn, it could be imagined they might be talking about it.

About her.

She'd *done* it. Offered herself to two disreputable rogues, agreed to a wicked covenant that would ruin her in the eyes of all society if it was discovered, and placed herself directly in the path of disgrace and scandal.

All in a good cause, a small voice inside reminded her with unswerving practicality.

Her sanity.

Her life even, if she cared to be melodramatic about it.

"I am sure they talk often. I've seen them." She feigned

her best dismissive tone, flicking an uninterested look at the two tall men across the room. "Are they not friends?"

"Surely, Lady Wynn, you've heard about their latest exploit."

"Do you mean that tedious bet?"

God in heaven, it was hot and it didn't help to have a phalanx of older, matronly women all around, virtually hemming her in. She had to quell the urge to leap up and run from the room as if all the devils in hell were at her heels.

One dark-haired devil in particular, balanced by one golden angel.

From beneath the shadows of her lashes, she watched them, finally permitted by the conversation, though she'd wanted to look ever since she'd arrived. Nicholas Manning, so gloriously attractive, his hair somehow managing to appear sleek and yet a little disheveled at the same time, his tailored evening clothes suited to his masculine beauty. Manderville also, like some Greek god, so handsome he seemed to warm the room with his presence, their mutual brilliance making them the center of attention with or without their current infamy.

"Yes, indeed, the wager. It's most de trop, don't you agree?"

Eight pairs of eyes fastened on her. The circle of widows, most of them two decades older at least, was her current bastion against any man who might approach. It was safe to huddle in the corner with them rather than chance accepting any of the offers to dance or—even less appealing—enjoy a flirtation.

She didn't have the slightest idea how to do the latter.

Caroline murmured, "I feel certain my opinion wouldn't matter to either one of them. Their mutual impertinence is legendary. I find the whole matter quite distasteful."

"Well said." The Dowager Countess Langtry nodded in crisp agreement.

"It's beyond the pale, no doubt. You are right."

Other voices chimed in, all agreeing with her. But as

much as the group might protest the behavior of the two gentlemen in question, they certainly didn't seem to have much trouble ogling the subjects of their conversation from afar.

She was, of course, the detached, so-removed, so-distant Lady Wynn. It was only natural she'd disdain even speaking about something so discordant to her own placid and reclusive existence.

If they only knew the truth.

God forbid, she thought with a small shudder.

In the end, she couldn't sit there and pretend the topic of the beautiful duke and the dashing earl bored her. She excused herself and made her way outside to the gardens behind the glittering mansion, taking in a great lungful of air as if it could heal and mend all the broken things in her life.

No, only she could do that.

There were a few other guests on the terrace, so she slipped away to where the formal flower beds and shrubberies were laid out. Wandering a darkened path, the smattering of stars above a diamond blanket in the night sky, she tried to assess her now-roiling emotions.

Was this really something she could do? A secret assignation to settle a bet made between two gentlemen who admitted to being under the influence of a great deal of wine at the time?

Her face heated and she was grateful there was no one to see it. The duke's unabashed masculine appraisal of her person back at the inn was not something she hadn't seen before, but her reaction to it was most unexpected.

Usually she felt infused with an unwelcome mixture of awkwardness and trepidation.

For whatever reason, he hadn't affected her that way. Maybe her part in the wager had set the dynamic of their interaction from the beginning. The meeting was her choice. What a novel concept, to have a choice.

Her skirt brushed the glossy leaves of some bush as she passed, and a white flower scattered petals across the fabric in a flurry, like a burst in a snowstorm. The fragrance was sweet, innocent, beguiling. She absently brushed them away, turning her face to a welcome breeze.

At least her would-be lovers seemed capable of honoring her request to keep her identity a secret. Neither one of them had so much as glanced at her in passing all evening.

This will work, she assured herself.

And prayed it was the truth.

Chapter Six

Did no one in London have anything else to talk about except that infernal wager?

The cup rattled into the saucer as she set it aside and a tiny slop of tea spilled over the rim. Annabel Reid gritted her teeth and hoped no one noticed, doing her best to appear as composed as possible.

Part of the current surge of interest had come, she knew, by the appearance of both the parties involved at the Branscums' ball the prior evening. They had stood talking for quite a while and, as usual, were apparently indifferent to the rising whispers. Together they were, as always, striking: the duke with his flagrant dark good looks and the natural air of power he wore so easily, and Derek Drake—whom she'd known since she could walk—with his devastating, refined handsomeness and effortless charm.

Only *she* wasn't charmed.

The man might be overwhelmingly attractive in every way a male could be, but she loathed him. That easy smile and genial air only cloaked the flaws beneath the surface.

Yes, she despised him.

Thoroughly.

Completely.

"I'm sorry, my dear Miss Reid, but aren't you related to Manderville?"

Annabel glanced up, realizing with belated chagrin she was being addressed. A group of eight ladies all looked at her expectantly, among them her future mother-in-law. The rest were Alfred's assorted aunts and cousins. She cleared her throat, unaccountably horrified by the question. "No . . . no. Not at all. His uncle is my guardian. That's the extent of it."

It was the truth. There was no blood tie. Thomas Drake and her father had been lifelong close friends, and that bond had been deep enough that her father had made provisions that in case the worst happened—and it had—her care would be entrusted to his old friend. She'd been a bewildered, bereft eight-year-old girl after her parents were killed in a sailing accident. Whatever she now thought of his infamous nephew Derek, Sir Thomas was a wonderful man, and he and his wife, Margaret, had treated her like their own child. In some ways, since they had never been able to have children of their own, Annabel wondered if she hadn't been as much a blessing to them as they were to her.

Either way, though she loved Thomas and Margaret, Derek was another story altogether.

"But you *did* grow up on the family estate, correct?" Lady Henderson gazed at her with unconcealed inquiry.

"I . . . well . . . yes, I did. In . . . Berkshire."

Why had she stammered out her reply, especially with so many people looking at her? The unwelcome subject was the last thing she wanted to discuss. She loathed gossip. If the whole scandalous issue would go away, she'd be more than happy. She sat in the drawing room of her fiancé's London home, all formal furnishings and far too crowded for her tastes, and that was bad enough without rehashing such an uncomfortable topic. Annabel liked books and solitude a great deal more than fussy teas. A nice copy of Voltaire and a sunny window seat were more to her liking than the current situation.

"I expect you saw him rather frequently." Lady Henderson's pale eyes held sly curiosity.

Everyone looked at her expectantly. Of course, because they were talking about Derek Drake, and if his name was mentioned in a roomful of women, it would not go unnoticed.

Damn him.

Yes, it was a little galling to know he actually owned the house she considered home. Her guardian was the youngest brother of the deceased earl, Derek's father. For that matter, she had an uneasy feeling Derek had provided her dowry. When Annabel asked Margaret outright, she'd been evasive about the matter, and Margaret wasn't one to lie, so that was answer enough. Thomas did well enough financially, but Derek held the true wealth in the family.

That was irony. The man she once thought she loved was giving money as an enticement for some *other* man to marry her.

"He's a decade older," Annabel pointed out, "so not that frequently. By the time I was eight, he was off to Cambridge and he seems to prefer London to Berkshire anyway. We rarely see him. Even when we are in the city, he has his own town house."

Another lady—she was fairly sure her betrothed called her Aunt Ida—murmured, "I can guess why. London is so much more . . . *populated.*"

Which meant more available women. The implication was clear, and though the last thing she wanted to do was defend a hopeless libertine like the Earl of Manderville, Annabel inexplicably did. "He actually has a lot of business interests and it is easier for him to have access to his solicitors and stewards while in the city. Manderville Hall is inconvenient. He's a busy man."

"I would guess so." A different lady, this one thin with unnaturally dark hair for her age, gave a sharp trilling laugh. "Though I doubt business is the first thing on his mind. Nevertheless, he is easy to forgive for his indiscretions since he is such a *beautiful* young man."

"More so than Rothay?" someone asked.

"Impossible," another one chimed.

Yes, Annabel's heart countered traitorously. *More than any man alive.*

She had so adored him when she was a child. With his mischievous smile and easy humor, he'd been a natural hero to a girl who'd been suddenly orphaned. In retrospect, she knew he'd been kind to endure her constant tagging at his heels. That a young man of eighteen had taken the time to give a child a pony and teach her to ride was a point in his favor, but still . . . the man was a despicable cad. The angelic good looks nature had bestowed on him were the worst possible kind of fraud. He should have two horns and a forked tail to go along with his mesmerizing eyes and those nicely chiseled features.

"How on earth could anyone decide which one is more handsome?" One of Alfred's cousins giggled, her young face showing a slight blush. "They are both divine."

"Hush, Eugenia," her mother said in reproof.

"If always swimming in the scandal broth," the thin aunt said again primly, but there was a gleam of malicious delight in her eyes. "Wasn't it just a few months ago that Lord Tanner threatened to name Manderville in his divorce proceedings against his wife on the grounds of adultery?"

Four months precisely since that unsavory rumor surfaced, but Annabel had absolutely no comment, feeling ill every time she thought about it. It was best she kept her feelings about the immoral earl to herself, lest she have to explain the reason for her intense dislike. She hadn't thought it possible, but the public accusation that Derek had participated in the breakup of a marriage made her opinion of him plummet even lower.

"And now this indecent competition. Though it's indelicate to even think about it, one does have to wonder just how they are going to settle their little dispute." The matronly Ida, for one who just declared the subject outré, certainly seemed determined to discuss it.

"I've heard that Russian actress, the one who played Ophelia so well even with her dreadful accent, is going to declare the winner." Lady Henderson—who did not need to increase the girth of her already ample waistline—plucked another sweet from the cart.

"Really? Well, I'd heard . . ."

Annabel blocked out the conversation with desperate concentration. Her efforts were ineffective and she probably came across as dull and overly quiet, but she did manage to decide what gown she'd wear later that evening.

So the afternoon wasn't a complete loss.

After the interminable tea was over, she was grateful to be handed into the waiting carriage. Soon she would be married and her association with Derek Drake would be severed once and for all. Well, not completely, because his aunt and uncle thought highly of him, and Thomas and Margaret were in essence her parents, but at least she would no longer have to endure his company very often. Besides, when she did, Alfred would be at her side and that would help.

Help what? The silent question made her gaze out the window as the vehicle rolled along.

It was best not to think about it.

About *him*.

Tenterden Manor was not her precise idea of a small country estate, Caroline thought with a glimmer of nervous amusement, but the duke had been right about one thing: it was secluded.

It sat in a wooded park, the mellow stone of the structure reflecting the wash of late-afternoon sun. An elegant facade showed Elizabethan influence in the outspread wings, parts of it obviously added over the years. Even if the duke was rarely in residence, the grounds were neatly kept and intensely green, and the clean gravel of the drive curved up toward the front door. Rows of shining mullioned windows were framed by ivy, giving the house a charming, almost fairy-tale effect, despite its great size. Mature trees stretched leafy branches over most of the grounds, letting dappled sunlight through to the clipped grass.

It was lovely and very private. Just what they needed for their little interlude.

Oh God. Nervousness fluttered in her throat, making it difficult to swallow.

It wasn't too late, she reminded herself, to ask Huw to turn around and take her back to London and just forget this mad escapade. Aside from the chance she was taking, after the next weeks were over, how was she going to feel?

Like a harlot for offering herself to two of the most celebrated rogues in society?

Perhaps. But then again, maybe she would finally feel like a woman instead, her inappropriate behavior giving some reward. The step she was taking to change her life was drastic indeed, but maybe drastic measures were needed.

How humiliating, though, should she prove a disappointment to the notorious Duke of Rothay.

On the contrary, she told herself firmly as the vehicle came to a halt and her stomach lurched, it was part of the wager between him and the earl that *they* were to prove their skill in the bedroom. She was merely supposed to cast her vote on which one could do it best.

It sounded simple enough.

The burly Huw was at the door of the carriage, holding out a hand to help her alight. His broad face showed no curiosity or censure, as blank as it had been when he'd driven her to the seedy little inn. She couldn't help but wonder what he was going to think when he realized the purpose of her journey was an assignation. He'd worked for her for several years and their relationship as servant and employer was a very comfortable one. More things might change from this reckless venture than just her perception of herself as a woman, she realized, wondering how much she should care about the opinion of a servant. Most of the beau monde would assure her she shouldn't mind at all, but Caroline wasn't sure she could be so blasé.

"Thank you," she murmured, climbing down, hoping her trepidation wasn't obvious.

"My pleasure, my lady." Huw inclined his head, his expression neutral.

The front door opened and the duke himself appeared as she went up the inlaid brick steps. In the brief note he'd sent with directions, he'd mentioned there was very little staff at the house since he didn't really use it, but she certainly didn't expect someone of his rank to ever play footman. It was startling. He was also dressed very informally in a loose-sleeved white shirt, black breeches, and polished boots. It made him look younger, but somehow not less formidable—but more. The casual clothing emphasized his height, the impressive width of his shoulders, and defined the muscular power of his long legs. The signature glossy fall of his dark hair brushed his shoulders, shining in the late-afternoon sun and framing those sinfully beautiful masculine features. It struck her that she was really seeing the man, not just the wealthy, handsome aristocrat with that breathtaking smile and compelling confidence. The more casual mode of dress also signaled an intimacy in their acquaintance that brought home the actual situation: she was going to spend the next week in his bed.

She felt a small shiver as he reached out to politely take her hand and bend over it, his mouth just grazing her skin.

He straightened and murmured, "Welcome, my lady."

"Good afternoon, Your Grace." Caroline managed to keep her voice level, though her pulse had picked up the pace. The duke towered over her, and his shoulders looked dauntingly wide.

His dark eyes regarded her with the faintest gleam of humor. "I hope you are prepared for a week of rustic living. As I warned, there is only a minimal staff. My arrival has the housekeeper somewhat rattled. Come, let's go inside. I'll order tea and we can get . . . acquainted."

So quickly? Caroline wasn't sure what he meant by that remark and her usual uncertainty took hold of her. Summoning every ounce of bravado, she murmured in a cool tone, "That would be acceptable, I suppose."

Now he definitely looked amused, his finely modeled mouth twitching. "Spoken like the true icy Lady Wynn. Please keep in mind I only mentioned tea."

She was well aware of her reputation for distance and lack of warmth. It was why she had embarked on her current mad course. "We both know why I am here, Rothay."

"Yes, we do." He still held her hand, his long fingers not relinquishing their light grip. It was a liberty, but given the circumstances, how could she object?

He bent forward, close enough his warm breath brushed her ear. "You are not going to be easy to thaw, are you?"

Those softly spoken words made her pull back and stare at him for a moment, unsure how to respond, an odd tingle in the pit of her stomach. Maybe honesty was best. "No," she admitted finally.

To her relief he said no more and released her hand. "Shall we go in?"

She stepped past him and walked into the foyer, more than a little rattled by the brief intimacy of their exchange. No matter how countrified he found the surroundings, she noticed—the diversion welcome—with its polished wood paneling, beautiful floors, and high ceilings, the place was both warm and gracious, with the air of an aging beauty. Fine bones under the mellowing exterior, a sense of belonging in the bucolic setting, the smell of wax and baking bread in the air . . .

"This is pleasant," she managed to say with aplomb, though his reference to thawing her had brought old persistent insecurities to the surface.

What if she was truly passionless and unable to respond to a man?

Nicholas Manning glanced around. The hallway led to an open area with a very large fireplace, with chairs and settees gathered into conversational circles. At the far side, a carved, graceful staircase curved upward. "More so than I remember," he admitted. "I have neglected to come here for a long time. I have eight houses scattered about various parts of England thanks to my illustrious ancestors. It seems every time a Rothay heir marries, we collect estates like children gather sweets. It is impossible to live in all of them, and besides, my presence in London is required too often for me to spend a lot of time in the countryside."

The dry tone of his voice told her his reference to his heritage was self-deprecating, and she gave a small laugh, liking him for the lack of conceit. "I doubt most people would feel sorry for you because of an excess of wealth, Your Grace."

"Perhaps not." He took her elbow and urged her down the hallway. "But it is not without its pitfalls, like anything else. Mrs. Sims will show you to your room and when you are ready, please join me for some refreshment."

The housekeeper was elderly, her soft-spoken voice carrying a hint of a Scottish brogue, and she escorted Caroline upstairs to a lovely room with a glorious view of the back gardens, with open windows that let in the sweet scent of blooming roses. For a country house the furnishings were certainly rich, if dated, and the large bed was hung with pale blue silk, the carpet luxuriant and patterned with ivory, rose, and indigo. The overall effect made her feel like an honored guest, but she could not help but wonder if the elegant suite wasn't supposed to be that of the lady of the house. Especially when she noticed the door that obviously led to another suite of rooms.

Honored guest? Well, she supposed she was. Nicholas Manning wanted her to think he was a superb lover.

However, it would take more than a beautiful room to achieve that end. She stared at the adjoining door and felt yet another quiver of trepidation.

Chapter Seven

Long mellow shadows fell across the grass, a scented breeze moved across the gardens, rippling the glossy leaves, and it seemed every bird in England had gathered to twitter and sing. A rabbit hopped across one of the gravel paths, nibbled at a blade of grass, and cocked one floppy ear, unconcerned with their presence on the flagstone terrace just a few paces away. It was like one of those settings he remembered from childhood books, where the world was perpetual sunshine and cloudless skies.

Or maybe his jaded soul spent far too much time in the city.

The usual fairy tale was not complete without a beautiful maiden.

Nicholas, propped in a comfortable chair, drank brandy, not tea, and observed his beautiful guest with what he hoped seemed like casual attention and not the rapacious interest he truly felt.

The night he and Derek had gotten so far into their cups was blurry, and when he realized in the light of the next day they'd made the bet public by placing it in the book at White's, he'd uttered an inward groan. The best way to handle the resulting furor of whispers and interest seemed to be with as much of a sense of humor as possible. However, sitting now across from the ravishing Lady Wynn, he wasn't so sure it had been such a drunken blunder after all.

Even the way she sipped her tea, with a lift of her hands,

her lips just barely touching the rim of the cup, was reserved and restrained. Her gaze seemed focused on some unidentifiable distant object, as if she was directly *not* looking at him.

Nicholas had met her in passing once or twice, but because of first her unmarried status, then her position as a young bride who had not yet produced an heir, and then the absence from society after her husband's death, he hadn't really paid much attention. Yes, he'd thought she was delectable in a lush, opulent way, her rich hair and flawless skin setting off those incredible silver eyes, but she simply wasn't anyone he would pursue. It was more like admiring a painting in a museum—it drew the eye and pleased you in an aesthetic sense, but you knew you could never possess it, so you didn't waste time thinking about it too much.

Except all of that had changed.

He *would* possess her in a very carnal way and he was looking forward to it to a degree that astonished him. Maybe it was the unusual situation, maybe it was that stupid arrogant bet, but he couldn't remember the last time he'd felt such an intense interest in a woman in such a short amount of time.

"Tell me about yourself." He held his brandy glass and watched her sip again from the dainty porcelain teacup. The sunlight showed the glorious reddish highlights in her auburn hair. She wore a fashionable dress of dove gray that exactly matched her eyes, and on any other woman the color might have seemed dowdy, but she carried it off perfectly because it emphasized both her vibrant coloring and the slender voluptuousness of her figure.

He couldn't wait to get it off her, he decided with uncharacteristic impatience. The swell of her bosom under the modest neckline drew the eye, eliciting less-than-gentlemanly speculations on how it would feel to touch and taste those tempting breasts.

Caroline looked a little startled. "What is it you want to know, Your Grace?"

"Call me Nicholas."

"If you wish." But she looked uncertain, hurriedly taking another sip of tea. The cup trembled just a little—but enough that he noticed—against her mouth.

And an inviting mouth it was too. Pink soft lips, the lower one a little fuller with a perfect sensual curve. Nice.

"Where are you from?" he prodded a little.

"York." She answered readily enough, though her expression held that detached, solemn look that made her seem so distant. "My mother died when I was a child, and my father was a busy man, so I actually spent a great deal of time in London with my aunt. She was the one who arranged my coming-out and my marriage."

Two sentences did not exactly sum up anyone's life. "No brothers or sisters?"

"No."

Prying conversation out of a woman wasn't usually such a chore. He quirked a brow and tried again. "What are your interests? Theater, opera, fashion?"

She hesitated, and then said simply, "I love to read. Anything and everything. Novels, the newspaper from front page to last, even scientific works if I can find them. It has always been a passion of mine. My governess was progressive. She encouraged my curiosity and loaned me books I am sure my aunt would have disapproved of my reading. Miss Dunsworth's father was a famous antiquarian and had collected works from all over the world. He left her impoverished in some ways when he died, but rich in others if you value knowledge. Everything had to be sold, but she kept his library."

Females with intellect did not bother him like they did some of the other males of his acquaintance. He also liked the word *passion* when she said it.

"Tell me your favorite author."

"Voltaire, if you force me to choose one." Her expression was animated, lighting up her lovely face.

"Who else?"

She liked the ancient Greeks, Shakespeare, Pope, the more modern works of some of the popular authors of the day—some of which he hadn't read yet.

The sun warmed him, the brandy was mellow and luscious, and he was . . . *charmed.*

By bluestocking tendencies? It was a revelation. Women usually served only one casual purpose in his life, but there was a spark in Caroline's eyes that drew him in. Since he learned her identity back at the inn, he'd been fascinated.

It wasn't until he steered the conversation back to her family that the enthusiasm faded from her expression and she studiously paid more attention to looking at her teacup. "As I said before, I lived with my aunt. She died only a month or so after Edward."

He waited. There didn't seem to be more information forthcoming, but after her note, he really was quite curious about her marriage. "I knew your husband, but only vaguely."

"Be grateful."

He couldn't help it; his brows went up at her clipped tone. "I see."

She regarded him over the rim of her cup, and then set it aside with what looked like deliberate care. Those luminous gray eyes, so lovely in the framing of thick, lacy lashes, were very direct. "Forgive me, but no, you don't. You have never been married off to a man you don't really care for. You have never been subservient to the whims of someone else, and please admit you realize the difference between the genders in our society that allows titled gentlemen to make extravagant wagers over their *lack* of virtue, while women are judged most severely on keeping theirs."

For a moment Nicholas had no idea what to say. Lady Wynn did not flirt—he'd already discerned that—and apparently she had the ability to get right to the point and be refreshingly honest. After a small pause, he inclined his head. "Point taken. I will refrain henceforth from making presumptuous assumptions."

His easy acquiescence seemed to disconcert her. She pursed her mouth, drawing his wayward attention to her soft lips again. "I—I'm sorry," she said with a small sigh after a moment. "I am a bit sensitive on the subject of my marriage.

That's why I have no intention of ever entering into such an arrangement again."

"There is no need to apologize, I assure you, for voicing your opinion."

A wry look flickered across her face. "I think I just scolded the Duke of Rothay."

"Who no doubt deserves it now and again." He grinned. "Maybe even more often than that."

"You're very"—she seemed to search for a word and finally found it—"gracious. Most men want a woman to agree with everything they say. I find it tiresome."

"Hence the discouraging attitude toward all those eager gentlemen gathered around you at every event?" Nicholas lounged in his chair, enjoying not only the warm, lovely late-afternoon breeze but also her unique lack of coquetry. He was used to women fawning all over him, not reprimanding his poor understanding of their position in the world.

"Let's just say I value my independence."

They might not know each other very well, but they had that in common. "As do I."

"So rumor has it." Her lips curved in a full, bewitching smile that made his body, already on full alert, take notice.

The change was remarkable. It turned her from a marble, distant figure into a soft and appealing woman.

Nicholas shifted in his chair, swelling a little in arousal so the material of his breeches felt tight. How odd. The lady didn't dissemble, she didn't even make a pretense of it, and he found he liked her directness. He said softly, "Don't believe every rumor about me, but that one is correct."

"There are plenty enough. Your celebrity is as infamous as any in London society."

"I can't think why."

"Can't you? The stories abound."

"So I understand. But truth and gossip rarely go hand in hand, my lady."

She regarded him gravely. "Are you trying to tell me that you—and I want to remind you that recently you made a very presumptuous wager about your supposed talents in the very area we are discussing—are more virtuous than the rumors imply?"

Was he virtuous? Nicholas was sure the term had never been applied to him, but in an abstract way, maybe he was. As a point of honor he didn't involve himself with anyone who might take the game of seduction in a serious manner. He smiled with deliberate lazy insouciance. "Perhaps. I admit I stopped defending myself years ago."

"But you *do* want your companions without strings?"

"Absolutely." Since Helena, he'd found amorous affairs were best kept simple and purely for physical pleasure.

Once upon a time—before he understood that romantic dreams were just that—he'd made a mistake of colossal proportions. One he was unlikely to ever make again. The lesson had been a harsh one, but he'd been young and foolish, and had idealistic expectations. Experience could be a bitter pill and left an aftertaste one didn't easily forget.

Apparently Caroline correctly interpreted his expression. "Well, no one knows I'm here, Your Grace. We're alone, anonymous, and free to do as we please."

"Nicholas," he reminded her with a slow smile, watching the way the light played across the fragile features of her face, along the slender curves of her shoulders, giving a delightful shadow to the tantalizing cleft between her full breasts, just hinted at by the neckline of her gown. "Do you want to go inside?"

She didn't misunderstand the suggestion, and her cheeks took on a rosy tint. "Now? It's the afternoon."

He stifled a laugh at her naive insinuation people made love only after the sun set. For a widow she was certainly sheltered. He murmured, "Why wait? We could talk more comfortably."

"Talk?"

"Among other things."

Her cheeks flushed a deeper shade of pink.

In bed, he meant. Though he usually didn't particularly want to talk in that environment, he was willing to do so if it made her more at ease. He didn't train virgins—not ever. Raised as a ducal heir, he'd been taught about the pitfalls of lost innocence from the time he was old enough to understand the concept—but he was getting the feeling she was as close to one as he might ever come until he married. It was evident that despite her composure she was very nervous, yet also aware of him as a man. It heightened his interest to a surprising degree.

Nicholas stood and moved to take her hand, pulling her gently to her feet. He gazed down at her upturned face and focused on her mouth. "I think you're very beautiful, Lady Wynn."

Gray eyes glimmered, her tone hushed as she replied, "You would say that, of course."

"Not if I don't mean it." He was sincere. Charming women into his bed did not include false compliments. He didn't need coercion, and if she thought he did, she was more innocent than he imagined. Surely someone of her exquisite beauty had been given enough poetic tributes to her looks to last a lifetime. "Since it isn't the first time you've heard it, why not trust my sincerity?"

Very lightly, he touched her hair, just a brush of the backs of his fingers over those vibrant silky strands. The color reminded him of fall, rich brown with glints of red. A few loose tendrils framed her oval face and teased the slender ivory column of her neck. The warm color suited her, despite her reputation for being chilly and distant.

He'd be willing to place another reckless wager that she wasn't actually cold in any way. Her husband had obviously been an oaf in the bedroom, but it was going to be Nicholas's pleasure to show her the benefits of mutual physical joy between a man and a woman.

Caroline gave him a quixotic smile. "I barely know you, Nicholas."

He liked his name on her lips. "Surely you realized that before you sent me the note. What better way to become acquainted?"

Whatever reply she might have made was silenced as he

lowered his head and took her mouth. His hands went to her slim waist, his clasp firm but not insistent as he very softly molded their mouths together. When it came to women, his instincts were well honed. He'd already sensed persuasion was going to be more effective than impetuous passion. There were plenty of ladies who liked to be swept away, who wanted their lover to not only possess but dominate them, but he had known Caroline wasn't one of them before he even touched her.

She tasted sweet, and felt incredible in his arms, her pliant breasts just touching his chest, but when he brushed his tongue into her mouth, she jerked in what could only have been surprise.

What the bloody hell?

For a moment he paused, arrested by a startling realization.

That a woman who had been married had never been kissed in an intimate way was impossible, but he could feel her tentative response to the exploration of his tongue, as if she had very little idea what to do.

That was an interesting facet to this country tryst. Nicholas continued, keeping the kiss undemanding, but subtly urging her closer so their bodies touched more fully. Normally he would have found that particular degree of inexperience off-putting, but—maybe it was the unique situation, maybe it was her compelling beauty, or maybe it was just how she seemed to fit perfectly in his arms; he wasn't sure—he found he was more intrigued than ever.

He murmured against her lips, "Can I once again invite you inside?"

By now she was nestled against his growing erection, so there was no mistaking what his suggestion entailed. But then again, wasn't that why she was there? Caroline nodded. Nicholas stepped away, took her hand, and smiled.

She didn't smile back but stared at him for a moment, her incredible eyes wide and her cheeks flushed. Not a bad sign, he noted as she allowed him to lead her inside and up the stairs to his bedroom. The house was quiet in the late afternoon, Mrs. Sims no doubt busy arranging preparations due to his unexpected visit. There hadn't been time to summon more staff, and since he knew Caroline valued anonymity, he hadn't brought any servants with him except his driver. Even his valet had stayed back in London so his bedroom was empty, and when he closed the door behind them, he knew they'd be left alone as long as they wanted. The housekeeper had strict instructions to not disturb them unless summoned.

"We have connecting doors." Caroline glanced over toward the wall separating their bedchambers.

"Convenient, isn't it?" Nicholas grinned, his heated gaze admiring how she looked, so graceful and feminine in the masculine setting of his bedroom. The furnishings were overdone in size—the huge bed sitting on a dais, the proportions massive—and the carved dark wood was centuries old. One of his august ancestors posed in lace, hose, and a doublet in a portrait over the fireplace.

In contrast, she was curve and shadow, alluring, and oh-so-conveniently there.

His erection throbbed from that one kiss, straining against the fitted material of his breeches. "Let's do this the right way."

She didn't resist as he loosened her long hair so it tumbled free down her back. It felt like warm silk as it spilled over his hands, and its summery fragrance was sweet and female. As he unfastened her gown, he kissed her softly in reassurance, taking care not to rush or alarm her. Lifting her in his arms, he carried her to the bed and stripped off her slippers and stockings with the same deft expertise, admiring her beauty with pure male appreciation as he sat down to take off his boots. He finished the task in record time and stood to finish undressing.

It surprised him, but he was actually in a hurry.

Clad only in her chemise, she was perfection, an auburn-haired Venus in the slanting late-afternoon sun coming in the tall windows, all supple limbs and flawless pale skin, framed by a tumble of shining tresses. Full breasts quivered with each breath, and her eyes looked darker, dilated, the unique silver color tempered by passion.

Or fear.

Nicholas realized it in a rush of consternation as his fingers stilled in the act of unbuttoning his shirt.

Yes, he thought as he fought disbelief. Fear. The trembling of the woman in his bed had nothing to do with desire.

Instead of flushed with arousal, her face was now a little pale. He dropped his hands, his shirt open to his waist, not sure how to handle this unexpected turn of events. "We don't have to do this, you know. Say the word. We'll go drink wine in the sun instead and you can leave tomorrow, if you wish."

For a moment she hesitated, and then she whispered, "Is it that obvious?"

He wasn't used to anything less than total eagerness in the bedroom, so the answer was a resounding yes. However, diplomacy seemed best. Nicholas said slowly, "I think it's obvious you aren't entirely comfortable, my lady. Our wager was a stupid moment between two foxed gentlemen who both had heavy heads in the morning. While the grace of your presence in my bed is appealing to me, you needn't go through with your offer."

In delectable dishabille, superimposed on the fine linens of the bed, Caroline gave him a faint smile. "No wonder your charm is legendary, Rothay, but did you think I volunteered lightly? Of the ladies of your acquaintance, I am probably the least likely to be found in your bed, but I am here, and it is up to you to seduce me, correct?"

She had a point. A fearful, edgy woman was *not* what either he or Derek had in mind, he was sure, but she'd come forward, they'd agreed, and he'd been the one so anxious to get her alone.

"Only if you wish it."

"If I didn't, I wouldn't be here."

Why the devil was she there, if the idea of sharing his bed made her go ashen and shake in trepidation?

She asserted with just a hint of desperation, "I want this."

Was that true? His unruly body urged him to continue, but still he didn't move. Every affair had its parameters, and every woman was different, but this situation gave him true pause. He had a feeling the amount of effort it cost her to lie there, compliant and willing, was enormous.

It was daunting.

What the hell had Wynn done—or not done—to her?

"Are you a virgin?" He asked the question quietly, not certain how he'd proceed if she said yes. He wasn't going to pretend he hadn't noticed her reaction to his kiss. This was no longer about the ludicrous bet. For her, he was beginning to realize, it never had been.

She looked away and swallowed visibly, the muscles in her slim throat moving. "No."

That one small word held a world of meaning.

More than a little at a loss, Nicholas still stood there. He knew all about the sexual games men and women played together, but not *this* one. This wasn't about lighthearted seduction in the least. He sat down and touched her, just a light pressure on her chin so her face turned toward him. Tears glistened on her lashes, he saw with a small shock of dismay.

"Seduce me," she whispered into the poignant silence. "Please."

Chapter Eight

If things kept going as they were, she'd be the only woman in the entire world who'd lain almost naked in the bed of the wickedly sensual and gorgeous Duke of Rothay and had him decline to make love to her.

She'd just practically had to beg him.

Mortifying as it was, she was surprised such a noted libertine had the sensitivity to know she was fearful. He looked as unsettled as she felt, and that was saying something. Under different circumstances she might have been amused.

"I want to, obviously," he finally murmured, a small wry smile curving his finely modeled mouth as he glanced down at the impressive bulge in his breeches.

Dear God, he looked . . . huge.

But weepy, inexperienced, frosty widows weren't his usual fare. He didn't have to explain. Who could blame him? No matter what she might look like, sensuality wasn't her forte.

But here she was, undressed, her hair unbound, in his bed. If she gave in to cowardice now, the opportunity would slip away.

"Kiss me again," she urged, looking into his midnight eyes. Through the gap in his unfastened shirt she could see the muscular hardness of his bare chest and it caused an odd feeling to coil in the pit of her stomach. Ebony hair, sleek and just a little disheveled, brushed his strong neck as his shirt hung open. His dark male beauty was compelling, but then again, her husband had also been a handsome man. Maybe not as magnificent a specimen as the infamous Rothay, but still . . .

No. She would not think about Edward. Not now.

Nicholas leaned forward and, to her surprise, instead of taking her mouth in another devastatingly wicked kiss, he touched his lips to the betraying wetness of her lashes. He gently kissed away her tears, and at the same time some of her fears. When he lay down next to her and gathered her close, she did her best to stay lax, even in the strong circle of his arms.

He smelled wonderful in some foreign beguiling way. Did all men have that spicy, intriguing scent or was it his alone?

"You're very lovely," he whispered, stroking her back, inching her chemise up so subtly she almost didn't notice what he was doing until his fingers smoothed over the curve of her bared thigh.

She reflexively started and he immediately removed his hand.

"Relax," he murmured in her ear, his breath warm, bewitching.

"I am doing my best." And a woeful best it was, she thought in bitter self-recrimination. Maybe Edward had been right all along, for if lying next to one of the most charming and handsome men in England did nothing for her, perhaps she was irrevocably flawed.

Well, perhaps not *nothing*.

His calm, even breathing and the steady beat of his heart seemed to ease the awareness of how his tall body dwarfed her much-smaller frame. To her surprise she felt her breasts tighten, and when he grazed his mouth across her cheek, she sighed and turned her head to offer her mouth.

"Maybe we should start slow."

She wished she had some idea of exactly what he meant, but she couldn't even hazard a guess. "Whatever you want."

How desperately she wished she could live up to that offer.

A mesmerizing smile curved his lips. "Kissing is an art. Would you like some instruction?"

"Why else would I be here?"

On his secluded estate, in his bed, clasped in his arms. Why else indeed except for the enlightenment she hoped it would bring her?

"Then it will be my pleasure, my lady."

Very slowly, he lowered his head again. Their lips touched, clung.

It was long, luxurious, tantalizing, forbidden. It was a real kiss.

His tongue gently dueled with hers, teasing forth a response as it explored her mouth, and Caroline began to relax into the kiss, especially since he simply held her and did nothing more. He was also still fully dressed, though she could feel the warmth from his bared skin through the gap in his unbuttoned shirt. His lips left hers, descended again, and this time trailed down her neck, lingering at the hollow of her throat.

The whim of sending that note—no, not a whim really, as she'd agonized over it—suddenly seemed very right.

This was exactly what she hoped she'd feel.

It was pleasant. No, not a good enough word. Better than pleasant. She shuddered at the teasing pressure of his mouth.

"All I am going to do is taste you." His voice held a light husky note as he whispered against her skin. "Nothing more. May I?"

She realized his fingers held the ribbon lacing the bodice of her chemise together, and he was asking permission to pull it free.

Asking. That was certainly unique in her experience. The notion her wishes would be considered at all was reassuring.

But the idea he'd want to see her naked was decidedly unsettling. It was a quandary. While the last thing she wanted was for him to simply shove her skirts up and get on with it, she was shy at the idea of being nude before him—or anyone for that matter—in daylight, no less. She'd known none of this was going to be easy, but as he waited politely into the lengthening silence, she felt an unusual glimmer of trust.

A good start at least.

Caroline nodded and felt the resulting tug with a wash of heat into her face as her chemise gaped open, baring her breasts. Nicholas looked at the exposed flesh and slowly reached between the parted cloth to lightly touch one nipple with a questing fingertip. She gave a small gasp.

"The color of a summer rose, delicate and perfect."

Caroline somehow managed to speak. "A true flowery compliment, Your Grace."

One dark brow arched upward in amusement. "But in this case the honest truth. Keep in mind also, Caroline, when you are in my bed, I am a man and you are the woman I desire. Use my given name."

She couldn't help but close her eyes at the stroking of his fingers across her sensitive skin. His warm palm now fully cradled her breast and to her surprise, the heated look in his eyes eased some of her misgivings.

Those eyes. Midnight dark, seductive as sin, framed by long, thick lashes in contrast with the chiseled lines of his features. Letting her lashes drift up, she met his gaze with a small jab of realization that he was waiting, doing nothing more than leaning up on one elbow and watching her expression as he cupped her breast in his hand.

Waiting for what? She had no idea. It was humiliating, and she despised Edward even more for her ignorance. "Am I supposed to do something?"

A quixotic smile touched his mouth. "Do something?"

Since it was obvious he'd been able to see through the guise of poised widow from the moment he kissed her on the terrace, it seemed pointless to dissemble. "Please don't laugh at me. I am sure you have already discerned—"

"I am not laughing at you." The interruption was soft and quiet. "I am admiring a delightful view, and also plotting my strategy. After all, I am supposed to acquit myself admirably and surely the first time is the most crucial, is it not?"

"You are not used to women like me, though," she responded with as much dignity as possible under the circumstances, "and therefore at a loss."

Because she was an utter failure in the bedroom. He was used to the urbane, sophisticated ladies he usually pursued. The distance between those skilled ladies and her ineptitude was an immense one.

"At a loss?" He grinned then, like a young boy, but the connotation of the intoxicating curve of his lips was pure adult male. Even in her unenlightened state, she saw the promise there with a small shiver of anticipation. "Definitely not," Nicholas told her, giving the flesh mounded in his hand a gentle squeeze. "I am merely trying to decide where to start. You are like a blank canvas, my dear, and that first brushstroke is crucial."

The poetic reference was just part of his well-developed charm, she reminded herself. "I am sure you are the supreme artiste, Rothay."

"Supreme? Have I won already so easily?"

"That was sarcasm over your arrogance." It was a bit difficult to sound cool and detached when his skillful fingers now massaged her tingling nipple.

"Do I sense derision?"

She liked his light teasing tone, and he was beginning to ease her apprehension. No wonder scores of women succumbed, she thought as a strange warmth built between her thighs. Despite his impressive height and obvious strength, he gave the impression of power without threat, of male charisma without dominance. Even his smile carried an overt sensual promise.

Maybe her impulsive scandalous idea wasn't a bad one after all. Oh yes, she'd be ruined forever if anyone found out, but this might just be worth it.

When he lowered his head and took the bud of her nipple into his mouth, she suppressed a shuddering sigh with effort, though she had the impression he still sensed it. The notion a grown man might want to suckle her nipples was startling, but as he ministered to one breast and then the other, Caroline realized it was wonderful. A luxurious feeling of enjoyment slowly began to captivate her body as he tasted and fondled, first one taut breast and then the other. His warm mouth traced the contours of the valley between them, the undersides, and back to the now tight, glistening crests.

But all she was doing was lying there and she was sure there should be more to it.

Or so Edward had told her in the most scathing way possible.

One of the duke's long-fingered hands slid along the side of her leg, caressing the underside of her knee. Somehow it felt delicious. Caroline had never thought that spot to be so sensitive. Slowly he lifted her leg so it was bent just a little, and then settled her foot back on the bed. As he took her lips in another one of those long, intimate kisses, his mouth lingering on hers, he did the same with the other leg, so she was now lying with her legs slightly apart, and though her chemise still covered her sex, the suggestive position made the hem slide to the top of her thighs.

The realization of her situation was like a lightning bolt. She was in the bed of the infamous Duke of Rothay and almost nude, her legs spread apart enough to give him access, if he wished it.

He did, she discovered a moment later as, with a delicacy of a touch so light she barely felt it, his hand slipped under the concealing material and he brushed the triangle of hair between her thighs. Caroline quivered and it was all she could do not to clamp her legs tightly together, but that would effectively trap his hand right where he wanted it to be. She took in a deep calming breath and managed to stay still.

Very still. Too still, because he said, "This should make you melt, lovely Caroline, not turn into stone. I see I am going to have to be very persuasive indeed. It would be ungallant of me to not pick up the gauntlet you tossed down before myself and Manderville."

He'd already called her icy, and it wasn't a far leap to frigid. That had been Edward's sneering opinion, and she opened her mouth to defend herself, but no words came out.

Instead she let out something between a gasp and a cry of outraged protest when her handsome seducer shifted position, put his insistent hands on her quivering inner thighs to widen them farther, and then lowered his head.

She lay rigid, in total shock, so stunned she didn't even object to the way he twitched her chemise upward, exposing her from the waist down. His mouth grazed her most private place, and then settled on it fully and the resulting sensation as his tongue delved between her feminine folds was . . . a revelation.

The Devilish Duke had his mouth between her legs, the dark silk of his hair brushing her inner thighs, and his wicked tongue began to do some very interesting things.

Tiny jolts of pleasure swamped her body and she twisted her hands in the bedclothes, as if holding on to something might keep her from flying away. Her affronted sensibilities held sway over her mind for only a moment and slid away in rapturous delight.

Oh God.

Nicholas chuckled, a brief sound that vibrated against her throbbing sex, and she realized she'd said the words out loud. Under normal circumstances it would have been enough to make her blush, but these circumstances weren't normal at all. He held her body in a thrall of erotic possession and she let her thighs fall even farther apart, lifting her hips a small fraction as a strange anticipation built.

This was *it*. This was why women whispered behind their hands, fluttered their fans, and spoke of the bonny dark-haired duke with reverent, sly innuendos and heated sighs. As erotic enjoyment swept over her, she shuddered in involuntary reaction.

There was no way she could keep back an unladylike moan and once it escaped, she found she didn't care about any other sounds, just the escalating mysterious need that built inside her. It was magical, elusive, captivating. Her blood warmed, her pulse raced forward, and she arched in an involuntary movement to increase the pressure of his bewitching mouth.

It felt too wonderful, something between agony and bliss, as if her wayward body yearned for something.

She found it, or it found her—a joyous burst, like being plummeted from a great height, knocking the breath from her lungs, making her give a small cry as the physical joy of it rushed through her and she shuddered and trembled.

It was, in a word, glorious.

Reality drifted back in hazy bits. The sun-drenched old-world elegance of the ducal bedroom, her dishabille with her chemise undone and the thin material bunched up over her hips, and *him*, the man who had just done the single most scandalous thing she could imagine—actually, she would never have imagined it—to her.

Nicholas Manning lounged next to her, lean and imposing, the bulge in his breeches prominent, though he made no move to touch her as he waited for her to recover. Except for his boots and undone shirt, he was still fully dressed.

A part of her wanted to wipe the self-satisfied smile from his face, but another part—the part that had set her on this course for this very reason, wanted to thank him from the bottom of her heart.

He said with an impudent quirk of one downy ebony brow, "Well?"

The woman sprawled so delectably on his bed was an enigma. Lush yet prim, inexperienced but obviously aware of an inner sensuality she wanted to discover, repressed but not eager to remain that way. Her beauty also was glorious; the contrast between the pristine white linen sheets and her lustrous auburn hair compelling, her breasts full and perfectly shaped, her legs slender and pale. Those soft full lips he'd kissed were the same shade as her nipples, both darkened to a deep rosy shade by his attentions. Everything, from the delicate arch of her brows, to the straight line of her small nose, to the shape of her chin, held an almost fragile femininity. He had to admit, he was captivated by her physical appearance.

There was also the very intriguing notion he knew he'd

just given her the first sexual climax of her life. Whatever had happened between her and her late husband hadn't been pleasant, he'd wager, because timid certainly wasn't her nature. The anger he felt toward a man already dead was futile, but it was there all the same. What had Wynn done to her? The realization she was physically afraid of him had been startling, but it explained a great deal.

If Lord Wynn weren't already in his grave, he might have found himself there anyway, for violence against women or children was something that particularly turned Nicholas's stomach, and his accuracy with a dueling pistol was undisputed. He'd certainly risen at dawn for less-worthy causes.

It made her offer to judge the adolescent contest not just the whim of a bored widow, but a lesson in courage. She had taken a great step to free herself of that innate fear that kept her so cold and distant.

Caroline stared at him with those striking silver eyes. She repeated as if still a little dazed, "Well?"

He could still taste her, the earthy sweet residue of her release on his lips. Nicholas smiled despite his rigid, uncomfortable erection. "I suppose it is unfair of me to ask how I am doing so far, so instead I'll pose it a different way. Would you like to get dressed and go for a walk in the gardens? They are quite beautiful here this time of year. I'd forgotten, since it's been so long, but I took a stroll while I waited for you to arrive and it was lovely."

"But you haven't—that is . . ." A vivid blush washed her cheeks and her hand crept to the hem of her shift, but she didn't pull it down to cover herself, though it was easy to guess she wanted to do so. Her gaze traveled to his blatant arousal, clearly visible through his breeches.

"I can wait."

"You don't look as if you want to wait, Your Gra—Nicholas."

His erect cock agreed with her wholeheartedly, but if he wanted her confidence, it was best to use restraint. He reached out, tugged down her chemise over her thighs, and took the ribbon on her bodice and regretfully tightened it over without a doubt the finest pair of breasts he'd ever touched and tasted. "We have all week."

Her smooth brow furrowed. "Did I do something wrong?"

The question amused him and was perplexing at the same time. "What makes you think so, if I may ask?"

Even as he said the words, he realized there *was* one thing she hadn't done yet. Even though he'd kissed her, tasted her delectable breasts, and brought her to climax with his mouth, she hadn't—not once—touched him. Not her fingers in his hair, not that telltale grasp of his shoulders, not even so much as a hand resting on his back.

Before this week was over, he'd change that, he made a silent vow. He had a feeling winning her trust on an intellectual basis was as important as wooing her gorgeous body.

This was an unexpected challenge.

She answered his question in an oblique way. "I do not want to . . . disappoint you."

The idea of it was so ludicrous he felt his mouth twitch. He looked into her eyes. "I promise you do not, and no, you did nothing wrong. I am intrigued by you in many ways, my lady. Now, then, shall we take a stroll in the garden and perhaps get to know each other a little better? Lovers should have more in common than the act of sexual intercourse, don't you think? Whatever they say, I don't value a woman just for the physical pleasure she might bring me."

It was true, but with a philosophical twist. Emotional closeness was not Nicholas's goal either. That was a disastrous path he didn't choose to tread. He liked to be friends with his lovers, no more. If nothing else, it paved the path for a more amicable parting.

Caroline sat up in a flurry of glossy auburn hair, a small smile gracing her very kissable mouth. "I see you are determined to win this wager. Who would guess the Devilish Duke has such romantic sensibilities?"

"Anyone who knows me well," he said in smooth repartee. "When I am with a beautiful woman, I want to know all of her, not just her body."

"As for the last part," she said wryly, "I think we've taken care of that in my case. I seem to be the only one undressed."

He'd barely begun to introduce her to the joys of the flesh. Nicholas grinned. "It's a nice place to start, I must admit. Never fear, I'll undress later."

Chapter Nine

If he slammed his fist through the wall, someone might notice, so perhaps it was best that he didn't.

But damn it all, he wanted to. Derek tossed down half a glass of wine in one gulp. The idea of enduring the rest of the evening made him want to bolt out the door. However, if he did that, his humiliating secret would be exposed to the world, and it was one he had to keep at all costs. If he couldn't have what he wanted, he would at least like to keep some vestige of male pride.

Bloody hell, though, did Annabel have to look so beautiful? Of course she did, he reminded himself in sardonic honesty. In sackcloth she'd be the loveliest woman in the room, and in a low-cut gown of pale blue silk that set off her eyes and golden hair, well . . . she was stunning. Though he did his best to look nonchalant in his casual pose with one shoulder propped against the wall, Derek watched her, his brooding gaze following her around the room as she mingled with the guests, accepted congratulations, and, the worst of all, favored her intended with one of those dazzling smiles. . . .

"It's turned out well, I think, don't you?"

Thomas Drake, his father's youngest brother, took a sip from his glass of wine as he joined Derek in the corner of the elegant drawing room.

Derek nodded politely. "Splendid party, Uncle."

"Annabel looks very fine, don't you think?"

Derek gritted his teeth. "Yes."

"Lord Hyatt is clearly besotted."

That was an understatement. The blasted man was drooling all over her. Derek chose not to comment. Hyatt wasn't the only besotted fool in the room.

"Your aunt Margaret thought maybe a quiet family party before the big engagement ball would be best. I agree it's very nice to all get together. When the formal celebration is given, there will be quite a crush. I am glad you could come."

Since he'd rather be dragged naked backward through a muddy field full of brambles and rocks by a runaway horse, Derek merely managed a brittle smile. "How could I possibly miss it?"

"The food was delightful, wasn't it?" Tall and lean, with a scholarly air, Thomas raised his brows just a fraction.

It might have been paste for all Derek knew. He'd drunk his way through dinner and not taken more than a few bites. He gave a grunt that might have meant anything, and looked around for more claret. It was true, the family gathering of thirty people or so was better than a ballroom full of guests, but only marginally. He still had to render a credible performance of indifference—or, worse, joy for the happy couple—plus dredge up the appropriate small talk with great-aunts and distant cousins. Hence his position on the fringe of the room, as out of sight as possible. If he could have ducked behind one of the elegant settees or crawled up the chimney of one of the several Italian marble fireplaces, he would have.

But he was the earl, his presence was requested by his aunt, of whom he was genuinely fond, and the best he could do was endure with as much equanimity as possible under the circumstances.

"For my part, of course, I wasn't sure about Hyatt for Annabel. She's on the headstrong side now and again and the man is a bit meek." Thomas chuckled. "Why am I telling you this? You've known her almost all her life. She has grown from a curious, mischievous child into a young woman who very much knows her own mind. I think we can agree she needs a firm hand."

What she needed, Derek thought in wayward contemplation, were *his* hands. On her, touching every delicious inch, bringing her exquisite, unforgettable pleasure . . .

He cleared his throat. "I am sure Hyatt can manage."

"She'll manage *him*, that's my prediction."

Having to attend the dinner was bad enough, but discussing how the woman he loved would handle her marriage to someone else was infinitely worse. Derek glanced across the room, noticed the way the candlelight gave rich golden highlights to her pale hair, and straightened. She *was* headstrong. Also bright, beautiful, and far too close even in a crowded room. He rasped out, "I need more wine. Please excuse me."

"Yes, I cannot help but notice you look rather miserable. But is wine the solution?"

Thomas's quiet question stopped Derek in the act of walking away. He froze and turned around.

Miserable was an understatement, but he'd thought he'd done a rather good job of hiding how he felt.

Thomas went on. "I tried to stay out of this, but have decided it is doing no one any good. Have you ever thought about telling her how you feel?"

Derek had a desperate moment where he wanted to act as if he didn't understand, but Uncle Thomas knew him too well. He'd been there as Derek assumed his responsibilities as the earl; he'd been like a father in many ways, since Derek had lost his own so young. He exhaled on a ragged expulsion of breath, ran his fingers through his hair, and didn't dissemble. "She despises me."

"You think so?" Thomas looked bland.

"She's made it clear enough." Derek heard the defensive note in his voice and did his best to temper it. "It's my fault and I'm suffering for it, but it is what it is."

"Mind telling me what happened? I've asked her about your apparent falling-out and she refuses to explain."

Did he mind? Hell yes, he minded. It brought back the

memory of Annabel's face that unlucky evening. Derek did his best to seem nonchalant, but his stomach tightened. "I'm afraid she caught me in a rather flagrant indiscretion with Lady Bellvue. I am sure you remember when she was our houseguest at Manderville Hall last year."

To his credit, Thomas didn't look disapproving. Neither did he seem surprised. "I thought it might be something like that. I remember the lady in question was in hot pursuit of you her entire stay. I suppose I am not astonished to find out you finally succumbed."

No, he shouldn't have. It might have been the weakest mistake of his lifetime. Derek said explosively, "Bloody hell, Uncle, don't excuse me. I shouldn't have touched Isabella, and I wouldn't have except . . ."

"Yes?"

Except he'd gone into the library that fateful afternoon. He could still remember the way the sunlight fell in blocks over the Oriental rug, how the air was heavy with the scent of yellowing paper and leather, how he hadn't been in the least surprised to find the room already occupied because Annabel frequently had her pretty nose buried in a book. She'd been there, looking uncommonly lovely in a day gown of white muslin embroidered with tiny yellow flowers of some sort, her shining hair caught simply with a satin ribbon at her nape. When he entered, she'd looked up and smiled, and he'd been more than a little caught off guard with the depth of his reaction.

To a smile.

Yes, he'd known she had a girlish infatuation with him. At first he'd been amused when he realized it, because while he was well used to females in pursuit and it was a game he enjoyed, he was not at all familiar with being the object of an innocent adolescent's adoration. Then several years went by and she no longer in the least resembled the engaging child who used to trot around at his heels, but had turned instead into a very beautiful young woman. More than just her physical transformation from girl to woman, she was also intelligent, articulate, and, as his uncle had pointed out already, capable of voicing her opinion on most subjects. Even when she was younger, she'd been adventurous, eager for life, and determined to overcome the horrendous tragedy of losing both parents at once in that terrible accident. Perhaps it was being orphaned at such a young age that gave her a resilient, self-reliant nature, or maybe it was just an innate part of her personality, but whatever it was, he liked her air of independence—he always had. In the girl, it had been endearing. In the woman, it was intriguing.

To his surprise, he'd found himself thinking about her often, even when he was in London and she was in Berkshire. Looking back, he realized now he'd gone to Manderville Hall more often than necessary—and Annabel was the reason why. Her laughter, the tendency she had to lean forward when she argued a point, the unfashionable intelligence that she made no effort to hide . . . all of it drew him.

How could it be? He, of all people, interested in a young lady barely out of the schoolroom?

No.

Or was he?

That fateful afternoon in the library, after making the pretense of looking for a book, making a few teasing comments so he could hear the music of her laugh, he'd done the unforgivable and kissed her. Oh, it was neatly executed, because he was quite experienced at the art of flirtation, and Annabel had been no match for him. He lured her to the window to admire the view of the rose garden, stood just a fraction too close for propriety, put his hand on the small of her back, and then angled his body just so and looked down at her. He could still remember vividly the slight widening of her eyes as she realized his intentions, and the soft willing feel of her in his arms.

The taste of her mouth had been strawberry sweet, warmth and innocence, and the tentative brush of her fingers against his neck made his entire body tighten with desire. With a woman's unerring instinct she'd swayed into him, surrendering everything, and he'd accepted the precious offer, damn him straight to hell.

Her first kiss and he'd been the one.

What's more, he'd *wanted* to be the one.

However, reality had a nasty habit of coming crashing down, and so it did, even as he lifted his head and stared into her eyes. They were blue, a pure shade he could compare to a cloudless summer sky, and held a dreamy look of happiness even as a brilliant smile touched her soft lips, still damp from his attentions.

Then she said it. *Don't stop.* In a singular breathless, innocent whisper that summoned a dash of icy reality.

Don't stop. Was she insane? Of course he had to stop.

What the hell had he just done?

He was twenty-seven years old and she was not yet eighteen. He was a rake with a formidable reputation for debauchery—some, though not all, of it deserved—and she was his uncle's innocent ward. Unless he wished to marry her, he shouldn't lay a finger on her, much less encourage her infatuation.

At the time, the word *marriage* scared the devil out of him. He wasn't sure it didn't have the same effect now, but it was with a different kind of perspective.

So, even more dastardly than kissing her, he'd mumbled some excuse, left the room abruptly, and avoided her the rest of the day, because he had no idea how to deal with the tumultuous feelings of guilt, confusion, and something else, something hard to define. When had it happened? When had the child turned into a woman and when had he noticed?

What's more, when had he been drawn in? Not just by her newfound maturity, not just by the way she looked and moved differently, but by *her*. The sparkle of her laughter, the quick vibrant wit, the unique look in her eyes as she gazed at him.

He'd seduced, charmed, and won his way through scores of women. This young woman—barely more than a girl—should have no effect on his life or his emotions.

But she did.

Later that evening, when Isabella Bellvue cornered him in the conservatory, he hadn't resisted her overtures.

Anything to get the image of Annabel's face out of his mind. It was his ill luck, or maybe fate, she had come looking for him.

The disillusioned look on Annabel's face before she turned and fled the room would be etched in his memory forever. The next day, he'd been even more of an ass and compounded his sin by leaving for London without saying a word. In the year that passed, Annabel had barely spoken to him and he didn't blame her. Twice he'd tried to offer some banal kind of apology, but both times she'd just walked away from him before he could get more than a few words out. After the second time, he told himself to just forget the incident, forget *her*, and that the world was full of beautiful women who did not despise him.

Intelligent words, but the ghost of that kiss lingered.

He'd come to the conclusion he wasn't going to so easily dismiss her from his life, but it hardly mattered now. She had dismissed *him* by becoming engaged to another man.

"Except I'm a damned fool," Derek said heavily.

"Upon occasion, I agree." Thomas smiled in his benign way. "But then again, most of us can say the same thing. The real question is how badly you want to remedy the damage done. In my opinion, Annabel's continued disdain is a symbol of her strong underlying feelings. When she was a child, she adored you, and as she turned into a woman, that sentiment seemed to deepen. Finding you in a compromising situation with another woman was probably hurtful. Maybe you should try to repair the damage."

"She'll barely speak to me, and besides, in case it has escaped your notice, she is very much promised to another."

Thomas looked across to where she stood next to her betrothed, his expression thoughtful. "What I've noticed, Derek, is that she isn't happy, no matter what kind of facade she presents in public. I think Hyatt is an amiable man and she likes him well enough, but it isn't a love match. Not on her part."

"Most fashionable marriages are not." Derek spoke with the authority of a man who knew he told the truth. It was part of life in the beau monde. Love was not required to make an advantageous match.

Thomas wasn't to be deterred. "We both know Annabel deserves happiness, not mere contentment."

This conversation *and* an empty glass? Neither was appealing. Derek made a helpless gesture with his hand. "It seems to me she's chosen her path."

"Maybe a different option would give her another direction. Tell me this. If she were free and you could persuade her to give you a second chance, would you marry her?"

"Yes."

Good God, he hadn't even hesitated. He needed something stronger than claret. Hadn't he just said he'd consider *marriage*?

Uncle Thomas gave him a glimmering smile and said drily, "You see, you aren't a fool all the time, your recent outrageous wager with Rothay aside."

"Not my finest idea," Derek admitted with an inner wince. "But Annabel's engagement announcement was in the paper that morning. Getting foxed seemed the thing to do."

"Like now?"

"Insensibility has its merits now and again."

"The thing to do," Thomas informed him, "is to change her mind. If she won't speak to you—and I am fairly sure she is still in that frame of mind—put that legendary talent to good use for a change. God knows you've been honing it in a myriad of bedrooms over the years. Don't let all that practice go to waste when something important is at stake."

Derek stared, nonplussed, as his uncle strolled off to mingle with the guests.

Had Thomas really just suggested he *seduce* Annabel?

Dinner was simple but delicious in the way only a country meal could be. The butter was freshly churned, the vegetables were just picked and cooked until meltingly tender, and the beef was flavorful and smothered in rich brown gravy. For dessert Mrs. Sims had made a fruit tart with pears from the estate gardens, and Caroline savored every bite.

She also, surprisingly, savored the conversation. They sat in a small charming room usually used for breakfast with a low ceiling and long windows, the table intimate, the space not at all grand but still very appealing. Lit tapers flickered light over a table that had seen use over the years, but as with everything else, each detail was well cared for from the polished dark wood floor to the mural of a spring garden on the wall. It was delightful and informal and not at all what she expected from an august duke with a vast fortune at his fingertips.

The lack of pretense was welcome. It also surprised her.

He surprised her.

She was still nervous over the coming night, but Nicholas Manning had a singular ability to manage to carry most of the conversation without monopolizing it, and she'd already noticed he was a rare breed of man who didn't wish to talk more about himself than any other subject.

His horses were another matter. It was clear his pastime was also an obsession and she'd seen firsthand at Ascot how successful of one.

"Norfolk won that day," he told her, a slight whimsical smile of reminiscence on his face at the end of one story, fingering his glass of after-dinner port. "With a cracked cannon bone. He couldn't walk out of the winner's circle. I've never seen such spirit. My trainer wept. I admit to a tear or two myself."

The Devilish Duke crying over an injured horse when he could buy another—or hundreds of others—with his fortune?

Caroline gazed at him from across the table. "Have you always been horse mad?"

He laughed in a flash of white teeth. "I think so. As a boy I contrived to avoid my tutor, but he knew he could find me in the stables if I mysteriously did not appear for my lessons. I still consider the bloodstock book more interesting than Latin and ancient Greek."

The idea of him as a child intrigued her. Why, she wasn't sure, maybe because her childhood had been so bleak.

"Do you have brothers and sisters?" Caroline could smell

the clean fresh scent of cut grass and flowers from the breeze sifting in the open windows, the serenity of the evening soothing.

"An older sister," he answered readily enough. "She is married to a baronet and they have three daughters. Charles works for the War Department in a capacity that no one really mentions."

Having spent her childhood bereft of family warmth, Caroline felt a twinge of envy at the affection in his voice. "And your mother?"

"Usually resides in Kent at Rothay Hall, but occasionally comes to London." He quirked a brow. "She's a formidable force and I admit I do my best to steer clear of an over-abundance of contact. I respect and adore her, but she never stops trying to arrange my life to her liking."

Her father and aunt had arranged things in her life, and it definitely hadn't been to *her* liking, so Caroline could sympathize with his caution. She murmured, "At least you are the duke and no one can force you into anything."

Nicholas regarded her with a level look. "I understand your sentiment, but make no mistake. We all have our obligations we don't relish. Titles are not a carte blanche to do as you please, believe me." He shifted, just an adjustment of his lean body, like a panther stretching after a nap in the warmth of a hot afternoon. "You said earlier your aunt passed on. What of your father?"

Fair enough. She'd asked him about his family. Caroline shook her head. "He is still in York, and without our discussing it, we have come to a mutual agreement to ignore each other. I wasn't a son."

"Ah." As heir to a dukedom, that one word said he understood probably very well.

The memory of Franklin's recent call came to mind and she suppressed a quiver of unease. "My husband's cousin— the current Lord Wynn—is about all I can really call family, and in his case, I'd rather not."

Her expression must have been telling, for Nicholas's brow furrowed. Sprawled in his chair, all indolent male, he had unintentional but definite arrogance in his demeanor, as if he were capable of changing things. "He's a difficulty?"

"He wants to be," she admitted.

"Can I help?"

Her life was her own and hard-won at that. "Why would you offer?" she challenged. "And why would I accept?"

After a moment in which they just looked at each other, he smiled. "I'm not sure on either count." He added quietly, "Except I like being here with you. This"—he indicated the cozy room, the table still scattered with dishes—"is nice."

What a simple statement. Yet so powerful. It wasn't flirtatious either, not in the smooth way she expected, but infinitely more persuasive because it evoked the possibility he might be sincere and not just out to charm.

"Nice?" She arched a brow and smiled back.

The Duke of Rothay edged back in his seat, long legs extended, his wineglass in his hand. "I thought the word appropriate. Should I rephrase?"

"No." The response was made before she thought it over. The memory of the glorious burst of pleasure he'd brought her that afternoon intruded. Several times, she'd caught herself gazing at him across the small table with a sense of disbelief. Not just that she was there, with him, doing one of the most—no, *the* most—outrageous thing of her life, but that he really was nothing like what she expected. Part of the persona was true; the charisma of the rakish aristocrat was very much there, but it was surface polish, and the man underneath didn't seem at all calculating or simply intent on selfish pleasure. Earlier he'd known she would have let him bed her, but he'd opted not to, even though she'd seen well enough he was more than ready. It could have been humiliating to know he had been able to perceive so easily she was nervous and afraid, but the sensitivity he'd shown was unexpected.

A perceptive libertine. Hmm. That was an interesting facet she didn't expect.

But then again, she hadn't known what to expect at all.

Between her indifferent father and her domineering, cruel

husband, she did not have a high opinion of men in general. Maybe sexual revelation was not all she would learn in this wicked week.

"In the morning we can ride out by the river, if you like."

Caroline jerked back to attention, feeling a faint flush in her cheeks at her introspection. "I'm at your disposal."

His eyes crinkled attractively at the corners when he smiled. "I like the sound of that, my lady."

The husky note in his voice unsettled her. "I meant . . . ," she started to say tartly, and then trailed off. Actually, she meant just what she said.

Nicholas lifted his brows. He just sat there, comfortable and relaxed.

"Does everything have a sexual connotation to you, Rothay?" She gathered her cool poise like an enveloping cloak. With the intimacy of the meal and the romantic walk in the garden earlier—where he'd picked her roses, actually tucking one behind her ear—it was easier than she imagined to let it slip.

"When I am with someone as beautiful as you, probably so." An unrepentant shrug lifted his broad shoulders.

"Does anyone resist you?" She had to admit she was curious. His reputation was formidable, but gossip was unreliable.

He toyed idly with the stem of his wineglass. The flickering candlelight played over his refined features, highlighting the perfection of his elegant bone structure and making his raven hair gleam. "I'm discerning in my choices."

"In other words, once you pick out a woman from your throng of eager admirers, she's yours?" She'd heard the twitters, seen the impact as he walked into a ballroom or rode by in Hyde Park.

His laugh was low and mellow. "How tawdry you make it sound. Like cutting out a mare from the herd."

She wasn't good at witty banter. There had been very little practice in her life. "I am sometimes honest to a fault," she admitted. "My aunt told me most of my life how unladylike it is, even though my governess encouraged free thought, and I suppose to a certain extent it is why I am so quiet when out in society. Lord knows I might very well say something all too blunt. It must come from spending a great deal of time alone as a child. There is no need to lie to yourself."

Nicholas lounged back in his chair, all languid male grace. His expression was hard to read. "I envy that, believe it or not."

"Envy what?"

"The notion you had some privacy in your youth, and your ability to be forthright with your opinions. From the cradle, I was hovered over every moment as the ducal heir and, believe me, taught to be politic with my speech from the moment I uttered my first word. The title comes with a certain level of responsibility and inevitable social criticism."

"I hadn't thought of it that way." Caroline tilted her head to one side, studying him. "It is hard to feel sorry for someone who is handsome, rich, and titled, but there are drawbacks to everything, I suppose."

"It is difficult to feel sorry for a woman who is exquisitely beautiful, an heiress, and who could have her pick of any man in London, but possible she still has her demons."

His insight was too close to the truth.

Yes, Edward was a demon, haunting her ability to live a full life. "Touché," she said coolly. "I am counting on exorcising one of mine this week."

"Having had a taste of your passion, I can say with all due honesty it will be my pleasure to help you do so."

He replied with such smooth facile assurance, she fought the vivid blush his emphasis on the word "taste" brought, and tried for at least some semblance of equal sophistication. "And next week you will have forgotten me. Isn't that how it works? Don't you tire of transient entanglements?"

Her implied criticism didn't ruffle his self-assurance. "I thought you weren't interested in permanence."

"I'm not," she hastened to agree.

"Then we are in accord and can enjoy each other without

reservations. I think this will be a very pleasant seven days."
He glanced at the window, where the stars were visible in
the velvet black sky, the draperies still open and the window
ajar to let in the fragrant night breeze. "And nights."

She was starting to believe he was right, though he hadn't
answered her question. Caroline folded her hands in her lap.
"I didn't expect to like you."

Nicholas laughed. "You *are* certainly direct, my sweet.
Please don't tell me I have a reputation for being an unlik-
able fellow."

"No, you are thought to be most charming. I just had my
doubts the charm was real."

"Ah, an affectation to lure young maidens into my bed, is
that it?" Something flickered in his dark eyes.

Annoyance, perhaps? No, she didn't know him well
enough to judge.

"Well . . . yes."

"Yet you agreed to spend an entire week in my company."

"We both know I have my reasons."

Nicholas gazed at her, his tall, lean body still and his expression enigmatic. "I see we are being very honest with
each other. I find it refreshing, to tell the truth. Too often
love affairs are full of intrigue and pretense. In the spirit of
that sentiment, I will say I don't usually favor women with
little experience in bed, nor do I sleep with marriageable
young widows who have obviously been roughly treated in
the past."

Maybe she'd been too forthright. Caroline felt a flicker of
alarm that the next thing he was going to tell her was he
wanted to call off their bargain.

To her relief, he went on, "But you are very tempting, my
lady, and now that I understand more fully your reasons for
being here, I am more than honored." He added almost con-
versationally, "Were your despicable husband still alive, I'd
thrash him within an inch of his worthless life."

She registered his sincerity with a start, because the grim
look in his eyes belied the casual tone of his voice.

She'd never had a champion. As a child, she'd been sheltered by her maidenly autocratic aunt, and she'd been barely eighteen when married. The arrangement had been completely negotiated without her consent, but she hadn't realized the devastating reality of it until her wedding night. When she discovered how ruthless and unfeeling the man she'd been forced to marry was, she'd left him and gone home to York. Her father had sent her right back and God knew she'd suffered for that lapse in judgment. The bruises had taken weeks to fade.

"I loathed him." It was difficult to keep her voice matter-of-fact, but she did her best. "Logic assures me all men are not like him, but experience sometimes outweighs good sense."

"So what you need are some good experiences to outweigh the bad."

The husky drawl of the handsome duke's voice caused a shiver to run up her spine.

"I agree. That's why I am here." Caroline squared her shoulders.

"Then maybe it is time we retire." Nicholas stood in one smooth athletic movement and held out his hand.

His unsatisfied body wanted haste, but if there was one thing Nicholas had learned over the past few years as he sampled some of the most beauteous ladies of the *ton*, it was sexual restraint. Women took longer to arouse; some were adventurous in bed, others demure, a few downright insatiable. Obliging his lovers in whatever capacity they needed had never been a problem, but Caroline was entirely different. Beneath that exquisitely beautiful exterior, she was damaged, and, though he'd established a fragile bond of trust earlier, still very much a challenge.

He wanted to carry her up the stairs in a dramatic romantic gesture, but rejected the idea because it would remind her of his superior size and strength. Instead he escorted her politely, her hand in the crook of his arm, as if leading her into a formal parlor or an evening at the opera.

The truth was, he was still very much out of his element.

She wasn't in hers either.

Why did it intrigue him?

Maybe it was ennui, but he really didn't think so. Caroline was somehow strong, outspoken, distant . . . and yet vulnerable, completely feminine, and, to his mind, courageous in a unique way.

Very much unlike a memory from his past. That particular lady had been anything but defenseless and he had been the one in over his head. Since then he made it a point to hold the upper hand.

Always.

When they reached the upstairs hallway, he decided on her room, thinking if they used his again, she would once more feel overpowered and on uncertain ground. "In here," he murmured, opening the door. "I apologize for the lack of a lady's maid, but I anticipated you wanted privacy more than convenience."

"The room is lovely," she said, hesitating only a moment before going inside. "And you are right. I can live without a maid."

He gave a cursory glance at the furnishings, not sure if he'd ever paid attention. Being unmarried, he hadn't cared much one way or the other about the adjoining suite. "I'm glad the room pleases you and I can be obliging. Let me undress you."

"Your reputation for being obliging is legendary."

Damn his reputation, Nicholas thought irritably, aware of what the gossips said about him, and still amazed, at twenty-eight, that anyone was so interested in his life. He replied almost gruffly, "I just meant if you need any help during our stay, please ask me."

"Did I just offend you?"

He took her shoulders and urged her with the slight pressure of his hands to turn around. "The fact I have a reputation offends me. I would prefer it if my personal life was not fodder for the gossip mill."

"Then perhaps you should not make outrageous public wagers on your sexual prowess." She said the words in a dry tone, but there was the slightest catch in her voice as he swept aside her hair and began to unfasten her pale, shimmering green evening gown. With practiced ease he undid the buttons, pushed the garment from her slender shoulders, and pulled the pins from her simple chignon. The silken mass cascaded over his hands and down her graceful back and he could smell her perfume, a haunting hint of lily of the valley. Lifting the warm weight of her tresses, he kissed her nape with slow, tantalizing pressure, allowing his mouth to linger as he felt her answering shiver.

"I'd heed your advice, beautiful Caroline, but if I hadn't taken Manderville's challenge, you wouldn't be here, would you? Maybe I should exchange drunken bets with him more often." He slid his arm around her waist and began to make love to her neck, nuzzling, kissing, tasting her smooth fragrant skin until she leaned back against him and he could see the rapid lift of her full breasts under the lace of her chemise, her nipples taut points against the sheer material.

"Can you feel how I want you?" He knew she could, his arm holding her in loose but insistent persuasion against his already rigid erection. "Do you have any idea how much sway a woman holds over a man when he desires her?"

"No." The whisper was poignant and soft.

Unfortunately, he was sure she just told him the truth. It did nothing to dampen his ardor, but it did temper his behavior.

"You have my entire attention, believe me," he promised. "Let me show you."

He did lift her then, carefully, as if she were a spun-glass creation, and he took her to the canopied bed. This time he removed everything, including her chemise, so Caroline reclined nude and lush in the glow of the lamps lit for her convenience upon retiring.

As she watched, Nicholas undressed with deliberation, removing jacket, cravat, shirt, and boots, giving her every opportunity to tell him to stop, or to cover her bared body.

She did neither.

Thank God, for he was on fire.

When he unfastened his breeches and pushed them down his hips, her lovely gray eyes went wide and she made no secret of studying his erection, her soft lips slightly parted in evident surprise.

That she had never seen an aroused male was disquieting. *Well, hell, another hurdle to jump.*

It was easy to guess now her husband had come to her at night, in the dark, to exercise his husbandly rights in a way Nicholas surmised amounted more to selfish brutality than anything else. Common opinion was that it was impossible for a man to violate his wife, for she was essentially his property, but he disagreed. If a woman was reluctant and unready, it was still a crime to take what wasn't given freely.

He climbed into bed next to her and did nothing more than touch her lower lip, tracing the enchanting curve with an exploratory fingertip. "Have I mentioned I think you are stunningly beautiful?"

"You have been very free with your compliments, Nicholas." Caroline's lashes lowered a fraction, but she didn't move away and seemed a great deal less tense than in their encounter during the afternoon.

"Every man in England would envy me if they knew where I am now."

"And no doubt every woman would feel the same about me. Especially the legions who have come before me and know what they're missing."

Discussing past lovers was never wise under any circumstances and he wasn't about to start now, not with carnal need so blatantly controlling his senses. What Nicholas coveted was a mere few inches away, her mouth warm and inviting, her voluptuous body his for the taking—only he needed to make sure she was equally involved. "Kiss me," he said with husky encouragement.

Let her take the lead. It seemed best, for he didn't want to frighten or rush her.

For a moment she hesitated, but then leaned in and brushed her lips against his. It took willpower not to crush her to him and devour her, but he stayed still and unmoving as she shyly pressed her mouth to his and then immediately broke away.

It was a small, promising start.

"That's a kiss?" He lifted a brow teasingly. "This afternoon I kissed you, remember? I'd like to see a better effort, Lady Wynn."

For a moment, she just stared at him, her vibrant hair spilling over her slim shoulders, her eyes a shade defiant. Then she leaned in again, this time actually placing her small hands on his shoulders and parting her lips. Nicholas angled his head a little to deepen the kiss and the tentative slide of her tongue inside his mouth made a small inner smile grow.

Despite her past, he had a feeling she was going to be an apt pupil.

Bare, soft breasts brushed his chest and he suppressed a groan, her long hair spilling over them both. Doing nothing but lightly touching her back, he traced the curve of her spine, letting her control the play. His fingers tangled in her long tresses, and a low sound of approval escaped his throat as she continued to kiss him with growing confidence.

They were both out of breath when she finally leaned back. "Better?"

"Much." His erection pulsed with each beat of his heart and Nicholas couldn't wait to be inside her, reluctantly amused when her gaze went right back to the stiff, swollen length against his stomach. She looked wary, but he was encouraged by a glimmer of intrigue in her eyes.

In a deliberate slow movement, he caught her hand and placed it on his erection. "I don't want to be a mystery to you in any way."

Slim fingers tentatively wrapped around his girth and she bit her lower lip. "My ignorance is mortifying."

He sucked in a breath as she squeezed a little. "Rest assured, you can ask *me* anything and I'll answer if I can. I've never understood why society seems to feel females should be kept in the dark when it comes to sexual matters.

Men discuss it at will. It tends to be a popular topic of conversation."

"In case you have not noticed, your gender has rights we are denied."

She had a good point, but it was hard to speak with her fingers exploring his whole rock-hard length. "I've noticed," he managed to admit, suppressing a groan as she wiped a bead of liquid from the tip and stared at her finger. "But keep in mind, part of the reason is possessiveness. Since we want to keep our daughters chaste and our wives only for ourselves, I think the general idea is the less you know about the pleasure men and women can give each other, the better."

"Are we going to start an intellectual debate on this subject? I don't think you're going to like my stand on the matter." She caressed him, peering down between his legs as she cupped his testicles. "They're heavy."

For someone with her lack of experience, she was certainly doing a good job of arousing him to a fever pitch. Heavy? He was about to explode from just her innocent touch and it startled him. He wanted to take his time, at least until she understood the game he knew so well how to play.

"I'm enjoying your curiosity," he explained with monumental effort at appearing relaxed when his ballocks were actually held in her hand, "but maybe it would be best if it was my turn."

All delectable lustrous hair and pale skin, Caroline looked a little confused.

"To touch you." He moved to take her in his arms and shifted so she was on her back and he was propped above her, his weight resting on his elbows. They should start simply, Nicholas decided, as he stroked her hip first, caressed her inner thigh, and then found the warmth of her sex. His fingers parted her soft feminine folds and immediately she looked away and tensed.

Damnation.

"I'm not going to hurt you," he whispered, tracing a line across her jaw with his mouth. "I want to make you feel good, beautiful Caroline. If you've been properly aroused, you'll enjoy me, I give you my word. You're already a little wet, which means your body understands what your mind wants to reject. Relax and I'll prove it to you."

He touched her then. Everywhere. Each stroke, each caress, punctuated by sugar-soft kisses and whispered words. The pulse point just above the dip of her collarbone. The tender inside of her elbow. His tongue flicking across her wrist. Taking her little finger into his mouth with provocative tenderness as he caressed her bare shoulder and held her close. It was an exploration, a journey of knowledge and persuasion. Both of them naked, skin brushing heated skin as he made love to her without actual penetration.

The first breathy sigh let him know his patience was being rewarded, the following moan encouraged him even more, and when his hand slipped between her thighs and he stimulated her with small practiced pressure, she clung to him with promising urgency.

His fingers grew wet, the reaction of her body to his touch not in question.

And he found it more powerful in some way because he knew it involved risk, trust, and a dozen things he had abandoned when it came to passion at least a decade ago.

It had an extraordinary impact. She didn't trust easily. Well, neither did he, so they had that in common, though his reservations were different. However, if the lift of her hips in supplication was any indication, she was overcoming that issue. On his part, he thought he had closed the door firmly on his ghosts.

Perhaps, though, he was wrong.

The past rushed in and crashed into the present and though he didn't thoroughly understand her motivations in being there, he felt a connection with his lovely bedmate that was more than unusual.

It was like their situation, as original as sin itself.

His care was rewarded when he finally coaxed her into a shuddering climax. And then another. Just when she began to relax, he did it again, sliding his fingers deep into wet, tantalizing heat and feeling those betraying contractions as she gasped and closed her eyes.

The exquisite tightness of her passage made him halt for a moment in a dizzying surge of need. Inner muscles clenched around his invading fingers as he tentatively began to explore the promise of paradise.

The expression on her face told him all he needed to know, and relief washed through him even as he felt sweat prickle across his skin from the effort it took not to move to climb between those lovely thighs—and take her. Caroline looked replete, dazed even, her mouth parted, her eyes wide, a faint flush in her cheeks from sexual release.

"Nicholas," she whispered in wonder, and let her lashes drift downward.

It was all the permission he needed to move. To adjust himself in place, use his new power over her to spread her legs even farther apart, and then take his pleasure.

He didn't.

A small voice—one he wanted to banish to hell—told him it wasn't the right time. Not yet.

In the languorous aftermath, he adjusted her in his arms, trying to still the treacherous need to possess her. She didn't speak, but he could feel her rapidly beating heart, the smoothness of her silken skin, the soft exhale across his chest as she moved a little and finally lifted her head.

"I . . . I . . ." She faltered, and then swallowed audibly.

He lay sprawled in resigned sexual tension next to her and smiled. When it happened, he'd try to make sure they climaxed together. "You what?"

"I liked that."

"I rather thought you might." He fought a grin he had a feeling would infuriate her and added softly, "And I'm glad."

She shook back her gleaming hair, the sight of her voluptuous nudity in the shimmer of the low-lit lamp a challenge to his resolve to wait. "You don't understand the depths of that compliment, Nicholas."

"*Au contraire*, darling, I have a feeling I do."

"You said earlier you would not make presumptions."

The spirit in her voice made him chuckle. "You cannot have it both ways. Either I understand women and that's why you decided to do this in the first place, or I don't know a thing. Which is it?"

"You don't know *me*." Magnificent eyes gleamed silver, but it was hard for her to pull off the haughty, distant Lady Wynn when she was in delectable dishabille right next to him.

His erection throbbed almost painfully. Jesus, restraint had a cost. This—when it finally happened—had better be worth it.

And perhaps he *had* been a bit smug.

He captured her slender shoulders and pulled her close for a slow kiss. When she melted against him, he felt a flicker of triumph. Moving his mouth to her ear, he told her in husky compromise, "All right, I concede I don't know you as well as I'd like to. We've all week and we've just begun to become acquainted. Does that intrigue you?"

Her resulting sigh fluttered across his throat. "Yes."

Chapter Ten

The sound of a deep voice stopped her cold in a wash of dismay.

Saturating every pore, every nerve ending, from her scalp to the tips of her toes, and Annabel stood stock-still outside the door to the informal parlor and drew in a breath.

No one had informed her Derek would be there for tea.

He never came for tea. Not ever.

God in heaven, wasn't seeing him the night before bad enough? Her face still ached from the effort of smiling through the small party Margaret had arranged. The celebration had been a thoughtful gesture, and she knew both Thomas and Margaret wanted nothing more than to support her decision to marry Alfred. The entire Drake family had always treated her as one of them and they had been wonderfully enthusiastic about the upcoming wedding, but unfortunately, it was expected that Derek would be invited to everything. He always was, but usually he declined the mundane entertainments. Except the night before, when he'd appeared unexpectedly, looking sinfully handsome *and* bored out of his mind. He'd left early also, escaping not long after dinner. She'd managed to be polite during their brief exchange of pleasantries, but did she really have to go through it again so soon?

"Forget something, child?"

She whipped around at the sound of her guardian's voice, to see Thomas smiling down at her, his good-natured face creased with his usual smile. He said, "It seems we're both a bit late, aren't we? I'm quite parched and a scone would be lovely right about now. Shall we go in?"

What choice was there? She should have run up to her room and pleaded a headache when she had the chance instead of dithering at the door. She could have sent her maid down with the news she would not be joining them for tea because she was indisposed. She just hadn't been thinking quickly enough. "Yes," she muttered in a bald-faced lie because her stomach felt suddenly in knots, "that sounds delightful."

They entered together and though she wished she didn't have to acknowledge the Earl of Manderville's presence, when he politely rose to his feet she gritted her teeth and managed a stiff nod. It was all so familiar—the clutter of blue chairs covered in brocade, the old pianoforte in the corner, the cream and indigo rug in an Oriental pattern, even the tea trolley parked by the polished antique table—but everything looked different with *him* there.

It was always that way. If he was in the room, she didn't notice anything else, and she felt a fierce resentment over the affliction.

Margaret, plump, pretty, and ladylike, smiled serenely, her cup in hand. "Derek stopped by at just the right moment and I insisted he stay for tea."

Annabel said nothing, averting her gaze, knowing there was no possibility that Thomas and Margaret hadn't noticed the current state of animosity between their nephew and herself. Once Thomas had even tentatively inquired over it, but it was hardly like she was going to tell anyone about either the fateful kiss or what she'd stumbled upon later.

It was still vivid enough in her memory, burned there with painful clarity. Derek bent over Lady Bellvue—who happened to have the nerve to be sophisticated and beautiful—her bodice unfastened, his mouth on . . .

At that point, tears had blurred her vision and Annabel had run out of the conservatory as fast as possible, before she broke down in a sobbing mess right in front of them both. No, she'd saved that for later. When she reached her room, she cried until there were no more tears left in her. It was ironic that the tender kiss in the library had been the culmination of all her romantic fantasies; then in the same day he'd destroyed her idealistic dreams.

She had grown up in that flat second when she realized the appearance of the young man with the easy smile and generous nature was a facade to conceal his shallowness and indifference to the feelings of others. She'd always thought of his innate good-humored intelligence as a measure of him as a human being, but now she understood his flaws far exceeded his virtues. The rumors were all true. All he wanted was a willing tumble. The callousness of it turned her stomach. How many hearts had he broken besides hers? What she thought she'd loved had been an illusion, no more.

". . . tart?"

Annabel looked up and blinked. "Excuse me?"

The subject of her thoughts gestured toward the plate on the tea cart. His vivid blue eyes were veiled, but there was just a slight glossing of a smile on his well-shaped mouth. "May I have one?"

"I am sure you've had many." The words just came out, and to make matters worse, the saccharine-sweet malice in her voice was a betraying sign of her antipathy.

Good heavens, had she really just said that out loud?

Margaret murmured, "Oh dear."

Derek's dark blond brows shot up. In a lazy pose in his chair, his long legs extended and one hand holding his cup, he looked infuriatingly amused. He was, as usual, impossibly good-looking in a dark blue jacket, tan breeches, and polished boots, his cravat as always tied to perfection. The light from one of the long windows gilded his hair with gold highlights and accented the clean line of cheek and brow. He drawled, "I admit to a fondness for tarts of all kinds, but with tea I prefer lemon."

Chagrined, because she promised herself every single day she cared nothing about what had happened between them any longer, Annabel grabbed the plate of sweets and thrust it at him. The confections slid dangerously toward the edge, but luckily none fell on the expensive floral-patterned carpet. She'd made a fool out of herself fast enough without making a mess as well.

Damn him, he took his time about selecting one, making her hold the plate like some groveling serving wench. No doubt he bedded those as well, she mused hotly, not sure if she was more angry with herself for losing her self-possession so fast or with him for finding it comical.

His confidence and ease always seemed to emphasize her lack of similar sophistication, but she was learning. She'd made an art form out of avoiding him ever since that horrible evening, and she'd wondered more than once if he wasn't making a conscious effort to decline invitations to events where she'd be present also. Naturally, on family occasions they had to interact a little, but neither of them did more than barely acknowledge the other's presence.

Derek *never* dropped in for tea. Especially not when he knew she'd be there.

"Thank you." He plucked a sweet from the tray and set it on his plate. The movement was graceful and elegant in a completely masculine way, just like everything else about him, including that irritating smirk on his face.

"You're welcome," she ground out, hating the rasp in her voice.

"I don't believe I've gotten a chance to congratulate you yet on your formal engagement, Annie. Last night you were very busy and I had to leave early."

Dear God, don't call me Annie.

He was the only one who used the nickname. He always had, ever since she was a child. But she wasn't a child now, she was a woman, and the soft familiar sound of the way he said it brought back memories better dismissed.

She stiffened but managed to nod. "I will tell Alfred you wish us well."

"He's a pleasant enough fellow."

She felt a flicker of irritation at the tone of his voice. Just the slightest hint of disparagement, as if pleasant went along with dull and stodgy. No, Alfred wasn't dashing or exciting, but he was steady. Defensively, she pointed out, "He's a true gentleman."

Her implication was clear that Derek did not belong in that category. Or she certainly hoped it was, for she meant it that way.

"I agree with Derek, Lord Hyatt is quite amiable." Thomas looked bland and sipped his tea. "A nice sort. Reliable and all that."

"Not a bad thing in a husband," Margaret said in agreement.

"Or a horse." Derek sank down a little more in his chair, the muscular grace of his tall body a contrast to the pastel color scheme of the room. If he was insulted by her snide barb, he—as usual—did not show it.

"A horse?" Outraged at the comparison of her fiancé to an equine, Annabel glared at him.

He looked as innocent as a depraved rake could manage. "Yes, indeed. Do you disagree? Which would you prefer to ride, a placid, dependable animal that will get you where you wish to go in an uneventful way, or a more spirited beast?"

She might be legions less experienced than he, but she couldn't miss the sexual innuendo. To her complete and utter mortification, she blushed.

Only Derek could say such a thing and get away with it. He was accustomed to using his looks and ease of manner to excuse himself for any number of sins. It worked on everyone else too, damn him. But not her. Not any longer.

The trouble was, she knew him. Knew that dry wit, the teasing glint in his eye, and in the past, she might even have laughed. However, they were talking about her marriage to another man and that he could joke about it . . . well, it was hurtful.

No, it wasn't, she argued inwardly, stiffening her spine. Derek no longer had that power over her. He'd abdicated it the day he'd kissed her and then shattered her heart with a casual betrayal that mocked her feelings.

Annabel looked him in the eye. "There is a lot to be said for dependable."

His smile faded and he countered softly, "Even the wildest creature can be tamed when the right touch is used."

"Not all are worth the effort," she shot back.

"It's hard to say if one doesn't try."

Margaret interjected in a lame effort to change the subject, "I thought the party went well, didn't you?"

Annabel nodded, but it was an absent gesture, detached from her. "It was lovely."

"You looked very beautiful," Derek murmured as if commenting on the weather.

No, he hadn't just said that. The compliment was so smooth, so sincere in the inflection in his tone, she was momentarily taken aback. He looked at her in the way only he could and for one single moment she forgot both Thomas and Margaret were there.

Like a stupid little fool.

Even if he meant it, what did it matter? Why did she care what such a disreputable, immoral man thought of her? Why had she chosen her dress with such care the night before just because she'd known he would be there?

It simply was not possible to stay so close to him for another minute. The realization swamped her, made a flare of panic tighten her throat. It was certainly more comfortable when they'd avoided each other, though she wasn't convinced he'd bestirred himself to that extent. One paltry kiss would not be significant to a libertine of his status. She was the one who had put too much emphasis on it.

But still . . . that kiss. The soft but firm touch of his lips as they possessed hers, the glide of his tongue, the tantalizing feel of his arms holding her close. His scent, his taste, his potent low sigh into her mouth, as intoxicating as any drink . . .

No. She didn't care to remember it. It was infuriating it still lingered in her mind.

"Please excuse me." Annabel rose and glanced at the clock in the corner, seeing the ornate metal hands were perched at some angle, not even really registering the time.

"I have a mound of letters to write, I'm afraid, and a slight headache. I think I will retire upstairs until dinner."

The afternoon was so warm that Caroline had removed the jacket of her riding habit, and it hung over the pommel of her saddle as their horses ambled along what barely passed for a path along the bank of a lazy river. Overhead the sky was pure, pristine blue, unmarred by a single cloud, and the air smelled of fragrant meadows as the slightest breeze brushed her face.

The idyllic day matched her spirits perfectly.

Caroline was well aware she was getting the brunt of the infamous Rothay's charm for a deliberate reason—the scandalous bet—but she was more than willing to accept the fantasy.

After a night of discovery and abandoned pleasure in his arms, they'd slept late, had a light breakfast together, and passed the rest of the day with similar casual, relaxed companionship, including their current late-afternoon ride.

It was a blissful change from her usual mundane existence and not all her enjoyment was due to her newfound sexual awakening. An attractive man paying attention to her was something she could get used to, especially since she felt surprisingly comfortable around him. Maybe it was just the sexual intimacy, but maybe it wasn't.

Though they hadn't yet culminated the actual act of intercourse, she was becoming less apprehensive and more and more curious. So far he had given her his full attention, the opulent pleasure of his touch enlightening, but he had taken nothing for himself.

Of course. All because he wanted to win the wager.

As if he could read her thoughts, Nicholas said, "I should do this more often."

She glanced over. He also wore no coat, the fine linen of his shirt spanning wide shoulders, the garment open at the throat revealing tanned skin, his seat in the saddle easy and graceful. He rode every day without fail and had horses sent ahead, since he didn't stable any in Essex. His mount was a magnificent bay that matched its rider, sleek and powerful, and her dappled gray mare the most well-mannered horse she'd ever ridden.

"Do what more often?" Caroline lifted a brow. "Whisk a stranger off to the country for sexual tutelage?"

His easy laugh rang out. "Well, no, that wasn't precisely what I was thinking, but now that you mention it, so far things have gone rather well."

Remembering the revelation of the night before, she could hardly disagree. It had been about sinful pleasure, every touch, taste, movement unique in her experience. His reputation was well deserved if he was always so selfless. The excess of sensation left her so exhausted she'd actually drifted to sleep while lying in his arms and if someone had predicted that a few days ago, she would have scoffed at the notion.

Unbridled enjoyment and a growing sense of freedom, even if it was born of nothing more than a masculine contest provoked by overindulgence in liquor, were exactly what she'd been looking for when she made her scandalous proposition. When this was over, she was going to be forever in his debt, for Nicholas Manning had at least shown her what *could* be.

"What were you thinking, then?" She brushed a loose tendril of hair from her cheek and watched his face curiously.

Never in her life had she asked a man what was on his mind. With Edward she would never have dared. Nor would she have probably wanted to know. With Nicholas, she already felt she could ask freely with impunity.

"That I spend entirely too much time in the city. Too much time up late at the parties and soirees, too much time at my club, too much time in my study and with my solicitors." He shrugged, his glossy dark hair holding a hint of blue it was so black, like a raven's wing in the slanting sunshine. "I keep telling myself, when the time comes to settle my life into a less hectic pattern, I will know it."

Inevitably, he meant taking a wife and begetting an heir. She felt an unexpected pang of realization. This wager was about casual conquest and her own enlightenment. What happened after their time together was over hardly mattered.

She did her best to sound nonchalant. "You are still young, though I imagine your family expects you to do your duty."

His profile was patrician and a little stern. For a moment, he didn't look at all like the sophisticated rakehell but instead almost grim. His voice even took on a chill. "Indeed they do."

It was none of her business, but somehow she found herself saying, "But you are reluctant?"

"I'm patently uninterested in taking a wife simply to procreate." There was a restive edge to his tone.

A curious position for a peer to take, since he'd probably known since he was in short pants he'd have to do just that. "You have romantic sensibilities."

"No."

"If I interpreted what you just said correctly, you want to fall in love."

His mouth twisted in a cynical smile. "I'm afraid you completely *misinterpreted* what I said, my dear. Falling in love is not something I expect will ever happen to me, nor would I want it. I don't think I even believe it is possible."

If ever she'd heard conviction in anyone's voice, those words echoed it. The assertion was a little incongruous from the same man who she now knew firsthand was capable of infinite and unselfish tenderness. "We all want to be loved," she ventured, though she was probably the last person on earth who was an authority on the subject.

"Being loved is not the same as loving someone else."

Her horse ambled around a small bush and she absently guided it back to the path. "I suppose that's true."

She didn't know much about men, but there was an uncharacteristic tightness in his tone that even she couldn't miss.

This discussion was personal on some level unknown to her.

He smiled again then, shaking it off, that glimmer of

wicked, compelling charm that captivated every woman in sight surfacing instead. "If you tell anyone you debated sentimental attachment with the Devilish Duke, I will deny it, my sweet, so please keep it to yourself."

If she told anyone, he would be more besieged than ever by eager young ladies wanting to capture not just his title and fortune, but his heart. However, she wouldn't. Caroline pointed out with unerring truth, "I am not supposed to know you except in the most casual and distant of ways, remember? I could hardly claim to know anything about your personal sentiments on any matter, much less marriage."

He gazed at her, their horses walking slowly past a copse of slender willows with long branches trailing into the sluggish clear water. The sun felt very warm on her back. "I have a feeling it is going to be a little difficult to pretend we don't know each other after this week is over. I am told a woman does not forget her first lover."

There was no doubt he was absolutely correct, because what Edward had done to her disqualified him from that label.

Nicholas couldn't be more different and though her body wasn't virginal, he was right—he would be her first lover.

It was amazing to realize it, but she was losing her apprehensive fears and looking forward to it.

Maybe even very much looking forward to it.

Caroline cleared her throat. "I am sure that is true, for you are right—I will not forget your . . . kindness."

Amusement made his mouth twitch. "Kindness? An odd word to describe carnal desire, my sweet. Since you are here for self-proclaimed sexual tutelage, let me continue in my role as instructor by informing you that your enjoyment when we lie together will be paramount to my own. To know he gives a woman pleasure is a powerful aphrodisiac for any man."

Unfortunately, she knew firsthand he was wrong. It was like being dashed with cold water. Quietly, she said, "Not all of them, Nicholas. I wish I could say that with less assurance."

In the resulting awkward silence between them, the dull thud of their horse's hooves and the trill of a songbird were the only sounds. He said finally, "I was just presumptuous again. My apologies."

She didn't want to think about her dark marriage, not on such a glorious day, not when she was with the most attractive man in England and they had the rest of what promised to be a very memorable week ahead of them. She gave him a mischievous smile. "I think, Your Grace, you were born presumptuous. Luckily for you, I find it part of your appeal."

"You find me appealing? Perhaps I made an impression last night after all." He seemed more than willing to shy away from the serious direction of their conversation and return to his usual lighthearted teasing. "Care to tell me what part you found most enlightening?"

That wasn't hard to answer and she owed him a great deal. "All of it."

It was true. Those devastatingly soft, persuasive kisses, the delicacy of his intimate touch, the gift of a pleasure she hadn't imagined existed.

Almost instantly, his face changed. Softly he said, "I think I might learn as much from you, my icy Lady Wynn, as you do from me this week."

Chapter Eleven

The dappled sunlight fell across the verdant grass in the small clearing, the quiet sound of the river soothing. Nicholas dismounted and turned to lift Caroline from the saddle, his hands lingering on her slim waist as he set her down. He smiled lazily into her upturned face. "This is a rather pleasant spot, isn't it? Private also."

Her dainty brows arched upward. "Is that important?"

It was damned important because since almost the moment they'd gotten out of bed that morning, he'd been assessing his overwhelming desire to get her right back into it. However, a bed wasn't necessary, not with a secluded romantic spot available, and he didn't want to wait until they retired to make love to her.

Restraint was all well and good, but how long need he hold back?

Unfortunately, the answer was simple. Until she was ready. There was a huge difference between what she would allow him to do and what she wanted him to do. At any time since her arrival she would have allowed it. But most certainly yesterday afternoon and the night before, she hadn't felt desire, he thought, just capitulation.

But if he had his way, and he intended to, she would learn.

He wasn't sure exactly why he was so fascinated with the lovely but inexperienced Lady Wynn, but he was. Part of it was her candor, part of it was her beauty, and to his surprise, he wondered if part of it wasn't also the hint of vulnerability when she looked at him with those glorious silver eyes.

Usually, that alone would make him run away as fast as possible. Vulnerable young ladies made his defenses shoot straight up.

"I thought we might sit a while in the shade." His lashes dropped a fraction and his gaze lowered to her mouth. "And admire the view. We could discuss literature, since it is one of your passions."

"Somehow I never pictured the Devilish Duke as someone who would perch by a stream and contemplate the beauty of nature or the structure of a poem. Society would believe that even less than he had an opinion on the subject of love."

"You will be able to attest they are wrong."

"Will I?" One brow arched up and she laughed. "I'm trying to imagine what your opinion on Homer or Rousseau might be."

Her smile was all too rare and it fascinated him. Like the woman, it was a mixture of reserve and underlying sensuality, he thought, gazing down at her. Lazily, he drawled, "Are you implying I'm a Philistine, Lady Wynn?"

"Earthy pleasures seem more your domain, Your Grace."

"Allow me to change your opinion of my character."

Her reply was *almost* flirtatious. "You can try."

Thus challenged, how could he back away? Nicholas chose a soft spot overlooking the meander of the river, the grass springy and fragrant there, the earth even. They sat and talked while their horses grazed—again, Nicholas found himself captivated by the way Caroline's eyes lit up when she fixed on a salient point to debate with him. Her old governess's independent views had been varied indeed, he discovered as they discussed everything from architecture to religion. Caroline said Miss Dunsworth—whom she recalled with a sentimental look in her remarkable eyes—had encouraged her education in every way possible, not just the usual interests of refined young ladies.

"She died of a lung infection," she said, a small catch in

her voice, "just near the end of my sixteenth year. I still miss her."

It gave him the opening to steer the conversation with deliberate intent back to her family.

He idly twirled a long blade of grass between his fingers, watching her face from beneath his slightly lowered lashes. "You have no desire to go back to York, I take it."

Without hesitation, Caroline shook her head. She looked delectable in a simple blouse, riding skirt, and half boots. Though she sat in prim ladylike decorum with her legs tucked to the side, she still managed to look adorably desirable. "I won't ever go back."

"That sounds definite."

"It is." A brief flicker of melancholy crossed her face. "Nor does my father want me there either."

"Then he's a fool." Nicholas reached out and touched her hand.

His prior restraint, he found, was slipping. Her increasing ease with him fueled his level of interest. Usually sitting and conversing about intellectual topics with a woman was not something he did, and he certainly never expected it to cause sexual arousal, but with her it was different. How curious.

She glanced at him. "How nice you have a sister."

Nicholas rarely thought about it, but the wistful look on Caroline's face made him conscious of his good fortune in his family. He wanted to comfort her, to promise she would find contentment and acceptance, but how the devil did he do that?

The only kind of real solace he knew how to offer her was physical and his body at the moment clamored for him to proceed.

Seduction was much more familiar than emotional indecision.

Leaning forward, he brushed his mouth against hers, ignoring her start of surprise. Other than lifting her from her horse, he'd made no move to touch her. He whispered, "There's something exhilarating about making love out of doors. It's more primal."

"Here?"

He kissed her in answer to that breathless question, amused at her shocked reaction, his hands already busy. He loosened her hair first, because he wanted to feel the satin weight of it when warmed by the sun, her fragrance tantalizing as he deepened the kiss. To his gratification her arms crept around his neck and while she didn't precisely cling to him, she rested in willing compliance in his embrace.

Compliance again, he realized with an inner grimace of resignation. This was certainly taking some effort on his part. The odd part was he was enjoying the challenge, despite a certain understandable level of frustration.

The swell of his erection was immediate and his heart already beat faster as he admired the compelling glory of her beauty. His enjoyment was enhanced by the sound of the gentle passage of the water barely audible above the quickened rasp of their breathing. Nicholas murmured, "Undress for me. I want to watch. There is nothing more arousing than a woman's body being revealed bit by bit."

Well, that wasn't precisely true. Watching a woman kiss her way down your body and take your rigid cock in her mouth might eclipse her stripping, but Caroline was not ready for that yet by any means. This week was supposed to be about her pleasure and not just because of that blasted wager either. No woman so beautiful and innately sensual should have to fear sexual intimacy.

He waited, one arm propped over his bent knee, his pose purposely casual except for the bulge of his growing erection filling his fitted breeches.

There was just a moment of hesitation before she stood and began to unbutton her blouse. Through heavy-lidded eyes Nicholas observed each fastening slip free before she tugged the garment from the band of her riding skirt and slipped it off. Boots, stockings, and skirt went next, her cheeks becoming more and more pink as she disrobed. Finally she pulled loose the ribbon on her chemise and lifted her chin, but didn't let the lacy material slide off her shoulders.

"Don't stop now," he said persuasively. "The best is yet to come."

"You have all your clothes on." She stood there, a bare-foot temptress, her hand holding the bodice of her shift together.

"Do you want me to take them off?" He held her gaze.

He wanted to make sure she knew—with him—she always had a choice. He usually preferred to take the lead in sexual games, but he was willing to make concessions to make sure she never felt overwhelmed.

"I am sure you are aware that you are considered to be very handsome. Is there some reason I cannot admire you in the same way?"

That was direct enough. Once again, no wiles.

"Whatever my lady wishes." He grinned and tugged at the heel of one boot, still keeping his gaze riveted on her.

With an artless, trembling smile, she let her chemise go and it pooled around her feet.

For a moment he stopped, boot in hand, and drank in the pure glory of her naked body, his admiration enhanced by the knowledge she was his for the taking.

He couldn't shed his clothes fast enough.

There was something about the woodland setting, the way the filtered sunlight touched her satin skin with a golden glow, the musical sound of the birds in the trees. . . . It took arousal to a new level. It *was* primal, elemental, and by the time he managed to get out of his breeches, he found to his surprise his hands were shaking.

That had *never* happened before.

He was going to have to analyze it. Later. After.

"Come lie with me." Nicholas reclined on the grass, the tactile sensation on his body an interesting contrast to his heated desire. Above the lacy canopy of branches, the sky was a cerulean blue.

"I want to." The hushed words were said with an underlying surprise as Caroline took a step toward him.

He sure as hell hoped she did, because he was more than ready. When she knelt beside him, he caught her waist and pulled her on top of his hungry body for a hot openmouthed kiss. It was less restrained than the night before, but she didn't seem to mind, her response not quite as hesitant this time. When she threaded her fingers into his hair, he felt a flicker of triumph through his arousal, and the hardened state of her nipples against his chest spoke volumes of how far she'd come in a very short time.

If he was a judge—and he felt qualified—she was going to be a very passionate bedmate for some lucky man when the week was over.

Of course, then she had her time with Derek. A quiver of dissatisfaction stirred inside him as he pictured his friend holding her luscious body as he did now.

To quell it was an emotional reflex. He was not a jealous man. Or he never had been before, at any rate. Considering their illicit bargain, this seemed like a poor time to acquire the habit.

He rolled over so her hair spilled against the grass in a luxuriant, gleaming mass. His mouth grazed her jaw, and he licked a path along her collarbone and nuzzled the elegant curve of her throat. Caroline arched beneath him, her breathing quickened.

Nicholas stroked her bare hip. "Talk to me."

Lacy lashes lifted and her mouth parted as a faint frown marred her smooth brow. "Haven't we been talking?"

"Yes, but let's change the subject."

"I could swear, Rothay, you wanted to do something else besides converse, or are you like this all the time?" She shifted suggestively against his rigid cock. "You seem to be."

If his smile wasn't wicked, he certainly intended it to be. "Oh, I am going to make love to you eventually—that isn't in question—but there is a wide variety of ways to do it. I just wonder if you realize how arousing it can be when lovers tell each other how they are feeling and, even more importantly, what they want."

Auburn curls moved as she shook her head, her eyes luminous as she gazed up at him. "I have no idea what you mean, but I suspect you already guessed that anyway."

He had. Bed play was as foreign to her as a romantic kiss. It would be his pleasure to change that.

"I'll go first." Propped above her, his weight balanced on one elbow, he moved his mouth to her ear as he stroked one glorious full breast. "I love the way you feel, your skin like silk under my fingers. You have the most beautiful breasts I have ever seen, full and firm but also soft and made for my hands."

A small shiver went through her as he gently squeezed the pliant weight of mounded flesh and waited, his thumb lazily circling one rosy nipple in slow circles, gratified by her physical response. He'd already learned she was intelligent, if a little shy. With a bit of instruction in the art of flirtation, she could have her pick of any man of the *haut ton*.

There were some blackguards out there and she was not only beautiful but an heiress. He hoped she'd choose wisely.

The notion he cared about what happened to her after their designated week was over startled him. Maybe he was simply trying to redeem his gender in her eyes, for earlier in their conversation he realized her father didn't sound much better than the deceased Lord Wynn. She hadn't said it in so many words, but he'd caught the underlying pain in her voice.

Yes, that was it. There was some remnant of chivalry left in him, despite what had happened with Helena.

Now was not the time to think of that horrible blunder.

"Your turn," he urged, nibbling on her earlobe. "Confide in me."

"I . . . I—" She faltered and then whispered, "I am beginning to think you are more than just a competent lover, Nicholas, but also a very nice man."

He went still in the act of caressing her nipple, arrested and nonplussed.

It was hardly a sexual innuendo or said with a flutter of her lashes and a seductive smile, but Nicholas was unexpectedly touched, not just by the simple statement, but by the sentiment itself. He was reputed to be a lot of things, he knew, but he doubted *nice* counted among them. People didn't care if he was a decent human being—wealth, looks, and an abundance of superficial charm were usually more than enough. The real man was not the focus of most of the women of his acquaintance.

He found he wasn't sure what to say and it unsettled him. She'd put him in that position more than once. Finally, he murmured, "Thank you."

Her sigh brushed his cheek. "That is not the sort of thing you meant, is it? I'm bad at this."

She was enchanting and unworldly, he thought, lightly brushing a curl from her pale shoulder, poised over her with his hard cock pressed against her thigh. "It was perfect."

"Are you ever ungracious?" Soft rose lips curved in an almost wistful smile.

He grinned. "I hate it when my horses lose."

"By all accounts that is rarely."

"I have an excellent trainer and the top jockeys in England . . . but darling Caroline, as much as I love the subject of racing, can we save the topic for when you aren't naked in my arms?"

Her soft laugh brushed his cheek. "You are the expert on what is supposed to be done in this sort of situation, not me."

Naked ladies in his arms, yes, he could modestly claim some expertise. Untried, fearful ladies . . . in that category he was not so skilled, but he was learning. Nicholas nuzzled her neck. "We will do what you want us to do. Nothing more."

"Kiss me."

That was certainly no hardship. He claimed her mouth, this time scandalously mimicking what he'd love to do to her body with small thrusts of his tongue. She responded beautifully, her fingers in his hair, her lissome warmth against him beguiling.

"Now touch me." Her breathless order was given in a gentle exhale across his cheek, a pair of slim arms twining around his neck. "Like last night."

A lazy summer afternoon, spreading trees, and a lovers' tryst in the fragrant grass. It was a sybaritic dream and if he was the satyr, the role probably fit. Just the slightest bit depraved, but that experience would only benefit his companion. Nicholas rolled a little, pulling her closer. "Whatever my lady wants."

His fingers wandered, they found what they sought, and she gave a small, telling shudder.

When she arched just enough her taut breasts pushed against his chest, he thought with amusement of all those discouraged suitors who muttered about her indifferent civility and detached icy dismissal.

Cold the lady was not.

Small blissful bursts swept through her body and Caroline couldn't help but make a low sound, pleasure still at war with a shadow of disbelief at her wanton behavior.

Well, she was nude in the embrace of the deliciously wicked Nicholas Manning. What woman wouldn't be wanton?

Had she really just asked him to touch her?

Yes, she had.

It was empowering, and even if the reason for them being together in the first place was both frivolous and a potential cauldron of disgrace, at the moment, with his arms around her and his skillful fingers working a captivating spell, she cast a vote it was worth it.

She could feel the hot press of his erection, the long rigid length of it between them as he held and fondled her. Twice before he'd denied himself, and she had the feeling he would do so again if she didn't initiate the actual consummation.

To her surprise, she wanted it. Not as some test of whether Edward's accusations were true, endured with gritted teeth and a fear of failure. No, not that way at all. She wanted it because she ached, she felt incomplete, and she knew intuitively that the man who held her so close had the power to heal her.

His touch was magic. What would a more potent part of him be like?

She shifted. It wasn't really conscious, just a subtle signal of this new yearning.

He understood perfectly. Those questing fingers slipped from between her legs and he murmured in her ear, "Are you sure?"

Since her current state of recklessness seemed not to be in question, she nodded. There she was, in the middle of the day, in some secluded glen without a stitch on, held in the arms of a notorious libertine after agreeing to give her body to two men she really barely knew . . . so, well, yes, why not only take the next step, but enjoy it as much as possible?

"I want you to . . ."

He nipped her throat, sending a shiver down her spine. "Yes. Say it."

"I want you."

"We have a lot in common, then, Lady Wynn, besides what we discovered earlier. I want you also."

This was where the nightmare would resurface. As he moved so he loomed above her, his knees pushing her thighs apart, she waited for the dread to hit her. The nudge of his hard length between her legs should have sent a jolt of revulsion and resignation through her, but she found instead an amazing anticipation building.

"Yes," she whispered, staring into his dark eyes. "Yes, please."

"Like I would refuse." Nicholas didn't smile, but instead he held her gaze as he pushed just enough so the swollen tip of his cock entered her.

And then more.

So much more. Deep, impossibly deep. All of him.

She was stretched, possessed, taken. His lean hips rested against her inner thighs, his arms were braced by her shoulders, and his mouth grazed hers in a slight gesture of reassurance. It was like nothing she ever imagined and most certainly not similar to what she'd experienced before.

Gentle fingers touched her face and he didn't move, his skin holding the flush of arousal, his dark eyes intense. "Caroline?"

She knew what he was asking. "I'm fine," she whispered,

unable to keep the note of exultant happiness from her voice. "Better than fine."

"I'll go slow."

"I don't think that's necessary." She touched her foot to the muscled back of his calf and rubbed suggestively. "I'm not fragile."

"If you—"

"Nicholas," she interrupted breathlessly, her nails lightly biting into his upper arms.

The message was apparently clear, for he slid backward in a tantalizing glide, only to thrust forward again in such a way that sensation prickled through what felt like every nerve ending in her body.

How the same act could be painful and degrading with one man and nothing short of rapturous with another was a revelation. Nicholas touched her with such soft persuasion, encouraging her to reciprocate his passion instead of using her as a vessel in which to quickly sate his lust.

Her fingers flexed on his hard shoulders, his size and strength not intimidating but instead as intoxicating as the plunging friction of his sex into hers.

It felt incredibly good and she let out another small moan.

Worth the risk . . . every moment of it . . .

Silky dark hair brushed his neck as he moved in that erotic rhythm and his face held a peculiar intensity. "Come with me, Caroline."

The way he said her name with such husky intonation as he moved in erotic rhythm within her heightened the sensual pleasure. The heat of anticipation singed her skin, brushed by the warm afternoon breeze. "Nicholas," she answered on a pant, lifting her pelvis, wanting him impossibly deep.

It was all impossible. Impossible to want something as much as she yearned for the exquisite burst of rapture, impossible to believe she was there on a riverbank on a sunny afternoon, nude and abandoned with her lover, impossible to experience such tumultuous joy.

He reached between them and caressed her and suddenly her world burst into flame. She screamed, an unrestrained sound, and was answered by his tall body going rigid in the cradle of her thighs, the force of his ejaculation filling her. They held there in the shattering moment until it ebbed and then he rolled to his side, keeping her close.

Replete in the aftermath, comfortable and quiet, she rested her head on his damp chest and wondered in wayward contemplation how many women he'd lured into paradise with his consummate skill.

Many. It was not just rumor, for he hadn't really denied it.

The fluid practiced lovemaking wasn't real, she reminded herself, listening to the strong beat of his heart. Because he was who he was—one of London's most profligate rogues—confident enough to risk a public bet on his bedroom talents, he made her feel wanted and desired in his arms.

It was deliberate and not personal and she needed to remember that, lest she be lured into a false sense of his intentions.

Not only was she just another easy tumble; she had brazenly asked for it.

"This was one of my more inspired ideas." He interrupted her thoughts with one of his disarming smiles, his dark eyes shadowed by half-closed lids. Filtered sunlight gilded the contours of his well-muscled body. Those high aristocratic cheekbones gave slight shadows to his cheeks. "We should take a ride every afternoon while we're here."

"Do you do this sort of thing often?" Caroline found enough strength to lift her head and watch his expression. The sweet scent of crushed grass rose around them, mingled with the even earthier fragrance of sexual intercourse.

There was a hint of wary question in his dark eyes. "Can you define the actual question?"

"I didn't realize it was unclear." She essayed a smile. "It isn't complicated. I meant spontaneous . . . and outside . . ."

"Lovemaking? No. The green stains on my knees are unique to you." With a light teasing fingertip he touched her lower lip. "I had no inclination to wait until later to touch you again, and why waste this beautiful day and this secluded spot?"

Was he sincere? She wasn't sure. "It's lovely," she admitted, their bodies still entwined, his arms strong and secure. "I've always liked the country much better than the city, but our country home was entailed to the estate, so after Edward died, it went with the title to his cousin. Luckily, I have the house in town free and clear."

The only decent thing Edward had ever done for her was leave her well enough off to be self-sufficient, and she suspected that was done to deliberately taunt Franklin, since the two of them had never cared much for each other. She'd been stunned when she heard the amount of her inheritance, but not half as surprised as the new Lord Wynn. Luckily, Edward had been as ruthless in his business dealings as he was in every other way and tied it up very neatly, so contesting the bequest had proved fruitless. In the aftermath of the dispute, Franklin treated her—as he had the other day after the race meet—with annoying condescension, and she disliked the calculating way he looked at her. To avoid him seemed best and she did so as much as possible.

"I understand your husband died of a fever."

Caroline gazed abstractly at a low-hanging branch fluttering green leaves above the water. The breeze caressed her heated skin. "They aren't sure what it was. He began to get pains in his stomach and became violently ill. It didn't pass. In two days, he was gone."

"I would say I'm sorry, but somehow I don't think you are anxious for sympathy over his loss."

"It would be hypocritical of me to accept any condolences. I didn't wish him dead, but neither did I grieve when it happened."

"You do realize that this time if you decided to marry again, it could be your choice entirely."

The bland tone of his voice made her tilt her head back and look at his face. "I'm wary of it, I'll not deny it. Who is to say what a man will become once the vows are said? Edward seemed charming enough upon first acquaintance, but you are right—he was not my choice. My aunt and my father contracted the marriage and I wasn't consulted."

The man holding her didn't comment. It was a common enough practice to arrange a union without input from the bride.

Caroline murmured, "Besides . . . I didn't conceive a child."

As much as she tried to sound detached and pragmatic, she still remembered Edward's disdain over her failure to bear him an heir. She'd always hoped for one too. Someone to love, and who in turn might love her. Since he wanted a son so badly, it was also a hope her husband would either be less sadistic in his attentions when she was pregnant or leave her alone entirely during her confinement.

Nicholas's arms tightened a little. "Possible infertility can be a consideration," he acknowledged in a quiet voice finally, "depending on one's duty. But there are plenty of men who would overlook it because of your exquisite beauty, Caroline."

What a diplomatic way of saying a man like *him* could not risk a barren wife. Not when it was his responsibility to continue the direct lineage of his family name and rank. She understood. Since her marriage, she was a great deal more knowledgeable about how the world worked.

Still, it stung a little.

It was forgotten in the next moment as Nicholas expertly adjusted their position and kissed her. He murmured against her lips, "We have hours before we have to return and dress for dinner."

Caroline wound her arms around his neck. "That sounds marvelous."

He smiled in a way that made something melt inside her. "I adore your enthusiasm, darling."

The endearment came so easily, used with the facile confidence of a man who knew women wanted to hear it from his lips.

Those gloriously talented lips. On impulse, Caroline moved up enough that she could lick the full bottom curve of his mouth. From corner to corner in a slow, provocative sweep. A flicker of surprised approval showed in his eyes and he laughed, his breath warm against her mouth. "The lady is a quick study, I see."

Was she? Maybe it was the warm afternoon and the setting that made her feel so daring. Perhaps it was the freedom of knowing all the nasty comments and cruel gibes hurled at her when Edward had finished and donned his dressing gown to leave on the nights he came to her room were false. It could even be that the very beautiful, indisputably virile duke truly was irresistible, not just to his usual parade of experienced bedmates, but even to someone as sexually ignorant as herself.

Whatever it was, she knew she wanted him again, wanted to feel his passion, his careful touch, to know she pleased him as a woman.

Even if it was all an illusion.

Chapter Twelve

"So, how goes the campaign? I daresay we've seen more of you the past few days than I have in several years."

Derek gave his uncle a jaded look of reproof. "You are aware it isn't going well, as you've been witness for most of it. Tonight at dinner is a perfect example. I don't believe she spoke more than a dozen words to me and then claimed a headache *again* and left the table early." Sprawled in a chair in the study, a glass of port at his elbow on a Moroccan table inlaid with a brilliant pattern of polished stones, he asked with what he hoped was idle inquiry, "Has she said anything?"

"To your aunt Margaret, you mean?" Thomas leaned back and shook his head. "Not that I'm aware, but there is a singular female conspiracy to silence about romantic confessions between them, I've learned—amazing in creatures not given much to silence in the first place."

Derek wanted to laugh at the dry observation, but he was a little too frustrated and dispirited. "I cannot believe Annabel hasn't remarked on my sudden presence here so often."

Good God, he sounded like a pathetic lovesick adolescent. He moved restively, annoyed with himself, and just annoyed in general. The situation with Annabel was bad enough, but the wager made going out to functions a bit of a trial, especially with Nicholas conspicuously absent.

London society noticed he was gone. The teasing questions about his whereabouts were an irritant Derek didn't need.

"I still say you should endeavor to talk to her alone."

"On several occasions I have tried. It's clear she isn't interested." He made a hopeless gesture with his hand, remembering those attempts with a chagrin that was uncharacteristic and unwanted. "You know, the furor over Phoebe Tanner coincided exactly with my realization that I needed to try to change Annabel's mind about my character. Though Phoebe's husband's radical decision to seek a divorce had nothing to do with me, the whispers didn't help. I'm sure it's merely confirmed Annabel's bleak opinion of me as a rakish scoundrel. There is nothing worse than being embroiled in a divorce petition. Luckily, not only am I innocent entirely of ever touching the lady, but Lord Tanner at least dropped his accusations. Too late, though, I'm afraid."

Thomas merely gave him a look of amused male sympathy.

"Annabel's opinion of me makes the bottom of the sea look like a mountaintop." Derek sprawled lower in his chair with a frustrated sigh.

"Ah."

Well, what the devil did that mean? Even if Derek hadn't ultimately been named in the lovely Lady Tanner's imbroglio, the timing couldn't have been worse. The Tanner divorce scandal had happened right as he finally admitted his inability to dismiss the incident with Annabel and go about his life. He was not going to be able to dismiss *Annabel*. And seeing his name trotted out as the likely source of Lord Tanner's outrage—though the rumor was false—hadn't helped his cause in the least. Phoebe Tanner had protected her real lover—who must resemble Derek in height and coloring, for the hapless gentleman had escaped out the window when they were discovered by her enraged husband, hence the mistake. Having a solid alibi for the night in question helped prove his denials of culpability were true, but what stuck in people's mind was not his proven innocence but the cauldron of scandal.

He'd written to Annabel several months ago, laboring

over the letter like a schoolboy, sitting at his desk for hours trying to think of how to explain his actions that fateful afternoon in the library, and, for his trouble, gotten no reply at all. He was fairly sure Annabel hadn't even bothered to read it.

Derek bit out, "Lighthearted seduction is quite different from . . . *this*."

His uncle's mouth curved in amusement. "You might try out the word."

"What word?" He resisted pouring another glass of port. Drinking too much wasn't solving his problems, though he had severely tested the method.

"Love," Thomas said mildly. "I think you are going to have to practice saying it."

There was a painting of a hound with a limp fox at its feet above the fireplace and Derek focused his attention on it as a diversion. Why any artist chose to depict dead animals on canvas for aesthetic purposes was a mystery to him. . . .

Love. No, he wasn't sure he could speak with eloquence on the subject. The letter had contained an apology and a request for a chance to speak to her but no flowery declarations. He knew how to please a woman with a well-turned compliment, how to whisper the right words in her ear when she was in his bed, how to make her sigh with just the correct touch, but he knew nothing about saying those simple three words.

I love you.

Thomas went on. "You must say it. Women need to hear it. They *like* to hear it and it's important to build a strong bond. Grudgingly admitting you'd marry her is vastly different from explaining just how you feel."

"It wasn't grudging," Derek objected.

"It took a year."

Well, that was a solid point. He'd come around, just twelve crucial months too late.

"How I feel?" he muttered. "That's easy enough. Wretched."

A benign smile lit his uncle's face. "Your current state of discomfort tells me you're sincere, Derek. But you aren't making much progress by simply showing up and glowering every time she mentions Lord Hyatt's name."

"I don't glower." He tried consciously to wipe the fierce frown from his face.

"No." A chuckle rang out. "Not at all."

"Your glee over my present distress is a little unsporting, isn't it? I thought males had an unspoken law that compassion was the order of the day for a fallen comrade." Derek shoved himself to his feet and paced restlessly over to the window. It was full dark outside and his image reflected back at him in the glass, the set of his mouth unhappy and tense.

"Trust me, I am not without compassion for your dilemma, Derek. I love Annabel as if she were my own child. I've been her father since she was eight years old, and her happiness is very important to me. I would also like to see you settled and content with the right woman rather than dividing your time between dull business obligations and frivolous love affairs. I doubt either leaves you very fulfilled."

The observation was very much on the mark and Derek gave a small grimace and turned around. "For the past year I've done my best to convince myself I had a small infatuation that would pass like any other."

"I believe Annabel has been busy doing the same thing."

"What if you're wrong? What if her feelings for Hyatt are genuine? After all, she agreed to be his wife." The last word came out a little choked. His cravat felt suddenly as if it was tied too tight and he loosened it with a careless tug.

Thomas folded his hands and shook his head. "Where now is the confident young man who does little more than glance their way and aristocratic ladies swoon into his arms? Surely you know far more about women than I do. I had a rather more staid existence in my youth and so my experience is limited mostly to my years of married life. But I can say with fair confidence that the way Annabel acts in your presence toward her intended is quite different from the more subdued persona I see when you are not there to witness her supposed bliss."

"You think she's trying to make me jealous?" He felt ridiculous even asking, but then he really wanted to know.

"The other night at the family celebration, she was most certainly more flirtatious and attentive to his lordship than usual. When you left, she was visibly more subdued. To be honest, I think Hyatt noticed and maybe even made the connection himself between your departure and her change in demeanor. On Annabel's part I don't think it was conscious, because she is not a vindictive person. But I do think she wants you to believe she's no longer taken with you in any way."

"She's succeeding." Derek gave a ragged exhale. "I'm both jealous and uncertain, and I loathe both states, for your information."

"I'm sorry for that, but quite frankly, I was starting to wonder if you would ever have more than a passing interest in any woman." Thomas calmly poured himself more port. "You seemed so determined to avoid any entanglement that might remotely become permanent. I suppose that's why I wasn't worried when I first realized Annabel's adolescent romantic feelings for you. Whatever the gossips say, I know you well, and you have more honor than to compromise her. I realize something happened, but I won't ask what. I trust you."

If Thomas knew some of the less-than-honorable fantasies he'd entertained about his beautiful charge, he might not retain his sangfroid, but in the end, Thomas was right: he would never have taken advantage of her infatuation.

Then.

The game was a little different now.

"A single kiss," Derek admitted.

"Ah."

"It scared me half to death." He could still remember with vivid clarity not only the sweet, beguiling taste of her mouth but also the shining hope in her beautiful eyes that made him realize he'd fallen off some figurative precipice and into an abyss.

Maybe it wasn't just that he was wary of shackling himself to one woman; it was an inner fear he didn't deserve such patent trust and emotion.

Thomas's brows went up and he laughed. "I doubt there're many in society who would believe the scandalous Earl of Manderville was frightened by a simple kiss bestowed on an innocent young girl."

"They'd be wrong." The whole thing was difficult to articulate in a way that made sense. He said in slow explanation, "It was more the look on her face afterward. I suddenly realized it was a turning point in my life. I could walk away as fast as possible and pretend it never happened, or I could consider an option I never had thought of before, which was marriage. I took the former, but it didn't work. The latter seems to now be my only choice."

Just how did one propose to an engaged woman—one who made a very convincing show of disliking you intensely?

The depressing reality was he had no idea.

Nicholas smiled at the delighted look on the face of the woman across from him. "I thought this would be more enjoyable than dining inside. It's really a beautiful night, isn't it?"

Caroline took the chair he offered, settling into it with graceful ease, silken skirts fluttering as she sank down and adjusted them with a slim hand. Her expression was a little bemused as she gazed at the giant sprays of flowers scattered in vases all over the terrace, the perfume of the blossoms filling the air. The table, too, had been done well. A pristine white cloth covered with gleaming china and silver was set over it on just the edge near the steps where they could gaze out over the gardens. As if nature were in full cooperation with his whim, the moon hung low over the tops of the trees, the air was warm, and the breeze nothing more than a pleasant whisper. The dozens of candles in strategically placed candelabras barely flickered.

Mrs. Sims—responsible for everything except the moon and the starlit perfection of the evening—deserved a very nice raise, he decided as he took a chair and reached for a bottle of wine to pour them each a glass. He didn't visit Essex often, but maybe after this interlude, he would use the estate more. To his surprise, he liked the quiet. As a youth, it chafed to be so isolated. As a man of almost thirty, his perspective was changing.

"It's lovely. What a marvelous idea." Caroline gazed at him from across the small intimate table. "I am quite impressed with your inspiration."

He was the one who was impressed. She usually favored greens and grays but this evening was more than dazzling in an indigo blue gown, the purity of her skin set off by the dark color, the heavy mass of her auburn hair upswept in a simple style that suited her classic beauty. A single sapphire nestled in the tempting valley between her luscious breasts, the size of the gem not ostentatious, but cut in a perfect oval shape and held by a thin gold chain around her slender neck.

He wondered with a twinge of unfamiliar emotion if her husband had given the necklace to her. Why the devil he cared he wasn't sure, but he felt an unprecedented urge to give her something even more dazzling. Maybe ruby earrings, as the gems would emphasize the subtle highlights in her rich hair. When they returned to London, he might just see about a gift. After all, he was thoroughly enjoying himself. He said, "You look stunning. I like that color on you."

"You are rather beautiful yourself, but thank you." A slight mischievous smile curved her mouth. "Lord Manderville will be hard-pressed to compete with a perfect moonlit evening and supper and wine on the terrace."

If the necklace bothered him, any mention of Derek even just sitting across the table from her brought a flicker of displeasure. He dismissed it as best as possible and grinned. "If you are willing to give me credit for the weather, I'll take it. I ordered this gorgeous evening just for you."

"And if anyone could coerce the elements into compliance with his wishes, you could, Rothay." Caroline laughed, accepting a goblet of wine, her slim fingers curling around the stem. "I am getting spoiled, I'm afraid."

"It's how it should be. Ladies as lovely as you are should have to do little more than decorate the world around them."

She gazed at him, her lashes slightly lowered, the glow of

candlelight vying with starlight to illuminate her face and graceful bared shoulders. "You are very gallant."

"With you it is very easy." Negligently he lifted his glass to his mouth and took a sip of wine.

"I wish . . ." She trailed off and bit her lip, then looked away for a moment. Her profile was suddenly distant.

Nicholas waited, curious as hell as to what she almost said, counting on her usual lack of duplicity to make her finish. When she didn't, he prompted softly, "You wish what?"

She just shook her head, tendrils of glossy hair brushing her neck. "I was about to say something I am sure you would find alarming and naive, so I am going to for once not be so forthright."

He set his glass back down with deliberate care. "I'm finding I like your lack of pretense. Tell me."

She gazed at him from across the intimate table, her soft lips just parted a fraction. Then she said quietly, "I was going to say I wish this was real."

She was right. A ripple of alarm surged through him. The trouble was, it wasn't an urge to immediately brush off any suggestion of romantic involvement, but a vastly more disturbing reaction: one small part of him—one he thought dead and gone after his experience with Helena—agreed with her.

To make matters worse, she elaborated, her lashes lowering just a fraction. "I mean, if the illusion is so pleasant, how much better would it be if we were truly—"

To his utter gratitude, the arrival of his Scottish housekeeper with the first course prevented her from finishing and excused him from having to make a comment. As he tasted the soup, he dismissed his unease over understanding just what she meant.

After all, he was the one who had engineered the romantic setting and seductive mood. He thought he was immune, but maybe the deliberately woven spell was taking effect.

They ate and talked quietly and drank wine as the sky became brilliant with stars and the insects settled into a soporific pattern of sound in the trees. The food was, as usual, simple, but so fresh and well prepared it didn't matter there were no fancy sauces or unusual ingredients. With dessert, he found himself somehow discussing his political views, his family, his horses again. Since she was so well-read, Caroline had a fascinating ability to actually engage him in conversation that did not involve meaningless gossip or, even more tedious, fashion.

Intellect could actually be as attractive as all the other delightful parts of a woman, he decided as he sat across from her and watched the moonlight gild her hair.

His mother would like her.

Good God, where did *that* thought come from?

"You have actually been to Rome?" she asked, bringing him back to their current topic of conversation, which was his travels after he finished university. "Seen the Colosseum, the aqueducts, the great churches?"

"I preferred Florence," he answered, enjoying the way her face lit with interest, giving her an animation more attractive than even her perfect, feminine features. "You'll have to make a point to go sometime. And Greece also was fascinating and amazingly primitive in some places for a country with such culture and rich history. Crete in particular has a wild feel, despite its complex ancient civilization reputed to have been destroyed and that quite possibly was the model for Plato's Atlantis."

At that point, Caroline leaned her elbows inelegantly on the table and stared at him. "Do you think the theory has any validity? A paper was presented recently to the Royal Society that suggested the same thing. At the time, I found the supposition intriguing. A catastrophic wave from a volcanic eruption miles away is supposed to have engulfed the major city and swept it away."

He was the one swept away by her candid interest. "I'm not an archaeologist by any means, but the hypothesis is interesting, isn't it?"

"I am intensely jealous of your experiences." For a moment her face was shuttered, but then she smiled and gave a rueful shake of her head. "As if you can't tell. I don't get much opportunity for discussions like this. Miss Dunsworth and I used to sit over tea for hours and she would tell me of her father's theories and his travels. I honestly don't think she even minded him leaving her destitute in exchange for the tales and artifacts he brought back. She gave me a great thirst for a broader world. I fear I've been plying you with questions like a curious child."

There was nothing childlike about her, he thought, his gaze drifting over her supple, enticing form. "I believe I already told you I'd answer any questions you have."

But that had been in bed, when he sensed her ignorance and uncertainty. She recalled the same thing, for a flustered look crossed her face. "So you did."

He lifted a brow in a lazy suggestive arch. "Anything else you wish to know?"

The sexual connotation in the question was unmistakable. Her mouth—that very delicious, kissable mouth—quirked. She said tartly, "I am sure if there was, you would be the person to ask."

"Any objections to my expertise?" He kept the question light and teasing.

An indefinable expression crossed her face, almost wistful. "No."

"Come," he said, rising, holding out his hand. "Dance with me."

"We've no music," she objected, but she rose obediently to her feet and her fingers clasped his. The silk of her gown brushed his legs.

"Do we need it?" He slipped an arm around her waist and brought her close—far too close for a crowded London ballroom, but just right for a secluded waltz on a starlit terrace in the warm darkness of the bucolic countryside.

She swayed into his lead, her breasts brushing his jacket, the lissome feel of her body as intoxicating as any spirit. "Just don't ask me to sing," she said facetiously, "or we will stumble all over the place. I am afraid my talents do not lie in that direction."

His laugh stirred her fragrant hair. "I'll imagine the tune in my head, then."

"That would be best, take my word on it."

"For a beautiful woman, you have a remarkable lack of conceit."

She gazed up at him with poignant uncertainty, the luminous color of her eyes striking. "I don't think I have had much practice with vanity."

He agreed. He didn't think she had either. An amazing truth when he considered her dazzling allure, but maybe not surprising if he factored in her past. Nicholas moved slowly, in small steps as they turned and whirled, and enjoyed the soft, luscious feel of her against him.

The dance went on, the moment having an idyllic quality that he didn't experience too often in his busy life. But what man, he reminded himself philosophically, wouldn't enjoy such an exquisite evening, holding a desirable woman, and having the knowledge that their silent, intimate waltz was simply the prelude to another type of dance when he took her upstairs to his bed? Already his erection swelled, stiffening against the constraint of his fitted breeches.

When his steps slowed finally, Nicholas leaned down to whisper in her ear, "I want you."

"I can tell." Her voice was also hushed, a breathy laugh escaping. "You are holding me scandalously close, Your Grace, and your *enthusiasm* is obvious."

"I'd rather be closer." He lifted her in his arms in a theatrical sweep, noting her cheeks were flushed and it couldn't be from their slow, swaying, twirling motion across the terrace. "Let me see what I can arrange."

In a few strides he was across the flagstones and shouldering his way through the French doors, ajar to the pleasant evening. Mrs. Sims was in the main hallway and she looked startled as they appeared, her concerned gaze fastening on Caroline. "Your Grace . . . is everything quite all right?"

Caroline made a small sound that he interpreted as embarrassment. He said in serene reassurance, "Everything is fine. Dinner was superb. Please tell the cook."

"Yes, of course." Mrs. Sims managed to compose her slightly shocked expression.

"My lady is fatigued. I suggested she retire."

The plain truth. She could sleep *afterward*.

Her mortification over having the housekeeper witness her lover's impetuous impulse to carry her up the stairs was tempered by the excitement flowing through her veins like honeyed wine.

Her lover.

However it had come about, however short a time it might be, the charismatic Nicholas Manning *was* her lover, even if it was only for one week.

The grand gesture that culminated their romantic meal was part of what Caroline felt must be some sort of idealistic dream. Carrying her off to his bedroom was the natural conclusion to a slow, seductive waltz.

"She doesn't think for a minute I'm just tired," she murmured, resting her head on one broad shoulder. Caroline knew her cheeks were bright pink, but wasn't sure just how much she cared. Nicholas smelled wonderful, all male, and the intoxicating effects of it made her nipples tingle and warmth pulse between her legs.

"The housekeeper's opinion doesn't really matter to me, though I do plan on rewarding her and making a remark or two on how I'd appreciate her silence over my visit." He seemed to carry her so effortlessly his breathing didn't even change as he took the steps with smooth athletic motion.

She wished she could share his indifference to others' opinion, but then again, he was very used to being scrutinized at every turn. The splendor of his dark good looks, the extent of his fortune, and the exalted rank of his title made him a natural target of interest. If society discovered her participation in the wicked wager, she'd be as notorious as he was, and that was a high standard against which to be measured.

No, Caroline assured herself quickly as he shoved the bedroom door shut with his booted foot. No one would find out.

He set her on the bed and his long fingers went to his cravat. "I need you naked."

The words weren't said with tenderness but instead with a compelling urgency. "Is that a suggestion or an order?" It was amazing how things had changed in just a few days. Had Edward said those same words to her, she would have wanted to run out of the room. With the Devilish Duke, she sat up and kicked off her slippers, boldly lifting her skirts to remove her stockings. His glittering gaze observed her every movement even as he shrugged out of his superfine jacket.

"Hurry," he said softly.

And somehow that one word was arousing. Caroline closed her eyes in a brief flash of sensation, and then lifted her skirts, bunching them above her waist. She brazenly spread her legs. "Is this fast enough?"

Nicholas gave a low inaudible curse, the sentiment clear enough without the words. He tore his breeches open. "It's perfect."

Why wasn't she afraid?

Because he wouldn't hurt her. She knew it. Fear was the last thing on her mind as he shoved his breeches down his lean hips and climbed on top of her. It wasn't in him to force her to do anything she didn't want, and she definitely did want this in every way possible. His entry was impetuous and even in the moment of impatient, complete need he paused, checked halfway through carnal penetration, and asked hoarsely, "Are you all right?"

"I need you." Caroline could feel the heat from his powerful body through the fabric of his shirt. Her fingers splayed across his chest, testing the muscular contours.

In response to her protest over his hesitation, he fully sheathed himself inside her, all the way so she could feel the entire rigid length of his desire, the extent of how she'd aroused him.

This is what it's like to be a woman.

Oh God.

Her hips lifted from a command she didn't even know she gave as he began to move. He slid backward and then surged into total possession again, so hard she gasped. Delirious sensation saturated her senses, took over her hungry body, and she gloried in it, his ostentatious carnal appeal like a drug. Under the fine lawn of his shirt his muscles were rock hard with tension.

Their first night she'd been frightened despite her resolve, but he'd held back and reassured her. The afternoon spent making love in the sun-filled glade, she'd been a little more free, less inhibited by her past, curious, and still cautious.

Now she was . . . eager. Wet. Needy.

For him. For his generosity and skillful dispensation of rapturous pleasure. Each stroke brought forth a low, telling moan and she arched back in response to his thrusts, somehow the decadent fact they couldn't wait long enough to undress inflaming her senses.

She felt wanton. It was wonderful.

Nicholas had made her wanton.

And she gloried in it.

Their rhythm increased, the flow of his body into hers became more frantic, wilder, and she clung to him with increasing urgency. Caroline let her head fall back as she moaned in pleasure and he muttered something she didn't catch.

Then he climaxed. She registered the stiffening of his tall body, the eruption of breath from his chest, his dark lashes lowering abruptly as he went still completely except for the deep pulsing eruption of his release. The burst against her womb was forceful and as rash as the way he'd swept her off the terrace and up the stairs.

The scorch of his breath brushed her cheek as moments later he gave a short laugh. "My apologies. Give me a minute or two and I promise I'll make it up to you. Apparently moonlit dances with beautiful auburn-haired ladies arouse my passions to an embarrassing degree. I can't remember ever spending myself so fast."

Though she doubted he realized it, the idea she'd made the smooth, experienced, and oh-so-devilish Duke of Rothay lose control was empowering, intoxicating. Caroline closed her eyes so he couldn't see the sudden sheen of tears. They were joyous ones, the stinging sensation evidence of her realization that all the hurtful jabs and derision she'd experienced at the hands of her husband were being erased with each tender touch, every flashing smile and wild, wicked kiss.

She wished this week would never end.

Nicholas withdrew and she stifled a sigh of disappointment that he had no trouble interpreting. His grin was a flash of white teeth. Lounging next to her on one elbow, his breeches unfastened, his dark hair a little disheveled, he was the picture of decadent, erotic promise. One finger traced a path down her cheek and across her lower lip. "Don't worry. In my current state of male mortification, I am determined to redeem myself in every way possible. Let me undress you and we'll begin again, my darling Caroline."

She liked the idea of being his darling.

A small smile curved her lips. In dishabille, her skirts still bunched around her waist, she felt languidly dissatisfied, though she doubted it would last. "You haven't disappointed me yet."

"The vote of confidence is appreciated." His fingers skillfully unfastened her gown as he shifted her into his arms. "I told you a woman has a great deal of control over a man when he desires her the way I do you."

"Too bad it's only because of the competition between you and Manderville."

He paused, going very still.

She was, in turn, horrified.

There she went, for the second time in one evening, saying whatever was on her mind. What did she expect? A declaration of affection from a man who barely knew her? He might have explored every inch of her body, but a few days in each other's company hardly constituted a deep relationship and their unusual circumstances had to be taken into consideration.

Her cheeks heated at her own audacity and gauche ability to say the wrong thing at the wrong time. It was why she usually stayed so quiet, so rigidly suppressed when it came to conversation in public. She might—as she had just proved—blurt out something embarrassing.

Luckily, he was much more practiced in the intricacies of the casual liaisons that can exist between men and women and he shrugged, seeming to pass over the implications of her ill-timed remark. The last button on her gown slid free and he smiled in his quixotic way. "That infernal bet brought us together, so I am not going to regret it. At this moment, you are here"—he slid her gown downward and exposed her taut breasts under her thin chemise—"and so very carnally available."

He kissed her as he continued to leisurely remove her clothing, long, slow, enticing kisses that seduced and beguiled and were a testament to his well-deserved reputation. In the ensuing hours he more than made up for his small sexual faux pas, bringing her to an orgasmic peak time and again, selfless and proving his legendary stamina was no myth but based in pure fact.

Later, replete and drowsy against him, she pondered the future with a sense of fatalistic introspection. It was easy for her to feel wanted while nestled in his arms, his rangy presence a symbol of the monumental change in her life.

She had to wonder if though she might be cured of her crippling insecurity, she could also be damned. With her level of inexperience, she had naively assumed the intimacy of making love could be disregarded. After all, Nicholas and Derek Drake both had a reputation of being able to seduce and abandon with ease, transitory pleasure their only goal.

What if she couldn't be as detached?

Next to her, Nicholas had slipped into sleep, all glorious male beauty, his even breathing lifting his chest in a steady rhythm. He was the problem, she realized, staring at where the night breeze gently lifted the curtain. Since all of this— all of him—was so new, so glorious, she found it hard to sift through the reality and the fantasy.

He *talked* to her. It was more compelling than his undeniable skill in arousing her body. Had he simply done what she expected in the first place and dragged her into the bedroom for the whole week, maybe she wouldn't feel so unsettled. Instead he'd been considerate, gentle, and attentive in every way.

She had an aching fear that now she couldn't walk away with ease.

Nicholas shifted position, pulling her closer even in deep slumber as if he'd done the same thing a thousand times with other lovers.

He probably *had* done it a thousand times. That should not bother her.

But it did.

Chapter Thirteen

Annabel turned obediently, the material of her elaborate wedding dress falling in folds around her, pins everywhere as the seamstress knelt on the floor and toyed with the hem. Margaret watched with a critical eye, occasionally making a comment or two.

Was it obvious, Annabel wondered, how distracted and indifferent she was to something that should mean a great deal to her?

She hoped not but was afraid the truth was written all over her face.

That fear was confirmed when they left the modiste's establishment an hour later and headed home. Margaret Drake was still lovely with soft brown hair slightly graying in a graceful way, her skin showing tiny lines that did not detract from the beauty of good bone structure and her fine, sparkling eyes. She settled into the seat of the carriage across from her and came right to the point.

"Is something wrong?"

Is anything right?

Annabel tried to look bland. "I'm not sure what you mean."

"You look tired, my dearest child, almost listless, and you pick at your food. Just now, when being fitted for your wedding dress, no less, you barely offered an opinion, even when asked directly."

It was all true, and since Margaret was like a mother to

her, Annabel found it difficult not to confess what was really bothering her. Except she couldn't. If she said it out loud, she'd have to really think about it and that was out of the question. "I never knew planning a wedding was so . . . involved," she explained, with a true twinge of guilt. It wasn't precisely a falsehood—the details were a little overwhelming—but neither was it the truth about her abstraction.

Margaret tilted her head a little, studying her, eyes just slightly narrowed. "Lord Hyatt agreed to whatever size of a celebration you wish. It needn't be so big if you'd prefer something a bit quieter."

That was part of the problem too. Alfred was a very accommodating, nice man.

Unlike someone else she could name, a certain earl who on the surface seemed beautifully mannered and utterly charming, but underneath the handsome exterior was selfish and unfeeling.

"I *want* a big celebration." The words came out too crisply, and with effort, she modified her tone. "What I mean is that marriage is quite a step and I want to share my happiness with my friends and, of course, my family."

Margaret lifted her brows. "All right, then, but you might show more enthusiasm for the details. And yes, one's wedding dress is one of those details."

She bit her lip and then sighed. "I'm very sorry I'm poor company this afternoon."

"My darling child, I'm not scolding you, just concerned. If you regret this engagement, now is the time—"

"No," Annabel interrupted swiftly. "I regret nothing."

What a terrible lie to someone she loved.

There was a long pause while the only noise was the rattle of the wheels over the street and the call of the occasional vendor hawking wares on a corner. Then Margaret nodded, upright on her seat, her face serious. "If you're certain you wish to go through with this, you know I will do my best to make it a wonderful event you'll always remember."

She would, Annabel never doubted it, and she felt doubly guilty for being deceitful. "Alfred is kind, generous, and gentle. Moreover, it's possible he'll actually be faithful, not something most wives can hope for. Why wouldn't I want to go through with it?"

"Are you actually asking me a question? If so, be careful. I might answer it."

It was Annabel's turn to narrow her eyes and stare. "What does that mean?"

"It means I'm concerned about you. I think that, for whatever reason, you are really not happy about this upcoming marriage, as much as you pretend otherwise. Thomas has even said something, and my dear, when a man notices and remarks on what a woman is feeling, it might just be obvious. They are not the most observant creatures."

She wouldn't be so rattled, so openly unhappy, if Derek all of a sudden wasn't everywhere she turned. In the past year she'd barely seen him, but in the past five days, he'd come to dinner three times and tea twice, and even shown up at a small musical performance given by the daughter of one of Margaret's friends. His unprecedented behavior lifted eyebrows all across the room, and the poor young woman was so flustered to have the infamous earl in attendance she stumbled through her renditions of Bach and Mozart in a way that would have made both composers wince. Annabel had endured it with gritted teeth, and it wasn't the discordant notes that bothered her but Derek's magnetic presence at such a small affair. The covetous looks the women there gave him were unmistakable. In elegant evening wear, his blond hair gleaming in the candlelight, he had an inscrutable expression on his face as he sat and listened and appeared to ignore the incredulity of everyone in the room over his attendance.

No one was as startled or uncomfortable as Annabel. She was afraid even Alfred might have taken note of it.

Derek's absence in her life made everything easier, but this sudden reappearance shook her world.

It shook her resolve to forget him, and she despised both

herself and, even more so, *him* for making her have even a single doubt.

It was that damned letter he'd written to her in part. It sat locked in a drawer in the bottom of her armoire, the contents inviolate, a symbol of her indifference.

But every single day without fail she wondered what it said, and it was more tempting than ever to tear it open and read it.

"Surely I'm entitled to a little nervousness over the wedding." She arranged her skirts with one hand, being careful to seem nonchalant. "I feel certain most prospective brides have a few misgivings now and then."

"Probably, I'll grant you that point as long as that is all it is. We do so want you to be happy."

Happy? When was the last time she'd felt happy?

The carriage turned a corner and Annabel caught the strap to steady herself against the sway of the vehicle. A vision came into her mind, unbidden and unwanted, of a warm, glorious summer afternoon, the quiet library at Manderville Hall, which she almost considered her own private retreat, and a magical kiss. Derek, so impossibly attractive with his fair hair just slightly rumpled and a look in his azure eyes she'd never seen before, turning to her, gazing downward and lowering his head with unmistakable intent . . .

And then the touch of his mouth on hers. Soft, tender, taking but giving, stealing the very breath from her lungs.

But then another memory intruded, this one of the same man who had taken her so gently into his arms embracing another woman.

Annabel banished both with ruthless determination and told Margaret, "I am happy."

Her surrogate mother just looked at her for a moment and then murmured, "If you say so, I believe you."

The street was crowded in the late afternoon, and Derek stepped out of his favorite tobacco shop on Bond Street and nearly collided with one of the pedestrians walking past the doorway. He murmured, "Pardon me."

"Manderville. How nice to run into you. Not in a literal sense, of course." The man's mouth twitched at his attempt at levity.

Good God, Derek thought with wry realization, of all the damned people to practically plow him down on the sidewalk, why did it have to be the man he wanted to see least of all in the entire city? "Yes, indeed."

Alfred Hyatt also carried a package. "Just come from the glove maker myself. Tedious business to run errands, but one must now and again, I suppose."

"No getting around it," Derek agreed with grim politeness. "Well, I suppose I—"

"Join me for a drink? There's a little tavern down the street that serves a decent whiskey." Friendly and urbane, Annabel's fiancé looked at him expectantly.

People streamed by, carriages rattled past, and maybe it was the noise and the distraction, or maybe he was just plain dim-witted at that moment because of the ironic notion of having a friendly drink with his adversary, but Derek couldn't come up with a swift excuse without it sounding churlish.

Devil take it, Hyatt probably didn't even *know* they were adversaries.

"A whiskey sounds like just the thing," he muttered, and that wasn't a lie. Maybe he'd drink an entire bottle, he brooded as they fell into step.

The tavern proved crowded, the patrons a mixture of well-dressed men like themselves and shopkeepers and tradesmen. They managed to find a quiet corner and sat down, and an efficient barmaid with an Irish brogue whisked off to fill their order.

Hyatt smiled in his usual pleasant way from across the worn surface of the table. Everything about the man, blast him to perdition, was pleasant. He was nice looking in a sort of unremarkable way, he dressed stylishly but without affectation, his demeanor wasn't posturing or foppish, so men liked him, and obviously if Annabel had agreed to marry the bastard, he appealed to women as well.

Damnation.

"Actually, seeing you today is fortuitous," Hyatt said, folding his hands on the table as they waited for their drinks. "I've been contemplating asking your advice on a matter of some importance to me."

That wasn't what he expected to hear. Derek raised a brow. "Oh?"

"In an area you are somewhat more of an expert in than myself." Hyatt gave a self-deprecating laugh. "Did I say 'somewhat'? I should have omitted that from my previous sentence. Let's just say I am reasonably sure for several reasons you will be able to help me with this dilemma."

"What dilemma?"

"Well . . . it has to do with females, of course. I am going to guess in the course of your . . . er . . . many relationships in the past, you have discovered just what pleases them when it comes to gifts. Add to that the simple fact you know Annabel well, and I wondered if you could guide me as to what to purchase for her as a wedding gift."

Derek stared, wondering just what bad deed he'd committed that fate sought to punish him by having the very man who was betrothed to the woman he loved ask him for advice on what would please her to celebrate their nuptials. Casting back quickly over his life, he decided that even in his less-than-angelic moments nothing came to mind that was bad enough to warrant this particular torture.

When he didn't immediately speak, Hyatt added, "I am at a loss, yet I want to get it just right, as I'm sure you understand."

Where the hell is that whiskey?

Derek cleared his throat. "What you would buy a paramour and buy a wife are two different things, I'm sure. I doubt I can help much. Annabel isn't vain enough to covet jewels or expensive perfumes, I'm afraid."

"You see, you do know her," Hyatt pointed out with unerring accuracy. "That's helpful already. Go on."

The barmaid arrived with their drinks like a gift from heaven. Even though she had pockmarked skin and was probably two decades older, Derek could have kissed her. He picked up his glass, drank so large a mouthful he nearly choked, and relished the burn as it went down.

The faster he finished it, the faster he could make a plausible excuse and leave.

"I knew her better as a child," he said, which was not quite the truth but close enough. The open, inquisitive child had given way to a woman, with a woman's dreams, and a woman's ability to beguile and fascinate. Had he understood her transformation a little better, maybe he wouldn't have ruined everything. "We don't really speak too often."

"Yes, I've noticed that." Hyatt took a reasonable sip from his own glass.

For the first time, Derek took note of the watchfulness in the other man's eyes.

Perhaps a reassessment of the situation was in order, he realized with a start.

Uncle Thomas said he'd thought Lord Hyatt had noticed Annabel's behavior at the engagement gathering. Maybe the man was perceptive in other ways also. Thomas had seen through Derek. Maybe Hyatt also sensed a rival.

As evenly as possible, Derek said, "We don't see each other often."

"She mentioned that to me once." Hyatt sat back a little in his chair, his gaze intent, and while not overtly hostile, his expression was set. "I have to say she becomes quite tense when your name arises."

Wonderful. They'd discussed him. Though Derek doubted Annabel would say anything about the kiss, he had no doubt she would have little complimentary to say otherwise. He wasn't sure how to excuse her derision, but he took his best stab at it. "I think once she was old enough to understand all the gossip, she decided I was rather less heroic than she thought when she was younger." He took another fiery sip from his glass. "She's absolutely right, of course."

"Quite." Hyatt looked bland. "Who knows how a woman will react to things?"

It was hard to know how to respond, so Derek declined to do so. Instead he finished his drink and set the glass down with a smart click. "I'm sorry I can't help you with a brilliant idea for a gift."

"Not at all." Hyatt waved a hand in a careless gesture, but the guarded scrutiny in his eyes didn't falter. "It was nice to talk, just the same. After all, we will shortly be part of the same family and see each other often."

And how the hell he was going to endure that, Derek wasn't sure. Worse than his visions of his lordship and Annabel in bed, he pictured her ripe with another man's child and it flayed him in a way he never imagined possible.

"Of course," Hyatt went on in the same mild conversational tone that barely rose above the noisy crowd, "I've thought about taking her away for a bit after the wedding. Italy, perhaps. Do you think she'd enjoy it?"

No. He *wasn't* going to discuss their wedding trip. The word "enjoy," in particular, grated on his nerves. Derek stood, summoning a false smile. "Annabel has always had a sense of adventure. I am sure she would. Now, if you'll excuse me—"

"Has that sense of adventure ever extended itself to you, Manderville?"

Derek went very still. He narrowed his eyes. "Excuse me?"

"Any man might wonder unless he was blind. I," his lordship added succinctly, "am not. She reacts to you. I suppose most women do, so maybe it isn't unusual. But maybe it means something."

This was the point where Derek should be able to declare he'd never touched her. But he *had* touched her, tasted her, and while one kiss hardly meant she was compromised, he still was not guilt free.

Looking the other man in the eye, Derek said tersely, "Rest assured, her honor is intact. Thank you for the drink."

He swung around and left the tavern, shouldering his way past the milling occupants, a light sweat on his brow.

Once outside he stalked down the street with purpose and it must have shown, for people stepped out of his way.

So Lord Hyatt had his doubts, did he?

Was it a good sign, or a bad one? Annabel might hate him all the more if he was the cause of contention between her and her prospective bridegroom. But Hyatt had mentioned *her* behavior, not his.

He needed to talk to her. There was no doubt about it.

Chapter Fourteen

It surprised him, but Nicholas found he liked the softness of the dawn. Not that he was slothful in any way—he had more to do than was possible some days—but he usually stayed up late and rarely rose just as the sun was cresting the horizon. After a few mornings of lying in bed and watching the sky lighten, he realized he enjoyed it.

Of course, it didn't hurt to have a captivating woman next to you either, he decided, and maybe that was the reason he'd suddenly developed a sentimental attachment to the sunrise after twenty-eight years on this earth of ignoring it completely.

Caroline slept like a child, on her side, one hand beneath her cheek, her breath even and slow. Except she was certainly not childlike in any other way, her nude, voluptuous body half-covered by the silken sheets, full, pink-tipped breasts exposed and all too tempting. Her rich hair tumbled over her pale shoulders and decorated the blanket in a glossy spill of disordered curls. In repose, she resembled what he supposed to be his ideal of the perfect woman, all graceful sensuality and earthy appeal.

And delicate feminine vulnerability coupled with an admirable inner strength that moved him.

Nicholas rose up and propped himself against the pillows, contemplating her lissome form with a faint frown between his brows. This was sexual, no more, he reminded himself sharply. At heart, he was a practical man.

But she woke early, and he'd discovered he liked waking with her.

Sure enough, as soon as the room lightened so the furniture was no longer vague shapes and the illumination against the drawn draperies gave the Oriental rug a warm glow, she stirred. Long lashes fluttering, she sighed, stretched just a little, and opened her eyes.

"Good morning."

Caroline rolled over to give him a sleepy smile. With a modesty that was a little too late and most unnecessary, she tugged the sheet upward over her naked breasts as she blinked awake. "Good morning."

"Always. When I wake with you."

"It's too early for your facile charm, Rothay." She laughed and stretched lazily again.

"What if I'm sincere?"

"We haven't known each other long enough for you to be sincere."

"It's always a possibility I am anyway."

Delectable and disheveled, Caroline was the picture of enticing womanliness. Close, warm, and beguiling. He had to flex his hands to keep from reaching for her.

He wanted to explain. That he didn't normally stay the night. If he'd drunk more than his share, or if the weather was bitter, he did sometimes sleep in the bed of the lady he'd entertained, but that was a mere practicality, not because he wanted to wake up next to someone.

But he said nothing. It was harder than he imagined to articulate true sentiment. With that, he had little practice. It usually wasn't hard to walk away.

His affair with Helena had taught him that. Keep attachment at a minimum because it could bring nothing but grief into your life. Trust was fragile, and so easily shattered.

Caroline sat up and tossed back her hair, sliding long bare legs over the side of the bed. Nicholas snared her wrist. "Don't get up just yet, my sweet."

With a laugh, she disengaged his fingers. "Forgive me but I need to . . ."

He grinned as she gestured at the screen discreetly concealing the commode from the rest of the room. "Of course. How ungallant of me. Hurry back."

Caroline arched a delicate russet brow. "You are in your usual state, I see."

His current level of arousal made a visible statement of just why he wanted her to return with all due speed, the outline of his erect shaft lifting the sheet pulled up to his waist. His mouth twitched. "It's a compliment to your incomparable allure. A direct cause and effect. The moment you woke, so did a certain portion of my anatomy."

And alluring you are, he thought as he watched her walk across the room to take care of a basic human need, all pale dewy morning skin and rounded perfect curves. When she returned a few moments later, he enjoyed the privilege of watching the sway of her breasts with each step, the luscious flesh beckoning for his mouth and hands.

She climbed back in beside him, an expectant look on her lovely face. He could smell the signature scent of her violet soap. Nicholas just gazed back and waited, his lashes lowered a fraction as he lounged against the pillows.

As her shyness and trepidation faded with each passing day, Caroline was beginning to explore her passionate side. It was fascinating to see the evolution, and it was his good fortune to be a participant in the journey. She'd come to him a virgin in every way except the physical one, and each time they made love she was a little bolder.

He wondered if when this was all over, she'd change her mind about marriage. At the least, he suspected she'd take a lover.

The idea of it made him narrow his eyes, a possessive surge of annoyance tempering his desire for a moment. Caroline, on her side next to him, those silky auburn curls spilling over her shoulders and back, bit her lower lip, her eyes widening a little. "Is something wrong?"

He *couldn't* keep her. This was transient lust, no more. It had always passed with any other woman, and would with her too. Besides, she was too young and marriageable to be his mistress, and the possibility she was infertile was too much of a risk for him to consider a different kind of arrangement.

Actually, he couldn't believe that option had even occurred to him, even offhand.

The moment passed. Nicholas smiled, wondering if even a few days in the countrified setting had upset the equilibrium of his sophistication. Maybe he'd breathed in too much fresh air or overindulged on home-churned butter. Or it could be his impetuous sexual need was in control of his brain with a beautifully naked and available young woman next to him and nothing to do all day but enjoy her warm willing body. Next week Parliament would be in session and he'd return to his normal routine. For now, he ought not to complicate things and just live in the moment. This many days of relaxation in his life was an anomaly.

"Nothing is wrong, quite the opposite." He reached out and touched her cheek first, then slid his fingers very lightly down the arch of her throat. "It's a glorious morning and I have you next to me naked. What could possibly be wrong, my sweet?"

"I don't know. For a moment you looked a little . . . fierce."

"The only thing fierce about me is how much I want you."

The moment slid past as he leaned forward and kissed her, brushing her mouth with his, tasting her lips. She responded as she always did, after that brief hesitation that signaled she was making progress in the world of carnal delight but had really just begun the journey.

He was more than happy to be her guide, so the notion of a morning between the sheets gave his world a rosy glow, banishing his brief uncharacteristic introspection on the subject of permanence.

"Like this."

The words, murmured against her mouth, were accompanied by the urging of his hands.

Caroline obeyed. It was frightening to admit it, but she'd

probably do anything he asked. Especially after the bone-melting kiss they'd just shared. Vaguely she was aware of the birds twittering outside, the cool scent of the early-morning breeze through the open window, the elegant silk hangings on the bed, and the growing glow in the room as the day came to life. . . .

But at the moment her whole world was *him*.

And what he wanted, it seemed, was for her to straddle his lean hips.

Nicholas looked like some decadent medieval prince with his dark hair disheveled against the white pillow slip and his classic, striking features. There was just the faintest flush under his skin and his muscular chest lifted with a slightly elevated rhythm. "Take me in your hand and guide me."

Her confusion must have shown.

"Inside you," he offered, just a small twitch of his mouth betraying his amusement over her ignorance. But his smile was tender and wickedly compelling. "The male does not always have to be on top."

The idea there could be more than one position was a little startling. So far, it had been completely different in every possible way—her sincere thanks to God—but the mechanics of the matter were still as she remembered with Edward. On her back, legs spread apart, Nicholas above her.

"Some women like it very much. Let's see if you do." His voice held just the slightest rasp she'd come to associate with sexual need.

Some women. Of course, she thought with an unwilling—and unreasonable—resentment, he would know. The Devilish Duke could probably draw charts and write dissertations on the sexual preferences of most of the ladies of fashionable society, including their ideal sexual positions.

His erect cock rose hard against his flat abdomen, the tip glistening with liquid evidence of his desire. Caroline wiggled forward a little, his hands still guiding her, and put her fingers around the swollen flesh as she rose up and positioned the tip at her female entrance.

He made a small, inarticulate sound and his fingers

tightened just a fraction on her hips as she sank down, his length slowly gliding into her until the tip rested against her womb. She found herself once again in the usual, frustrating position of not knowing exactly how to proceed, but Nicholas helped her, with small whispered phrases and words of encouragement as she began to move. Under her palms his chest felt warm and hard as she rose and fell, settling into a rhythm finally, awkwardness replaced with pleasure.

If she angled her body just so, it felt so divine that she trembled in response. The friction was deliciously slick and hot, and they watched each other as their bodies climbed the mutual pinnacle. Up, down, up again . . . dear Lord, she couldn't take it, especially when he moved his hand between them and did something very wicked with his thumb in just the right spot.

"I think now would be a good time, my sweet." The words were said in a hiss between his clenched teeth. His hips thrust upward to meet her downward slide.

Her world collapsed. So did her quaking body as she gave a small scream and clutched his shoulders, pressing her face to his strong throat as wave after wave crashed and receded until she was left limp and shaken in the wreck of orgasmic aftermath.

Nicholas, holding her tightly, groaned and went still, impaling her impossibly deep, and she could feel through her haze the surge of his ejaculation.

Panting, damp, silent, they lay together in a lazy post-coital sprawl. Finally, he gave a low laugh. "I'm going to say you enjoyed being a little more adventurous. There's more to learn, you know, and we still have three days."

A wayward part of her brain translated that. *Only three days?*

"I feel confident you know all there is to know, Rothay." She managed to lift her head and hoped her expression was as bland as she intended. She wanted to be detached, to be indifferent—more like the women he was used to, because if she could effectively impersonate one of those sophisticated society beauties, then maybe she could assume their blasé attitude over superficial sexual liaisons. A perverse part of her was intensely curious, and she asked the question that had been at the back of her mind almost since the moment she met him. "Tell me, with all those women, was there never someone special?"

It was probably an ill-advised question and, despite their intimate position, none of her business, but she wanted to know.

"All of them." The teasing flippant charm in his voice was familiar, but a muscle tightened in his jaw.

There it was again, a flash of something in his face, something she didn't quite understand.

She gave him as skeptical a look as she was capable of in her languorous blissful state, her body still humming and his sex still inside her.

"This isn't my favorite subject," he admitted in somber candor a moment later, his handsome features expressing what she interpreted as a hint of regret, the look in his dark eyes difficult to read.

Since he'd already confessed he wasn't interested in marriage, she understood, and she tried to ignore the irrational flicker of sorrow that apparently she was included in those countless numbers of past amours. It didn't matter, she reminded herself with swift relentless logic. She understood the game she'd joined and he'd certainly fulfilled his part of the bargain.

He was gentle, ardent, skilled, and generous.

This was the most lovely week of her life, but he was going to forget her and a poignant sense of sadness filled her over that undisputable truth. He wasn't a constant lover and he certainly hadn't ever promised to be, so she had no right to expectations of any kind.

There was a small bead of sweat at his temple and Caroline wiped it off with a fingertip in a playful gesture, determined to savor every second and dismiss any thoughts that interfered. "You do realize, Your Grace, you are going to be hard-pressed to outdo your romantic gesture of last evening."

If she came away with nothing else from this, she'd forever have memories of a moonlit terrace and strong arms around her as they moved in a silent, beautiful dance.

An ebony brow lifted and his smile was slow and infinitely devilish, a true tribute to his nickname. "Is that a challenge, Lady Wynn?"

"I suppose it could be interpreted in that way."

"Hmm." His fingers traced her spine, to the curves of one bare buttock, and his hand gently squeezed as he cupped her bottom. "I am going to have to be inventive, aren't I?"

"To best Lord Manderville? You know him better than I do, but I would guess since he is part of the wager, he will put his best foot forward."

It came again, to her surprise. A certain dark flicker of an expression across his face she could describe only as irritation. When she thought about it, he'd mentioned the earl only once or twice and not at all in the past few days. The bet itself hadn't been a topic of conversation. He muttered, "His foot isn't what I'm worried about."

That drew a laugh she couldn't suppress, but she had a feeling her smile was a little tremulous. "Not to feed your arrogance, but I doubt you have to worry anyway."

"I've impressed you?" His finger tipped her chin up a little, the roguish curve of his mouth familiar. She had the sinking feeling it would haunt her dreams.

It would have been better if she was a good liar. Instead she said simply, "Yes."

He rolled her over and impressed her again.

Chapter Fifteen

Desperation was a powerful force when it came to inventive methods, Derek decided in wry self-mockery as he hauled himself onto the ledge and caught his breath. What he was doing was both undignified and foolhardy, but it would hopefully demonstrate his determination and the depth of his feelings.

All he wanted was to have a short civil conversation.

Well, that wasn't *all* he wanted, but he would settle for a chance to be able to declare himself.

The window was ajar because of the warm night, which he'd counted on. He perched on his narrow vantage point and heard the murmur of voices inside, waiting for Annabel's maid to leave. When the soft sound of the door clicking shut came, he braced himself, hoping the object of his visit wouldn't scream down the house.

Lucky for him her back was turned as he pushed aside the drapes and slipped into the room. At her dressing table, she didn't notice his precipitous entry until she caught sight of him in the mirror and her eyes widened.

Quickly, he said, "Don't. If you scream, everyone in this house will know I'm in your bedroom."

Her mouth, which had opened, snapped shut. Annabel whirled around on the chair so violently she almost toppled to the floor. She caught her balance and leveled an outraged glare at him. Her cheeks blazed pink. "Get out of here."

Since he hadn't expected a warm welcome, Derek was unfazed. "No. Not until we talk for a few moments."

"Are you mad? You just crawled through my window. If you wish to speak to me, just ask in the normal way." She added stiffly, "My lord."

He almost laughed at the attempt at formal address. Since Annabel was a child, she'd always called him by his first name, but Derek was so far beyond the point where he found anything about his current state of misery funny, he simply gave her what he hoped was a neutral look. "I've tried. In case you haven't noticed, I've drank more cups of insipid tea this week than in the past year. I've gone to parties I'd never consider attending when perfectly sane, and slogged through dinner here more than a few nights. You, my dear, are impossible to get alone for even a minute. This is my solution. Unless you want a scandal, you can't announce my presence."

She stared at him as if he really were insane and he wasn't sure it might not be true. Bloody hell, it was his uncle's house and he could walk through the front door at any time with impunity and full welcome. However, even the easygoing Thomas would not allow him in Annabel's bedroom.

He expounded with obvious cynicism and bitterness, "Have you forgotten my letter? Please don't try to tell me you didn't get it, Annie."

"I didn't read it. I threw it away."

The confirmation did absolutely nothing for his confidence. His voice held a hollow ring. "I see. I'm glad I bothered to take the time."

"Why did you? Why are you doing this?" As if she suddenly noticed she wore nothing more than her nightdress, her hand crept to the bodice and flattened there. "Alfred would not appreciate you here."

"I didn't ask his permission, did I?"

Sod Lord Hyatt. Derek *loved* her.

"I ask you once again to leave."

Devil take it, she looked delectable in nothing but white lawn and lace, her golden hair loose around her shoulders, her face averted so he could study the perfection of her profile. Long lashes sent shadows on her cheeks.

"Not until I say a few things." Derek didn't move from his pose by the window but instead propped one shoulder against the frame. If he approached her, he wasn't sure he could promise gentlemanly conduct. "May I speak?"

"Can I stop you?" Her voice was full of resentment. "You've already barged in and threatened me. I can't see how I have a choice."

"I scaled the wall of my own uncle's town house and risked breaking my neck." He crossed his arms over his chest. "Does that tell you it's important?"

Annabel lifted her chin, still clutching her nightgown together at the neck as if he were a blackguard and might pounce on her. "I can't imagine what we have to say to each other. I'm engaged, and you're . . . *you*."

It stung, especially when said in such a scathing tone.

You're you.

In a lethal voice, he said, "Yes, I am. A man. One who has the normal failings of every other man."

"Normal? Not all men fornicate indiscriminately with every female they might stumble across." She rose, pacing to the opposite corner of the room to whirl to face him. Her eyes, so lovely and blue, were full of both accusation and outrage. "Whatever you came here for, you aren't going to find it. I lost all faith in you a year ago *and* I realize to begin with that faith was misplaced. I know now how naive and foolish I was to fall in love with you at all, but I'm not the same besotted innocent I was."

Not innocent?

Derek felt his chest constrict in rejection of the notion. He involuntarily took a step forward. "He's compromised you?"

She flushed crimson at the accusation in his voice. "Of course not. If you mean Alfred, he never would. Not everyone is like *you*."

There was that word again, flung at him like a barbed arrow. Relief surged through him anyway. No, Hyatt hadn't touched her, hence the man's resentment and suspicion during their not-so-companionable drink. Derek had no perspective when it came to her, no distance.

Her contempt made him cringe inwardly, though he hoped he didn't show it. He gritted out, "I'm no saint. I've never claimed to be one. But neither am I without a conscience. That's why I am here now. I've never had the opportunity to apologize for what happened except on paper and it apparently isn't enough for you."

"Happened?" Arched blond brows rose.

"In the library," he clarified in brusque explanation.

"Oh." The one-word reply was cold as a stone in winter.

A low breeze rustled the curtains behind his back. He said with quiet intonation, "I kissed you. Do you remember?"

He knew she did. She knew *he* knew it. Annabel's eyes flashed. "As a matter of fact, I do remember that day. *All* of it."

"I hurt you." It was a soft observation.

"Don't flatter yourself, my lord."

She was lying if she denied it. As much as he'd seen her wide-eyed happiness after the kiss, he remembered in full measure the blanched horrified look on her face as she'd stumbled out of the conservatory where she'd found him with Isabella. It didn't really matter, he supposed, that he hadn't actually done more at that point than give Isabella his regrets and leave. The damage had already been done. It hadn't been an auspicious evening. Isabella had been most vocal over her seething disappointment at his withdrawal after Annabel had run from the room crying. If it was possible to feel more like a worthless cad, he wasn't sure how. He'd taken a bottle of brandy to bed that night, but not Lady Bellvue.

Fighting for a calm he didn't really feel, he said, "That is what we need to discuss, Annie. Both the kiss and what happened afterward, for they are directly related to each other."

"I can't see how one simple kiss could be related to your sordid, disgusting behavior later." Her hair shimmered in the illumination from a single lamp, the fair strands framing her fragile features. Dark blue eyes stared at him with overt accusation.

"I know I disillusioned you, but it wasn't intentional. Besides, that kiss was anything but simple and we both know it."

Her lips trembled just a fraction. "Just one in a thousand for you, I'm sure. Please don't try to tell me it was meaningful in any way. I *saw* you later, Derek. And from all accounts, you haven't exactly lived a monkish life since then either. Irate husbands everywhere could give credence to that supposition if Lord Tanner is an example. When that story surfaced, I admit, I wasn't surprised."

"I've never aspired to sainthood. All I can say is the Tanner affair didn't involve me. It never did. I'm not sure what else you've heard, but believe me, what I have done the most this past year is think about you."

"All because of one kiss? Forgive my skepticism but know it is hard earned."

Hoping she could hear the sincerity in his voice, he told her the truth. "That kiss changed my life."

How could he do this to her? This last week had been torture, because Derek suddenly seemed to be everywhere, impossible to ignore—and now this? He was right. Annabel deliberately avoided him as much as possible because the last thing she wanted was to be reminded of her ill-fated infatuation with the faithless, notorious Earl of Manderville.

But there was certainly no avoiding him now. Not when he stood there, in her bedroom of all places, the stark masculine beauty of his face shadows and hollows in the low light, his thick blond hair brushing the collar of a fine linen shirt that emphasized the impressive width of his shoulders. Black breeches and Hessians called attention to the long length of his legs, but he wore no coat or cravat for his risky climb.

That he'd done it at all was bewildering, and his last declaration had her speechless.

Derek repeated in the same husky tone, "That kiss—the one that never should have happened—changed my life, Annie. On my honor, I swear it's true."

Did he just use the word *honor*?

Because the memory was so painful still, like a raw wound that refused to heal properly, she said with bitter conviction, "I am sure you could tell any manner of untruths with your honor offered as proof of your conviction. Since it doesn't exist."

His mouth tightened a fraction and she knew she'd drawn blood. "I suppose I am not surprised you have a low opinion of me, because you've made it clear enough. But we've also known each other a long time, so can't you give me the courtesy of hearing me out?" His eyes, so vividly blue, held an uncharacteristic look of supplication. "Surely you're curious as to what I have to say that is important enough I'd risk my neck to tell you."

She was, but admitting it seemed like a weakness. His ability to charm was not in question.

Besides, she lied outright about the letter.

The uncertain thing was her ability to resist. Perhaps she wasn't even close to his degree of sophistication and experience, but she was at least intelligent enough to realize it and know it was foolhardy to let down her guard for even one moment. Derek Drake was dangerous to her current state of tenuous contentment over her upcoming marriage. "No," she lied. "I'm not in the least bit curious."

A muscle twitched in his jaw. "My family—and I—have provided for you all these years and it should count for something."

"That's not fair." She stiffened, staring at him. "Is it my fault I was orphaned?"

"No, of course not." His implacable expression didn't change. "But I think I am a bit beyond fair. You at least owe me a chance to speak. Shall we talk?"

He was the earl, his title making him ultimately responsible in a financial way for the estate that she considered her home, and yes, his family had been more than generous to her; she knew it. If not for his sake, for Thomas and Margaret she owed him something. Ungraciously, she inclined her head. "Fine."

A ghost of his usual beautiful smile hovered on his mouth. "First I am reduced to begging, and then blackmail."

"Just say whatever it is you think is so blasted important and then leave. If anyone found you in my bedroom at any hour, even fully dressed, I would be ruined."

Unfortunately, that was all too true. As accommodating as Alfred was, she doubted even he would understand.

Thus given permission, Derek seemed to hesitate. After a moment, he said simply, "Nothing that happened that day was as I intended. I didn't intend to kiss you, and later, I didn't intend to so much as touch Isabella Bellvue—and that was as far as it went. If you recall, I'd been avoiding her for days."

She did recall the flirtatious countess because she'd watched jealously as Lady Bellvue shamelessly pursued Derek with such blatant purpose that even a seventeen-year-old ingenue couldn't miss it. "You certainly weren't avoiding her that evening in the conservatory," she said acerbically.

"That's because I'd kissed you earlier."

"I've never heard anything so nonsensical in my life."

"No? Well, listen on." His voice held a sort of grim amusement. "If you want nonsensical, I can provide it. That afternoon, when I held you in my arms, I realized I had only one choice when it came to you, and that was to retreat or proceed with honorable intentions. I am not trying to hide that the idea of the latter thoroughly rattled me. When Isabella approached me later, I was still trying to deny I had to make a decision. The notion my life was going to change so dramatically wasn't easy to acknowledge. I am not the first man to shy away from the idea of love, much less marriage."

Did he—Derek Drake, infamous for his detachment—just use the words love *and* marriage *in the same sentence?*

What's more, she well remembered the look on his face before he left the library so abruptly. There was a possibility he was even telling the truth.

He went on. "I suppose I thought an interlude with a willing woman might cure my momentary madness."

The realization her heart had begun to pound faster was irritating. "Did it?" she asked in as cool a tone as possible, but her palms were damp. There was a set to his mouth she'd never seen before and though he was still imposingly tall and all too male, there was a hint of vulnerability to a man she'd always seen as invincible.

It was the very last thing she needed.

He said quietly, "No. As I just said, nothing more happened than what you saw. When you left the room, I did as well. Isabella was incensed, believe me."

Annabel snapped, "Forgive me for not having a lot of sympathy for her. Still, what happened already seemed like more than enough to me. She was half-undressed and you were . . ." She stopped, embarrassed. Undoubtedly he'd touched the breasts of so many women the event held no significance for him.

To her chagrin, he understood the falter in her speech for what it was. "That's because you are still so innocent, which is part of our problem. Trust me, there is a lot more."

"Trust you? Please. Besides, we don't have a mutual problem. There is nothing we share." She spit out each word deliberately.

"Come on, Annie, that isn't true." The expression on his face was stark, almost accusing. "You avoid me. God knows I've tried to stay away from you. It isn't working. Not for either of us. Other people have noticed. Your fiancé has noticed, for God's sake."

"Leave Alfred out of this . . . ridiculous discussion. I am not sure why we are having it in the first place." Her hands curled into fists and her stomach felt strange, as if she'd swallowed something indigestible. "How could you possibly know what he thinks anyway?"

"Men have a more direct way of communicating than women." His smile was faint and ironic. "Usually if there is something on our minds, we simply ask to settle the matter. If the answer isn't to our liking, we sometimes use our fists or pistols at dawn. Barbaric, I know, but we tend to be more straightforward in our dealings with the world around us."

Annabel stared at him. "He asked you about me? About . . ."

"Us?" he supplied. "I'm afraid so."

Yes, her stomach definitely felt queasy. "What did you tell him?"

Derek lifted a brow in an infuriating arch. "Nothing. I'm a gentleman, despite your opinion to the contrary."

"You truly expect me to believe that?"

"What else can I offer but the truth? It's why I am here."

He just stood there, still impossibly handsome even without his notable charm in evidence. Instead the expression on his face was exposed, open, nothing like his usual lazy charismatic allure.

There was no doubt her knees had begun to wobble. Annabel did her best to look composed, but in reality, her mind was whirling. "Let me see if I understand what you have gone to such great lengths to tell me. After you kissed me that afternoon, you worried any further dalliance would put you in peril of having to do the unthinkable and marry me, and so instead, you callously used another woman to assuage your lust. Am I correct?"

He sighed and ran his fingers through his thick hair. How it could make him even more attractive to have it rumpled she wasn't sure, but it somehow seemed to happen. "Put that way, it certainly sounds bad enough. You aren't going to make this easy on me, are you? And as I said, I didn't assuage anything."

"Is there some reason I should make this easy on you?"

"I behaved in an abominable fashion, so I suppose not."

Acutely conscious of her state of undress, she crossed her arms over her chest. "Finally there is a point we agree on."

"Annie, I love you."

What did he just say?

She stopped breathing.

Damn him, she thought dimly, he should not still be able to do this to her.

But he could. God help her, he could.

"I love you," he repeated softly. "It's all I think about and quite frankly, it is driving me mad. It took me a year and your damned engagement to realize the depths of it, but I swear to you it is true."

Blindly she groped her way toward her dressing table and sat down. Inhaling a deep shuddering breath, she asked, "Is that why you placed a wager in front of all of fashionable society that you were the most talented lover in England? That sort of boast does not come from a man who would ever be faithful to only one woman."

"On the contrary, it is exactly the sort of idiotic behavior produced by the infamous emotion I just declared for you, my dear." His smile was rueful. "In this case, it was inspired by the announcement of your engagement in the paper. For a long time I'd been trying to come to grips with not only my feelings but the idea I'd alienated you so completely, and there in print was proof I'd never have the chance to do anything about either problem. Throw a good deal of claret into the situation, and a man might just do something quite stupid."

He couldn't be serious. *Please don't let any part of me believe he is serious.* "It *was* stupid," she muttered.

He took a step forward. "Rather like clambering up a wall in the dark and climbing through a window like a character in a romantic novel."

Even as she rejected the idea he might touch her, a traitorous part of her wanted it. Three more steps . . . maybe four, and he could take her in his arms again and . . .

Her spine stiffened. She reminded herself of that terrible

betrayal a year before and the resulting misery. "Don't come any closer. Please, just . . . leave."

He went still, his arms at his sides. The angles of his face were etched in the uncertain light. "Annie."

Ignoring the husky plea in his voice was the single most difficult thing she'd done in her life. "Please."

If he touched her once, just once, she might fall apart.

To her utter horror, a tear slid down her cheek in a slow, hot glide and dripped on her hands, which were clasped so tightly in her lap the knuckles ached.

And to think she'd vowed to never shed another tear over him. How dare he make a liar of her after all the rest of his myriad offenses.

For a moment he just stood there, and then to her surprise he nodded and did as she asked without saying another word, slipping out the window and disappearing from sight.

She was alone.

If he'd fallen and broken his neck, he would at least be out of his state of current frustrated misery, Derek decided as he walked the two blocks to his own town house, but he hadn't. Besides that, his brilliant plan had failed all because of one teardrop.

He couldn't bear to make her cry.

He had many faults—too many to count probably—but he wasn't cruel. The look on Annabel's face had told him all he needed to know about what he'd already put her through, and if he had gone ahead and followed through with a seduction, he would have hated himself afterward.

Worse, she might hate him too.

The only cheery part of the whole thing, he thought as he let himself in and went toward his study, was that he *could* have seduced her. It was there in her eyes as she gazed at him, in the panicked reaction at that one step toward her, in the tension in her oh-so-desirable body.

So the game wasn't lost. He just needed to rethink his strategy.

Helping himself to a glass of brandy, he sat down behind his desk and brooded at the empty hearth.

For one thing, he would concede that ludicrous bet. He wasn't going to go off for a week with the delectable Lady Wynn. He might as well face it. What if there was the slightest chance of Annabel changing her mind and he ruined it by further enhancing his already less-than-pristine reputation? He hoped Nicholas was enjoying himself, but Derek seriously doubted he could approach the matter with equal enthusiasm. Not with his entire future happiness hanging in the balance.

The only woman he wanted was Annabel. With or without her, he had a feeling his days as a rake were over.

Chapter Sixteen

The missive brought with it a very real sense of disappointment. Nicholas read the note a second time, and then set it aside, weighing his options. There really was only one.

"Bad news?" Caroline gazed at him from across the table, concern furrowing her brow.

He'd looked forward to another ride along the river and perhaps coaxing her into a late-afternoon swim. She'd confessed she'd always wanted to learn how. Caroline, naked in the water, had some tantalizing possibilities.

"I'm afraid I have to go back to London."

"Oh, I see." For a moment she looked away as if fascinated by something outside the window, but then she turned back with a resigned expression on her face. "I hope nothing is amiss."

Though he usually didn't explain himself, especially to casual lovers, he found himself reacting to the sudden distance in her eyes. "The prime minister wants to meet with me. I head a committee and apparently there's an issue he'd like for me to address with the other members before we convene next week."

Her smile held a wistful quality. "I thought a week away was rather ambitious for a man of your stature to give to someone else. I wondered how you were going to manage it."

Did she really feel he had given her something? He looked at her, realizing how comfortable it was to sit and enjoy something as mundane as a simple cold luncheon merely because he liked her company. The extravagance of her beauty aside, she was unusual in that she played no feminine games. As far as he could tell after spending five pleasurable days constantly in her company, Caroline Wynn was completely without pretense. His fortune and title didn't overly impress her either, and perhaps for the first time with a woman, he felt she truly didn't want anything from him other than what they'd already shared.

"Come back with me," he suggested, reaching over to take her hand. "This matter is pressing, but it should require little more than a few hours. You still owe me two days."

"And how are we supposed to manage that with any measure of discretion, Nicholas?" Slim fingers lay cool against his palm. "Not that I wouldn't love to say yes, but it seems foolhardy."

There it was again, the refreshing honesty he found so captivating. "We're going to have to devise a way. Nothing is impossible."

She raised a brow. "Spoken with true ducal assurance. I'm sorry to disagree, but some things *are* impossible. What are you going to do, smuggle me into your bedroom in your pocket?"

She was right, of course; servants talked. His home was out of the question. "We could meet somewhere."

"Not in London, not with any measure of safety. You have very little to lose if we are linked together in a scandalous way. I do. So I am afraid I must refuse."

The sunlight coming in the long window lit her glossy auburn hair to warm fire. She wore a pale yellow day gown of frothy muslin that made her look very young, like an innocent schoolgirl. But Nicholas could attest after the recent satisfying days of sexual edification that there was a passionate woman under that demure exterior. Men were going to sense it, for what before had been aloof poise was now replaced with a womanly confidence. They'd flocked around her when she was supposedly distant and standoffish. Now they'd besiege her.

It chafed to realize that any man could approach her, but

the very nature of the past days they spent together and the infamous bet meant that *he* had to publicly keep his distance.

Hell and blast.

A dilemma to be sure. Especially since she was supposed to spend an equal amount of time with Derek.

Damnation, he was starting to think *that* reality made him downright unhappy.

Perhaps this separation was for the best. He was disappointed, but to have their interlude cut short might at least stifle his irrational twinges of what could only be jealousy. Who was he to ask her to not go through with the second half of the bargain? He didn't have any claim on her and she'd just calmly declined any further involvement.

There was no denying the fine line a woman had to walk in their judgmental world, no matter what side she chose, virtue or otherwise. If she preferred her ice-cold persona, so be it. He was certainly capable of—and more experienced than she was at—detaching himself from sexual entanglements.

Nicholas let go of her hand and pulled his watch from his pocket. "As soon as my driver can get the carriage ready, I'll depart. Please feel free to stay another few days as my guest if you wish."

She nodded, those long-lashed gray eyes unreadable. "I have had such a lovely time. I suppose I should feel promiscuous—"

"Indeed you should not," he said, cutting her short. "You are a beautiful, sensual woman. There is nothing wrong with that. Just the opposite."

"We live very different lives, don't we?"

An understatement. He had the freedom of his title and wealth, and while she was also of the upper class, there was no similarity in their circumstances.

"In many ways," he admitted, thinking back on how right away he'd argued to be the first one to take her away, how quickly he'd arranged his affairs so he could. He felt another one of those unfamiliar glimmers of insight.

He was going to be sorry to leave her.

The unexpected fascination was hardly over.

It was disquieting, made worse by the fact she refused to chance a clandestine relationship once they were back in London. He understood her reasons. Especially if she would ever consider marriage again, her reputation was important.

Abruptly, he got to his feet and gave her a small bow, knowing he needed to get away from her at once. "Please excuse me."

Caroline stared unseeingly out the window at the spacious green of the park surrounding the house. She was packed and as soon as Huw brought the carriage around, she would depart. It had been a good decision to leave, because almost the minute Nicholas's vibrant presence was gone, the house felt unbearably empty. One stroll in the garden told her she wasn't going to be able to endure staying on. It was probably a little foolhardy to arrive back in London right after his return because it might call attention to their mutual absence, but she simply could not accept his invitation to remain his guest.

There was prudence, and then there was melancholy. She'd known way too much of the latter in her life already.

The Duke of Rothay had a profound effect on her good sense.

From where she stood, she could see the terrace where they'd first sat and had tea—well, he'd drunk his usual brandy—and then later waltzed to an invisible tune.

Maybe she should have agreed to meet him again. If she had, would she not feel so . . . bereft?

Her hand tightened on the fine fabric of the curtain. The complication of forming an infatuation for the devilishly handsome and sensually talented duke was not something she'd seen coming. She wasn't the first, and she could hardly suppose she would be the last, but there was no denying he was going to be hard to forget.

Nothing about him had been as she expected, except for his legendary sexual skills. The man had lived up to his reputation there with ease. What she didn't anticipate was the thoughtful look on his face when they discussed his visit to the Byzantine mosques she'd only read about, his indulgence over her breathless questions, his congenial attitude over her unworldly and cautious approach to society. . . .

He wasn't snobbish, and with his bloodlines and fortune, he certainly could be. She'd even caught him one day out by the stables, chatting with her driver, Huw, and sitting on a bale of hay, his shirt partially unbuttoned, the straw on his boots showing he'd helped muck out the stall of his restive big stallion. Nobleman and servant had laughed at the same time, and Caroline had felt an inner warmth for the man that had nothing to do with his persuasive sexual expertise.

If she was honest with herself—and it wasn't easy—she knew very little about love. Her cold father certainly didn't inspire that emotion, her aunt had been neither warm nor motherly, and Edward had been a nightmare. Maybe the whole problem was that for once in her life someone had treated her with courtesy, with tenderness, and, above all, as if she was a person with thoughts and feelings of her own. In and out of bed they'd discussed everything from politics to history, and if she disagreed with his opinion, he was interested in why. The concept of a friendly argument was a new one, and Nicholas, with his formidable confidence and keen intelligence, was not at all the self-centered rascal she'd anticipated. It was confusing and she knew she was woefully susceptible, which didn't help matters. The game he was so adept at was new to her, and being a tyro, she'd done the unthinkable and fallen in love.

At least she suspected that was her current ailment. In just a few short days. Even when she knew he was deliberately exerting himself to captivate her.

It made her feel foolish and gauche and unsophisticated. Even if he did want to pursue an affair, it didn't mean she was anything but an unusual diversion from his regular diet of experienced lovers, and she was pragmatic enough to know it.

"My lady, I think everything is ready."

Caroline turned, startled out of her reverie. "Oh, yes. Thank you, Mrs. Sims."

The housekeeper nodded. As usual she was neatly dressed, with a crisp apron over her plain dark dress, her graying hair in a severe chignon. "It was rather nice to have His Grace here, I must say."

It was easy to respond with complete honesty. "He's a very charming man."

"He is that, I grant you. Ever so polite and congenial always, despite his place."

"Yes."

"I hope you enjoyed your stay, my lady."

Since Mrs. Sims managed the household, she surely knew she and Nicholas slept together each night, for only one bed had been used. Caroline fought a blush with only partial success. "It was lovely, thank you."

"I always rather hoped His Grace would develop a fondness for this old place. It's very pleasant here, though I suppose not very exciting for a young man. I remember him as a boy and he was always a bit precocious, able to wheedle extra sweets from the cook and trick his tutor out of his lessons. Threw his mother into fits, he did, but he's turned out a fine man, whatever they say about him."

Not sure if she was more surprised the woman lingered to talk to her or that she knew so much, Caroline couldn't help but ask, "You knew him when he was a child?"

She could picture a dark-haired little boy, exuberant and playful, and her heart tightened a little.

"Oh yes. I was at Rothay Hall for years." The housekeeper smoothed her already perfect apron in an absent mannerism. "When I wanted something less taxing, he offered me this. My joints ache something terrible sometimes and 'tis quiet enough here."

It was. It had the peaceful beauty Caroline preferred, and more than once she'd considered selling the town house in London and buying a lovely secluded place just like it.

"His Grace wished for me to tell you that if you'd care

to use Tenterden Manor at any time, you will always be welcome."

More than a little surprised, Caroline wasn't sure what to say.

Mrs. Sims gave a small brisk nod. "Told me you miss the country, my lady, and you're to visit whenever it suits you. I hope you'll consider it now and again, when the city bothers you."

The thoughtful gesture made tears spring to her eyes. If she didn't already feel like weeping stupidly over his departure, this did it. One chance remark and he'd remembered it.

His virtuosity in bed aside, that was what truly had her undone. Whether it was part of the bet or not, he acted as if he cared how she felt about things.

If she wasn't doomed before, she certainly was now.

Caroline blinked and cleared her throat. "Thank you, Mrs. Sims. That is very generous of the duke. Another visit sounds wonderful."

He'd had a restive journey home; the meeting he had to attend was first thing in the morning, and really, the last thing he needed was the news his mother was in residence. Nicholas adored her, but she also had no compunction about trying to interfere in his life. Travel-weary and a little disgruntled, he strolled into the informal drawing room and essayed a smile. "Good evening, Mother."

"Nicholas." She rose from an embroidered settee and crossed the room to offer her cheek with gracious poise. It was a richly furnished room, with Turkish carpets, a scattering of comfortable chairs in the style of Louis XIV, and some artwork that could grace a museum wall. His mother suited the surroundings, always regal, always polished and perfect with her dark hair upswept, able to command attention with both her beauty and her poise. Her elegant bearing contained a canny mind, and she often surprised and discomforted him with her insight. He was well past the age when he needed guidance from his mother in certain areas of his life. Unfortunately, those were exactly the areas she was most interested in.

She wished to see him married and settled, and though they didn't precisely argue over it, the point came up often enough to exasperate him.

With dutiful affection, he kissed her and then straightened. "This is a pleasant surprise."

"I arrived this afternoon. Althea is with me. The children stayed in Kent with their nanny. She's upstairs changing for dinner and Charles is going to join us. He's been in London for three weeks and she missed him. It is why we are here."

So his mother, his older sister, and his brother-in-law. It seemed now he'd be dining *en famille* rather than as he'd imagined. He glanced at the clock with what he hoped wasn't obvious dismay. A quiet evening with dinner at his club was out of the question now. "It sounds delightful."

"Yes, you look delighted, darling." The Dowager Duchess of Rothay cocked her head a little in amused reproach. "I take it we're interfering in your plans. You needn't stay and eat with us if you don't wish. I realize we didn't inform you of our impending arrival."

His disquiet had nothing to do with any plans, but more so with one very lovely young woman who had occupied his thoughts all the hours home. Had Caroline chosen to stay? His feelings on that were decidedly mixed. He could clearly picture her sleeping in the bed where they'd shared so many hours of pleasure, and it made him restless.

Why? He wasn't sure. Usually he left and didn't look back.

"I don't have specific plans, but I just got here as well. I've been out of town."

"So I understand." With shrewd insight his mother gave him a quizzical look. "Who is she?"

"What makes you think there's a she? I have a dozen reasons to leave town and do so often enough."

Silently, she regarded him with thoughtful inspection.

Lord, this was not what he needed. Were all females so perceptive or was it just mothers with their sons? He smiled and shook his head. He was a grown man and disinclined to discuss the matter, especially since Caroline was the subject. "I am not going to comment. How was your trip?"

"It was fine."

At least she accepted the dismissal, though he had a feeling the discussion was far from over. They exchanged a few more pleasantries before he excused himself. "I'll be delighted to have dinner with two of my favorite ladies and you know I like Charles. Just let me change. I'm a trifle dusty. The carriage didn't appeal to me this afternoon and I chose to ride."

He bowed politely and went upstairs, finding the familiar confines of his bedroom at least a little soothing. His valet, alerted to his arrival, was ever efficient and waited, saying, "Good evening, Your Grace. Hot water will be up shortly."

Nicholas nodded. "Thank you, Patrick."

Diffident and earnest, with thick red hair and a freckled complexion, the young man hurried to pick up each item of clothing as it was discarded. "I trust you had a pleasant trip."

More than pleasant actually.

"It was . . . satisfying."

Satisfying. It seemed an appropriate word choice.

The real question was, would he stay satisfied?

Caroline had clearly refused him further contact, so he had no choice.

He had to admit, he wasn't used to it and it chafed. However, he was an experienced man and realized she'd gotten under his skin in an unusual way. The conclusion had become crystallized as he'd ridden away from Essex, the vivid image of how sweetly she'd kissed him before he left embedded in his mind, her slender arms around his neck, her soft mouth warm and receptive.

It had been one devil of a good-bye kiss. Was it his imagination that she'd clung to him for just one fraction of a second too long before they broke apart?

Shaking off the memory, he quickly bathed and dressed, going downstairs to find his brother-in-law had arrived already. Charles Peyton was ten years older with an affable disposition and a keen mind. Nicholas wasn't sure exactly what he did for the War Office, but he knew he was highly regarded in all circles and suspected the secrecy meant something to do with military intelligence.

"Nicholas . . . good to see you." Peyton wandered over with a glass of claret and gave him a bland look over the rim. "I understand you've been out of town."

"For a little while," he confirmed, since apparently it was common knowledge. Then, as Caroline's seductive image rose starkly in his mind, he murmured, "Not quite long enough."

"Does this have anything to do with your little competition with Manderville?"

Why he was surprised anyone could guess so easily, he wasn't sure. Especially Charles, who was as sharp as a honed rapier. "Are people still discussing that idiotic moment?"

Charles chuckled, his pale blue eyes full of sympathetic humor. "Oh, indeed. Your precipitous absence without explanation has not helped quell the rumors."

"I was gone all of five days and I don't owe anyone an explanation, by God." Very rarely did he feel his privileged status made him immune to the same rules that governed those of lesser rank, but in this he did. Why should he account to anyone for his whereabouts? England got quite enough of his time as it was.

"I didn't say you did. But everyone wants to hear the grand announcement of the results."

"I'm glad you find this amusing."

"To a certain extent," his brother-in-law admitted with a twitch of his mouth. "Allow us long-married men to live through your exploits, won't you? There are more speculations on who might judge your unorthodox contest than there are on the outcome. Quite a fair amount of money is being wagered on your little contest."

"Well, hell," Nicholas muttered, careful to make sure his mother didn't hear the profanity.

"Ah. Quite."

With Charles, that could mean anything, and Althea's arrival in a swirl of violet silk, lustrous pearls, and expensive perfume stopped the conversation cold.

He gave a silent prayer of thanks at the interruption, hoping no one noticed Caroline's absence coincided with his own unexplained trip and suspected the truth. They wouldn't, he quickly reassured himself. Not of the reputedly cold, disdainful Lady Wynn.

She was safe enough.

Chapter Seventeen

Annabel gazed out the rain-streaked glass at the view of the wet street, the occasional splash of a passing vehicle coming over the persistent sound of the downpour. A glowering sky sat just above the rooftops. "I'm afraid I'm spoiled. Our weather has been so fine I almost forgot how dreary it can get."

"You do seem quieter than usual this afternoon, my dear." Alfred smiled at her. "I am glad to hear it's the weather and nothing else is wrong."

If he only knew. Everything was wrong.

Everything.

According to Derek, Alfred had noticed the tension. Worse still, he had *confronted* Derek about it.

She looked at her fiancé and wondered why she was having doubts. He looked the same as usual, elegantly dressed in the latest fashion, his boots polished to a high sheen, his chestnut hair brushed neatly back from a face that, while not handsome precisely, was certainly very nice looking. The same brown eyes, the same nose, the same mouth, but instead of being reassured by his presence, for some insane reason, Annabel was shaken from her conviction this upcoming marriage was what she wanted.

It was Derek's fault. She blamed him entirely, and when she thought about the other night when he'd climbed into her bedroom through the window, she was utterly furious.

How dare he ruin her happiness?

I love you.

Needless to say, she didn't believe him, and even if she did, it wouldn't matter. He was not the type of man who would be faithful, and she was not the kind of woman who could be married to someone who wasn't. That was the end of it.

Not that he'd mentioned marriage anyway. Derek Drake wasn't the type to offer honest marriage to any woman. All he wanted was the transient use of women's bodies. From that one devastating kiss a year ago she knew he was attracted to her, and she suspected his impetuous invasion of her bedroom and subsequent declaration stemmed from the notion he couldn't have her.

Because there was no way on earth she would be so foolish as to believe he was sincere.

". . . hardly crossed the street before he stumbled and fell headlong at her feet. What are the odds of that?" Alfred chuckled, the heavy signet ring on his finger winking as he lifted his cup to his mouth.

Annabel blinked, realizing she hadn't been listening to the anecdote, and a sense of guilt compounded her already churning emotions. "That *is* amusing," she said in a dismal attempt to pretend she'd heard what he'd said.

"It truly was at the time." Alfred set aside his tea and regarded her with a steady gaze she found disconcerting. "But I can tell you are not in the mood for frivolous little stories. Would it be best if I called another time?"

"No," she protested. Then, after a moment, she sighed. "Maybe it would, my lord. May I offer my apologies for being such poor company?"

"None needed, my dear, you know that. We will be married for many, many years and I imagine we'll both have our fair share of adverse moods."

Many, many years. Somehow, that didn't help her dilemma. Before they were even wedded, here she was sitting and thinking about another man. Devil take it, she didn't *want* things to be this way.

Alfred stood. "I'll call for you tomorrow morning and if

the weather improves, perhaps we could take a short drive."

The gloomy weather matched her current mood *exactly*. Annabel nodded.

Her fiancé came over and took her hand, lifting it to his lips, just brushing the backs of her fingers with his mouth before releasing it. He said, "Until tomorrow, then, my dear, and I hope whatever is blue-deviling you gets resolved. If there is anything I can do, you know all you have to do is ask me."

That long-ago fateful moment in the library was certainly part of the problem. Inspiration seized her. She stood up suddenly. "Kiss me."

Alfred looked unaccountably startled. "Annabel, we are in the drawing room. I hardly think—"

She tilted her face up and asked in what she hoped was a soft persuasive tone, "Don't you wish to?"

"Yes . . . well, yes, dash it, of course, but the only reason we are relatively alone is because Thomas trusts me to remain a gentleman."

He was right, and the door stood wide open for any passing servant to see them, plus Margaret could come bustling in any moment, but Annabel didn't care. If there was anything she could do to erase that plaguing memory, she was willing to take the risk. Besides, they were supposed to be married in a few months. Surely no one would be that scandalized.

"A kiss is hardly a horrible breach of conduct. Not when the woman is going to be your wife." Since her bow in society, she'd learned quite a bit about the art of flirtation and she gazed up at him from under the veil of her lashes with as much provocative invitation as she could summon.

In turn, he stared at her mouth and then put one hand very lightly at her waist. "I suppose you're right."

Kiss me. Make me forget that first kiss, make me forget him. . . .

When he lowered his head, she shut her eyes and waited, her breath fluttering in her throat.

Unfortunately, it was over all too quickly. All he did was press his closed lips against hers for the space of two, maybe three heartbeats, and then he stepped back.

This time the earth didn't shatter. This time—with the man she'd agreed to marry—the kiss was quite a pedestrian experience. He smiled in his usual earnest way, looking vaguely triumphant. Annabel did her best to conceal her crushing disappointment. It was one thing to ask for a kiss; it was quite another to tell him he'd hardly acquitted himself well. Naturally, he was a very proper young man, so he would never coax her mouth open and ravish her with his tongue and lips in a sinful bewitching way that left her weak-kneed. What had she been thinking?

As brightly as possible, she said, "I will see you tomorrow morning, then, my lord."

After he'd gone, she sank back down miserably and stared at a crystal vase of hothouse roses that sat on top of a polished parquet table across the room. Alfred had brought them to her a few days before and several of the yellow blooms had begun to wither, going brown around the edges, their heads just beginning to droop.

He was really a very thoughtful man. Considerate, polite, and very eligible. He would make a good dutiful husband and treat her with respect and affection.

Was he in love with her? He'd never said so, and she doubted there were real passionate feelings behind his proposal of marriage. She was from a good family and well dowered, and she knew he admired her looks. In short, she was very suitable and he was looking for a suitable wife.

Good God, *suitable*. How she suddenly loathed that word.

Derek heard the familiar hum of male voices punctuated by the occasional laugh and nodded at the steward. "Is the duke here, Frederick?"

As immaculately dressed as any of the patrons of the club, the young man inclined his head. "Good evening, my lord. Yes, indeed he is. At the usual table."

"Thank you."

The air held the smell of tobacco with an overlying hint of brandy, and he passed several tables of acquaintances who hailed him, delaying his progress. When he finally reached the corner of the room, he saw Nicholas sprawled in his usual careless pose, a slight frown on his face. He nursed a glass of spirits, his long fingers wrapped around the bowl.

Without preamble Derek dropped into the opposite chair and reached for a glass. The whiskey he preferred had already been delivered, a testament to the efficiency of the staff. "I got your note. You're back early, I see."

"At the prime minister's request."

"Ah. Always a difficult one to refuse. Lord Liverpool calls and we answer."

"Indeed."

Actually the tone of Nick's missive had been a little brusque and Derek was understandably curious as hell about his friend's week in the country—and the arms of Lady Wynn. "Tell me, was it a relief to leave? You'd been there . . . what? Five days? I still say that's a long time in the company of one woman."

"Depends on the woman."

That was a new sentiment from a known rake. "Does it, now?"

Nicholas finally lifted his glass and took a sip before answering. "Actually, I was disappointed to have it cut short."

With sharpened interest, Derek said, "I take it our luscious Caroline lives up to her beauty."

"And then some, yes." Nicholas gave him what could only be described as a quelling look.

"That's a little surprising. While she is very attractive, of course, I wouldn't have expected her to turn out to be a hot little piece between the sheets."

"If you wish to hear details, think again, Derek."

The curt, warning tone was hardly what he expected of a man who'd whisked off a lovely woman for a week of sexual pleasure. He settled back a little in his chair. "I didn't ask for details, Nick. A bit touchy, aren't we?"

The answer was a small grunt that didn't give much in the way of information, but Derek had already surmised something unusual was going on. He'd been surprised enough by his friend's unusual impatience to get the lady to the country in the first place, and now Nicholas seemed downright surly to be back.

He'd been surly himself lately, but that was due to his untenable situation with Annabel.

They were well used to being honest with each other, so Derek said bluntly, "You're in one devil of a foul mood."

"Look who is speaking. If I had a coin for every time you've sunk into a black humor in the past months, I'd significantly increase my fortune."

Well, that was hard to deny; instead Derek took a hefty drink from his glass. He wasn't ready yet to tell his friend about the debacle a year ago and the ensuing blunders that just seemed to make it all worse. Thomas knew, and that was enough.

Annabel knew, and it *wasn't* enough.

With unnecessary vehemence, Nicholas said suddenly, "Her husband should have been horsewhipped."

Derek blinked before he said cautiously, "Lord Wynn? What did she tell you?"

"She didn't have to tell me anything. Let's just say Caroline's response to our infantile male posturing involved some measure of courage. I admire her for it."

In the background someone laughed heartily, the raucous sound rising above the usual murmured conversation. Derek felt confused. "At the risk of seeming obtuse—which has certainly happened before—can you elaborate?"

"He was a vicious bastard."

"Oh, I see." The tone of Lady Wynn's note took on a whole new meaning.

Whatever the devil *had* happened in Essex, it had been more than a simple sexual rendezvous. Derek tried to look noncommittal and finished off his first glass of fine whiskey as he assimilated this new development. He gestured to have it refilled.

"I suppose, now that she's back in London, you'll . . . well, I suppose you'll make arrangements." Nicholas rubbed his lean jaw, an irritated expression on the handsome face so many women admired. For his meeting with the prime minister he wore a fitted green velvet jacket, the embroidery on his waistcoat a matching emerald, beige breeches, and highly polished boots. His ebony hair was a contrast to his pristine white cravat, just edged with lace, but the faint scowl detracted from the impression of elegant courtier.

Bloody hell, the infamous Rothay was jealous! Derek realized it with no small measure of shock.

Even though he had no intention any longer of touching the lady in question, he couldn't pass by this opportunity to test the waters and see if he might be right. "I can't wait," he fibbed, leaning back in his chair in a languid movement and fingering his glass as the waiter hurried away. "I've been bored lately and could use a good fuck."

Sure enough, something glimmered in his friend's dark eyes at the deliberate crudity. Nicholas growled, "Refer to it that way again, and I'll . . ."

Derek waited, one brow lifted.

Oh yes, definitely possessive of the formerly standoffish Lady Wynn.

Nicholas muttered, "I sent you the note to meet me because I wanted to tell you to be careful with her. That's all."

"Careful?"

"Yes, careful. Gentle. Don't rush things."

"Are you truly *instructing* me on how to bed her?" His incredulity was tempered by sympathetic amusement.

"I'm just saying . . ." For the second time Nicholas trailed off, his fingers tightening on his glass. Then he added ferociously, "Bloody hell."

He stood suddenly and stalked off without so much as a good-bye.

Derek pursed his lips in a silent whistle as he watched the duke's tall form exit the room.

Since Derek had once committed the unforgivable sin of resisting his own feelings, he understood all too well how it could affect a man's life. But he also knew old habits died hard. Perhaps Nicholas wasn't ready to admit he was at the least smitten, and quite possibly more.

Well, Derek might not be able to resolve his own problem with Annabel, but maybe he could aid Nicholas. As he sat there, a germ of an idea occurred to him and he mulled it over, staring at his glass of whiskey but not drinking it.

Women fell for Nicholas like autumn leaves drifting from a tree. If the gorgeous widow had once been in a horrible marriage, how had she reacted to the seductive powers of one of England's most accomplished lovers? Judging by the way the Duke of Rothay had just acted, something momentous must have happened.

Now, this was truly interesting.

Yes—though not for the original purpose Nicholas insinuated—maybe he should make arrangements to see the lady.

Chapter Eighteen

The hour was late, she was tired, and her visitor wouldn't give her butler his name. Caroline frowned at the scrawled cryptic letters on the plain card, and then realized who it must be with a flicker of consternation. "Yes, Norman, I'll see the gentleman. Please show him into Edward's study."

The elderly man, clad in his dressing gown, inclined his head, showing no curiosity over the very unusual event in a normally quiet household, but she could guess what he was thinking. Her recent absence, too, was not usual for her.

EofM. It had to stand for the Earl of Manderville. She'd asked for discretion and was fairly sure an evening visit to her town house didn't qualify. The man must have heard from Nicholas they were back already.

He certainly didn't waste any time coming to see her. It was hard to decide whether to be flattered or annoyed. As luck would have it, she was still dressed, because she'd dozed off in the sitting room while reading after dinner. Taking a tray in her room was easier than going through the formal ritual in the dining room by herself. The staff hadn't expected her back yet either, so cold chicken, cheese, and fresh bread could be eaten just as easily upstairs. She did it often enough. Even sitting at the long table all alone was better than dining with Edward, but still, it made her feel downhearted and emphasized she was alone.

Like she needed that. She had to wonder if the idyllic tryst with the beautiful Rothay had made life more difficult, instead of working as a cure to her melancholy.

Caroline glanced in the mirror, smoothed her hair, and then went down to see what Derek Drake wished to discuss with her that couldn't wait until a more civilized hour.

At first glance into the study she was a bit startled, then relieved, and then amused. She went into the room and quietly shut the door. "Good evening, my lord."

He turned and noted the laugh quivering on her lips, a rueful smile touching his well-shaped mouth. "Good evening. You see, I can be as inventive as you, my lady. I walked also, just to be sure no one paid any attention to horse or carriage."

It was true. He was dressed like a tradesman in plain garb, a drab coat hanging off his wide shoulders, worn trousers encasing his long legs, and somewhere he'd found scuffed old boots. A battered hat lay on a chair. He stood by the window, tall and imposing in spite of his state of dress, and though at a glance one might believe the disguise, she guessed much time in his company would belie the plebian image. It was that same easy confidence in the way he held himself that Nicholas had, so much harder to conceal than physical appearance.

She murmured, "I'm pleased, naturally, that you took care to make sure no one would recognize you, but am a bit puzzled as to why you are here, much less at this hour."

She wasn't looking forward to telling Derek Drake that she'd changed her mind about her part in the wager. He would want to know why. A sophisticated rogue like the earl was probably going to be very amused at her naïveté if she told him the truth. Though she was sure she wasn't the first woman to tumble so quickly into love with the Duke of Rothay, she was still trying to understand her feelings and be as objective as possible about the situation. Another unfortunate part of her decision was that if Derek and Nicholas decided the bet stood and still wanted to settle it, it meant Nicholas would entertain some other woman with his lavish charm and glorious skill in the bedroom.

It hurt to think of it, which made her doubly a fool.

What did she expect? That after her he'd be celibate? He'd asked to see her again and she'd said no. It was the end of it.

"I could have waited until tomorrow," Derek said abruptly, "but calling at night made being recognized less of an issue and what I need to discuss with you is much better done face-to-face. I've waited long enough to do something and what I've chosen so far hasn't worked."

A little confused, Caroline chose a chair and sat down, folding her hands in her lap. Despite her resolve to stay cool, she blushed. "I know we need to arrange our . . . well, week, but—"

"Excuse the unforgivable interruption, but it isn't about that." He made a restless movement with his hand. "Well, indirectly, I suppose. What happened between you and Nick?"

What a question. She stared, her face heating further. "I beg your pardon?"

Whatever was in her expression, he understood it. Of course he did; he was very suave with women and familiar with their moods by all accounts. He gave a short laugh. "I'm not asking for specifics, believe me. I understand how it all works. Not what happened between you in the bedroom, but what else? I saw him earlier and he's not at all himself. He's rattled. More than that, I think he wanted to warn me off. To cancel our challenge."

He did?

The study around her, with its vague lingering scent of leather and whiskey, seemed to fade. Caroline looked at the tall man across the room and felt a twinge of . . . what? Hope? Happiness?

"I can't go through with it anyway." She made her confession in a small voice as she tried to comprehend what he was telling her. "I was going to send you a note. I'm sorry to renege, but I . . . must."

To her surprise, Derek's expression seemed to lighten at her mumbled words, even though she hadn't directly answered his question.

"Why must you cancel?"

No, if she said it out loud, she'd become emotionally involved. A verbal acknowledgment would make it painfully true. He might even tell Nicholas she thought she had fallen in love with him.

No.

"Personal reasons," she said with what she hoped was succinct dismissal of the subject. "Once again, I apologize for backing out."

"Do these personal reasons revolve around one very stubborn and independent duke?" There was a disconcerting shrewdness in his blue eyes.

For years she'd fooled everyone into thinking she was cold and unfeeling. Now it appeared she'd lost that ability. Caroline cleared her throat. "Please do not ask me that."

"A resounding yes, if ever there was one. Excellent."

It was a bewildering comment. Caroline felt more lost than ever over the purpose of his visit. Did she misunderstand or had he just intimated he thought it was a good thing she had a hopeless penchant for a man well-known for his emotional detachment when it came to love affairs?

He went on. "Don't apologize for the loss of our time together, Lady Wynn. It wasn't going to happen anyway, with or without whatever is between you and Nick. I am through with meaningless liaisons with women who value only transient pleasure. Let me be brutally honest with you. The wager was the direct result of a frustrated moment due to the announcement the woman I love with my heart and soul is going to marry another man."

Had the clock in the corner always ticked so loudly? She handled her accounts in this room and never noticed it before. It was the only sound to intrude on the dead silence as she stared at her visitor in undisguised surprise.

Had Lord Manderville actually just said he was in love? Unbidden, Caroline's laughter spilled forth, her uncontained mirth breaking the moment. It was part genuine amusement, part the release of a stockpile of nervous tension that had built over the past few days.

His dark blond brows winged upward. "That's amusing? I'm glad you think so, but for my part, I'm the most miserable man in London."

She managed to shake her head and catch her breath, her hand going to press against her stomach. "No, my lord, I am not laughing at that unfortunate part of your speech. But you must admit this is all so comical in a way. Nicholas essentially told me while we were in Essex he only wants to marry for love. Here *you* are, telling me your supposedly inviolate heart is being broken. No one in fashionable society would believe it."

The earl looked disconcerted but had the grace to smile. "I suppose you're right."

Caroline had to admit, she was curious. "Who is she?"

"Annabel Reid, my uncle's ward."

She registered the information with disbelief. Miss Reid was very young and the quintessential fresh-faced ingenue. *That* was who had captured the heart of the wicked Angel? A young chit out of the schoolroom and his uncle's ward, no less? Not that the young woman wasn't very pretty, but he didn't dally with marriageable young ladies. It was common knowledge.

"You're surprised," he said, correctly interpreting her expression. "Well, so am I, but it's the truth. I'm surprised over Nicholas's reaction to you too. However, maybe this is all meant to be. I'm rather hoping we can join forces. That is, if you are as taken with Nicholas as he seems to be with you."

She was more than taken—that was the problem—but she tried to equivocate. "I don't think the duke and I have known each other long enough to be able to gauge the depth of our feelings."

Lord Manderville gave a small snort. "He was jealous this afternoon when he talked to me. I recognize the emotion only too well. Concerned about you, unsettled, unhappy, irritated with himself, confused . . ."

"You make it sound like an awful disease, my lord." Caroline stifled another unwilling laugh at his pained expression and battled an unreasonable flare of optimism.

"It is, take my word." His mouth twisted and he hesitated for a moment. "Look, my lady, I've known Nick a long time. From that first moment in the parlor at the inn, there was a spark between you two. I noticed then, but thought it might just be the unusual circumstances that intrigued him. Now I wonder if it isn't a good deal more."

Could he be right? It was irrational to hope so. Still, she gave him a helpless, confused look. "How can we help each other?"

"Maybe if we work together, it will help us both. My uncle is convinced Annabel feels the same for me as I do her, and I think—I pray—he is right. Yet she is engaged to Lord Hyatt and my last attempt to explain myself to her was a disaster. I wondered if you, from the slant of your own experience, could persuade her to see that a loveless marriage is the road to misery."

Did she actually feel sorry for one of the most handsome, wealthy, charming men in England?

Well, yes. He looked desperately sincere and after all, he had donned a ridiculous disguise and come to see her in the middle of the night. Not to mention he'd declared he had no intention of going through with the wager, even if she had still been willing.

Caroline said, "I can only speak from my own experience. I have met Lord Hyatt and doubt he would be a cruel husband. But you are right, my lord. I do believe a marriage without love wastes a precious part of a person's life, and it is doubly unfair if one of the parties involved is in love with someone else. I suppose I am willing to try."

"Excellent." His smile was genuine for the first time, a mesmerizing curve of his mouth that no doubt had turned many a woman's knees to water. He arched a brow and the smile slid into a devilish grin. "I, in turn, will take great pleasure in making Nick acknowledge to himself—and you—that his heart might be engaged at long last. I don't want him to make the same mistake I did. If I thought a simple lecture would work, I'd try it, but men are more obtuse than women."

"If you think for a moment I am going to argue with *that*, Lord Manderville, you are mistaken."

"I doubted you would," he said drily. "My point is that something that bludgeons him over the head will work better than subtlety. I have a plan."

Caroline was beginning to realize why Nicholas was such good friends with his notorious cohort. "I imagine it is very inventive, but there is one very big problem. If you hadn't been so honest just now, I wouldn't ever discuss it, but . . ."

Even having said that, her voice trailed off and she swallowed against the tightening of her throat. She glanced down at her intertwined fingers in her lap for a moment, and then squared her shoulders. "Despite my offer to judge the wager and the past days I spent with the duke, I am not interested in a casual love affair. Since there is every chance I am barren, nothing else is possible between us. Besides, he and I have known each other such a short amount of time. Less than a week in each other's company is surely not enough to judge true emotion."

Manderville leaned one broad shoulder against the wall and folded his arms. "I think you are entirely wrong, Lady Wynn. I've known Annabel for more than a decade and even I couldn't see what was happening between us. There is no time standard against which to measure falling in love. I think it happens to some people the instant they meet, and I think it takes others years to gradually grow into it, and there is every possible scenario in between. As for the possibility of your never conceiving a child, I acknowledge having an heir is an important consideration for anyone who has a title to pass on, but even if Nicholas were to marry some virginal miss, he would still be taking that chance."

That was true. Before she married, she had certainly never considered she might not conceive. "With me, he has the evidence of my previous failure."

"So your argument is that he'd be better off marrying

some insipid untried young chit? I thought you just told me he wants to marry for love."

Was she really having a deep discussion with a known rakehell on the subject of romance and marriage?

Neither Nicholas nor Derek Drake were the men they were perceived to be. Caroline pointed out, "We do not know he has any feelings for me at all beyond physical attraction."

"On the contrary, you did not see him this afternoon." Derek straightened. "Tell me this, my lady. If you had only one word to describe your time with him in Essex, what would it be?"

One word? It would be impossible to sum up sunlit glades, indescribable pleasure, breathtaking smiles, and silent waltzes with one word.

But she could try.

She said finally in an almost inaudible voice, "Magical."

He nodded, the look in his eyes telling her how poorly a job she'd done of hiding her feelings. "So then, would you like to hear what I have in mind?"

Chapter Nineteen

Two days. The refrain played in his head even when he was in the simple act of heaping marmalade on a piece of toast. Unlike the simple sunny breakfast room at the estate in Essex where he'd dined with Caroline, the lofty ceilings, huge gleaming table, and bevy of servants moving discreetly in the background in his London home as they replenished rashers of meat and eggs reminded him that nothing was done on a small scale. Nicholas was used to it—had rarely even thought about it—but the ducal pomp came sharply into focus because of his preoccupation with one very lovely, unattainable widow.

Caroline had preferred her toast plain. She drank milk in her tea, but took no sugar. When the sun hit her hair, the shimmering color was unique, like . . .

"You certainly are in another world, darling. What has you so distracted this morning?"

Nicholas looked up with a start, his cup halfway to his mouth. Good God, he'd been daydreaming like some besotted idiot.

What should he do? Tell his *mother* he was absorbed with the notion Lady Wynn owed him two more days of carnal delights to settle their bet? He had no illusions; his mother must have heard about the wager, but so far she hadn't said anything. Not that he wasn't grateful she didn't bring up such an indelicate masculine challenge, for he was sure she disapproved. She probably *should* disapprove, for that matter. However, what had happened couldn't be changed. Not the bet duly listed in the books for London to whisper over, and not those five telling days with Caroline.

Those he *wouldn't* change, but seven was the bargain.

Yes, she owed him two more. She'd refused, but maybe he could change her mind. He was becoming obsessed with the thought.

"It's been a busy week." He set his cup down with exaggerated care next to his plate and touched his napkin to his mouth. "I'm sorry if I am ignoring you. Please forgive me."

"I forgive you, darling, but I'd prefer to know what put that expression on your face." From across the table, she frowned at him, idly stirring her chocolate.

"What expression?" He gave an inner resigned sigh. After all, it was his fault for sitting there and thinking about Caroline in the first place. If an interrogation was on its way, he had only himself to blame.

But he couldn't seem to put her out of his mind.

His mother gracefully picked up the beautiful porcelain pot in front of her and added rich liquid to her cup, but her attention was all on him. "You looked as if you were recalling something quite pleasant. It made you smile."

The Dowager Duchess of Rothay had always been perceptive. But Nicholas wasn't in the mood to answer questions and even if he were, he doubted she'd like the answers. Maybe she wouldn't even believe it. He was never preoccupied over women.

Until now.

She went on thoughtfully, her fine dark eyes reflecting curiosity. "You seem as if your mind is elsewhere. And you've been quiet all week and declined to accompany us anywhere."

She was right. He'd passed on attending the usual round of soirees and various entertainments, mostly because he wanted to avoid Caroline.

And at the same time, he had this perverse, discomforting urge to see her too. Usually he knew his own mind. His current state of unrest reminded him in an unsettling way of how he'd felt about Helena a decade before. Only then the interest had been prompted by boyish infatuation and he was no longer a boy.

"I'm extremely busy right now," he said with as little inflection in his voice as possible.

His mother wasn't fooled. An arched brow went upward and her patrician features were a caricature of skepticism. "You are always terribly busy, Nicholas. That can't be it. Althea has noticed as well. You seem a bit . . . I don't know . . . distant."

That was what a man needed, he thought in resigned sardonic amusement, every female in his household analyzing him. "If I've been distracted, blame it on the current state of political conflict. We're debating everything from Wellington's request for more soldiers to agricultural sanctions."

"That makes you go to bed at a reasonable hour and rise at dawn?" His mother gazed at him with intent scrutiny that made him feel as if he were five years old again and caught in a blatant lie. "You usually have quite an opposite schedule. The debates in Parliament are always there. It is what it exists for, actually. I think you are being evasive and I wonder why."

Since his return from Essex, he *wasn't* sleeping all that well. He had quickly adapted to his new affection for the break of day, but it wasn't nearly as satisfying as when he had Caroline warm and willing next to him and he could celebrate the arrival of the sun in the most pleasurable way possible.

"You are planning on attending Harrison's ball this evening, aren't you? I believe Charles and Althea are going to the opera instead and I wouldn't mind the escort."

Thus asked, how could he refuse?

"I would be honored to oblige. And please, stop worrying over me." He rose from the breakfast table, kissed her cheek with affection that was not at all feigned even though he was uninterested in staying for further interrogation, and left the room.

He hadn't lied. Not precisely. It wasn't that anything was

wrong; it was that something wasn't right. The ridiculous preoccupation wasn't limited to wandering thoughts during breakfast either. The night before, he'd dreamed of creamy, satin skin next to his, lustrous auburn hair spilling over his chest, and heated pleasure mixed with the elusive scent of lily of the valley. To his mortification, he'd woken perspiring, twisted in the sheets, not to mention rock hard and erect, something that hadn't happened to him from a dream since adolescence.

The vision had a face, delicate, beautiful, and intimately familiar, framed by that silken mass of hair and dominated by large, incredible silver eyes.

His arousal he'd dealt with himself, thinking of her. It wasn't something he did often. Really, he had no need. When it came to sex, there were willing women ready to take of him.

A point he might remember later. For the moment, however, he wanted to check on his horses. He hadn't been to the stud lately, and this coming week promised to be packed with meetings, and the hectic schedule involved wouldn't allow much time for contemplating what the incomparable Lady Wynn might be doing.

With Derek.

No, luckily, not. It was perversely satisfying to know Derek couldn't get away immediately. He was just as occupied with political matters. Whatever arrangements he might make with Caroline would have to be postponed for a short while.

As he ordered his horse brought around, Nicholas found he gritted his teeth at the thought of their upcoming assignation, the slight ache in his jaw a direct result. With an inner shake of his head over his reaction, he consciously dismissed her. The memory of how she'd turned him down was still fresh in his mind. There was no question she'd meant it. Neither could he blame her for not wanting scandal in her life, so . . . it was all settled. Not necessarily to his satisfaction, but settled.

Wasn't it?

The ride to the outskirts of town wasn't pleasant because

of the wet streets from all the rain in the past few days, but
it felt good to be outside nonetheless. He'd had enough of
stuffy meeting rooms and the confines of his study. His stable master greeted him with a broad smile and an informal
slap on the back from a beefy hand. The rank he held mattered not at all when it came to his bloodstock, for in the stable O'Brien held court like a king, his decisions inviolate,
and Nicholas—after win after win—trusted him implicitly.

The stables were meticulously maintained, built of stone
and polished wood, the orderly stalls in long rows, all accented by the smell of hay and oats, and just the slightest inevitable tinge of manure. It was sophisticated by any
standards, worthy of some of the finest horses in Britain,
and Nicholas always felt a certain peace among the animals
he regarded almost like children.

"How's Satan's foreleg?" he asked. His current favorite
was always the first one he inquired about.

"That feisty lad is right as rain. Let's go see him, shall we,
sir?" Red-haired and boisterous, O'Brien was a wizard with
his expensive charges.

"And Baikal?" One of his youngest acquisitions was still
an unknown quantity, but the Irishman had insisted on buying the colt for a somewhat exorbitant price and Nicholas
hadn't hesitated for even a minute.

"I can honestly say you're going to be impressed. Did a
mile in one fifty, and he's young yet."

"Is that right?"

The next hour was spent touring the facility, getting up-
dates on the welfare of each animal stall by stall. It was
pleasant to forget about his outside life and immerse himself
in his passion.

He almost—almost—forgot, for a short while, about his
other passion, until he was sharply reminded when something small, furry, and extraordinarily clumsy galloped in
front of him and he nearly tripped over it.

"Sorry, Your Grace." A young stable hand scooped up the
offending party and held the wiggling animal in the crook of
his arm. "He's the rambunctious one of the lot, he is."

Nicholas eyed the squirming puppy, but instead of seeing a pink tongue trying to furiously lick the boy's face and a furry canine, he instead pictured a wooded glen and a very beautiful, nude woman in his arms as they lay in the lazy aftermath of exquisite erotic pleasure as he yet again tried to pry more information about her life from her.

My father has never cared to be bothered with anything he deems a nuisance. As a child I desperately wanted a puppy, but he always said no and my aunt wouldn't hear of it. . . . It doesn't matter now, of course. . . .

But even then—even in the haze following an excess of carnal largesse—he'd heard in Caroline's voice it did matter. He'd discerned something else as well. Her father had included his only child in the category of being a nuisance. Driving to York and wringing the man's unfeeling neck held a certain allure.

But maybe Nicholas could restore that childhood dream instead.

After all, she *had* challenged him to be even more romantic than arranging an impromptu dinner on the terrace. On impulse, he asked, "Is there a litter, then?"

The young man nodded. "Six of them."

"Old enough to be weaned?"

"Only just, Your Grace."

Pleasantly, Nicholas said, "I'd like to see them, if I may. I have a friend who has always wanted a dog."

In the end he chose the wild one who had literally crossed his path, and though it looked more like a mop of hair than an actual dog, he had to admit the creature was endearingly affectionate and enthusiastic. He should know, for he was forced to ride back through London holding on to the damned thing, and at the point when it piddled on his formerly immaculate breeches, he wondered if he wasn't nothing more than a sentimental fool.

He confirmed that suspicion with a wish that he could be there to see Caroline's face when it was delivered. But that was impossible, and to desire it made him more idiotic than even the act of carting some mongrel halfway across the city indicated.

To give the hapless footman who opened the door credit, he kept his expression schooled as Nicholas gratefully deposited the dog in his arms and said, "See that it's fed and bathed and I'll give you an address to deliver it."

"Very good, Your Grace."

He paused a moment, Lady Wynn's quest for discretion coming to mind. The ducal crest on the side of his carriage was out of the question. "Take a hired hack, if you will, and leave my name out of it. The lady will guess it is from me."

"Of course."

Smiling, he went upstairs to bathe and change. He might smell like horses and dog piss, he thought with inner sardonic humor, but it had actually been a satisfying afternoon.

There was no question he'd been waiting.

No, she could adjust that observation. Spying.

Caroline had little choice but to let Franklin take her arm as she ascended the steps, for he'd appeared like an apparition out of nowhere. If she wasn't sure the notion was ludicrous, she would have accused him of loitering in the alley by the town house, anticipating her return.

"How fortuitous we should arrive at the same time," Franklin murmured, escorting her to the door. "I've called on several instances, but I understand you've been visiting a friend in the country."

Visions of that *friend* came to mind. Dark windblown hair, a sinful smile that both dazzled and captivated, a lean body that covered hers as they moved together in the oldest communion possible between a man and a woman. Was Nicholas a friend? Actually, yes, she did think of him that way, his sexual prowess aside. When she considered it, she'd probably talked to him more in those five days than she had to any other person in the course of her whole life. It was his fault, because he'd seemed interested in what she had to say.

"Yes, I was with a friend."

If the clipped tone of her response bothered the new viscount, he didn't show it. Those familiar Wynn family features, angular and defined, revealed nothing about his feelings. All too well she recalled that same quality in her late husband. Once she'd understood what Edward really was, his physical appearance held absolutely no appeal whatsoever. A monster was a monster, no matter what face it wore.

Though to have to offer the politesse made her feel a very real flicker of irritation, she said, "Won't you come in?"

"I wouldn't have called if I hadn't have anticipated I would."

The smooth smugness in his tone annoyed her more than ever, but several years of marriage to his even-more-overbearing cousin had taught her a great deal of self-control. She hoped her smile was as remote as she willed it to be. "Of course. This way, my lord."

"I fully know the way. At one time, I imagined this residence would be mine."

His words were said with supposed humor, but Caroline remembered well how much of her inheritance she'd surrendered to the solicitors who'd argued her bequest was legitimate.

There were no illusions. He was not a friend, but at least his vindictiveness was a great deal less overt than Edward's had been. When she settled opposite him in the formal parlor and rang for refreshments, she sat silent, waiting for him to state the purpose of his visit. He had one: of that she had no doubt.

Franklin stared back, his pale eyes unreadable. "You look lovely, Caroline. Your visit must have done you good."

"Thank you."

"I have always appreciated your beauty, you know."

His calculated interest did nothing but make her skin crawl. Her time with Edward had taught her that a man could desire a woman in a carnal way and have absolutely no affection or kindness toward her.

When she didn't reply to the comment in any way, a faint

smile curved his mouth. He sat in causal repose, as usual elegantly dressed to the point of being dandified in a peacock blue coat, his pristine cravat sporting a diamond stickpin, fawn breeches tucked into polished Hessians. "Let's be frank. You distrust me after the disagreement over the disposition of my cousin's estate. I think I have made it clear I wish to settle it between us."

"We needn't ever discuss it again." It was a neutral thing to say. The truth was, she suspected Edward had disliked Franklin because they were a little too much alike.

He spread his hands in a supplicating gesture. "Indeed we do if it is a source of discord between us. After all, we are family and I do not want to shirk my responsibilities toward you. As I have pointed out before, I'm your nearest male relative and it is my right to have some say in your life."

The tedious theme was not one she wanted to talk about again.

"We are merely cousins by marriage. It's hardly a close tie and not a blood one at that. Besides, I have my father."

"I've spoken with him."

She stared, shocked at the presumption. "What?"

Franklin merely looked back, his face impassive. "Of course. You already know I am concerned about you. His position is that the day you married Edward and became a Wynn, his obligation to you was over."

Obligation. It stung to think her parent would put it that way, but unfortunately she could imagine him saying exactly that. Caroline could feel her hands clench into fists in the material of her gown, crushing the fragile silk. She consciously relaxed them. "I am a grown woman and a widow. I do not require help financially nor do I need protection from anyone."

He merely looked amused in his cold way. "Every woman needs protection. Since your mourning is over, more than one man has approached me on the subject of offering for your hand."

It made her furious to think that not only did he arrogantly assume he could interfere, but others did as well. "How kind of you to screen my suitors for me."

He didn't blink an eye at the dripping sarcasm in her tone. "Your future concerns me. You are too young to be unwed."

"In your opinion only, my lord. In mine, my age gives me the freedom to wait and decide if I should ever want to marry again."

"Your position on the subject is progressive, my dear, but—"

"My lady?"

The interruption to the rising argument made them both glance at the doorway. Norman, fastidious and tidy always, stood there, looking comically aghast. In his hands he held what appeared to be a riotous ball of brown fur. "Forgive me, but this was just delivered for you. The man who brought it said there was no note, but you would know the source of the . . . er . . . gift. What shall I do with it?"

For a moment Caroline was speechless, staring at the puppy in her butler's hands, its woolly wiggling body shedding hairs on his neat waistcoat. Even as she wondered who on earth would send her such an unusual gift, the truth came in a flash like lightning in a summer cloudburst.

Nicholas. During one of those lazy, divine afternoons, her head pillowed on his bare muscled shoulder, the fragrance of water and grass and earth around them, she remembered confessing how, as a child, she'd always wanted a dog but been refused. It wasn't like she wanted to talk about her childhood, but he'd managed to coerce out of her more details than she had ever told anyone. Maybe it was his wayward charm, or maybe it was the catharsis of finally telling someone she felt held a genuine interest, but she'd found herself confessing small things like the thwarted desire for a pet.

She wanted to laugh with delight over the gesture.

She wanted to burst into tears at the same time; she was so touched.

Caroline rose and went over, taking the small creature from Norman, who looked grateful. Two soulful dark eyes looked up at her, and what passed for a stubby tail wiggled frantically. A tiny pink tongue began to swab her hand.

She fell in love for the second time in her life. "Oh my, isn't he adorable?"

Norman, who liked the household to run in a sedate, orderly manner, looked doubtful over the new addition. "If you say so, my lady."

Franklin said in a peevish tone, "Who the devil would send you a mongrel?"

Since the truth would hardly do, she didn't answer. Instead she bent and set down her newfound friend, who promptly scampered under an embroidered settee and then emerged a moment later to run back to her and plop at her feet. It gave a short bark, as if asking for approval for that wondrous feat. She gave it, bending down to stroke one downy ear. "I've never had a pet."

"It's a rather presumptuous gift, if you ask me."

Caroline laughed at the appropriate choice of words. She couldn't help it. The gorgeous and sensual Duke of Rothay was presumptuous to a fault, but in this instance, his gesture touched her heart with inexplicable deep emotion. Had he sent her diamonds, she would have thought him generous and romantic, but this was truly a splendid thing, for it meant he'd listened to more than just her words when she told him of her childhood disappointment. He'd heard what lay beneath the detached speech and small shrug.

She prayed Derek was right, and if there was a way to coax Nicholas into thinking of their relationship in a present permanent way instead of a past casual one, she wanted at least to try.

Even at the risk of shattering her heart if it didn't work.

"If I had known what it took to bring a smile like that to your lips, my dear, I'd have scrounged a dirty ill-bred dog from some nasty gutter myself. I can't see a woman making such a gesture, so I do wonder who else might come up with an unorthodox idea to bestow such a present."

His soft, almost menacing tone made her glance up and straighten, a flicker of alarm twisting in her stomach.

Nicholas couldn't have known Lord Wynn would be there when the puppy was delivered, but the timing was terrible. Franklin regarded her with narrowed eyes, his mouth a trifle tight.

"It's from Melinda, I'm sure," she improvised, knowing she wasn't a good liar, hoping he didn't notice the flush in her cheeks. "I believe she mentioned one of her husband's spaniels was a bitch about to have a litter."

"That is hardly the progeny of a purebred hunting dog."

He was undoubtedly right. She murmured, "Who knows who sired him?"

Franklin got to his feet. "Since you seem currently occupied, I'll take my leave. Think about what I said."

Joy was replaced instantly with resentment. "If you mean marriage, I'm sorry, but it isn't in my future plans at this time."

With elaborate deliberation, he adjusted his cuff. "That will change."

She stared at the doorway after he left, wondering what he could have meant by that cryptic remark. It made her uneasy, because while she vowed to herself he couldn't force her to do anything she didn't want, he seemed to have an equal measure of assurance he could.

A sharp tug on the hem of her gown drew her attention downward and she scooped up Nicholas's gift and held the exuberant bundle close. A little unconditional love in her life would be nice, she thought, unable to suppress a smile as she dismissed Lord Wynn from her mind.

Chapter Twenty

The gaming room was, as always, held in a thrall of tobacco smoke imbued with the smell of brandy and claret, and windows open to the warm evening did little to clear the air. The conversations were occasionally raucous, punctuated by outbursts of laughter, but at their table the atmosphere was subdued. Derek watched in silence as the man across from him tossed down his cards and collected the winnings of yet another hand.

It seemed the Duke of Rothay was having a lucky night.

Only, for a man with the devil's own fortune smiling on him, he didn't look particularly overjoyed. Nicholas had a singular set to his mouth that anyone who knew him beyond casual acquaintance would recognize as irritation. Derek had a feeling he knew the reason.

"I say, Rothay," young Lord Renquist grumbled, "mind sitting out a hand or two so the rest of us have a chance?"

Nicholas's dark eyes held just the slightest glitter of what could be inebriation. If the number of times he'd had his glass refilled since he'd taken his seat was an indication of what he'd been doing before he arrived at the ball, it wasn't a bad guess. He drawled with only marginal civility, "I'm not dealing the cards. Are you implying something?"

The young man might be a little foxed himself, but not so far gone that he didn't recognize the hint of measured warning in Nicholas's voice. "I wasn't implying anything. Just a joke."

"Was it?"

Renquist's face paled just a little. "Not a good one."

"Let's just play, shall we?" Nicholas picked up his cards, his long fingers expertly fanning them out, his expression holding that uncharacteristic hint of sullen ill humor.

Derek saw two of the other players glance at each other in an unspoken but clear agreement to not cross the normally unruffled and smooth-mannered Duke of Rothay that evening. If such an innocuous remark could cause offense, perhaps it was best to stay quiet.

After two more disastrous hands, Renquist excused himself with careful politeness and moved on to a game of dice. Derek didn't even mind losing a little, as he was determined to play the role of watchdog for the evening. Under normal circumstances he trusted Nicholas to behave himself, but the situation was not usual at all.

Caroline was in attendance, out in the ballroom as they played cards. On Derek's advice, she was even dancing, something she did rarely. This evening she was lovelier than ever, dressed in a low-cut gown of cream lace with a pale underskirt of lemon silk, her gleaming hair and ivory skin set off to advantage. Something unidentifiable had changed about her since she had returned from her sojourn with Nicholas, and though she seemed just as serene, she had a different air about her.

Men had noticed. Not just the dancing, though it had been remarked upon, but the more subtle difference that softened her usual icy shield.

Hence the duke's unsettled ill humor at a guess, because no one knew better than Derek how it felt to be near the woman you desired and not able to approach her. Caroline was there, Nicholas knew it, and he had to stay away while other men waltzed and flirted with her. A posture of restraint heretofore unknown to a man who could usually have what he wanted, especially when it came to the fairer sex.

Not that *he* was in a better predicament, Derek thought, for Annabel was there also, lovely in pink tulle, her pale hair upswept to show off the graceful line of her neck and satin shoulders. He could, of course, ask her to dance, since no one would think much of it, given his familial connection to her guardian, but he wasn't at all sure she wouldn't give him the cut direct if he tried to approach her. Being snubbed in public would cause gossip and, while he didn't care so much for himself, he doubted it would make her happy to be the subject of backhanded whispers. He had no illusions; she would blame him.

So, like Nicholas, he had to keep his distance.

One of their friends took Renquist's open chair at the table and asked to be dealt in. Derek said in a neutral tone, "Just a word of warning, George. Nick is lucky as Satan himself tonight. He can't get bad cards."

"Thanks for the warning. I won't play too deep, then." George Winston, heavyset and gregarious, settled down and grinned. "Speaking of luck, how's the contest between you two going anyway? When do we hear the grand announcement?"

A muscle visibly clenched in Nicholas's jaw, but his voice was pleasant enough. "It isn't settled yet."

"Should be in the next few weeks, though," Derek said with a deliberate lazy grin. "We don't want to rush the matter."

It could be a mistake to needle Nicholas in his current mood, but making him acknowledge his jealousy was part of the plan.

Good-natured but always too talkative, Winston winked. "You don't want to rush the lady, you mean. You've got to know everyone's having a devil of a time trying to figure out who she is. Give us a hint, now."

Nicholas stared at his hand as if it were the most fascinating thing on earth. "No."

"Is she beautiful?" George wasn't interested in being put off. In fact, all the men at the table looked both amused and curious.

"What do you think?" Derek lifted a brow.

"I assumed. Big tits?"

Nicholas lifted his head like a wolf scenting its prey.

If there was a discreet way to tell George that speculation like that might make him a very sorry man indeed, Derek would have done so. Across the table, in a deceptively casual voice, Nicholas said tersely, "As gentlemen, we refuse to discuss it."

Clearly a warning.

The cold look in his dark eyes declared the subject to be closed.

Then he tossed his cards on the table and got up. "Excuse me, gentlemen, I'm out."

There was a brief silence after his abrupt departure. He left the room with determined steps, as if he had a definite destination in mind. One of the other players muttered, "I say, not quite himself this evening, is he?"

A very promising sign. Derek said merely, "He's been meeting with the prime minister every day this past week and his family is in town. It could be he's just tired."

George snorted. "The Devilish Duke? I've seen him stay up until dawn drinking and do nothing more than change his clothes, leave for a race meet, and do the same thing the next night. Nick doesn't *get* tired."

Derek would wager the markers piled in front of him and then some that George was wrong. At the moment, he'd guess the legendary Rothay was very tired of being near the off-limits Lady Wynn and unable to so much as touch her hand.

The carriage door opened and Nicholas sat motionless, hoping he hadn't just made the impulsive mistake of a lifetime by listening to his unruly cock. Caroline began to climb in but stopped dead as she caught sight of him, her soft mouth parting in shocked surprise.

He said quietly, "Please get in and I'll explain."

"Nicholas, what are you doing?" She hung there, not quite inside the carriage, the question an outraged whisper.

"I talked to your driver. He'll take us the long way home. So, please, get in before anyone wonders why you won't."

That brought her inside finally and the young Welshman

who'd driven her to Essex shut the door. She settled on the seat in a graceful rustle of silken skirts and a moment later the vehicle pulled away. Luminous silver eyes stared at him, but it was dim and he couldn't quite gauge the level of her opposition to his presence. She said finally, "I certainly hope no one saw you talking to Huw or, even worse, getting into my carriage."

"I was careful." He had been and was damned glad he'd taken the time to speak to the young man during the time Caroline had stayed with him in Essex. He and her driver discussed horses, a natural mutual love there leveling aristocrat and servant with ease. Besides, Huw obviously knew exactly where his mistress spent her nights, so he hadn't blinked an eye over Nicholas and his request.

"I am not sure you know how to be discreet, Rothay," she said in a tart tone, but a small smile curved her mouth.

"For you, I am willing to do my best." He relaxed a little, familiar with that soft expression on a woman's face.

Not that knowing a woman wanted his company had ever been quite so important to him before, but with her, it was. Very important. As incredible as it might seem, he wanted to know she'd missed him the way he'd missed her.

She still primly reprimanded him. "I believe I told you no. I realize you are unfamiliar with the word, but in this case, I'm afraid I'm sincere. I do not want to take the risk of trying to have a clandestine affair with you. There is a long enough list of people who know about my trip and stay at your estate as it is. Besides Huw, there's Mrs. Sims, the maids there, not to mention Lord Manderville."

"Derek won't say anything, no one in Essex was told your last name, and only you can speak for your driver, but he seems loyal enough. We won't be discovered."

Her lacy lashes lowered minutely. "It must be nice to always have such assurance life will go your way."

Being born to wealth and title probably did give one a certain confidence that wasn't so much inbred as imposed, but he really didn't want to debate the matter, not with her so deliciously close. The light fragrance of her perfume put his body on full alert and he could see the luscious curves of her breasts framed by the décolletage of her gown. Big tits? No. Perfect firm womanly breasts that fit in his hands and mouth? Yes. When Winston had started speculating over her physical appearance, an all-too-vivid image of her nude body beneath his had come to mind, and at that moment he'd made a decision, unable to help himself, which he was going to have to look at later when in a calmer frame of mind.

When not in full rut, a more civilized wry voice in his mind observed. His growing erection just from being close to her was irrefutable proof his body agreed.

"I am very much hoping *this* evening will improve, true." He held her gaze and patted the seat next to him. "Come sit here."

"I shouldn't." Her response was quiet. "You shouldn't be here."

"You should. We're alone. Your driver will postpone our arrival until I give him a signal. I want to introduce you to the joys of making love in a carriage. It's a bit cramped, I'll concede, but can be done with delightful results."

"I somehow feel quite sure it's an art you've practiced often enough." Despite her dry tone, she did as he asked and moved to take the proffered seat. A soft gasp escaped as he changed his mind and lifted her onto his lap instead. Her tempting bottom nestled against his groin and he hardened further.

Nicholas nuzzled her neck. "You danced tonight. You don't often."

"You watched me?" Her throat arched back to give him greater access, the question soft as a gossamer cloud.

Admitting he hadn't been able to help it seemed as imprudent as sneaking into her carriage. The retreat into the gaming room hadn't helped either. He murmured, "I noticed."

"I noticed you too."

The admission was made in a hushed voice and her eyes sparkled like jewels in the dim light.

So, they watched each other. He didn't want to think
about it too much. It was becoming a distraction in his life
and what he should do is stay away from her until the fever
passed. But instead there he was, stealing a few moments
of her time like some vagabond thief who had nowhere
else to turn.

Which was ridiculous. He had dozens—more—places to
turn. Lady Whitmore had earlier issued a blatant invitation
as they'd waltzed, but he'd been on the floor in the first
place only because he wanted to brush past Caroline.

He'd declined in the most polite way possible.

And instead spent almost an hour sitting in a dark carriage. Waiting.

For this.

"You smell like flowers," he told her, his mouth tracing
the sensitive hollow under her ear as he tried to dismiss his
unsettling thoughts. "Hmm."

"Nicholas—"

"Shh."

He took her mouth in a searing kiss because he didn't
want to talk, to analyze the why and wherefore of his presence, his tongue seeking entrance, finding it, and brushing
hers. Caroline's arms crept around his neck and she leaned
into the embrace, the pliant slender weight of her negligent
in comparison with his much larger frame. At least her fear
was entirely gone, he thought as he explored her mouth with
leisurely heated pleasure, and, from the way she kissed him
back, her willingness not in question.

The carriage rattled along, swaying slightly as they took
a corner, their bodies and mouths together so they moved
as one against the motion. Nicholas realized he was breathless when he lifted his head, his erection now an iron
length that protested the confinement of his tailored
breeches.

Soon.

First he eased the material of her gown off one slim feminine shoulder and pulled it down, lower and lower until a
full, taut breast spilled free. He bent his head and licked

the ripe peak, tasting her nipple, teasing it, making Caroline shift in his arms.

"Oh . . ." A throaty moan rippled out.

It was shadowed secretive pleasure, the gentle sift of her fingers through his hair and the arch of her spine as he suckled her breast bringing deep pure male satisfaction. A bed would be preferable, he thought as he subtly aroused her, easing one hand under her gown and gliding his fingers along a smooth warm inner thigh to find wet tantalizing heat, but he'd take this if it was all he could have.

Maybe she was right. Maybe he was spoiled by his past encounters with his lovers; maybe he did take for granted the risk she'd incur in any involvement because of his cursed notoriety.

And maybe he shouldn't fuck her in a moving carriage simply because he didn't have the self-restraint to accept her refusal.

In the act of lifting her skirts, the soft fabric bunched in his hands and his straining body clamoring for speed, he hesitated. It was an unfortunate moment to have an attack of conscience, but it seemed that was what was happening. He took in a deep shuddering breath. "How many times in our acquaintance am I going to have to beg forgiveness for my arrogant presumption? Do you want this, Caroline?"

She exhaled in a small laugh, her breath warm against his cheek. "Don't I seem enthusiastic?"

"Not when you climbed into the carriage."

"That was in objection to the implications of your presence, not your actual person." She leaned closer and kissed him, their lips softly clinging, her half-bared body rubbing against him. When she drew back, she whispered, "The risk has been taken, so please don't waste it. I've been thinking about you, Nicholas."

"I'm a selfish ass, as the risk is all yours and I didn't give you a choice."

Her hand slipped downward and she touched the bulge between his legs. "Can we debate this in a few minutes, please?"

"You're sure?"

"God, yes, Nicholas . . . hurry."

The fluid power of the man who held her would once have made her feel intimidated and vulnerable, but now Caroline reveled in it as he shifted her easily, unfastened his breeches with swift deftness so his hard cock was free, and grasped her waist.

"Lift your skirts." The rasp of the command indicated his need and she gloried in the idea he wanted her, even if it was only a physical communion. Caroline complied, pulling them above her waist, and she spread her legs as he lifted her up so she was poised above his lean hips. They joined slowly, her hand guiding his rigid length as he lowered her, the sensation spectacular and sinfully reckless in the confines of the moving equipage, surrounded by the city streets.

She felt wicked, but she also felt an odd freedom as she sheathed his erection in her needy body. Straddling his lap, she began to move at his urging, small upward slides and downward motions. Strong hands held her hips and he thrust into her as she rose, obviously impatient but still controlled, their gazes locked as they moved toward a common erotic goal.

Desire soared to new heights, her senses saturated, the rocking motion of the vehicle part of the rhythm of their lovemaking. Nicholas held her, somehow a combination of leashed strength and gentleness, giving as he took with the glitter of fierce desire in his dark seductive eyes. His heady male scent added fuel to the fire already lashing through her body, familiar, evocative of haunting memories of the same beguiling, unforgettable pleasure.

Her lips parted as she began to gasp, trying to stifle an open moan but reaching that place where she no longer cared if Huw heard them, or even if all of London were witness to her abandoned rapture. The pinnacle was there suddenly, white-hot bright and pulsing. She clung to him as the first orgasmic ripples took her prisoner and held her in a vise grip, and she muffled a scream against his fine velvet coat.

In turn, his hands tightened almost painfully and his hips shifted upward with a turbulent surge and she could feel his tall body shudder. Once, twice, and a third jerk as he ejaculated and they hung suspended, fused together in mutual, overwhelming ecstasy.

Half-insensible, Caroline went limp against him, only partially conscious of his mouth against her hair, of the now tender, easy clasp of his arms. They stayed that way, still joined, their breathing gradually slowing. A low laugh eventually rumbled from his chest under her ear. "I believe I'd like nothing more than to ride around in carriages the rest of my life."

"Feel free to invite me to join you." The words were a low mumble, her body so lax against him she felt boneless.

"Don't tempt me. As you may have noticed, self-control isn't my strongest attribute when it comes to you. Suggestions like that won't keep me at bay."

There was an edginess to his soft tone and he moved, just a slight shift, but she felt it acutely.

So far, she had a feeling Derek's idea to prod Nicholas's usual effortless detachment with jealousy seemed to be working, but was it just simple lust? A moment ago it had felt like it, but the way he held her now, cradled against him, suggested otherwise. "You know my reasons for wanting to keep even the suggestion of a passing acquaintance a secret," she said, listening to the strong beat of his heart through the layers of his fashionable clothing.

"Yes."

"But you don't agree."

"I understand. It still doesn't make me happy about it. Obviously."

"Or you wouldn't have contrived to hide in my carriage." That he taken such action made her smile, though it was rash and ill-advised.

"Not my usual way of approaching a lady, I admit."

It was a dash of icy reality to hear him say "usual." It reminded her of what and who he was, and she willed enough strength into her body to sit up. She was still open-legged across his lap with his sex inside her, the froth of her skirts bunched around them. She could feel the material of his breeches against her inner thighs.

"I'm very grateful to you but . . . wary."

In the muted darkness, his sculpted features were a little mysterious and his expression could have meant anything. "Of scandal. Because I'm Rothay."

Why lie? "Yes."

"I'm wary of you too, my chilly Lady Wynn."

Caroline lifted her brows a fraction, hope flaring, her palms suddenly damp against his tailored coat. "How so?"

There was a palpable hesitation.

"Well, my impulse to lurk uninvited in carriages for one." His teeth gleamed white in a slow, lazy smile. "My grand consequence would be compromised should anyone find out. So you see, your secret is very safe with me."

And she realized at that moment he'd dismissed any serious tone to the conversation. He was very, very good at it too.

She smothered her disappointment, reminding herself with cool practicality that he was the most unlikely man on earth to fall to his knees and spout poetic declarations of love so easily. It appeared she'd given him what he wanted and it was more than enough. Incipient lust was assuaged, he was content, and she was a distraction that could be forgotten. If he'd been jealous, it was a passing thing, like a child seeing someone else playing with his favorite toy.

Caroline murmured, "I don't believe I've thanked you for my inventive gift. My butler isn't quite as charmed to have a puppy underfoot, but I must admit I find it vastly entertaining."

"You're welcome. It seemed like an endearing enough creature and you mentioned wanting one."

"It was very thoughtful." She touched his cheek, just a light brush of her fingers.

"Or a calculated bribe, to keep me in your good graces perhaps." The corner of his mouth twitched in amusement.

With the same athletic ease he'd used to place her there, Nicholas lifted her from his lap. Gallantly he offered her his handkerchief to wipe away the residue on her thighs, refastened his breeches, and then rapped three times on the roof of the carriage. In a neutral tone, he said, "I told your driver to drop me off several blocks from your town house. I'll find a hack to take me back to the ball. No one will ever know we were together."

Except *she* would know, she thought in pragmatic despair.

And she'd better face the reality that Lord Manderville could be horribly wrong. When Nicholas had arrived earlier, he'd had a lovely older woman on his arm, their family resemblance so strong she knew even before they were announced, they were mother and son. The arrival of the dowager duchess had shaken Caroline's nerve to proceed with Derek's plan. Melinda Cassat was always a font of gossip and it hadn't taken much prodding to get her friend to reveal the details of the lineage in the Manning family. With Nicholas an only son, the next in line was a distant cousin residing at this time in the colonies. It was important to his family for him to have an heir, and according to Melinda, the closer he got to thirty, the more the hopeful mamas and eager young debutantes became he might make a dynastic marriage.

A barren widow was probably not at all what the elegant duchess had in mind for her handsome, extremely eligible son.

Caroline finished adjusting her clothing and nodded, unable to speak.

If she could ever get him to consider marriage in the first place. The gamble was for high stakes and at long odds. But when they rolled to a halt and he kissed her a lingering farewell before he clambered out of the carriage, she decided since her first venture with the Devilish Duke had turned out so well, this was also worth a try.

Chapter Twenty-one

The name on the card made her feel very real surprise. Annabel frowned, not sure how to interpret the unexpected visit from a woman she barely knew, but nodded, for she could think of no reason on earth to not see Lady Wynn.

On the other hand, she could think of no reason the young widow would call either.

She told the footman who'd brought her the card, "Please show her into the drawing room. I'll be right there."

Thomas was out on some errand and Margaret had gone to the milliner's, so it fell to her to play hostess. She set aside the book she'd been reading and rose, hoping her muslin skirt wasn't too wrinkled because she'd been sitting there for hours, immersed in a novel in which someone else's woes made her forget her own.

A few moments later she entered the formal room, seeing her guest had taken a seat on one of the chairs covered in pale green silk, the shade a foil for her vibrant coloring. Delicately beautiful in a cream-colored day gown embroidered with tiny blue flowers, her lustrous hair caught up in a simple, heavy chignon, Lady Wynn regarded her with those signature long-lashed gray eyes, her cool demeanor typical. "Good afternoon, Miss Reid."

"Good afternoon, my lady."

"Thank you for seeing me."

"Of course. How pleasant of you to drop by."

If Annabel could recall, they'd been introduced once, but

often crossed paths at social events. However, their acquaintance barely qualified in the nodding category and Annabel was mystified over the reason for Lady Wynn's visit.

"I didn't precisely drop by. I came to see you with a specific purpose. I hope you will not find it objectionable."

This was becoming more intriguing by the moment. Annabel sat down opposite her unexpected guest, self-consciously smoothing her rumpled skirt. Only a few years older than she, still Caroline Wynn exuded a sort of smooth, detached composure that made Annabel feel like a schoolgirl. She couldn't help but ask, "Objectionable?"

"I would appreciate if what we are about to discuss would remain between us."

That was an interesting statement.

"If you wish to share something in confidence, I will honor your request." Annabel spoke slowly, with no attempt to hide her surprise. "Though, I admit, I am puzzled. We are not strangers but barely more than that."

What could be described only as a wistful smile curved her visitor's mouth. "No one can have too many friends, and I find I have too few at times. Who can tell? Maybe we will surprise each other. I think we have quite a lot in common, after all."

"We do? How so?"

"Well, for one, we are not far apart in age. Also, both of us are virtually alone in the world in some ways. You due to the death of your parents, and myself since my father ignores my existence. Let's not forget, I married a man I did not love and you are, by all accounts, about to do the same thing."

Put that way, it sounded awful. Annabel felt her reaction to such blunt observation in the way her spine stiffened and her mouth grew tight. "How on earth can you know how I feel about Lord Hyatt?"

Caroline Wynn looked unfazed at the acid in her tone. "I don't. That's why I came here to talk to you."

To say Annabel was confused was an understatement.

"With apology, my lady, I cannot see why you'd be concerned."

An auburn brow inched upward. "I was in a terrible marriage. I really wouldn't wish the state on anyone."

"Nothing about Alfred is terrible." *Except that passionless kiss, of course,* an insidious voice whispered.

"I agree. He's a nice man as far as I can tell." Lady Wynn gave a small, telling sigh, little more than a breath. "But do you love him?"

No one had asked her that. *No one.* Not her guardian, not Margaret, not even Alfred himself. It shook her, and Annabel was already shaken enough when she thought about her upcoming nuptials, thanks to Derek. Upon her life, she couldn't think of how to respond to the question she never expected to be asked.

Beautiful silver eyes glimmered with what looked like understanding as the silence lengthened. Finally, Lady Wynn murmured, "I see."

Annabel swallowed convulsively. "He's kind."

"He does appear to be that way."

She hated to hear the agreement made with a touch of sympathy. "And generous."

"I'm sure."

"And suitable." Oh drat, had she really, really used that horrible word, flinging it out there as if it were something admirable?

"He is that." Caroline Wynn smiled faintly.

Why was this happening now? Why had some woman she didn't even know suddenly appeared to address her most telling doubts? It was the worst timing possible.

Or maybe the most fortuitous considering her lingering dilemma.

There was no possible way she could sit still any longer. Annabel got up and walked across the room. She leaned an arm on the pianoforte and took in a long, calming breath. "Can I please ask why you feel this is any of your business at all?"

Lady Wynn hesitated and then squared her shoulders.

"Lord Manderville asked me to speak with you on his behalf."

Derek.

Damn him.

Annabel turned in slow wooden motion like a puppet and stared at her guest. Of course. Lady Wynn was exquisite with all that gleaming red-brown hair and her voluptuous figure, slender but curvaceous, temptation incarnate for a randy male like the lascivious Earl of Manderville. She said heatedly, "He sent you here to plead his case?"

"Have I pleaded?"

Well, Lady Wynn had a point; she hadn't, but still Annabel felt outraged.

And jealous. Very jealous in a way that involved her soul, her mind, and very definitely the pit of her stomach. There a small black ball sat, heavy as lead. She steadied herself. "I have never heard any whispers attached to your name, madam, but I can only assume what kind of friend Derek Drake might be to you. You are desirable and female, and that says it all."

Composed and still looking at her in that unnerving empathetic way, Lady Wynn shook her head. "He hasn't as much as touched my hand. What's more, he hasn't even attempted."

The situation was getting more bewildering by the moment. "Then how could you be friends with him?"

A becoming blush crossed the perfect features of the woman across the room. "It's rather a complicated story, but the short of it is I think he is actually a very decent man and, beyond a doubt, more than a little in love with you. Hence my presence here. Yes, he wished for me to speak with you because by his own admission his usual charm has no effect."

"That is because you are wrong. He is an appalling blackguard with the morals of an alley cat."

But the protest wasn't said with enough conviction. Annabel could still see him, standing there in her bedroom, and hear that poignant declaration. *I love you. . . .*

She wanted to believe it, and it was heaven and hell at the same time to feel that flicker of hope it might be true. Either way her doubts about marrying Alfred now were very real, even without the observations of her unexpected guest.

"I understand the earl's reputation gives you pause. It tells me you are not just interested in his looks, title, and wealth. He isn't perfect, but sometimes those are the very rogues we fall in love with."

Annabel asked in a voice that wasn't quite steady, "Do you speak from experience, Lady Wynn?"

The young woman standing a few paces away had an almost accusing look on her pretty face, her blue eyes dark and wide, her small hands clenched into fists at her sides.

It had taken quite a bit of resolve to walk through the door of the Drake town house, and it would be even harder to admit to her current state of infatuation with Nicholas Manning. However, Caroline had promised Derek to help him, and from the expression on the face of Annabel Reid, he was completely right about her feelings for him. The posture of her body indicated a certain vulnerability in her poignant distress, and she had flared into defensive anger at just the mention of Lord Manderville's name.

He was right. Miss Reid was not at all indifferent. From the high spots on her cheeks, she was quite the opposite.

"Yes, I do." Caroline feigned a nonchalance she didn't feel. "But I am hardly here to talk about my folly, but yours instead. Tell me, do you think you can marry Lord Hyatt and not regret the decision?"

"If I didn't think he was a sensible choice, I would not have accepted his proposal."

"Forgive me, but the word 'sensible' lacks any resemblance to a romantic ideal."

Soft lips compressed into a hard line. "I had a romantic ideal once, Lady Wynn, and found out it was based on a fable, a myth I'd created in my own foolish mind. Since it is obvious Derek has spoken to you about me, you might already know I fancied myself in love with him at one time. His looks and charm turned my head and I hadn't even had my coming-out yet, so I was particularly susceptible. I dreamed one day he might return my feelings. I knew of his reputation, but somehow it didn't matter. Like a fool, I fantasized that for me he would change."

Caroline couldn't help but murmur, "I believe I understand perfectly."

Annabel shook her head, some distant memory making her eyes shimmer, and she blinked rapidly a few times. "I was very wrong."

"He told me his version of the story and I must admit I believe he's sincere in his regret over both hurting you and losing your regard." Lord Manderville had not spared himself in the brief recital, citing his own behavior as insensitive and selfish. Caroline could only guess at what it cost him in male pride to be so blunt about his feelings to a virtual stranger, but she felt he was being so candid because he was truly desperate for her help. The incident in the carriage with Nicholas seemed to prove that the earl was doing his part, so Caroline wanted to return the favor. Even if she hadn't promised him, the bleak look on Annabel Reid's face would have moved her.

She knew all too well how Annabel was feeling.

The young woman standing by the polished pianoforte smoothed a trembling hand on her skirt in an absent gesture, her gaze very direct. "Yes, he did hurt me, and yes, he lost my regard."

"And you believe Lord Hyatt can mend your broken heart?"

The question hung there in the quiet of the room.

The silence was the answer.

With dignity, Annabel finally said, "I believe he will treat me well, give me children, and we will get along together. He isn't in love with me either, as far as I can tell, and actually, it is a relief. It means we want the exact same thing out of our marriage. Companionship and a family."

"What about passion? What if there are no children? I can

say with some measure of authority there is no guarantee. Then it will be just the two of you . . . forever."

"We are friends." The protest was swift, but something flickered in the other woman's eyes.

Doubt? It might be.

"Which is pleasant, I agree, but hardly enough." Not at all used to discussing her feelings, much less something as private as what she'd shared with Nicholas, nonetheless Caroline braced herself to be frank. After all, she'd arrived uninvited and presumed to discuss something very personal. "Though I have never told anyone the truth about my own marriage, I am willing to do so with you. I know I was woefully uninformed over what to expect and the results were disastrous. Our circumstances aren't identical, but there is enough similarity I feel it might help you, regardless of the decision you make over Lord Manderville. However, if your mind is firmly made up, I will take my leave."

For a moment Annabel appeared to hold an inner debate, but then she came back and sat back down across from her on a brocade settee. "I am not sure," she confessed in a voice that held a faint wobble, "exactly why I want to hear what you have to say, but I do."

Perhaps it was the coward in her, but Caroline had half hoped to be dismissed so she wouldn't have to speak about something she'd done her best to forget. She nodded and glanced away, taking a moment to gather her composure. Clearing her throat, she looked back and smiled in wry acknowledgment. "This might be embarrassing for both of us, but I will do my best. Let me start with the simple statement that intimacy between a man and a woman can be many things. The wrong man can make it a shocking and awful experience, and the right one can make it more pleasurable than you could ever imagine. I hope you will not judge me too harshly when I tell you I've experienced both, as it is common knowledge I have only been married once."

Annabel regarded her with those very lovely dark blue eyes. "If your husband was the wrong man, I would hardly blame you for seeking solace elsewhere, my lady."

"My husband, quite frankly, was a terrible man, and a woman is never more vulnerable than when submitting to the sexual needs of a male. Yes, we know they tend to be taller than we are, and are built differently, but as sheltered young ladies, we are not quite aware of how much stronger they are. We are also not aware—or I wasn't—of the actual mechanics of the act itself. If you are like I was, you must have wondered, but it is this great mystery, kept from us because it is indelicate to discuss."

A soft flush had come into Annabel's smooth cheeks. "Even Margaret won't say much about it to me. She vows to explain before the wedding."

Though she was only a few years older, Caroline felt vastly more sophisticated and the cost of her education had been dear. "Make sure she does, or feel free to ask me. A little knowledge can help a great deal when initiated to something so . . . personal. My point now is not to explain the process in anatomical detail, but to illustrate the emotional trust involved. As a leap of faith it is a huge one. Can you imagine lying naked next to Lord Hyatt for the rest of your life? Can you imagine having him touch you everywhere, even the most intimate of places? Do you want to be held in his arms, taste his kiss, or are your visions more of him passing the rack of toast at the breakfast table?"

"I have considered my wifely duty, of course." Annabel looked pinker with each passing moment.

"Duty?" The deft expertise of Nicholas's touch came to mind, and the ripe, overpowering splendor it evoked. The way she trembled with him, the feel of his need inside her, the impetuous pleasure of his mouth against her skin. Caroline raised her brows. "It should have nothing to do with duty or you are cheating yourself."

Somewhere she'd touched a nerve, for Annabel said defensively, "Most marriages in society are not based on love but practicality."

"Indeed they are. And look at the results. Both husbands and wives stray, trying to find what they don't have within their bedroom walls. How do you think Lord Manderville and the Duke of Rothay built their formidable reputations for vice? Not by seducing eligible young women. That is for certain or they would have been dragged to the altar long ago. They were even able to make their outrageous bet and have the *haut ton* think it both amusing and intriguing."

The woman across from her stared at the patterned carpet, her face shuttered. "Derek claims the bet was made in a drunken moment because of my engagement."

"I have confirmation he is telling the truth."

Almost as soon as she said the words, she regretted it. Annabel was no fool and her gaze sharpened as she looked up. "From the duke?"

Yes, she'd definitely said too much. Hopefully Miss Reid was trustworthy, but Caroline had just associated herself with both men. She stifled the urge to grimace and tried to emulate her best image of the cool unapproachable widow. "The source doesn't matter. I believe him. The question is, do you? Derek Drake claims to love you, and with his title and fortune he is hardly an ineligible man, not to mention you just told me you don't have deep feelings for Lord Hyatt."

Annabel made a helpless gesture with her hand. "Am I supposed to sever my engagement on the faint chance Derek is really serious about this? Let's not forget my conviction he would never be faithful, even if he was sincere. What does a man like him know about love?"

"I would think"—Caroline chose her words carefully, considering her own disquiet on the subject—"he would most definitely know the difference. Between his usual detachment and his vast experience with it, surely he of all people would recognize it is different with you."

"Vast experience is right," Annabel muttered, though her face was no longer set in a militant expression of anger and denial but more a pensive look of near despair. "Tell me, Lady Wynn, if you were in my place, would you believe him? Would you risk your entire future and throw away a chance at a safe and secure marriage with a nice man to hinge your hopes on a known libertine? Just recently all of London was agog as his name was bandied about with that of a known adulteress in an extremely scandalous divorce. His claim to innocence might or might not be true."

Nicholas despised his notoriety also, and had mentioned how much of it was spun out of thin air. Caroline shook her head. "Gossip is unreliable and there is no evidence the allegation is true."

Annabel looked unmoved except for the quiver of her mouth. "Fine, I concede that, but even if he thinks he means what he says about his feelings for me, who is to say it will last?"

The argument was valid. Caroline couldn't deny it.

Annabel went on, almost as if talking to herself. "He feels guilty about me. He's admitted as much. So now he has conjured up a way to fix it and excuse himself from what happened before. Well, I'm not sure I'm willing to forgive or forget, and his capacity for constant love is still a very real question in my mind."

At least there was a glimmer of speculation in the lovely Miss Reid's voice.

"I know." Caroline understood very well. She was all too cognizant of the ramifications of being in love with someone with a weighty reputation like Manderville. The Duke of Rothay hadn't even declared deeper feelings for her, so she was one step behind.

For a moment they just looked at each other and seemed to draw a common breath of unique sisterhood.

Annabel smiled, a tentative offering. "Though I am not sure about how I feel about your visit, Lady Wynn, would you like a glass of sherry?"

"I'd love one and please, call me Caroline."

Dearest Annie:

Am I entitled even to ask you to forgive me for my actions at Manderville Hall a few months ago? I have pondered the question at length and cannot give myself an answer. All I know is I wish I could erase the memory of how you looked when you left the conservatory that evening. If I could eradicate the act that caused it, rest assured I would. I assume full responsibility. After all, I am older, but apparently no wisdom has come with those added years.

Even more compelling is my recollection of our kiss. Perhaps I should apologize for it, but in all honesty I cannot. I am not sorry it happened, I am only sorry for my ungentlemanly conduct afterward. Please accept my deepest apologies.

I cannot tell you how I yearn to see you smile at me again.
Yours in complete sincerity,
Derek Drake, the sixth Earl of Manderville
Dated this day, November 21st, 1811

Annabel let the piece of vellum slip through her fingers, her hands shaking. She watched the letter drift to the floor and settle there as she swallowed the lump in her throat.

What might have happened had she read this when it arrived? The point was moot, because she had still been in a shocked state of disillusionment, but surely it was significant she hadn't thrown it away. Could part of all this be her fault? After all, Derek hadn't asked to become her mythical knight, the gallant prince of her dreams, the handsome hero of every girlish fantasy. He was just a man, and therefore fallible.

He isn't perfect, but sometimes those are the very rogues we fall in love with. . . .

She had built a picture of him that wasn't quite real, and when he didn't conform, it had shattered her world. He wasn't exactly without fault, she reminded herself, thinking of the countess in his arms, but then again, maybe it wasn't *entirely* his fault either.

The difference was, he had apologized.

She hadn't.

Chapter Twenty-two

The stuffy meeting room was less than ideal, and Derek felt restive and shifted in his chair. The session had gone on interminably and he was beginning to get a headache. Not until the yawning in the chamber took on epidemic proportions did Lord Norton seem to realize how long he'd been droning on and he finally wound down without ever having made a valid point.

If the alacrity with which the peers exited the House of Lords was any indication, Derek hadn't been the only one bored to near tears. It was a relief to step out into the afternoon sunshine.

There had been a short note from Lady Wynn about her talk with Annabel a few days ago that expressed her hope it had gone well and she had done her best. Like some inexperienced schoolboy, Derek had paced around his study that afternoon, and later sat restlessly through a very terrible opera in which he had no interest. The only redeeming part of the evening had been that the woman he loved *hadn't* appeared on the arm of her fiancé. At least he hadn't been forced to sit there and studiously avoid looking at them. One small grace in a situation that seemed utterly set against him.

So now Derek had two choices. He could don his ridiculous costume and visit Caroline in the wee hours to beg for details on their conversation, or he could crawl into Annabel's bedroom again and ask her.

Neither held much appeal. Both ideas had been rash the first time.

Derek was a man who was never rash. That is, unless he was kissing young innocent ladies in libraries or invading their bedrooms to give unwanted and unreciprocated declarations of love.

Well, maybe he *was* rash now and again.

Damn.

It was clear he was going to have to *assume* it went well. But why should he think it did? No reason at all. Annabel had coldly dismissed him.

Well, no, she hadn't. Not coldly. She'd dismissed him with the shimmering path of an unwanted tear on her cheek, and her voice hadn't sounded in the least like her own.

It gave him hope. Maybe it was false hope, but he didn't wish to give up. If this failed—if whatever Caroline had said to Annabel made no impression because he'd ruined things to the point of no return—he still intended to help Nicholas.

There was no way through the fire without getting burned a little.

Rothay House was an impressive mansion in Mayfair on Grosvenor Square with all the requisite galleries and palatial doorways, and a stone facade worthy of a royal residence. He instructed his driver to wait and climbed the stairs, hopeful that Nicholas had been just as anxious to get home after the debate as he had himself. The duke was in, he was informed by the stiffly formal butler, and if his lordship cared to wait in the study as usual . . .

Yes, Derek did. He helped himself to a drink too, before he settled into the usual chair by the fireplace. The room smelled familiar, of whiskey and old books.

"Not that it isn't pleasant always to see you, but didn't we just spend an excruciating afternoon together?" Nicholas entered and closed the door behind him. "If you came here to complain about Lord Norton's point, I'm going to have to confess I lost sight of it halfway through his speech."

Derek laughed and shook his head. "No, not for that.

Don't ask me either. When the prime minister drifts off and begins to snore, let's be frank, you've lost your audience."

"True." Nicholas settled in behind the desk, long legs extended casually, his face unreadable. "So I guess politics do not play a role in this visit."

"No. Caroline and I will leave Monday. I've secured a room at a secluded inn near Aylesbury. Not far, but not too close, and just right for a discreet rendezvous. Everything is in place."

The Duke of Rothay wasn't a legend without reason. He remained relaxed in his chair, but his dark eyes held a certain glitter that Derek was sure he recognized. There was a small, almost infinitesimal pause. "Then may the best man win."

"That has been our intention all along, hasn't it?"

Derek heard the clash of an imaginary sword, the jar of metal on metal almost audible in the quiet of the venerable room.

"*Exactly* our intention." Nicholas sounded as cool as ever. "You have no objection?"

"Why would I with no claim on the lady?"

Why indeed? The question of the day. Derek wasn't fooled. Or at least he hoped not. "You seemed a bit involved after your return."

It was a neutral statement. Nicholas flicked a glance at the window. "As you know, the term *involvement* is ambiguous. I felt a little involved. It passed."

Was it true? No, it wasn't. If so, his friend wouldn't be so carefully nonchalant. Helena's perfidy had left some permanent scars. Derek understood, but he recalled the look on Caroline's face when he asked her if her feelings were engaged. He also remembered Nick's terse instruction that afternoon at White's.

Be careful with her. . . .

"Once this is over, we at least won't have to deal with this ludicrous bet any longer," Derek said in a musing, introspective voice. "It was a daft idea to begin with, but the attention we've received has made going out in society downright uncomfortable."

"Quite so."

"After this next week, it will be settled."

"You'll find her enchanting." Nicholas shifted again, as if he couldn't get quite comfortable.

Stubborn idiot.

"I imagine I will." Derek took a casual sip from his glass.

Nicholas opened his mouth to say something else, but snapped it shut and remained silent. He tapped his fingers on the desktop in a restless gesture, and then stopped that also, as if he realized the movement betrayed his feelings.

An objection? A request to call it all off? Derek understood to an excruciating degree the measure of Nicholas's inner war. It was a simple equation. If Nick called off the wager, it would be a declaration of his deeper feelings for Caroline Wynn.

Satisfied all had gone according to plan, Derek got to his feet. "Just thought I'd drop by and let you know we'd made our arrangements. The two of you have been back for almost two weeks now, right?"

"Eleven days." Nicholas caught the precision of his answer. "Or so," he amended.

Derek just barely managed to choke back a laugh. It wasn't that he enjoyed the torture his friend was going through, but he felt a sympathetic male understanding that he knew Nicholas wouldn't appreciate until he came to terms with it himself.

"So I suppose we'll see what the lady has to say when this is all over, then."

That ought to plunge the dagger deep.

"I suppose."

"Better watch out, Nick—she'll have forgotten you by that first night."

His friend didn't bat an eye. But neither did he give his usual quick repartee.

Derek left, reflecting that at least the seeds were planted. The question was, would they bear fruit?

The room was filled with bolts of fabric, chattering assistants, and the overpowering smell of the modiste's gardenia perfume. One dark-haired girl knelt at her feet, adjusting the hem of her gown.

Annabel just stood rigid, her back straight, her hands laced together, misery like a lump in her throat.

"It's quite glorious, Madame DuShane." Margaret gave the hovering woman a smile of approval. "You'll be an angel, Annabel."

Did she have to use the word *angel*? It evoked images of a man with dark gold hair who was laughingly christened that epithet, though hardly for his saintly pastimes. A man with eyes so blue, looking into them was like gazing into a crystalline sea, and a smile so mesmerizing, no female within his range was immune to its power.

Should she really be standing there in her wedding dress and thinking about Derek Drake?

But what choice did she have? Annabel finally forced herself to turn and look in the long mirror. Yes, it was a lovely creation, the ice blue underskirt done in satin, a lace overlay giving an ethereal effect. It tucked close at the waist and then shaped upward to a modest bodice, showing just a hint of the top curve of her breasts. Small pearls had been sewn along the cap sleeves and the neckline, the shimmer catching the light.

The dress was stunning.

She, however, looked awful in comparison. She was ghostly pale, the faintest hint of shadows under her eyes from lack of sleep, and her mouth trembled as she fought an unbearable urge to burst into tears.

Why had she read that letter?

Margaret stepped behind her, reflected in the glass. "Annabel?"

"I can't do it."

The words came out only as a thin whisper. Margaret's mouth parted and a flicker of alarm crossed her face. "My dear child, I—"

"I can't marry Alfred." Annabel whirled back around. "I'm sorry. . . . I am so sorry. . . ."

Madame DuShane was a disheveled-looking woman with

a sharp chin and small black eyes. Her hands fluttered up in a dramatic gesture. "It is natural to be nervous, no? All brides feel so. It will pass. You are a vision in this gown. He will fall on his knees with love for you."

The flawed logic that a piece of clothing could inspire an emotion she was pretty sure Alfred did not feel for her in the first place gave Annabel the macabre urge to laugh, but she didn't. Instead her hands fisted at her sides and she shook her head. "It isn't nerves, madame. The dress is very beautiful, but I doubt I'm going to need it."

Margaret, realizing they were in a public venue, said quickly, "Darling, why don't we have one of the girls help you out of the gown and dress. We can discuss this at home and then return for a last fitting at some other time."

With swift efficiency Annabel undressed, replacing the wedding gown with her yellow day dress—the one she'd chosen because she hoped the cheery color would lighten her spirits—and followed Margaret out of the shop to the waiting carriage. They had planned on making several other stops, but Margaret gave the driver instructions to take them back home.

Annabel braced herself for a well-deserved lecture, given in Margaret's understated and elegant way. Instead, the woman who'd raised Annabel like she was her own simply lifted her brows once the carriage was in motion. "Madame DuShane is a wonderful seamstress but also a terrible gossip. I think once we are home, you need to speak to Thomas right away so Lord Hyatt can be informed before he hears it from someone else. He's a nice man and he is about to be jilted. The less humiliating you make it for him, the better."

Margaret was right, of course. Lord, why did this have to be so complicated? Why couldn't she just love *him*, not someone else?

"You aren't surprised?"

"Dearest Annabel, I have eyes. Did I not ask you after the last fitting if you still wished to go through with the wedding?"

"Yes," she admitted on a sigh. The tears were still there,

stinging behind her lids. What else had Margaret noticed? The kindly sympathy in the older woman's eyes further flustered her.

"Besides, when a potential bride turns a certain shade of green every time she tries on her wedding gown, something is markedly wrong."

"I know."

"I am just glad you came to this realization before the wedding and not the day after."

"Thanks to Lady Wynn." Annabel could recall clearly the firm conviction in the young widow's voice as she spoke of the trap of a loveless marriage. It might be a romantic view, especially in the upper class, where arranged unions were commonplace, but the lady seemed to speak from bitter experience.

"Lady Wynn? An odd mentor. I was unaware you were friends."

If she weren't so off-balance from her hesitancy in settling into a firm decision to sever her engagement, Annabel would never have blurted it out, but she said, "We weren't particularly, not before the other day. She is a friend of Derek's."

They rocked along, Margaret's expression reflecting skepticism. "I would normally not discuss such a subject with you, but I doubt that's true. I haven't heard a whisper."

"Not his mistress." Annabel was well past worrying about whether the subject matter was considered appropriate for her ears. She'd aged a decade in the past few weeks. "She stated quite frankly he'd never approached her in an amorous way."

"Good heavens," Margaret muttered. "What an interesting conversation that must have been. I am puzzled at her motivations but not ungrateful. I have been worried about you. Thomas is concerned as well."

Her hands clenched in her lap, Annabel stared at the floor. "You are, as always, too good to me."

"Nonsense. In every sense of the word except for your actual birth, you are our child." Then Margaret added in a tentative tone, "We are equally as fond of Derek. It is always a trial to judge how much one should meddle in the lives of others. I have been trying to let you two figure this out for yourselves. It was not easy to do so, I have to tell you."

So . . . they knew. Of her infatuation, of his supposed feelings—and it seemed logical to assume they were aware of the disillusionment she felt as well.

They knew of her shattered heart. How did she think she'd been able to hide it?

"How does one trust a man with his reputation?" Annabel asked with a horrible tremor in her voice. "And I pray at this moment you do not give me a reformed-rakes speech, for I cannot answer for a ladylike response. This is the same man who recently made an outrageous gamble based on his . . . well . . ."

She blushed. Even though she might have had a few—well, an embarrassing amount of—fantasies about what it would be like to be held in his arms, it was another thing to talk about it.

Margaret seemed to understand. "Young men—or for that matter all men—are not always the most prudent of creatures."

"An understatement," Annabel grumbled.

Her companion gave her a pointed look. "Rather like rash young ladies who agree to marry someone they have less-than-deep feelings for just to prove an absurd point?"

"It is hardly the same."

"Tell me how."

Given her behavior at the dressmaker's, how could she argue? Annabel whispered, "What do I do now?"

Margaret leaned forward and patted her hands, still tightly wound together in her lap. "Love is a miraculous thing, my dear child. Do not underestimate it."

Chapter Twenty-three

A long fingernail trailed down his bare chest, making him pry open his eyes. Nicholas blinked, started to sit up, then groaned and fell back. "Good God, what time is it?"

"Eleven, darling."

"Damnation, is it really?"

Elaine Fields laughed in a low musical sound. "Yes, really. Tell me, how much do you remember about last night?"

He looked at the woman sitting on the edge of the bed—her bed, for God's sake. The room was resplendently pink. Pink curtains, pink hangings, pink wallpaper, it even smelled pink if such a thing were possible. The day must be sunny, because hot blocks of light lay across the rug. His head hurt and his mouth felt dry and unpleasant. After a moment, he admitted, "Not too much."

Elaine arched one delicate, finely plucked brow. She was a luscious redhead with opulent curves, a decade his senior, and though they'd had a brief, very casual affair years ago, they had managed to stay friends. When her elderly husband died and left her in a financial battle with creditors, he'd used his influence to help her stave off their high-handed, greedy tactics. Being the Duke of Rothay had its compensations now and again.

There were downfalls also, if you considered how Caroline wouldn't even be seen speaking to him.

Elaine murmured, "I'm not surprised. Rarely have I seen you truly foxed, Nicky. I should have realized it when you arrived, and forgone offering you more brandy. I suspect you'll feel the consequences all day."

He had the ominous feeling she was right. What the hell had happened the night before? How had he ended up with his former lover? He'd gone to a small gathering, heard some dreadful chit desecrate Bach on the pianoforte, and then . . . was it Manderville who suggested they haunt one of their favorite gambling hells? It might have been him—he just couldn't recall.

Didn't he know better than to overindulge with Derek, of all people?

"I can only pray you're wrong," he said in cynical resignation. "Please tell me I wasn't too boorish."

"Not at all. I've never had such an interesting conversation in my life."

"Conversation?" As he said it, he realized two things. The first was though he was bare-chested, he still wore his breeches. Someone thoughtful had removed his boots, thank God, since he doubted he'd been sensible enough to take them off himself. The second was that she'd brought tea and Nicholas had never been so grateful to see anything in his life as the tray and steaming pot.

She noticed the direction of his attention and moved with a small smile to pour him a cup. "You were very philosophical, darling."

With effort he levered himself up to a half-sitting position and accepted her offering with gratitude. After a blissful sip, he muttered, "All right, go ahead, what did I say?"

Dressed in bronze-colored silk with fine white lace at the bodice and cuffs, with just a slight smattering of freckles across her nose, Elaine sat back a little and regarded him in open amusement that sparked a glimmer of alarm. "You wanted to have a deep, meaningful discussion about a subject I didn't think you ever contemplated."

Love.

She didn't even have to say it.

"I was drunk." His excuse sounded like the protest of a petulant child.

"Yes, indeed, you were. You must have been, because you told me her name. I admit I had a hard time believing it at first."

Devil take it, he'd broken his word to Caroline. His head ached worse than ever, though he knew he could trust Elaine to be discreet.

She went on with a serene laugh. "You needn't look so stricken. I won't say anything about your unusual involvement with Lady Wynn."

He was an ass. A drunken ass who betrayed confidences. It did not improve his mood to realize it.

"Thank you. And I suppose I should also thank you for putting up with my liquor-induced ramblings as well. My apologies."

"No need. And were they?" Elaine patted his knee.

"What?" He drank more tea, feeling a little less queasy.

"Just the ramblings of a man who had overindulged? You seemed shockingly sincere."

"Sincere in what way?" His question was cautious. Who knew what he'd said? How he'd ended up in the pink hell of her bedroom was even a mystery.

"That you think you've fallen in love with the beautiful cool widow of the late Lord Wynn."

He really *had* been drunk. "I said that?"

Elaine nodded, a slight smile hovering on her mouth. "More than that, you meant it."

"Brandy is a catalyst for stupidity."

"Yes, indeed, but it is also a truth serum." She sat back a little and gazed at him with open speculation. "Are you really going to allow her to go off with Manderville for a week if you are so opposed to the idea? Why don't you simply tell her the truth?"

So, the perfidy was complete. He'd not only revealed the truth about their time together in Essex; he'd confessed about the wager itself and Caroline's part in it. *Bloody fucking hell.*

Even though it was scalding hot, he took an overlarge mouthful of tea. It burned all the way down until it hit his unsettled stomach. "If I could figure out the truth, maybe I would."

"The truth? That's your problem, darling Nicky. You *have* figured it out."

Former mistresses turned confidants turned philosophers were not easy to handle when one's head felt like a ball of lead. He sipped more of the steaming liquid in his cup and struggled to repair whatever damage he'd already done. "Please, Elaine, I'm out of my depth. She's different, I admit it. She captured my attention, not to mention we seemed to have a certain communion in bed. However, she doesn't want to be openly associated with me and destroy her respectability, and who can blame her? Unless I offer marriage, it's over."

Silence.

Elaine simply looked at him.

Had he really just said *marriage*?

Yes, he had.

Damnation.

His mouth tightened. "She isn't *interested* in getting married again. She made it quite clear."

"The woman in question is young and sheltered. Your ramblings about her husband tell me she had a horrific experience, but her agreement to go with you to Essex in the first place shows she isn't resigned to forever avoiding males. From the sound of things, you changed her mind in a way only you can, darling. Didn't the two of you get along . . . famously?"

"It will be infamously if anyone finds out." His temple throbbed and he rubbed it. "And who knows? Maybe she'll like Derek just as well."

It was torture to picture them together and he could feel his face tighten into an involuntary scowl.

Elaine didn't miss it. She asked gently, "Would you like to hear the advice I gave you last night now that you are in a condition to remember it?"

His smile was rueful and heartfelt. "Since I had the discourtesy to barge in on you uninvited, drank myself into a stupor, and slept in your bed, I suppose it would be churlish to refuse."

"You need to put Helena behind you once and for all."

The smile vanished.

Now, *that* name was hardly something he wanted to hear while his head was pounding like a snare drum at the front of a French column. "You," he said with what he hoped sounded like calm dismissal, "place entirely too much emphasis on something I've all but forgotten."

"Somehow I doubt it. I watched it happen, remember? It's why you ended up in my bed, short-lived as that was. After it was over, you suddenly became the Devilish Duke, casual seduction taking the place of what I know from memory was a much more open and less cynical approach to life."

"I was stupid then and apparently haven't improved all that much." He drained his tea and considered one of the scones on the tray but decided against it. Just the mention of Helena's name had that effect on him. The queasy feeling in his stomach wasn't entirely due to the excess of the night before.

"She betrayed you."

Yes, indeed that was the truth. Helena had captured his youthful passion and then shattered his faith in love. She was also a widow—a very attractive one—and she'd lured him with both sexual provocation and the pathos of her supposed plight as a defenseless woman all alone.

Only she hadn't been lonely. He'd found that out in a way that shook his world.

It was a valuable lesson. Vulnerable beautiful ladies were likely to bring you nothing but grief. So . . . enter another tempting widow with an untapped potential for passion and wounded trust, and there he was again, acting like a green boy despite his experience.

No. Caroline was nothing like Helena. He was sure of it. Almost.

"We needn't discuss this." Nicholas levered himself up and swung his legs over the side of the bed. "Where the devil are my boots?"

"Maybe *we* needn't discuss it, but maybe you should talk to *her* about it."

"I haven't even known her a month."

A ghost of a smile touched Elaine's mouth. She moved to retrieve items he sought with her usual languid grace, plucking the discarded boots from the floor. "I think it is a good sign it took so little time to have your feelings so engaged. She sounds perfect for you, if you wish my opinion."

"I don't," he grunted, and accepted a boot.

Good God, his head hurt.

"You did last night."

He glanced up in the act of tugging his boot over his foot. "When I marry, it will be strictly because of duty. I can hardly choose a woman who not only has made it clear she has no interest in a second such arrangement but who also by all appearances is infertile. I have a small lustful obsession that will pass. It always does."

Elaine looked at him with troubled eyes, her expression solemn. She said softly, "I fear very much you are letting Helena make a fool of you for the second time."

This had better work.

Caroline alighted from the carriage and self-consciously glanced around, seeing nothing but a long, quiet street and thatched roofs, the tame setting incongruous with the nature of the rendezvous. It might not be the most notorious tryst in all the history of England, but it was the current talk of society to be sure.

The inn itself was small and unassuming, with a plain front and a somewhat lopsided sign, faded from sunlight and weather. It hardly looked like the place where one of society's most renowned lovers would plan a seduction.

Huw, as usual, said nothing but merely escorted her into the establishment, his demeanor as reserved as ever. When he turned to leave, however, he halted and swung back around. "My lady?"

Caroline had been surveying the modest taproom, nothing but wooden floors and plain tables. It was attractive because though it was simple, it did have a quaint quality and thankfully was clean. She lifted her brows. "Yes?"

"Are you quite certain you wish to do this?"

Her gaze turned into a stare as she looked at the young man. His skin had taken on a dusky color.

Of course. Huw knew about the wager and her part in it. He had stayed in the servants' quarters at Tenterden Manor during her five days with Nicholas—he must have easily guessed. Huw stood there with his hat in his hand, a light coating of dust on his uniform from the drive. His hair was dark and curly and framed a face with an expression that was a mixture of embarrassment and concern.

It was touching.

Still, she tried to prevaricate. Faintly, she asked, "Do what?"

"It isn't my place to say, madam, but the duke . . . well, he wouldn't be pleased you're here, if you ask me."

Since this was the same young man who had driven them around London while they made love in her carriage, she couldn't help but blush. But still she bristled a little at the assumption Rothay had any say over what she did. After all, the man had made no declaration of feeling for her whatsoever.

He wanted her, which was something else.

She wished for more. Yes, she did, or she wouldn't be now meeting Lord Manderville at some unprepossessing country inn.

Servants knew everything. It was a point she often forgot because in the past there was nothing about her to know.

Caroline smiled ruefully. "Why do you think I am here in the first place? I am hoping His Grace doesn't like it at all."

Huw's face broke into a tentative smile. "I see."

The man actually looked relieved. Such was Rothay's compelling charm. She remembered the two men chatting about horses once or twice in her hearing back at the country estate. It had impressed her he addressed the Welsh lad with the same easy camaraderie as anyone else.

Huw liked him. She liked him too. She liked him too much for her peace of mind. Nicholas was infinitely likable.

That was not in question. Too many women could testify to his magnetic allure.

Whatever she might have said next was silenced by the entrance of the very man she waited for. Well, that wasn't accurate. She was expecting Lord Manderville. She waited—and hoped—for Nicholas.

Derek looked dashing as ever even dressed less formally than his usual style, his cravat simple white linen, his coat draped over his arm instead of spanning his shoulders. His hair was boyishly tousled and his blue eyes were alight. A smile graced his aristocratic features. He inclined his head politely at Huw and bowed to her. "My lady."

She nodded at her young driver in dismissal, touched admittedly by his protectiveness. "Thank you, Huw."

He hesitated for a moment and then left.

She turned to the earl. "I see we arrived at about the same time, my lord."

The innkeeper hadn't missed the aspect of a liveried driver or the way the two of them addressed each other. He was a rotund man with a bald crown, a florid face, and a nose with a reddish hue that indicated perhaps he imbibed quite a bit of ale himself. He hurried forward.

Derek took her hand and gave her fingers a small squeeze. One eyebrow went up in a haughty arch as he addressed the proprietor. "We'll be staying a few days. My correspondence should have reached you last week."

"Our finest room, yes indeed, milord." The man wiped his perspiring face with a handkerchief, shoved the cloth back in his pocket, and led them to a small flight of stairs.

They followed, Caroline conscious of the earl's light grip, aware that something about him was different. She didn't know him well, but even she could sense it.

They entered an attractive room with half-timbered walls, a large bed with a patterned quilt in various shades of blue and green, and two small windows that overlooked a stream bordered by a meadow full of grazing sheep. A small back garden full of vegetables looked promising at least as far as the menu might go.

Of course, it was her hope not to stay too long.

Would Nicholas care enough to come and stop what he was supposed to think was going to happen?

Derek's theory was he would. She didn't have the same easy confidence, but in some ways, she supposed, she didn't know Nicholas as well as his friend. But she wanted to know him. God in heaven, how she yearned for another moonlit balcony dance or, even better, to wake up in sleepy dishabille next to him again, his arm around her, the wisp of his breath against her cheek as he slept. . . .

"Annie has severed her engagement."

Caroline, who was staring out the window at a ewe with two small lambs flanking her on either side, turned around and smiled. "I rather thought you seemed lighthearted when you arrived. Now I know why."

"What you need to know is you have my undying gratitude. Whatever you said to her had the desired effect."

Caroline took a seat on the chair by the small fireplace. "I simply told her the truth. That it was a disservice to them both if she married Lord Hyatt when she was in love with you."

Derek chose the bed, settling down with casual ease.

Naturally, Caroline thought with a twinge of wry observation. He was hardly a novice at sharing small rooms at inns with a variety of ladies. For her the stakes were much higher. She was putting her reputation in as much jeopardy as when she'd gone to Essex. Not for passion but as a ruse.

She felt unsure, but Derek had sworn it would be a success.

"Did she admit she was in love with me?"

"No."

His lordship looked crestfallen. Yes, a first-caliber rake with a reputation to make any maiden blush looked like a child who had just had his sweet taken away. "I see. I rather hoped—"

"Did you honestly think she'd tell me, a mere casual acquaintance, something so personal? I did almost all the talking, but to be honest, my lord, I think she was already inclined toward breaking it off with Lord Hyatt." Caroline cocked a brow. "I doubt, even with her engagement over, it is going to be easy for you to win her back. Her love for you isn't in question; it's her trust. That is a commodity that once destroyed is not so easily replaced."

"I realize that." He shifted a little from his perch on the side of the bed, his booted feet scraping the floor. "I've agonized over it, believe me."

He'd *agonized* over it. Annabel was lucky.

"Women have romantic notions over how we should be wooed and won."

His smile was a glimmer. "Are you going to lecture me now about women, my lady? I am rumored to be an expert, I warn you."

His charm was certainly a palpable thing. No wonder Annabel Reid had fallen for it. If Caroline were not so involved with Nicholas Manning, she would probably have been susceptible herself. She smiled. "If it were not for your reputation—and Nicholas's—we would not be sitting here, would we?"

He gazed at her across the room. "If it were not for the bet, you and Nick would still be nodding acquaintances, Annabel would still be planning her wedding, and I would still consider myself impotent to change things. I find I cannot regret the wager now."

"Will he come?" Her question came out involuntarily and she looked immediately away.

Derek chuckled. "Oh yes."

His confidence was reassuring, but she wasn't sure she shared it. "Why are you so certain?"

"Because of several things, but mostly because of eleven days."

Caroline wrinkled her brow. "Eleven days?"

"He knew exactly how many days had passed since the two of you left Essex. Whether or not I know women, I know about the male of our species, since I am one myself. Keeping track of such a thing is not normally in our nature. He counted the days. It says it all."

Caroline was still an ingenue when it came to intrigue of this sort. "That means something?"

"It does. Take my word."

"I have, for quite a lot of things. If I did not have faith in your integrity, I would not be sitting here now."

"I suppose not." Azure eyes regarded her with what looked like resigned humor. "Nicholas finds your approach to society's censure an annoyance."

"An annoyance to his purposes, you mean."

"He likes his liaisons without strings, I admit."

"And most women bow to his whims." She sat up straighter.

Derek gave her a level look. "Which you have not. Look how it has brought him to his knees."

"I haven't seen much evidence of that."

"For Nick, his distraction and irritation is evidence of itself. I know I've never seen it before. Well"—he hesitated—"let's say I haven't seen it but once before. It proved disastrous then. He's understandably wary."

She was intrigued and recalled when she asked if there had ever been anyone special, how flippant Nicholas had become. "Who was she?"

"If he wants to tell you, he will."

Men, Caroline thought in irritation. When they closed ranks, it was impossible to glean information.

Lord Manderville grinned, his well-shaped mouth boyishly curved.

It was angelically infectious. Caroline could not help it. She grinned back. "So, what do we do now?"

He said succinctly, "We wait for the grand entrance."

Chapter Twenty-four

He'd waited too damn long. Nicholas pulled his horse up and cursed under his breath. Yes, he'd hedged and procrastinated and tried to deny his overwhelming urge to follow his gut, but he'd finally succumbed.

Good God. He'd followed them.

All the way to Aylesbury. Several pointed questions of loquacious and only marginally informative residents told him he had located the right inn.

Hell and blast, he was making a fool of himself.

It was modest and small, set at the edge of town, with a pitched roof and flowers in boxes beneath the windows. It was not quite what he'd have chosen, but it wasn't his right to choose it either. Derek was trying to be discreet at Caroline's request, no doubt.

Derek and Caroline. Together.

Dismounting, Nicholas tossed the reins to a young lad that came out of the stables, and stalked to the door. Inside, the place was adequate in a countrified way, he supposed, for a romantic fling.

Which might be just what Caroline wanted, he reminded himself.

Had she given him any indication of wishing for anything else?

In the carriage the evening when he'd been reduced to asking favors of servants and hiding like a thief in the night just to see her, he'd disappointed her. Caroline wasn't sophisticated enough to conceal her expression when he'd confessed to being wary of her and she'd asked him why.

The answer was clear, he thought with grim self-reproof: because he was leery she'd make him do ridiculous things like riding at top speed for hours to some little countrified inn to stop her from settling a very ill-advised, juvenile wager.

He loved Derek like a brother. This interference was as much to save their friendship as anything else.

No, it wasn't, he told himself with rueful honesty. It was selfish, because he could not bear the thought of the two of them together.

In bed. Touching, kissing . . .

He hoped like hell he wasn't too late.

A small plump man had stopped wiping one of the tables at his entrance, reacting to the hint of impatience and purpose in Nicholas's expression.

Nicholas said in a clipped voice, "I'm looking for two guests. A beautiful woman with auburn hair and a tall blond man. Where are they?"

The proprietor eyed his expensive clothing and gauged his social status. "My lord, I can't—"

"You may call me Your Grace," Nicholas corrected with a lethal edge to his tone. If his title held weight to get him expedient answers, he'd use it. "And please answer my question or I will simply pound on all the doors until I discover where they are."

"First room to the right at the top of the stairs." The innkeeper understood the impatience in his tone very well. The towel dangled limply from his pudgy hand.

Nicholas nodded and turned, but then swung back around. "How long have they been here?"

"Several hours, Your Grace." The confession ended on a squeak.

Under his breath, Nicholas muttered a curse. Why the devil had he waited, pacing in his damn study, for so long? It was already beginning to get dark outside.

He took the stairs two at a time, as if haste at this late hour could make a difference. At the correct door he stopped, rigid and arrested, as he heard a small breathless laugh.

Feminine and familiar. In Essex he'd heard it often enough, usually sighed in his ear as they lay in bed together. Spontaneous and free and as lovely as the rest of her when she wasn't rigidly holding everything in an icy facade of detachment.

Nicholas lifted his hand to knock and paused, another scene coming back, like a ghost drifting past in the subdued lighting of the hallway.

Helena had disappeared. He knew because he'd been so acutely aware of her every movement, the fluid grace of her body as she danced, the curve of her smile, the sway of her hips as she walked.

Where was she?

Outside for a bit of fresh air? Certainly it was warm enough; certainly the closeness of the room was a good reason.

Why had he gone looking for her?

Because he'd known. It had happened to him, after all. That alluring glance, the brief pressure on his arm, the delicate and subtle scene of seduction.

Yes, he'd known.

So instead of looking on the terrace or in the gardens, he'd gone quietly upstairs. And stood there, on the wrong side of a closed bedroom door, and heard them.

Dear God, he'd heard them. She was supposedly in love with him, yet here she was enjoying a passionate moment with another man—he didn't even have to walk into the room to know it was true.

He recognized that light, breathy exhale of pleasure. . . . He knew it. It was branded in his brain, his nerve endings, his heart. . . .

Twice damned as an idiot, he'd opened the door then, and he thrust it open now with more force than he intended, sending it back against the wall with a loud bang.

With his heart pounding and his jaw set against the worst possible scenario, he found instead the woman he was obsessed with sitting demurely in a chair by a brick hearth, a glass of sherry arrested near her lips and her eyes wide at his abrupt arrival.

Fully clothed, every female frippery in place, her hair still neatly coiffed in a simple chignon. Derek too, perched on the bed, was dressed right down to his Hessians and even his neckcloth.

No, not at all the same scene he'd invaded a decade ago. Praise God.

Relief had him speechless. Or maybe it was something else, something akin to mortification. Into the resulting silence, he managed to say brilliantly, "Good afternoon."

It was Derek who responded. His old friend got to his feet in one lithe movement, a small smug smile on his mouth. With studied precision he tugged a watch from the pocket of his waistcoat, glanced at it, and tucked it back away. "You took longer than I thought, Nick."

What?

Nicholas wanted to glare, but he couldn't manage it, even after years of practice in controlling his emotions. He said coolly, "Care to explain that remark?"

"Care to explain your presence here?" Derek sauntered toward the doorway. "Not to me, of course, since I'm leaving. I am sure Lady Wynn would like to hear what you have to say, though. Call on me when you get back to London."

What the devil is going on?

Nicholas stepped out of the way as his friend shouldered past him. Derek had a faint but unmistakable smile of open amusement on his face.

Yes, as if Nicholas weren't scoffing at himself already, that's what he needed, someone else laughing at him.

But it was hard to be too irritated if he was suddenly alone with Caroline. Alone. With her. In a remote country inn.

A dream come true. No, make that a male fantasy come true. Or maybe a combination of both.

She looked positively enchanting in a simple gown of pale rose muslin, her attire rumpled from her journey, those silver eyes luminous as she gazed at him from across the small room.

The bed, he noted, looked comfortable enough.

He'd thank Derek for his choice in accommodations later. "You expected me?"

Her voice was hushed. "I . . . hoped."

She hoped. Dear God, he was in over his head.

"I don't know why I'm even here." He thrust his hand through his hair in aggravation and exhaled raggedly. "Except I really could not take the idea of your going through with the second part of this bargain."

"So you came to save me?" She sat there, the small glass dangling in her fingers, her face unreadable. Usually, he understood what women were thinking. No, that was wrong— he could guess what women were thinking, but understanding it was something else.

Now he really had no idea.

Nicholas moved into the room and shut the door behind him.

At that moment he banished Helena's ghost into not only the hallway but the forever past. "I came for you," he said in simple honesty. "What it means exactly you are obligated to help me understand."

"Obligated?" Auburn brows rose, but Caroline looked becomingly flushed. "Rothay, you do *understand* that just because you are a skilled lover, handsome in every way, and could charm a snake out of a basket, I am not necessarily one of your conquests."

"Aren't you?" He grinned.

Why had he ever hesitated over this?

"Well," she said in that same pragmatic, prim, very Lady Wynn voice—though the heated anticipation in her eyes belied it—"I am not convinced of it."

No one knew how to issue a challenge like she did. No one. In one note she'd managed to turn his life upside down. Look at what she was doing to him now. She was still halfway across the room and yet he could feel his erection grow, just from the promise of being close to her.

This wasn't just simple desire. *That* he'd felt before. Many, many times. It was the fodder that fed the gossip mill; it was what kept him from thinking about Helena; it was in the past.

This was different. It had been different from the moment he'd kissed her that warm afternoon on the terrace in Essex and had the first taste of her tentative but eager passion.

Or maybe when she'd lifted off her hat and veil back at the seedy little tavern . . .

Oh hell, who the devil cared when? It had happened.

It just had.

He looked magnificent.

Surly, a little disheveled, out of sorts, irritated, and yet the gleam in his beautiful dark eyes was one she recognized with a vivid clarity.

Desire.

The scandalously delicious Duke of Rothay wanted her.

Was it too much to hope that wasn't the only thing that brought him all this way?

From the bulge in his breeches as he deliberately shrugged out of his jacket, it was hard to be sure. But, as Lord Manderville had pointed out, if the Devilish Duke wanted a woman for base purposes, he needn't ride any distance to find her.

But he'd come.

The risk had been worth it.

He advanced purposefully across the floor. Caroline took a compulsive gulp of sherry, never taking her eyes from his lean form. He was just as tall, just as masculine and powerful as she remembered, and just as intimidating as the last time they'd locked gazes across a crowded ballroom.

Except that he halted before her chair and extended his hand instead of doing something more presumptuous like sweeping her up into his arms.

Just that. One extended hand.

It was symbolic of what she hoped he offered. Not just transient pleasure but a more meaningful joining. Nicholas had come from London to prevent her from following through with her judging offer, and Lord Manderville had exited as planned, leaving them alone. Everything so far was going well.

The slow pound of her heart throbbed in her wrist and throat.

Caroline took his proffered hand, entwining her fingers with his as she allowed him to gently tug her to her feet. "Like I said, I hoped . . ."

She stopped, faltering, not sure how much she was supposed to volunteer.

Nicholas had a faint smile on his face. A dark lock of hair hung over one brow. His breeches and boots held dust from the road. He took the glass of sherry from her hand and set it aside. "You hoped what?"

After all, what did it hurt to say it? Well, maybe it was a risk, but Nicholas had come a fair distance to interfere, and though Derek swore it would happen, it still both surprised and thrilled her. "I hoped you'd come."

An ebony brow went upward. "I hoped I wouldn't," he said on a low mutter before he crushed his mouth to hers.

It was not in the least a gentle kiss. It was intense, demanding, yet somehow yielding at the same time. Caroline leaned into him, letting him have his way with his tongue and lips, and found her hands on the lapel of his jacket and her breasts against his chest. Since he was obviously there despite his better judgment, she could forgive even that gruff tone of voice.

The Devilish Duke was not all charming at the moment . . . and she loved it. Loved the hotspur need in his embrace, loved the lack of finesse. He was capable of persuasive planned allure, of tantalizing seduction, but this was something else entirely. His hands roamed over her body and they melted together.

Ebony hair brushed her cheek. A hot demanding mouth possessed hers and she felt the rigid length of his erection even through the layers of their clothing. The small room didn't matter; the darkening sky held no meaning; all that was her world was one man.

That said it all.

One man.

"Nicholas," she murmured against his lips.

He whispered back, "I'm here. Heaven help me, I couldn't stay away."

Yes, he was there. It made her body taut and needy. "I'm glad."

"Let me demonstrate just how much I am here." He backed her toward the bed.

His hands worked their magic. She didn't stand a chance, but she didn't want one. Her gown was unfastened and pushed from her shoulders so quickly she was barely aware of it slipping free and pooling on the floor. Chemise, stockings, and slippers were disposed of just as fast and he scooped her up to deposit her nude body on top of the coverlet.

"Now, that is worth riding all the way from London for," he said as he began to undress deliberately, his gaze roving over her body.

How she'd missed it. The blatant audacity in his stare and the resulting curl of excitement deep in her belly. He fairly jerked off his clothing and for a moment he just stood there as if he realized with the same frantic force of need how important the moment really was to them both.

Then he climbed onto the bed and into her arms, sliding fully on top of her, his mouth claiming hers again. This time the kiss was slow and wicked, his erect cock hard between them. Caroline rubbed against that long length, winning a small rumble of approval from deep in his chest.

She loved the skillful way his hands moved over her body, the warm feel of his mouth on her neck as she arched into his embrace, the scent of his skin. Already she was wet and receptive, eager to feel him inside her. It was natural to spread her legs, an invitation he didn't miss. Nicholas braced his weight on his forearms and accepted the offer, his knees opening her thighs wider as he poised to enter her.

For a moment he paused, the restraint it took evident in the tension in his muscled form. "I'm never possessive."

That he was still having trouble defining his actions was no surprise.

Caroline gazed upward, a languid pleasure assaulting her senses as anticipation hummed through every nerve ending. "I know."

The tip of his erection rested against her opening, but he didn't move. "The idea of you with Derek—oh hell, you and anyone—was more than I could take. It was torturing me."

More than any sentimental words, the dark look on his all-too-handsome face made her smile. Caroline touched his cheek. "I wouldn't have done anything anyway."

"Why not? Tell me."

She caught the deepened, hoarse tone of his voice. That Nicholas Manning, the devilish lover of so many women, his suave, practiced charisma whispered about behind gloved hands wherever he went, was urging her into some kind of declaration first was poignantly amusing. He was good at every aspect of making love, but love itself seemed to be something that shook his usual unruffled calm.

She wasn't good at it either. But she tried. "I can't imagine being with anyone but you."

"Why wouldn't you have lain with Derek? That was the agreement. Women find him infinitely attractive."

Was Nicholas—*Nicholas*—truly insecure about her?

That was a euphoric realization.

"The agreement was before," she told him, her tone quiet and direct.

"Before what?" His eyes narrowed just a fraction. She could feel the heat from him, the evidence of his desire pressing against her yielding flesh, the slight tremble in his arms showing the amount of control it took for him not to complete the act they both wanted so desperately.

"Before you, Nicholas."

"Go on." The restive tone demanded something. The look

on his face said he'd ridden after her, and the statement that made needed a firm reason for her to support it.

Caroline had never in her life declared her love to anyone, but then again, she didn't think she'd ever loved someone before. Her mother maybe, as a child, but she didn't really remember her. Her cold, stern, distant father, her unfeeling, dutiful aunt, and least of all Edward, whom she loathed, hadn't inspired warm feelings. Nicholas had wooed not only her body but also her soul with his gentle, skilled touch and compelling smile.

One silent, moonlit dance on a terrace and she had been lost.

She struggled to say the right thing. "Once you touched me . . . since Essex . . . I just knew I couldn't. I told Derek as soon as we got back that I withdrew my offer."

"So this was a trick?"

The last thing she wanted was for him to feel *that* way. She reached up and touched his mouth with a fingertip. "No. I don't know what to call it, but not that. I think Derek speculated it might make you examine your feelings if you thought I would still go through with it."

"Did it occur to him I had no desire to examine my feelings?"

She couldn't help but laugh at his disgusted tone, but she still felt shy when she said, "I'm glad it did because"—her hips lifted a little to emphasize the point—"we are here now. Like this. Would you mind . . . ?"

Her inadequate declaration seemed to satisfy him, for his smile held a wolfish quality. He growled out, "I don't mind at all."

His entry was fast, impetuous, hard enough to make her gasp. He sheathed his entire rigid cock deeply, the blissful sensation making her quiver. Her eyes shut. "Yes."

They moved together, their bodies communicating what they apparently couldn't say with words. The rhythm was unconstrained, wild, and Caroline reveled in it as she climbed toward that erotic paradise.

No, she could not imagine doing something so intimate,

so wonderful, with anyone but the man who moved with her now, both of them seeking . . . finding. . . .

The completion was rapturous, the pleasure so acute she felt as if the world stopped and the sky fell. They shuddered together, enveloped by sensation, limp in the afterglow as they sprawled in a tangle of arms and legs, both of them reluctant to speak once their breathing began to slow to normal respiration.

Nicholas had come after her. Even naked in his arms, her body damp in the aftermath of tempestuous passion, some part of her held stunned disbelief it had really happened.

One long finger traced a path along her jaw and caressed her lower lip. Dark eyes regarded her from under the veil of half-lowered lashes. Nicholas smiled, but it wasn't the usual lazy calculated curve of his lips. Instead it seemed almost wistful, which was not a word she would ever have applied to the Duke of Rothay.

"Are you still wary?"

Caroline stirred, which took some effort because she felt so marvelously sated and content. "What?"

"That night in your carriage, you told me you were wary of me."

She shook her head, her hair moving across her shoulders and bare back. "I said I was wary of scandal."

"Aren't you still?"

Did that mean he was never going to offer her more than what they just shared? Not sure how to answer, Caroline rested against him, silent, uncertain, her happiness fading a little.

"Caroline?"

Slowly, she admitted, "If you are asking me to conduct an affair with you again, I hope that is not the question you rode here for. Those days we spent together were a revelation for me. That isn't a secret to you. Sexually, yes. But not just the enlightenment I found in your bed. Remember when we were in the clearing and made love for the first time? I realize I did not make the suggestive comment you wished for, but I told you the truth. You are a very nice man, Nicholas.

All of the trappings of title, birth, wealth, and sexual skill aside, you're . . . you."

Gently, he touched her chin, forcing her face to tilt up so they stared at each other. "And what does that mean?"

How she wished she could be nonchalant. But she couldn't. She whispered, "I fell in love with *you*. That man, not the Devilish Duke, but the real one."

Chapter Twenty-five

Three days. It had been three days since he'd returned to London from that little inn where he guessed Nicholas and Caroline were still enjoying themselves immensely.

Derek, on the other hand, was not having a good time. Staying away from his uncle's town house had been torture, but he hardly wanted to arrive on the doorstep like a vulture lighting on a doe the minute the dissolution of Annabel's engagement became public, so he'd waited.

Three very long days.

Dusk had descended with insidious purpose and then darkness and still he sat, morose and uncertain. His normally neat desk was cluttered with paperwork he'd barely glanced at because he didn't have the ability to concentrate. A waft of the night breeze carried in scents from the street and garden, the smell an eclectic mixture of chimney smoke and overblown roses.

It was late. Maybe he should go out to White's or Brooks's, find a corner and bottle of whiskey, and . . .

And what? Sit *there* and think about her instead? Yes, that would be productive.

The slight scraping sound woke him from his abstraction and he frowned, startled as he turned to look at the open window in his study. The rustle of fabric told him he wasn't imagining things, and he sat transfixed as he saw one slender leg slide over the sill.

He might have been alarmed, but very rarely, if he had

to guess, did intruders have such shapely calves. Nor did they wear evening gowns of cream-colored silk. Riveted by surprise, Derek sat frozen in his chair.

But his heart had begun to pound.

Annabel landed on the floor, her breathing audibly agitated, and then straightened, shaking out her skirts. The curtains behind her moved in a flutter, framing her slender body. As if it were the most natural thing on earth for her to crawl in his study window, she said merely, "I saw your light."

Belatedly—because he was still in disbelief—Derek thrust himself to his feet, nearly toppling his chair. "Annie, what are you doing?"

She stood there, all golden hair and ivory skin, her chin tilted up at a slight angle, the look in her blue eyes defiant. "Isn't this our current method of calling on each other?"

He stared back, wondering if he was having some sort of absurd hallucination. "The devil it is. If you want to call— and ladies don't call on gentlemen—come with a battalion of chaperones and through the front door."

Her chin went up a little more. "I see. One set of rules for you, and another one entirely for me. It's perfectly fine for you to crawl through my bedroom window if you have something to say, but I don't have the same latitude?"

Derek shoved his hand through his hair. "Good God, Annie, you know you don't. Do Thomas and Margaret know you're here?"

"Of course not."

He felt himself pale. "Please tell me you didn't walk."

"I could hardly call for the carriage, could I? It isn't far and I'm not a cripple."

A young woman alone on the streets at—he glanced at the clock and saw it was well after midnight—this hour, even if the neighborhood was fashionable and quiet, was reckless enough to make him feel weak-kneed. "Jesus," he muttered. "You little fool."

"I need to talk to you."

Headstrong was far too tame a term for her. He spoke

harshly, because he was still reeling from the chance she'd taken, with not just her reputation but her safety. "I'm going to see you safely home."

"No." She took in a shuddering breath, and shook her head. "I have the courage to do this now. In the morning I may change my mind. Besides, I want to move forward and not spend one more minute immersed in this inner battle I cannot seem to resolve. Aren't you interested in what brought me here?"

It was the same question he'd posed to her the night he'd been desperate enough to crawl into her bedroom.

She had told him no.

But it hadn't been the truth. He'd seen it in the vulnerability in her eyes.

There had been enough misunderstanding between them without adding more lies to the mixture. Derek said simply, "You must know I am."

Thus given permission, she hesitated, so lovely in the faint glow of the lamp that had burned low, the cream color of her gown making her look more innocent and young than ever. Except it was cut low enough to modestly show the upper curves of her full breasts and there was nothing childish any longer about her. She was an alluring woman in every way, her independent spirit included.

And it was captivating, which he didn't need. He was already her captive.

He helped her by saying, "I heard."

She didn't try to pretend she didn't know what he was saying. "Yes, I imagine everyone knows by now I severed my engagement with Alfred. I felt terrible doing it, but not as terrible as if I'd done him the disservice of marrying him. He wasn't even particularly surprised, I think, just like you said."

Derek just looked at her. Slowly he raised a brow.

"Don't be smug," she said.

It would have been more effective if her voice hadn't cracked. It wasn't much, just a single hitch in her speech, but it was enough.

For hope.

"I shall contrive not to," he murmured. "I am not even sure I have any reason to be smug. Is there? Except, perhaps, your unconventional arrival and presence here at this hour."

"I'm still angry with you." She didn't quite answer the question.

"I've noticed," he conceded in grim humor. "Never have I paid so dearly for a mistake."

She looked at him with luminous eyes, her mouth trembling just a little. "I don't even know why I should speak to you. I have spent the past year trying to reconcile the man I thought I knew with who you really are, and I haven't enjoyed the exercise. Give me one logical reason to trust you."

No part of him ever thought this was going to be easy. There was a certain advantage—and disadvantage—to knowing someone very well. She loved fully, but felt betrayal with the same amount of passion. Derek took a moment, and then said quietly, "Annie, I understand I was both insensitive and a fool last year. Please, label me both without argument. But, on my part, can't *you* understand what was happening between us felt both forbidden and foreign? You were so young, and there I was, with this reputation I can't shake that half stems from my father. Let's toss in an ill-advised penchant for my uncle's ward. I was hard-pressed on how to act."

"So you fell right into the countess's eager arms." The accusation in her eyes was unmistakable. She *was* still angry.

But she was also there. *She'd* come to *him*.

"I've explained why and apologized." He groped for the right words, something to ease the tension visible in the set of her slender shoulders. "Permanence was not something I had ever considered before."

"Before?"

The delicately asked question challenged him. Very well. She needed to hear it. He supplied, "Before you."

"But you are now?"

"Adjusted to the idea of permanence?"

"Yes." She swallowed, the muscles visibly rippling in her throat. "I need proof."

Well, that was hardly an easy order to fill, but she deserved at the least what Hyatt had given her and even more. He said hoarsely, "Marry me, Annie."

She took a step toward him, the expression on her face difficult to interpret. "You want me to marry you?"

"I just asked." Derek couldn't believe he'd said it so easily, relinquishing his freedom without hesitation or regret. "Yes, I want you to marry me. To be my wife."

"If you are sincere, let's settle this." Her face wore a determined look, her fine brows just slightly knit, her soft mouth compressed. "So, take me."

He went still, every muscle in his body tensing. Stunned and shaken, he stared at her. "What?"

"Is your hearing impaired?" She moved closer and he didn't miss the gentle sway of her hips, provocative whether she did it consciously or not. "Take me to your bed. We have until dawn."

Speechless, he felt his body react, though emotionally he was resistant to the suggestion. After a moment, he managed, "I have no intention of treating you with dishonor."

Her smile was unexpectedly provocative for an untried young woman. "You are supposed to be the most skilled lover in England, correct? I believe that's what you've put forth before all of society. You even wagered what is reputed to be a small fortune on that claim."

"I was—"

"Yes, I know," she interrupted, gazing up at him, her delicate features shadows and curves in the flickering light. "You were inebriated at the time, but still the notion must have come from some inner conviction and I want you to prove it. To me."

"Annabel." The reproof lost its effect when his gaze dropped to her mouth against his will. "Don't tempt me, please."

"Why not?"

"Thomas will have my head, for one."

"Let's not tell him." She came close enough to place her hand on his chest. Through the fine linen of his shirt he could feel the slight pressure. "I want this for myself. No doubts, no chance you'll change your mind, no going back for either of us. If there is one thing I do know about you, it is you don't seduce innocent young women. Even when I told myself I hated you, I didn't count that as one of your sins."

He didn't, it was true enough.

"So," she went on as if what she was suggesting was logical and made perfect sense, "if you do this . . . if you compromise me, I'll know your proposal is genuine."

"It is genuine," he protested, not sure how to proceed, because being propositioned by a normally proper young lady was out of the realm of his experience. Her doubt was insulting to a degree, but he hadn't given her much reason to trust him either.

"Then you agree?"

"We can wait until our wedding night." Desperation to act like a gentleman vied with his swelling cock. She was so close, so tempting, so much the focus of his every desire. . . .

"I don't want to wait. This is important to me."

The conviction in her voice undid him. Bloody hell, what was he supposed to do? Apply for sainthood? The woman he wanted more than anything on earth was petitioning him to take her to bed. Besides, a traitorous voice whispered in his brain, there was gossip enough over her severed engagement and she couldn't immediately become formally engaged again without the whispers rising to deafening proportions, so a quick, quiet wedding was in order anyway.

Derek tried one more time. "I'll see you home."

"No. You claim you love me. Prove it." Her mouth trembled. Not much, but enough he noticed.

He said in a choked voice, "I don't just claim it. I do love you."

"Then kiss me."

He wanted to touch her, to kiss those soft rose lips, to hold her against him and make her wonder what could be.

What *would* be. He knew how to give a woman pleasure, how to coax those heated sighs and subtle movements, how to bring her to the brink of ecstasy and slide her over the precipice at just the right moment.

Annabel looked up at him, so beautiful it made his breath catch in his throat. "Do you understand how this is for me?" Her voice was muted, her eyes misted.

"Over the past year," he informed her, a little thin-skinned himself, "I've come to understand a great deal about thwarted love, Annie."

"Show me. I think I understand it too."

He couldn't take it. The urge to hold her was too much. As was the azure shimmer in her eyes. Derek caught her against him. He smoothed his thumbs over the sides of her cheeks, now damp with betraying wetness, feathering his lips over her brows. "Let me define it for you. We can compare notes. It is torture, but yet again the greatest bliss. It is heartache but also joy. It is wonder and despair at the same time. Am I close?"

A nod, almost imperceptible, moved against the cradle of his hands.

"Annie." He lowered his mouth.

"Yes."

Their lips met, touched, parted, and yet met again. Through all the legions of women, through all the detached dalliance and lighthearted repartee and careless moments in forbidden bedrooms, he'd never felt this way. Never such welling tenderness, never such agonizing need, never such an aching desire.

Usually he prided himself on his finesse—that was public knowledge—but as Annabel swayed into him, her slender body quivering, he lost all real sense of what he was doing. All he could think about was how warm and silky her mouth felt against his, how the shy delicate brush of her tongue sent a jolt of pure desire straight to his groin, how she tasted like heaven.

The planet could have stopped spinning on its axis, every bird on earth fall silent, the oceans all drain away, and his world could not have changed more.

He prolonged the moment, tasting, teasing, whispering

her name in her ear, one hand at the small of her back gently holding her close against him.

But finally, there was no use for it; he had to lift his head and look at her.

Into her eyes, hoping, praying to see that same shining light that had been there a year ago before he darkened and destroyed it.

His eyes were such a vivid blue, with those absurdly long lashes, his nose straight, the line of his lean jaw masculine and perfect. And his mouth, capable of both that devastating smile women twittered over and such tender, persuasive kisses her knees felt weak—well, she couldn't even begin to describe it.

However, at the moment Derek wasn't smiling at all. He stared down at her, as if in unspoken question.

I love you.

When he said it this time, there was no hesitation. No sense he felt as if he were stepping off a precipice to fall to a painful death, no echo of uncertainty.

Derek loved her. When she reflected back on all the girlish—and then not-so-girlish as she got older—fantasies she'd had over this moment, she could not help the smile that curved her lips. "I've always thought my imagination to be excellent, but you've now convinced me otherwise."

His arm around her waist tightened almost imperceptibly. "How so?"

"That was a most romantic kiss and I didn't think you could possibly outdo the first one. I want to know more."

"This time is going to be nothing like what happened last year, I promise you." The altered tone of his voice made her feel a shiver of anticipation.

"I need that promise." Her fingers feathered down his arm. Through his shirt, she could feel the tension in his muscles.

"I know you do." He kissed her again, but lightly this time, just a brush of his lips on hers. "Tell me what else you want. All your dreams."

The man didn't ask much. A leap of faith into his arms and bed and her dreams too? Annabel hesitated until he said huskily, "Help me. I'm uninterested in making any more mistakes that take a year to correct."

She might not be experienced like the women he usually became involved with, but she was nestled close enough in his embrace she could feel the hard bulge in the front of his breeches. Heat filled her cheeks and she pressed her burning face against his chest.

He wouldn't let her. Long fingers caught her chin and tilted it up so their gazes locked. "Annabel?"

"I want *you*," she confessed.

"Oh, you have me," he responded, his embrace tightening, his breath warm against her temple.

The cost of it had been high, but how she'd yearned to hear him say those words. Maybe even a year of misery, denial, and disillusionment was worth it to have this moment.

He smiled. It usually made the heart of every woman in the room flutter, but this time it was for her alone and she was the only woman to see it.

She wanted this. Wanted him.

"Don't stop," she said. They were the same two words she'd uttered a year before, but they now held so much more meaning.

"I won't," he assured her. His eyes were darkened, his lashes lowered. "I couldn't if I tried. If you mean this, come with me." Derek gently tugged her hand and led her from the room down the darkened hallway until they reached a stairway. The hushed quiet of the house felt forbidden, but then again, what she was doing was very forbidden and yet she'd demanded it.

We can wait until our wedding night. . . .

Her husband.

She was going to marry the wicked Earl of Manderville. The furor that would ensue once society got wind of the match was daunting, but not as daunting as the prospect of holding his hand and allowing him to escort her up to his bedroom.

Because *she* had asked for it as a trial by fire.

There was no going back now, she thought as she took each step, feeling the warm, firm clasp of his long fingers around hers. Well, that wasn't exactly true, because even though she'd felt the state of his arousal when he kissed her, she knew he would let her go if her courage failed her.

"You're still sure?" he asked as if reading her thoughts, his hand on the ornate knob of the first door in the upper hallway. "I can still take you home and hopefully you could slip inside undetected, but either way—"

There was no way she would back out now. She'd broken things off with Alfred, she'd risked her reputation by sneaking out of the house, and she'd bared her soul and made this outrageous offer. "Derek, I'm sure."

He kissed her then. He kissed her as he urged her inside, he kissed her as he backed her to the bed until it bumped the backs of her legs, and he kissed her as he began to unfasten her gown. Annabel felt the material loosen only in a vague way, the only thing in the world the hot, hungry urgency of his mouth against hers. She threaded her fingers into the silk of his hair, felt the heat of his skin against her palm, and reveled in the knowledge he wanted her. They were so closely pressed together that the strong beat of his heart made the tips of her breasts tingle. Each thud reverberated through her very soul.

"Annie, Annie," he murmured against her mouth, his hands dispatching garments, moving across her flesh.

There was no time to be embarrassed or shy, she discovered as he stripped her bare and lifted her onto the bed. It was wide, soft, spacious enough so that even when he jerked off his shirt and peeled his breeches from his body, when he joined her—all large and imposing and aroused male—there was still room.

He was magnificent. Hard, sculpted, beautiful.

"I need you." His gaze seared her and she knew he spoke the truth, the throbbing heat of his erection against her hip. Strong arms gathered her close and though maybe she should have been afraid, she just . . . wasn't.

"I'm going to pleasure you until you scream," he promised, nipping along her neck. "Until you call out my name."

Annabel arched, in disbelief she was doing this—giving herself to Derek at last. She gasped, "Do it."

"Because you want to be compromised. Because you want no going back." His breath tickled her ear.

"Yes."

"Because you want . . . me?" His tongue whirled in an interesting arc along her neck. "Enough to surrender your virginity as an offering to seal our pact? It's an effective strategy, let me tell you, my love."

My love . . .

She might have objected under other circumstances to the implication she planned any of this when in truth she'd paced her room, brooded, been angry, and then pensive and then angry again. Not until the clock struck midnight had she gathered her courage and left the house like a thief in the night, creeping down the back stairs and out the servants' entrance, running along the street to reach him. The light in the downstairs window of his residence had been a boon, a gift. She had pictured having to knock and ask for him, waking half the household.

This way was better.

This way was like a dream come true.

His mouth found her bare breast. Wet heat closed over her nipple and she gasped, arching back onto the softness of the pillows, her body suddenly on fire. Derek suckled gently, swirling his tongue around the taut tip until she felt as if she stopped breathing, and she realized this was really happening. They were naked in each other's arms, his blond head bent over her, his mouth doing magical, magical things.

"Oh." Annabel clutched at him, her body tense, feeling the effects of his ministrations in the pit of her stomach and deep between her legs.

Was this what it was like? Was this what women whispered over?

"God, Annie, I want you so." The faint bristle on his face brushed her skin. His hands caught the mounded fullness and shaped it, and his thumb brushed the erect tip of the opposite breast.

"Derek." Her voice was strained, uneven.

"I need to taste every inch of you."

The harsh rasp in his voice increased her quivering reaction to his seductive touch. He leisurely explored the other breast with lips and tongue and then nuzzled the valley between the flesh cupped in his hands.

She wanted to cry out with pleasure and barely managed to stifle it. Catching her lower lip between her teeth, she smothered a whimper. Was it supposed to be like this? she wondered. Those drugging kisses, the hot, wicked sweep of his mouth on her skin, the feeling of abandonment and surrender.

Yes, she decided a moment later as he licked a hot path across her collarbone and made a sound low in his throat. This was exactly why he and the sinful Duke of Rothay had made that wager in the first place. Because he knew just what to do. He must, for *she* had no idea and here she was, beneath him, her body available for his carnal pleasure . . . or was it hers? The edges of definition were blurred, indistinct, her senses captivated.

When he moved lower, raining kisses across her stomach, she didn't understand until . . .

Oh God, until she realized his mouth was in a place she never dreamed anyone would want to taste and he really meant it when he promised everywhere. The fiery rapture produced from the scandalous kiss between her open thighs made her mind spin. Derek pushed her legs apart for better access, lowered his head again, and won a telling cry she could not help from deep within her.

"Perfect," he murmured, his mouth still moving against her sensitive flesh. "Flow with it, Annie. Let it take over. We are going to do this the correct way. I want you bound to me forever."

Let what take over . . . ? Oh God, she jerked in response to the invasion of his tongue, whimpered at the deft flick of it in just the right spot, and felt her hand shake as she grasped his head to push him away.

Or pull him closer. She couldn't tell; her body was in such a thrall.

It came then. Like a tall wave, moving forward, held suspended, and then dipping in an overflowing crash. She twisted, fought for air, and shuddered as it rippled through her in rapturous pulses.

It was . . . incredible.

So overwhelming she was barely aware as he adjusted his position, sliding upward, sliding inward. His sex penetrated her, at first just a blunt pressure, and then more fully as he began to take real possession of her body.

"If you want proof of my devotion, you surely feel it, Annie." He kissed her, a brief hard contact of their mouths, and shut his eyes. He looked more beautiful than Michelangelo's *David*, all marble defined muscle and sculpted features, his expression indicative of supreme control. "I'll take what you want to gift me and intend to give back twofold. Open for me just a little more. I'll be as gentle as possible."

Still shaken from the depth of the pleasure he'd given her, Annabel didn't resist, still drifting in the aftermath, letting him part her thighs wider.

"I've never done this before," he whispered against her lips, sinking in a little more, stretching her female passage with his inexorable entry. "If I make a mistake, forgive me."

Annabel fought the urge to laugh, inappropriate to the moment. "But you've . . ."

She stopped on a short breath as she felt the stinging pressure of her maidenhead being torn, and then he rested fully inside her.

All of him. All of her. Together. It was uncomfortable, but the pain was negligible compared with the marvel of being so joined, so close. "I'm sorry," he whispered, kissing her cheek, the tip of her nose, the corner of her mouth. Then he murmured against her lips, "You're mine now . . . forever."

"I've always wanted to be," she told him, fiercely triumphant, her nails lightly biting into his muscled shoulders. "Forever."

He held still, impaling her but not moving. Derek's face

wore an uncharacteristic intense expression at odds with his usual lazy charm. "You haven't said it. This seems like the perfect moment. I know I'm selfish, but even though you just gifted me with the most precious thing a woman can give a man, I want more than your innocence, Annie. Please tell me."

She stared into his azure eyes, moved by the plea in his voice. "I love you. I always have. That was part of the problem. Even when I told myself I hated you, I knew deep down I still loved you."

"At this moment," he said softly, and his eyes held a suspiciously bright, liquid look, "I feel like the luckiest man on earth." He shifted his weight to one elbow, and brushed her cheek with the backs of his fingers. "I *am* the luckiest man on earth."

Was the notorious Earl of Manderville truly moved to tears?

He was, she noted, reaching up with wonder to touch the feathery lashes at one corner of his eye as she gathered a minuscule bit of moisture. "Derek."

One hand slid over her shoulder, his long fingers gliding in a persuasive caress. "We'll talk later. Agreed?"

Annabel lifted her hips a little without thinking, glad the discomfort was easing as her body adjusted to the sensation of fullness and possession. "Is it over?" she asked, her voice breathless for a reason she didn't quite understand, an odd excitement replacing any sense of trepidation.

"No." His familiar grin surfaced—the one she'd so missed—impudent and boyish, the curve of his lips as intoxicating as a glass of fine wine. "Now that our mutual declaration of our feelings is done, let's finalize this as you requested. Believe me, we are not nearly finished. Let me show you."

Derek began to move, fluid, powerful against her—in her. His hardness slid backward and then surged forward and, to her surprise, the friction was at first an interesting sensation, and then became something else entirely.

Exhilarating, she decided as her body began to accept and

respond to the rhythm of thrust and withdrawal. His hand slipped between them, touching her, rubbing as he continued, and she felt flickers of pleasure with each touch, each stroke.

"Again, Annie," he urged, his eyes heavy-lidded. "For me. Again."

What did he want? she wondered frantically until she felt that interesting tension, her spine arching. Her thighs tightened around his hips and she made a very unladylike sound, the moan torn from her throat.

It felt so . . . good. Very good.

Incredible.

Unbelievable.

Her hands fisted in the coverlet, she stopped breathing and the world flickered away. She shuddered and clung to him, damp skin to damp skin, her body trembling with pleasure. Derek groaned and went still, his muscles hard and rigid, and she felt a curious warm fluid pulse deep inside her.

The bedroom was quiet except for their harsh breathing. Annabel, for whatever reason, began to laugh, a weak sound because she still wasn't sure she could breathe. She clasped her arms around Derek's neck and murmured against his throat, "I believe you now. You do want to marry me."

His lips feathered across her brow. "I've never been so sincere about anything in my life."

Chapter Twenty-six

Into every Eden must crawl some serpent.

The calling card arrived on a silver tray and Caroline glanced at it with disinterest at first, but as she recognized the engraved name, a sense of foreboding made her stomach flop over. Though she would normally have refused him, today it didn't appear to be an option, according to her butler.

"He is very insistent, my lady, and claims to know first-hand you are at home."

How that was possible she wasn't sure, but the last time they'd spoken, Franklin had appeared out of nowhere at just the right moment.

Or wrong, depending on a person's point of view.

Norman, hardly in his youth, was not someone to cast out Franklin Wynn, who was two decades younger and infinitely more determined. Caroline gave a very unladylike inward curse and murmured, "Very well, show him in."

"There's no need. Good morning, my lady."

Startled at Franklin's audacity in following the butler without waiting for her response to his call, Caroline stared at the man who brushed past an outraged-looking Norman into the room.

Her cousin—not that she claimed the relationship gladly—wore plum this time, she noted as he strode into the room. It was impossible to miss. A dark purple coat, a lighter embroidered waistcoat, lavender breeches, and even his shoes were that shade below white silk stockings. His pale eyes glittered with the usual ice, and his mouth curved in a way that made her breath catch in apprehension. Dark hair waved away from his coldly handsome features and one lip curled upward just a fraction.

She liked nothing whatsoever about his expression.

"You are home from the country, I see." Without invitation or more than a brief, negligible bow, he tossed his tailcoats up and took a seat. Very comfortably. As if the room were his, not hers. "That's the second trek in a month, isn't it? Unusual. I wasn't aware you traveled so often."

How the devil did he know where she'd gone?

"Yes," she said with very little inflection.

His next words chilled her to the bone. "How *are* Rothay and Manderville?"

Oh. Dear. God.

Her mind went blank for a moment. Blank.

Think. . . .

She had been going over her correspondence in the morning room and carefully set aside the letter she'd been reading so he wouldn't detect the tremor in her hand. "I beg your pardon?"

"The two lascivious rogues that are the talk of the city right now. How are they?" Franklin leaned back triumphantly in one of the chairs, a supercilious smirk on his face.

Did he really know something or was he fishing?

Caroline shook off a chill despite the warm morning sun pouring in the windows and giving the airy room a mellow glow. "I'm confused, my lord. How should I know?"

"My speculation would be, of course, that you, despite all outward appearances that would make anyone disinclined to believe it, are the judge for their boastful contest. Why else would you be meeting them both at a dreary little inn?"

Her stomach lurched. "That, sir, is a lie."

He leaned forward with his hands on his knees. "Is it?"

"Of course. Where did you get such an extraordinary notion?"

"Where indeed?"

It was going to be very difficult to maintain some absurd cat-and-mouse game with her heart pounding like the hooves of one of Nicholas's fabulous horses in the stretch. "It seems a very straightforward question."

Yet he didn't answer it. "I am very interested to know the outcome. Tell me, did Manderville fail to perform adequately? I understand he arrived first but did not stay long. On the other hand, you and the duke spent several nights together. I take it Rothay wins?"

She felt faint with the horrifying realization that he truly did know. Of all people, Franklin was the last one she would want to have leverage against her. She tried desperately to keep her composure. It had been her only defense against Edward and she certainly needed it at this terrible moment.

In a credible voice, she said, "Do you have some reason for coming here and leveling this scandalous accusation at me?"

Franklin clucked his tongue. "Dear me, you look quite pale all of a sudden. Can I get you something?"

Leave, her mind screamed. *Get out.* But on the other hand, she didn't want him to go until she understood his purpose for coming in the first place.

"I'm quite well, thank you."

"Indeed. You are lovely. I like that color on you, but your beauty is undeniable no matter what you wear. Or don't wear, I'm sure. I suspect I'm going to find you even more appealing when you are naked in my bed, your legs spread, like the pretty whore you've proven yourself to be."

Bile rose in her throat. Her trembling hands were clenched together so tightly her knuckles ached. For a moment she could do nothing more than stare at the sadistic and gloating look on his face. The resemblance to Edward was like reliving a nightmare. She had seen that lascivious glitter in those similar pale eyes before, and experienced what it meant.

"No matter what foul things you threaten to say about me, I will not be your mistress," she said with full icy conviction.

"Nor do I want you to be." His tone held a mocking edge and he smiled in a way that would make a reptile look appealing. "I'm proposing marriage. Your loose morals are something I can overlook when I consider the fortune I stand to gain."

A second marriage with a man who reminded her so much of her brutal, callous husband that the mere sight of him made her feel ill? The idea was so repugnant she had to stifle a hysterical laugh. Social ruin was much more preferable.

Caroline looked him in the eye. "Never."

His pale eyes narrowed and his sallow cheeks took on a flush. "I believe you misunderstand me. You have no choice."

"I have every choice." She stood and indicated the doorway. "Please leave *my* home."

The emphasis had the desired effect and his mouth tightened. He got to his feet as well, but made no move toward the doorway. Instead he took a step closer. "I'll destroy you. Blacken your name so no hostess will ever receive you. So no decent man will look your direction unless he wants a quick tumble with an infamous harlot."

"No one will believe your malicious lies, my lord. My reputation for virtuous distance is well-known." It was a bluff, but she didn't care. All she wanted was him away from her.

"I have the evidence of the men I hired to watch you, my dear Caroline. In addition to a written statement from the innkeeper. He says you arrived with one man and left with another. Did you think it would go unremarked? If it makes you feel better, the wife of the innkeeper thought the duke's dramatic arrival rather romantic, but then again, I understand most females fall under Rothay's spell. She was able to describe all three of you perfectly."

"Why would you have me followed?" The last thing she wanted was to engage in further conversation with him, but he was clearly the enemy and dealing with Edward had taught her it was good to be able to gauge their tactics. It had helped her survive with a minimum of damage, or she hoped so.

"You have something I want."

"The money." Should she buy him off? For a moment she

wondered if it would be worth it to hand over the fortune she'd inherited to be rid of him.

Then he raked her body with a deliberate insulting perusal. "Two things I want," he corrected softly.

That was out of the question. "Get out," she ordered, proud that her voice was steady and definite. "And your protestations of a family tie mean nothing to me, so please feel free to never call again."

He took another step forward and was close enough to touch her. Menace glittered in his eyes. "This house should have been mine. So should you. Everything that was Edward's should be mine. The title means little without the fortune he left to you instead. I am determined to gain it one way or the other."

His cold tone sent a chill up her spine. Alarmed, she still refused to retreat. "I am going to call for someone to escort you out, my lord."

"No, you aren't."

The sudden lunge took her off guard. It wasn't that she trusted him, but gentlemen callers in lavender breeches with lace at their cuffs and embossed cards did not often grab their hostess and clamp an unrelenting hand over her mouth.

Outraged, she began to struggle, an awful sense of how disparate their sizes were swamping her with dreadful memories of this very thing, where she felt overwhelmed and powerless. When he dragged her to a small sofa in the corner and forced her down on it, she went almost limp, her limbs frozen, her mind seized with a horrific sense of the inevitability of what might happen.

Franklin thrust his face close and hissed, "You ice-cold bitch. All along looking at me as if I was some parasite, avoiding my calls, pretending not to be home when I knew full well you were in residence. My cousin must have enjoyed you very well to leave you his fortune, and I wish a taste of it too. I insist upon it, no matter how you try to deny me. Afterwards, you will be obligated to accept me or banish the idea of a respectable life."

No.

No. She'd endured it too many times to let it ever happen again. The delicacy of Nicholas's touch, his wicked enticing smile, the passion in his dark eyes, swam into her memory. He hadn't exactly proposed marriage, but with his extraction of a promise of love from her, she hoped maybe—maybe— he would, despite her flawed body's inability to produce a child.

She bit down, managing to catch the palm of her assailant's confining hand with her teeth so she tasted the iron bitterness of blood. For one moment Franklin loosened the pressure and uttered a curse, and she gave a small, choked scream.

"You little witch." Franklin's face was contorted with anger, just inches above hers, and she was certain he would have struck her if he hadn't been more concerned with keeping her quiet. She squirmed, fighting the pinning weight of his body, trying to claw her way free. His hand raked her thigh as he jerked her skirt up.

No, not this. Not this. Please.

Would he really ravish her in her own home? In the warm little room she used as a sanctuary for a morning cup of tea and some introspection as she went through the daily post?

No.

All of a sudden she heard a crashing sound and Franklin groaned, his grip loosening. Then he went lax, his weight a stifling burden, his head lolling to the side. To her surprise Caroline found herself drenched in water and rose petals.

Annabel Reid's face swam into view, concerned and grim, her blue eyes holding a murderous hint of outrage. She said succinctly, "Sorry for the mess, but I do hope I've killed him."

Annabel felt no remorse as she stared down at the man who toppled to the floor as Caroline Wynn struggled to push him away. The other woman sat up shivering. To think Annabel had pondered her impromptu visit because the hour was a little early to drop in, but she had been anxious to thank someone she considered a newfound friend and share the news of her upcoming marriage.

She supposed, as she surveyed the broken shards of glass and water droplets on the floral carpet and the blood seeping from the gash on the man's head, that walking in on what looked like a very shocking attack and bashing the villain would constitute an act of friendship.

So maybe her thanks were said, albeit in a rather violent way.

Lady Wynn was ghastly pale, her usually lovely face drawn into a ghostly mask. Stray damp strands of auburn hair were plastered to her slender neck, and her gown clung damply to her body, thanks to the impetuous impulse Annabel had to use a handy vase to whack her assailant with a robust blow.

"Are you all right?" Annabel plucked a handkerchief from her sleeve and handed it over. The square of lace was insufficient in size, but it was better than nothing.

"My lady!" The elderly butler who had answered the door looked aghast in the doorway. "His lordship, that vile black-guard . . . dear me. I would never have allowed him in if I had known. . . ."

"It's hardly your fault, Norman." Caroline shuddered and moved to sit on a less wet part of the sofa that was farther away from Franklin's prostrate form. She dabbed at her face with Annabel's offering. It was hard to tell if the wetness was from tears or the water to keep the roses fresh. She looked at Annabel with silver eyes that shimmered. "Thank you."

"Not at all."

Dewy lashes clumped together, Lady Wynn murmured, "No, I mean, *thank you*."

Yes, definitely tears. Not that Annabel blamed her. She'd be weeping buckets herself under similar circumstances. She sank down next to her, ignoring the damp fabric of the settee, and took the other woman's shaking hand. "Of course I would help. I was just telling your butler my name when I heard you scream. Normally, I would never call this early in the morning, but now I am glad I did."

"It was excellent timing." The other woman smiled faintly.

"I suppose that's undeniable. By the time I realized his intentions, it was too late to summon help."

They both surveyed the man prone on the floor as if he were a distasteful pile of rubbish.

"I suppose," Annabel said in a matter-of-fact voice, "we will need to do something with him."

"I suppose we will." Caroline gave a weak laugh. "Can I mention again how glad I am you arrived when you did?"

"I can only imagine."

A shudder shook Lady Wynn's slender shoulders. She seemed to realize her skirts were disheveled and adjusted them more demurely.

"My lady, what would you have me do?" The butler looked more than just a little chagrined at what had almost happened to his mistress. "A magistrate would be in order to my mind."

Caroline shook her head. "Give me a moment to think. I fear I am now embroiled in a scandal no matter which way I turn."

Annabel said with force, "Please do not let me hear you will allow him to get away with this. I am a witness if he tries to deny it."

A small groan told them he was already coming around.

"I know him." Caroline looked whiter than ever. "He will make this more unpleasant than it already is if I am not careful. I am going to have to deal with this." Caroline squared her shoulders and her crisp tone indicated she had made a decision. "I don't seek to make it worse without trying to circumvent the damage, but one can only try." She looked at the hovering butler. "Can you please arrange to have someone come in here to put Lord Wynn in his carriage and send him home?"

"Certainly. Of course." The man bustled off, looking relieved to be given the reprieve of actual duties. He was efficient too, for in moments two young men hurried in, hauled the semiconscious man up off the floor, and bodily carried him out of the room.

Annabel stared curiously at the woman who had so

calmly arrived on her doorstep less than a week before and taken the time and trouble to dissuade her from making what in retrospect was a huge mistake. Marrying Alfred would have made her miserable and bereft, and maybe even ruined both their lives. Knocking the apparently despicable Lord Wynn over the head with a vase full of flowers was a good start in repayment of a grave debt, but she was willing to do more.

Despite being doused with water and nearly ravaged on her own couch, Lady Wynn was able to draw a mantle of reserve around her. Annabel said plainly, "I do not see how you can possibly ever rest easy if that man does not pay for his affront. I agree that charges before a magistrate are the best course. You do not seem to me like the kind of woman who would let him get away with such a dastardly attempt."

Caroline gazed at her with those remarkable silver eyes. "I can't protect myself from every eventuality. He tried to blackmail me, and when it didn't work, he attacked me. I think maybe it might be best if I just gave him the money he desires so much. Perhaps he will then leave me alone."

"Or perhaps you will be even more powerless against him," Annabel pointed out. "Hire a guard. Or several. Take it public the way he just treated you."

Lady Wynn shook her head. "I wish it were that simple."

Why wasn't it? Annabel knit her brow. After a moment, she said slowly, "I'm confused. You mentioned blackmail. How could he possibly—"

"The wager," Caroline interrupted her, looking resolute yet still pale.

The wager. For a moment Annabel didn't understand and then it dawned on her what the other woman might be saying.

"You?" Annabel was stunned, and she felt a stab of jealousy. "You said Derek never touched—"

"He didn't." Lady Wynn pursed trembling lips together. "He's in love with you. Trust me, he wouldn't. I think at the beginning the earl thought he could . . . but things changed."

"Why would you ever do such a thing?" Considering the

circumstances, and because Derek was involved, Annabel felt she had the right to ask. "Forgive me, but it seems rather out of character."

Caroline's smile was brittle. "I had my reasons. Tell me, if you wished to know if you were truly passionless and wanting as a woman, who better to turn to than two men who claim to be superlative lovers? I knew the risks, I suppose, so the current state of affairs is entirely something I brought on myself. They both promised me anonymity, but I underestimated Franklin's interest in my inheritance. He wants to marry me to gain it, and when I declined his charming offer, he tried to force himself on me. He will be more vindictive than ever after this."

Annabel realized the implications of being labeled as the wanton critic in the contest murmured over by everyone in a society inclined to judge women with unforgiving exactitude.

Lord Wynn had somehow discovered his cousin's widow's secret participation. Even if she and Derek had never engaged in the act itself, her involvement in any guise would serve to make her as notorious as Derek and the duke, if not more so because of her gender.

Annabel murmured, "I see your dilemma."

Caroline pressed a hand that shook to her forehead and took in an audible breath. "My reputation will be in tatters by nightfall. I could try and brazen it out, I suppose, but I don't think I am stalwart enough for that. When Franklin starts spreading the word, everyone will remember I was gone at the same time as Nicholas not long ago. Denial would be futile."

Annabel couldn't help but recall how the woman sitting next to her explained the differences there could be between two lovers in their previous meeting. If her former husband had been a horrible man—and it seemed to run in the family—that meant the dashing Duke of Rothay was the man who . . . how had Caroline phrased it? Made making love more pleasurable than was imaginable? Since Annabel now knew full well what she meant, she had to wonder about the lovely Lady Wynn's relationship with the infamous Rothay. She asked quietly, "What about the duke? Surely he'd help you deny the accusation."

With what looked like infinite weariness, Caroline dropped her hand back into her lap. "No. I am a grown woman and entered into the agreement of my own free will. I'll not ask him to lie for me, and besides, he has given me more than you can imagine already."

The beautiful, usually distant Lady Wynn had fallen in love with the Devilish Duke, Annabel realized with a start. It was there in the poignant expression on Caroline's face, etched in the set of her mouth and the hint of sadness in her eyes. "Has he?" she murmured, a new understanding of the situation settling over her.

Caroline nodded. "Though I hoped his feelings were as engaged as mine, it doesn't seem to be the case. To tell you the truth, I've thought of moving to the country. Perhaps all this is a sign I should go through with that plan."

"I don't think running away will solve anything," Annabel said in objection, trying to think of a way to help.

With quiet dignity, Caroline disagreed, "I don't think I have much of a choice. I responded to Lord Manderville's and the duke's wager in the first place because I wanted to change my life. It worked, but, as with most things, not exactly as planned." She rose, graceful but obviously still pale and shaken. "I hate to be an ungracious hostess especially after what you just did for me, but I think you can understand I need to begin to make arrangements. Will you excuse me?"

Chapter Twenty-seven

Nicholas battled an uncharacteristic feeling of disquiet and studied the famous mural on the opposite wall of the formal drawing room. Who had painted it? Off the top of his head, he couldn't think of the name. The peaceful scene of water and wood presented a soothing ideal, complete with a playful cupid peeping out from behind a Grecian folly, bow in hand.

Real life was not that simple. There were no cherubic nymphs with well-poised arrows . . . or maybe there were. Hard to say. He had been stricken, that was for certain, and though he'd come to the conclusion that wound was not something he could recover from, he still had to deal with the realities.

He cocked a brow at the mischievous-looking figure with laurel leaves in a ring on his little head.

"You wished to speak to me?" His mother entered the room, an inquiring look on her face, as lovely as ever in rose silk, her dark hair coiffed and perfect. Diamonds glittered at her throat and wrist.

He bowed. "Mother. I appreciate the audience."

Her brows shot up. "That sounded frightfully formal, Nicholas. So did your note. Why send up a footman when you can come see me yourself at any time? Darling, do you mind enlightening me? You've been a bit odd since your return from your trip."

Once he did this—once he told her—it was going to be

official and the thought made him restive. She was right; he was probably wandering around like an idiot. Certainly he wasn't getting much accomplished except brooding over the situation. He cleared his throat, prepared himself to simply tell her, and then muttered instead, "I need a brandy. Would you like something?"

"Do I need something?" She sank down on an ecru satin settee and stared at him. "I must say your expression is making me uneasy."

"Try being me," he said darkly, and dashed brandy into a glass, took a solid sip, and then set the glass aside. The truth was best.

He turned, met her gaze, and steeled himself. "I have something of import to say. I thought it best if we were alone and this formality"—he gestured at the elegant salon— "seems appropriate to the moment."

She rested her hands in her lap, her dark brows raised. "You can only imagine my curiosity. What is it?"

"I'm . . . well . . . considering marriage."

Her mouth opened slightly and her eyes widened. After a prolonged moment, she said, "I see. I must be out of touch. I wasn't aware you were courting anyone. As a matter of fact, I am sure I would have been told if you were. Society pays such close attention to your every move."

"My reputation requires discretion. She isn't interested in being openly associated with me."

His mother bristled. Dark eyes flashed and her tone was frosty. "Last I checked, being the Duchess of Rothay was one of the most coveted positions in England."

The maternal show of defense made him smile wryly. "The beginning of our relationship hardly matched my intentions now. Let me rephrase. The lady has an impeccable reputation and mine is quite the opposite. I know you are aware of this. I'm labeled a rake, and in part maybe it is deserved."

There was a short silence and then his mother sighed. "I'll not censure you, though I haven't always approved of all the gossip. However, handsome young men with titles and fortunes do tend to have more temptations than some others. Perhaps it is just a mother's excuse, but I've always discounted most of the whispers as exaggerations."

He felt a twinge of amusement. "I won't confirm or deny anything specific and we'll leave at that, shall we? Anyway, I intend to propose soon and wanted to tell you."

Dark eyes glimmered with curiosity. "I'm delighted, naturally. The secrecy is a bit confusing, though. Any family I know would welcome an honest suit from you. There is a difference between what a man does in private when he is a bachelor and when he decides to choose a wife. I've seen how the society matrons trot out their daughters in front of you, reputation or no. Who is she?"

This was the tricky part. First of all, he wasn't completely sure Caroline would accept him. She'd said she didn't wish to marry again, but she also said she loved him. There was also the other issue to resolve.

He said quietly, "Caroline Wynn."

"The viscount's young widow?" His mother sat very still, surprise etched on her features.

"The same."

She digested it. "She's lovely . . . well, more than lovely, so I can see the attraction, but . . ."

"But?" he prompted as she trailed off.

"I don't know. I am rather taken aback by this, Nicholas."

"It isn't an advantageous match in some ways, I realize that. However, before you point out bloodlines and pedigrees and social alliances, let me say none of that has ever appealed to me anyway and I've made my feelings clear on the subject before, I believe." His voice was curt, so he tried to temper the tone. "I've thought this through, believe me."

His mother shook her head, the late-morning light catching the silver glints threading through her hair. "I wasn't going to say any of that."

"No?" He lifted a brow. He braced himself for the objection. Yes, he was Rothay, he could do as he pleased, and his family could do little about it, but still, he loved them and wanted their approval. Concern for Caroline also made him want them to give their wholehearted support. She'd borne the brunt of enough neglect from her own family, such as it was. To have his relatives object to her would hurt her more and he just couldn't have it.

"I was going to ask how you even know her. I haven't heard a breath of insinuation at a relationship."

That damned wager. Well, he wasn't going to confess the truth. He said instead, "We move in the same social circles. *You* know her."

"That's my very point. I've met her. Knowing her is something else altogether. She's quite distant."

Nicholas shook his head, recalling Caroline's warmth and directness, not to mention the passionate side she hid so carefully from the world. "She's anything but distant once you get to know her. Moreover, she's intelligent, well-read, and articulate. There's nothing venal about her, so my fortune isn't any part of this, and I doubt my title matters to her in the least." He ran his hand across his face and added on a breath, "I am not at all sure she'll accept me when I ask."

"Why on earth wouldn't she?" His mother looked indignant.

"Her first experience with marriage was a disaster. She's told me outright she doesn't intend to marry again." He paused for a moment and then added in a calm voice, "Which brings up another issue I'm sure will occur to you, if it hasn't already. There's the possibility she's barren. During the course of several years of marriage she never conceived."

There was no response, just silence, and Nicholas took another swallow of brandy. He went on, "I was hoping you'd approve anyway. Althea will like her. You'll like her, I'm sure. More importantly, *I* like her. I am not indifferent to my duty, Mother. I realize the title and entailed portion of the estate would go to a distant cousin should I fail to have a son. It's a devil of a dilemma to have to decide if sacrificing personal happiness is worth the gamble of marrying some young chit who might—or might not—give me a male child. I've never found the idea of it appealing in the first place and less so now. I only have this one life."

"And she will complete it?" The question was said softly, his mother's gaze fastened on his face.

Nicholas had done nothing but ponder the issue since his return from Aylesbury. "I think so. When I found myself contemplating the idea of being able to see her every day, I started to question my level of detachment. We . . . talk. The first time I met her, she quoted Alexander Pope, and I was struck by her lack of flirtatious affectation. We've discussed the latest mechanizations of the War Office, debated over the works of Horace and Virgil, and"—he couldn't help it; he smiled remembering the argument—"we both like Herr Mozart's work, but she thinks Haydn the greater master."

"I . . . see." It was a quiet statement.

Did she? He wanted her to understand. "Combined with the same level of enthusiasm as I feel over her undeniable feminine appeal, it was somewhat of a revelation. She interests me."

His mother sat back a little, her sharpened gaze on his face. "That unique smile tells me you are in earnest."

"I believe I am," he said deliberately. "But I am concerned. If I ask, and if I am lucky enough she agrees, I want her accepted fully and with warmth. I can't subject her to further indifference or hurt."

"And you are protective. What a promising sign." The dowager duchess gave him—to his relief—a brilliant, if somewhat misty, smile. "Darling, I am delighted for you, of course. What mother doesn't want her child to be happy?"

"You approve?" Here he was, a grown man, an influential duke, no less, desperate for his mother's approval. Still, it was important to him his family embrace the match without reservations.

She lifted her brows in a haughty way only she could manage, designed to send a chill through the air. "If she refuses you, let me talk to her. She'll agree, mark my word. As for her childless state, we can only wait and see. Though everyone usually blames the woman, it could be her husband was the culprit. Perhaps it isn't an issue. For that matter, fertility isn't a guarantee anyway. The Earl of Wexton has six daughters and no sons, poor man. Their marriage portions alone will bankrupt him, I'm sure."

The idea of six young females to manage was a bit daunting and Nicholas would have said something to the effect, except behind him someone cleared his throat loudly.

He turned to see one of the footmen there. "Begging your pardon, Your Grace, but there is a young man outside who insists on seeing you immediately. He refuses to state his business but says to tell you his name is Huw. That's all he'll say. I would have turned him away, but he swears you'll wish to talk to him."

Caroline's young driver had come to see him? That was unconventional enough to send a flicker of alarm right through him and the word *immediately* didn't help. Nicholas nodded. "Please take him to my study and tell him I'll be right there."

"Yes, Your Grace."

Nicholas gave his mother an apologetic look, a different kind of anxiety replacing his earlier trepidation over telling her about this new turn in his life. She'd been remarkably supportive, so his doubts there were assuaged. He went over swiftly and bent to kiss her cheek. "Forgive me, but I have a feeling this is important. I'll see you at dinner."

"Is something wrong?" she asked, correctly reading his expression, concern furrowing her brow.

"I hope not," he answered grimly. "Excuse me."

He walked swiftly across the polished floor of the hallway, his booted feet ringing in sharp staccato, the feeling of foreboding building. It could be nothing, he reassured himself. Maybe Caroline wished to see him but didn't want to send a written request and used Huw as a medium of communication instead. After all, their parting after Aylesbury had been open-ended. He hadn't proposed then, mostly because he wasn't prepared. He'd had no ring, no speech ready, no idea even he was contemplating such a permanent change in his life. Caroline hadn't petitioned him for a similar declaration of love or even a promise of a future meeting, and because his feelings had been in such turmoil, he'd gratefully accepted her silence on the subject of the future.

But on the ride back to London, he'd realized the depth of his emotions. How he would be unable to see her in public and stay away, how he longed to wake up every morning with her at his side. All those miles he contemplated the word *marriage* with growing certainty. With the problem of his mother's possible disapproval out of the way, all he needed to do was persuade Caroline he might make a suitable husband.

As he'd told his mother, Caroline wasn't interested in his financial or social status, but he knew full well she disliked his reputation. That alone—without her opposition to relinquishing her control over her own life—might make her refuse him. Infidelity was a given in their class, especially for the males. Certainly he'd never considered faithfulness except in the most abstract of terms, but then again, he'd never promised it to any woman either.

He would offer it to her, if she would accept him.

Was that love?

Huw waited by the fireplace, his cap moving nervously in his hands, his curly dark hair rumpled, an unhappy look on his face. Nicholas came into his study, closed the door behind him, and said without preamble, "What's wrong?"

"My . . . my lady doesn't know I'm here, Your Grace," the young man stammered out. "I took this upon myself."

Another twinge of apprehension hit him. Nicholas crossed to his desk and sat down behind it, indicating a chair with a motion of his hand. "This is between us, then. Tell me."

Huw looked uncomfortable, glancing at the velvet-covered wing chair as if afraid he'd soil it, but then he perched on the edge of it and cleared his throat. "It's him, sir. Lord Wynn, the bastard. I thought you should know."

Nicholas recalled how Caroline had mentioned the man with distaste. He said curtly, "What about Lord Wynn?"

"He's always sneakin' about. She doesn't want to see him, so he waits, or sends one of his footmen to wait and see if she's home." The young man's hands crushed his hat, the knuckles visibly whitening. "And this morning, he barged in, pushing right past Norman, and then he . . . he . . . well, Your Grace, there ain't no good way to say this. He tried to have his way with her, he did."

Nicholas felt a flame of rage explode in his brain. "Is she hurt?"

"No, sir. A young lady caller bashed his high-and-mighty lordship over the head. Jones and me tossed him into his carriage and told his driver to take the rubbish home. I imagine he's there now, nursing one hell of a headache. But he'll be back for her, mark my word. In fancy clothes or in rags, I know his kind. He wants her money. It ain't no secret. Since she won't have nothing to do with him, he meant to ruin her and force her to marry him."

Though he wasn't conscious of standing up, Nicholas realized he was on his feet. "Thank you for telling me, Huw." He added with lethal promise in his voice, "I'll take care of Lord Wynn."

Margaret gazed at Derek with resigned censure over the rim of her teacup. "The words *the sooner, the better* make me jump to a certain conclusion."

He lifted his brows, too happy to feel properly chastened at her implication. Even the day reflected his mood, sunny and warm, the afternoon pleasant and the informal parlor holding a golden glow. He said neutrally, "I've waited for Annabel a long time. Do you blame me for wanting a swift wedding now that she's agreed?"

His aunt sighed. "I suppose not. A special license is probably in order anyway. Still, your hasty marriage right after her broken engagement is going to cause a tidal wave of gossip."

Thomas, who had been silent so far, chuckled. "I am not sure Derek has ever concerned himself overmuch with what people say, my dear. Besides, happiness wins over the opinions of people who will soon see it is a love match and lose interest. Controversy holds society riveted. Marital bliss bores them all to tears."

A cynical truth, but accurate, Derek thought. "I'm glad there is no objection, then. How about tomorrow afternoon?"

Margaret looked flustered, her teacup rattling into the saucer. "Derek! Tomorrow?"

"I've talked to Annabel and she agreed that whenever I could secure the arrangements, she wanted to proceed. Tomorrow was the earliest possible."

"How much did that cost?" Thomas just looked amused. "A small fortune, I wager."

It had, the price of expedience never small. Annabel was worth it, and he found being so close to having her bound to him in every way, including legally, made him impatient. "I didn't care," Derek admitted, not bothering to dissemble. "Who could think of something as mundane as money in comparison with having her as my wife?"

Margaret and Thomas exchanged a glance. It was an unspoken communication, moving and obviously intimate. Thomas reached over and took his wife's hand, raising it to his lips for a moment. "I believe," he said, "I know just what you mean."

And after their many years of marriage, Margaret still blushed. "You've always been hopelessly sentimental."

"I suppose I am," Thomas responded with a small unrepentant shrug. He turned back to Derek. "You have my permission to wed Annabel, of course, but you've had that all along. It was your own mind you needed to reconcile to the idea."

The arrival of the subject of their conversation in a flurry of sprigged muslin, golden hair, and breathless agitation halted the discussion and Derek stood at once. He smiled, but Annabel didn't smile back.

His stomach tightened. Surely she hadn't changed her mind? After the sweet, warm passion they had shared . . .

"Good afternoon." She gave Margaret and Thomas a perfunctory greeting. "Sorry I'm late. I was with a . . . friend. I . . . well, Derek, can I please talk to you?"

He had been surprised at her absence, but Margaret said she was out with her maid, running a few errands, and his aunt didn't seem concerned, so he hadn't thought too much about it.

"Of course." His voice was a little thick.

His fiancée grabbed his hand. "A walk in the garden, then?"

Puzzled, he nodded, bowed to Thomas and Margaret, who looked just as surprised, and allowed himself to be led outside into the small walled garden behind the town house. In the sun-warmed embrace of flowering trees and stone paths, the expression of the young woman clutching his hand was incongruously somber.

But it was promising she still kept their fingers clasped together. "Away from the house," she suggested. "I don't want to be overheard."

"Whatever you wish, of course."

"I'll explain, just give me a moment." A pretty frown creased her brow.

Since he'd walk hand in hand with her off the end of a cliff, he didn't argue. After a moment, when they were close to the back at the corner farthest away from the house, she let go of his hand and turned to him.

Her blue eyes—the ones he thought were so lovely with those dark gold lashes and deep cobalt hue—stared at him accusingly. "By your own admission, *you* started this. You need to help her now."

Not even wedded yet and he was already in trouble.

Mystified, he asked, "Help who and started what?"

"I know Lady Wynn was the one to pass judgment on your wager."

Bloody hell. He opened his mouth to say only God knew what, but Annabel forestalled him. "She told me nothing ever happened between you. Considering her feelings for the duke, and her reasons for entering the contest in the first place, I believe her. The trouble is, what you put forth as a playful challenge to Rothay now threatens to destroy her. In a way you are responsible, and indirectly, so am I."

He was culpable over the wager but had no idea what she was talking about. "Destroy her how?"

"Lord Wynn knows she volunteered to be your judge. I can say firsthand he is a conscienceless blackguard. He threatened to ruin her socially but not before he tried to ruin her in truth." Annabel paused and then shrugged her slim shoulders. "I'm afraid I knocked him unconscious."

"I beg your pardon?" Derek stared down at his bride-to-be in consternation. "Annabel, do you mind clarifying what you are talking about?"

Her story, told in quick concise words, made him feel a surge of anger as he heard about Caroline's brush with Wynn's nefarious intentions. When Annabel was done, Derek was furious and he could only imagine how Nicholas would feel. "If he follows through with his threat, Wynn just made the last mistake of his miserable life," he said through his teeth. "Nick will tear him limb from limb. More than that, he'll call him out."

"I certainly hope so." There among the gardens, her feminine figure surrounded by glossy green leaves and delicate blooms, Annabel looked not just indignant but fierce. "She refuses to tell him unfortunately. I suggested it, but she would not hear of sending for him."

"Why the devil not?" Derek understood women when it came to their bodies, their susceptibility to romantic gestures, their sensitivity to a look or a glance, but he would never claim to fathom their logic.

"She doesn't want to draw him to her that way. When and if he comes, she prefers it not to be because he feels a responsibility to save her from what she terms 'her own folly,' but because he loves her and freely acknowledges it. I empathize completely."

A wry smile curved his lips. "Yet you still wish for me to interfere, correct?"

"Absolutely."

Chapter Twenty-eight

"You misunderstand," Nicholas said in his best aristocratic tone, icy cold and unrelenting. "I do not care if Lord Wynn is receiving or not. I *will* see him."

The servant correctly registered both the look on his face and the conviction in his voice. He was young and a half foot shorter than Nicholas, his dismayed expression showing he felt ill equipped to handle the situation. The footman cleared his throat and rasped out, "He's indisposed, Your Grace."

"I imagine he is, by all accounts. Nonetheless, show me in and tell him I'll search the house to find him if he is too spineless to come down."

In the face of such determination, the servant acquiesced, probably because, Nicholas thought as the young man stepped back and held the door for him to enter the foyer, a man like Wynn did not inspire much loyalty.

He was shown into what passed for the formal drawing room, the furnishings spare and not quite shabby, but wellworn. Since he knew Caroline had inherited the Wynn town house, the place was probably rented anyway. Nicholas didn't sit down but stood instead by the fireplace and glanced at the clock in the corner. He told himself he would give Wynn five minutes, and tamped down the urge to pace.

Very rarely did he lose his temper. His self-control was part innate, part learned because his position and responsibilities demanded it, but even raising his voice was not a common occurrence. Of course, he couldn't really remember feeling so murderously angry either.

The man had touched Caroline. More than that, he'd undoubtedly frightened her.

"What the devil do you want, Rothay?" The question was snarled from the doorway. "How dare you force your way into my home?"

Nicholas turned, focusing his gaze on the man who came into the room, noting with satisfaction his lordship did look a trifle white around the mouth, as if he was in pain.

He said pleasantly, "I'm tempted to kill you."

The sneering expression on the other man's pallid face froze. After a moment, he sputtered, "I have no idea why. I don't know what that cold little bitch told you, but—"

Nicholas stepped forward at the insult. "I still might," he said reflectively, his eyes narrowing, his posture undeniably threatening. "Considering my current frame of mind, I advise you to adjust your form of address when referring to Lady Wynn. It would be my pleasure to tear you into tiny pieces with my bare hands."

Wynn stiffened. "Over a woman? You?"

"Over *this* woman, yes."

"Come, now, Rothay, isn't she just another one of your casual bed partners? You change them like you change your shirts. Besides, I find it hard to believe this matter affects you at all. She's a whore, offering to spread her legs for two different men. Why would you care if she gave me the same favors?"

Nicholas felt his hands clench into fists, a red haze momentarily obscuring his vision. He took a deep breath, knowing if he touched Wynn now, he might just snap his neck. Through his teeth he said, "If you had the slightest notion of how much I am tempted to disregard the fact murder is a crime in England, you would shut your mouth this moment. As it is, I can call you out and kill you at dawn tomorrow morning with no more remorse than if I stepped on an insect. Now, you'll be quiet and listen to what I have to say, understand?"

For a moment he wondered if the other man, who hadn't sat down either, would turn and run. Lord Wynn seemed to at last comprehend his true danger, for he lost that air of bravado and turned a sickly color.

"Good, that's better," Nicholas said softly. "I think we understand each other. Here is the bargain. You stay away from her. Far away. Don't look at her, don't contact her. If she attends a function and you are there, you leave at once. For the next few months at least, I suggest a sojourn in the country until my temper cools. If you are in town and we run into each other, I can't answer for my self-restraint. I think that part is clear enough."

Wynn opened his mouth as if to object, but wisely closed it. His pale eyes had narrowed to slits and his hands shook. Men who terrorized women were rarely anything but cowards, and Wynn was no exception.

"Let me go on. If you say one vile word about her, I'll destroy you. Socially, financially, in every way possible. The Manning family has influence in every corner of England and, for that matter, the Continent as well. The prince regent is a friend of mine. You'll be shunned, destitute, and banished. If it appeals to you to test my word, just spread the rumor Caroline was involved in any way with that wager."

"If he does, he'll answer to me also."

The lazy interjection had a steely undertone and Wynn jerked at the sound of another voice, whirling around. "Manderville," he choked out, looking positively ill. There were now beads of sweat on his brow.

It *was* Derek. He stood in the doorway, leaning one shoulder against the frame. "Your footman seemed disinclined to refuse me entrance with Nick here already. I see he has everything well in hand, though I admit when I heard the Duke of Rothay had arrived, I expected bloodshed."

"It could still happen," Nicholas said, enunciating each word carefully, "if he insults the lady again. What brings you here, Derek?"

"My fiancée." Derek made the announcement with casual aplomb, looking at Wynn. "I think you two met this morning when she delivered a vase of flowers to your thick skull, Wynn. I was ordered to also disabuse his lordship of any notion he might bother Lady Wynn and not suffer for it. I see you beat me to it."

"I could press charges against her for assault," Wynn said, but it was a weak attempt at defiance, belied by the look in his eyes. "What she saw was a romantic moment and she misunderstood. Caroline enticed me, and when we were caught, she denied it. I—"

Nicholas moved then, in two strides catching the man by the shirt and slamming him up against the wall so hard the painting above the fireplace wobbled. "You might just have pushed me too far."

Wynn gasped as Nicholas brought his forearm up. The man's face turned a dull red, his breath whistling out as Nicholas applied enough pressure to make sure his sincerity wasn't misunderstood.

After a moment, Derek drawled, "I realize killing him holds a definite appeal, but if you intend to let him live out his miserable life, you might want to let him go now, Nick."

His friend was right, and Nicholas managed to loosen his grip with effort, stepping back. Wynn drooped, his hand massaging his windpipe, his pale eyes watering.

Nicholas said tersely, "Remember every single word I said. Caroline is under my protection in all ways, including my name."

"I think you've made your point," Derek observed drily.

They left together, rapidly striding out of the town house past the nervous footman. On the sunny street outside, Nicholas glanced at his friend. "Thank you for wanting to step in on Caroline's behalf."

"I went to tell you about the morning's events first, but apparently you'd already been informed." Derek grinned. "I feel rather useless after all, but I could have helped you dispose of the body. I doubt somehow he'd be missed."

"Her driver came and told me. Huw seems to have a genuine affection for her and I am grateful."

"*You* have affection for her too if your arrival in Ayles-

bury or your current state of affront are any indication."
Derek paused. "When you said she was under the protection
of your name, did I interpret it correctly?"

"She hasn't agreed yet, but I have my hopes Caroline will
marry me." Nicholas cocked a brow. "Speaking of such
things, did I not hear you say your 'fiancée'? When did this
come about and who the hell is she?"

"This came about recently and is the direct result of the
wager in many ways. Annabel has made me reexamine some
of the priorities in my life."

Nicholas registered surprise. "Your uncle's young ward?"

"The same." Derek hesitated and shrugged. "I've been in
love with her for quite some time but was too stubborn to
admit it. I almost lost her."

"I see." Nicholas had met Miss Reid of course, but in
view of the fact she was an eligible young miss, he had
steered clear of further association. Since he knew she'd become engaged recently, he now understood some of Derek's
preoccupation in the past few months.

They looked at each other as a carriage rolled by on the
street, the warmth of the afternoon a cocoon, mutual amusement lighting their faces. Nicholas said, "I'm glad for you.
She's a lovely girl."

"I'm happy for you as well."

"It isn't settled yet," Nicholas muttered, "but hopefully it
soon will be. I'll let you know how it goes."

He swung into his carriage and rapped on the ceiling.

What a disaster. Not just the day, but her life.

Caroline stared in the mirror, seeing the remnants of tears
on her cheeks, the disordered state of her hair, and the hollow look in her eyes. She'd set things in motion already,
sending a letter to an agent about listing the town house for
sale. Afterward she'd gone upstairs to lie down and eventually fallen into an uneasy sleep.

It was hard to define her roiling emotions, she thought as
she plucked the pins from her hair and reached for her brush.
Catastrophe had struck—she shuddered at the memory of

Franklin's bruising hands on her—but even though she'd been rescued by Annabel's resourcefulness, she had no illusions her husband's cousin would keep his knowledge about her role in the wager a secret.

The undeniable truth about her relationship with the Devilish Duke would be made public, and even if Derek Drake denied any involvement with her, all the *haut ton* would know she offered. Her status would go from unattainable to promiscuous the moment the word got out, and she doubted Franklin would waste much time.

A traitorous, illogical part of her didn't care about the whispers. When weighed against her never having lain in Nicholas's arms, never having tasted his seductive kisses, or felt the warmth of his smile . . . well, the cost of social ostracism was high, but she knew it was worth it. She'd gone from existing to living.

She murmured in abstracted self-mockery,

> *Dear, damn'd, distracting town, farewell!*
> *Thy fools no more I'll tease:*
> *This year in peace, ye critics, dwell,*
> *Ye harlots, sleep at ease.*

Pope's "A Farewell to London" took on a whole new cynical meaning, even though it was one of her favorite works.

The sharp rap on her door was perfunctory, because it opened before she could answer it. As she turned around, Nicholas stepped into the room, looking tall and very male in the sanctuary of pastel colors and dainty furnishings.

She couldn't help a small gasp of surprise at his audacity, though she knew him well enough by now to expect such reckless acts. This situation became more scandalous by the moment. Now the Devilish Duke was in her bedroom. The entire household would be agog.

And tomorrow, no doubt, all London would be talking about it.

Perversely, she was happy to see him despite the arrogance of his arrival in her bedroom uninvited. He stood there, his gleaming raven hair slightly ruffled, his dark eyes holding a somber light. As always, she was struck by the magnetic power of his presence. If she had even tried to speak, she would have no idea what to say. His ill-advised and unexpected arrival left her completely without words.

He spoke first in simple explanation. "I needed to see you. To be sure you were unharmed."

When she still didn't say anything, he added, "Huw told me what happened."

Caroline found her voice, his calm intrusion into her bedroom still a shock. "Did it occur to you I might come downstairs if word was sent up you wished to see me?"

Nicholas just smiled at the outrage in her tone. "Had I thought it over, perhaps. I didn't want to wait."

Why did he have to do this to her now? When she was so vulnerable and shaken. "You shouldn't be here," she said, but it wasn't with conviction. Her hand had started to tremble and she quickly set aside her brush. "I'm not even dressed."

"I like you best undressed," he responded, his gaze riveting, heated. He moved toward her. "Did that bastard hurt you? Everyone says no, but I thought you might need me."

Did she need him? God, yes. More than she realized, and every objection she had to his assumption he could simply walk into her household and invade her bedroom vanished. If everything was already in shambles, what did she care if Nicholas was reported to all and sundry as feeling he had the perfect right to stroll in unannounced while she wore only her chemise? Regardless of her actions, all London would hear about their association soon enough and the comfort of his arms beckoned.

"I . . . ," she began, but stopped, not at all certain what she was going to say. A small sob escaped.

She rarely cried. Since the first night of her marriage, she had dismissed tears as useless.

"My love." Nicholas was there, sweeping her up, settling onto the small bench in front of her dressing table with her body cradled in his arms as if she were something precious and breakable. "It's over. I've taken care of it—of him. You're safe. With me."

Had he just called her his love? Of all the endearments that flowed so easily from his lips, he'd never used that one before. Caroline rested her head against his chest and allowed herself the luxury of thinking he meant it. The scent of him evoked memories of idyllic interludes and luxurious pleasure.

The rest of his speech registered a moment later. "What do you mean you've taken care of him?"

Nicholas pressed his mouth to her temple in a gentle caress. "There are some advantages to being high placed and wealthy. I paid Lord Wynn a call this afternoon. Let's say he and I came to an understanding. He's still alive, for now anyway."

Shocked, she stirred, lifting her head so she could see his face. "Nicholas—"

He meant what he'd just said. She saw it in the glittering anger still in his eyes, despite the tender hold of his arms.

His smile held no trace of humor. "I'm confident he was convinced, especially with my hands at his throat. I suppose my reaction was barbaric, but warranted, I think, considering my feelings for you. I'd have had him prosecuted and punished except I was sure you wouldn't want to endure the publicity of the ordeal. The same for calling him out. Your name would still be bandied about and I promised you discretion."

Her heart had started a slow, hard pound. His thighs felt like iron under her bottom, his arms strong and sure.

. . . my feelings for you . . .

Nicholas whispered in her ear, his breath warm, "Did you not say you love me because of who I am, not what I am? Not the duke, but the man himself."

She could feel her lips tremble as she attempted a smile. "You know I did."

He gathered her closer, his arms cradling her. "Once, a long time ago, I mistook the words *I love you* as an interest in my heart, not my title and fortune. I was young and brash and stupid and she was older and supremely venal."

Caroline had wondered exactly what had made him so wary of any emotional involvement. She rested in his embrace, silently willing him to tell her.

His mouth curved in that humorless smile, his dark eyes shaded by those long thick lashes. "I discovered Helena's true nature the hard way, by having the privilege of finding her in bed with another man. I learned later she'd planned all of it, from our very first meeting. She confided in one of her other lovers well before she and I ever met she had her eye on my title and the fortune and prestige that went with it. So she deliberately wheedled a friend to introduce me to her, fell into my arms with convincing enthusiasm, but neglected to discontinue her other associations. You might find this a little hard to believe, but at eighteen, I was naive and a romantic."

She had experienced a similar disillusionment at the same age when she married. "I understand."

"The humiliation when I realized just how many people knew exactly what she was doing and how easily I was led is hard to shake. I then embarked on a mission to destroy the persona of Nicholas Manning, the susceptible young duke."

It was difficult to imagine him other than easily confident and sophisticated in every way. Nicholas's devil-may-care charm was like polish on a precious stone.

Caroline smiled and touched his jaw. "I think you succeeded."

His mouth twisted. "God knows I tried. For the past decade I have played at love in the physical sense, but kept my distance otherwise. I vowed I would never make a mistake like that again." He made a small gesture of uncharacteristic helplessness with his hand. "But despite my wariness, I believe you aren't lying about your feelings. I wouldn't hurt you to save my own life and you've made it clear being lovers is out of the question. I think we have no options left but the obvious. I've thought of nothing else lately and it has my life upside down."

"I vowed to never trust any man enough to marry again." Caroline felt the horror of the day fade, the frustration and bewilderment in his tone more persuasive than any honeyed words of love. "So, see? We share the same misgivings."

His eyes held a grave light. "What if we both broke our inner promises? Is that a good way to begin a life together?"

She felt a welling emotion, so powerful she could barely speak. "I think, considering the nature of the promises and why they were made, yes, I believe it would be an excellent way to start over."

Finally it came. A lift of the corner of his mouth first, and then a wicked glint in his eye. The Devilish Duke resurfaced. "As if I was going to give you a choice. Even my mother told me I'd be an idiot to not insist upon a swift wedding. She is very free with her advice and I take it sparingly, but in this singular case I agree with her."

He'd discussed her with his family and they approved?

"Does she realize I'm barren?" It hurt to say it. God, how it hurt.

"She pointed out you are young yet, and there is no absolute proof of the matter. Besides, I believe she is so relieved to see me contemplate marriage with something other than grim resignation and detachment. She finds my feelings outweigh her concerns over the legacies of titles and money."

Caroline felt dizzier than ever, but now it was happiness that had her head whirling. "What will she think about the scandal?"

"What scandal?"

How like him not to worry over it.

"If Franklin—"

"I told you I took care of it. He won't say a word, trust me."

"I do trust you."

It came so easily, because it was true. Nicholas moved, standing up and settling her back on the small seat as he went down on one knee before her, his handsome face still and serious. He took her cold hands in his and held them in gentle persuasion. His gaze was seeking, searching, and she felt it to the depths of her soul. "Do you? Enough to take a chance on a man who has a reputation like mine?"

Was the Duke of Rothay really kneeling at her feet, offering marriage? Every woman in London would swoon to be in her position. Perhaps every woman in England . . . or on the whole Continent . . .

"Nicholas." Her voice was nothing but a husky rasp.

"I could use a 'yes' to ease some of my nervousness, Caroline."

Nicholas Manning nervous? She could feel the slight tremor in his long bronzed fingers as they held hers, and there was a strained look around his mouth she'd never seen before. Gone was the arrogant aristocrat and in his place was the man she'd fallen in love with so easily, the gentle, considerate lover who had denied himself to reassure a fearful woman, the man who spun dreamlike moonlit evenings and romantic dances on terraces and sensual, clandestine carriage rides.

"Yes."

The tension eased, his fingers tightened momentarily, and the flash of his smile held reckless triumph. Still kneeling, he told her, "I've been racking my feeble brain trying to think up the most romantic way possible to do this. None of my ideas included that blackguard Wynn being the catalyst." He paused and said with wry inflection, "I'm afraid I have never proposed before."

"I've never been proposed to either," Caroline admitted, her throat thick with emotion, "but in my judgment you did a fine job."

Nicholas lifted one of her hands to his mouth and brushed a kiss across the backs of her fingers. One dark brow quirked upward. "Forgive me for sounding like an autocratic husband even before our new vows are given to replace our old ones, but your judging days are quite over, my love."

Epilogue

The silk wrap slid from her shoulders and Caroline swallowed a lump of nervousness that lodged suddenly in her throat. The footman whisked off with it and she felt the slight pressure of her husband's hand at her back.

Nicholas peered down into her face. "Are you quite sure you are up to this? You didn't feel well this morning. I can always summon the carriage back around."

She smiled and hopefully did a credible job. "This must be done sometime. Now is as good as any."

It was better done now, though he didn't know it yet, than in a few months. The suspicion she might be with child filled her with an exultant joy she couldn't yet trust. Her courses had always been very much on time, but she was late, and there were a few other things pointing a finger in that direction, including her earlier indisposition. While emptying her stomach into a basin each morning wasn't exactly bliss, the idea of being pregnant with his child was heaven.

That afternoon in the glen in Essex. It had happened then. Somehow, she was sure of it.

"I agree. Let us get this over with as quickly as possible. Though I am not much looking forward to it." Next to her, Annabel Drake, the new Countess of Manderville, smiled nervously. She looked dazzling in a peach-silk gown that set off her fair coloring to an advantage, her golden hair swept into an intricate coiffure. "Ever since the announcement in the paper appeared that due to unforeseen circumstances the two of you have canceled the wager, Margaret says all of the beau monde is quivering to know why. I imagine this evening will be interesting, to say the least. Everyone will be talking about us."

Beside her in elegant brown and cream evening wear, his blond hair framing those features that set so many female hearts to fluttering, her tall husband had an amused look on his face. Derek drawled, "I assure you the worry over this is for naught. There will be an initial few twitters and then everyone will forget about the four of us."

"Exactly." Nicholas adjusted his cuff and looked unruffled. "I have to think this is a rather brilliant plan if I do say so myself."

"Since it was all your idea," Caroline murmured, and shot him a rueful glance. "It sounded good at the time you proposed it, but right now it is daunting."

It *had* been his inspiration. Two special licenses, a double discreet wedding, since none of them had any interest in either a long engagement or more scandal, and no public announcement of their nuptials in the society section of the newspaper. The subterfuge had spared them more drama so they could enjoy a few days alone together before the *haut ton* caught whiff of the titillating news that the two most notorious rakes in London society had married on the same day.

One of them to a standoffish widow who had a reputation for being unattainable but had been lured into Rothay's bed, and the other to a young woman who had severed her engagement to give in to Lord Manderville's persuasive charms. Or similar versions, embellished into a cloud of speculation, no doubt.

It was easy to imagine the rumors that would fly. Caroline took a deep breath and clasped her husband's arm. The wager also would come up. Of course it would. A united front for the four of them did seem best.

"Ready?" Nicholas, more dashing and handsome than any man had a right to be in black-and-white tailored clothing, flashed a reassuring smile. "Just act as if we are the only people in the room."

"I'll try." She lifted her chin and affected her most detached expression.

Derek and Annabel went first down the sweep of the staircase. The ballroom below was crowded and noisy, but when the butler announced in his lofty, stentorian voice the Earl *and* Countess of Manderville there was a sudden lull in the hundreds of conversations.

Caroline braced herself as they followed.

"The Duke and Duchess of Rothay."

The room fell silent. Even the orchestra stopped playing.

Oh yes, not nerve-racking in the least, Caroline thought with cynicism, hoping she looked as collected and composed as ever, but her color was high. She could feel the warmth in her face under the stunned gazes of several hundred people.

As if half of London wasn't gaping at them, Nicholas murmured in a noncommittal tone, "I do hope the champagne is not too warm. I detest the stuff unless it is properly chilled."

That's what he was worried about? The temperature of the beverage he might be served? Caroline couldn't help it; she laughed. The sound floated out into the hushed quiet and something snapped, the unearthly hush replaced by a babble of voices.

Perhaps not such a bad plan after all. If Caroline could endure this evening, then the worst was really over.

The surge of the well-dressed guests eager to give their congratulations—and of course hoping for some sort of juicy tidbit on the secret romances—was overwhelming, but Nicholas stayed at her side, fending off the obvious questions in his inimitable way, usually with little more than a lifted brow. After the grueling first hour, he managed to extract them from the crush and pulled her onto the dance floor for a waltz.

"Some answers," he said, "are better done with actions than words."

At first she wasn't sure what he meant.

Until she noticed how close he held her. Very close. Rather like the evening on the terrace at his estate in Essex when they were alone. She'd thought it scandalous then. In this setting, with the eyes of all the *ton* upon them, it was even worse.

They didn't call him the Devilish Duke for nothing. Her first urge was to put a decent distance between them. They were going to be talked about enough already.

"No." The circle of his arm didn't ease as she tried to push away a fraction. "Let them see."

"See what?" Caroline argued on a low hiss of protest. "That being the subject of every gossip doesn't bother you? That, they already know. It does, however, bother me."

"Let them see I love you."

She stumbled over the hem of the diaphanous gown of midnight blue she wore at his request, her skirts swirling around his legs as they moved. But his arm was around her waist keeping her upright with inflexible support, and his dark eyes held hers, poignant with emotion. As the music rose and fell, she lost track of the intent crowd, the whispering, the avid stares. A happiness she didn't think possible turned the night from a trial into a triumph.

Nicholas bent his head so his mouth brushed her temple as they moved into a turn, the warm caress much too personal a gesture for hundreds to witness.

She didn't care.

I love you.

He hadn't said it before and she hadn't demanded it either.

Maybe he was right. She was sure the gossips were wondering how the distant Lady Wynn had captured the handsome, wicked duke without society ever seeing them do as much as exchange a glance.

If it hadn't been for one very indecent proposition, she wouldn't have.

Were her feet even still on the floor? If so, she couldn't tell. She murmured, "Have I mentioned before how grateful I am for the existence of claret?"

He laughed, catching her reference to that fateful night when he and Derek had made their challenge, but there was a serious look in his eyes. "Is that all you have to say?"

"No."

"Then?" He gracefully spun her into a turn.

Heedless of the scandalized audience, she whispered, "Hold me closer."

Read on for an excerpt from
Emma Wildes's next novel,

*Lessons from a
Scarlet Lady*

Coming from Signet Eclipse
in January 2010.

*If you have not captured his attention in the first place,
how can you possibly hold it?*

—*the entire preface to* Lady Rothburg's Advice,
published 1802

The vestibule was full of well-dressed people milling like jeweled birds in their finery, just as she'd hoped. Brianna Northfield let her husband slip her velvet cloak from her shoulders and deliberately kept her back toward him, smiling and nodding at several acquaintances in the throng. Her husband handed the garment to a nearby attendant, greeted Lord Bassford, who was an old friend, while Brianna waited, still strategically turned away.

This was the first step in her plan and she certainly hoped it worked, for she felt exposed.

Very much so.

Colton finished his conversation and took her arm, his gaze thankfully intent on scanning the crowd for a way to proceed toward their private box. "This way, my dear. I think we can squeeze through over by where the Earl of Farrington is standing."

"That young woman with him is not someone I know," she murmured, noting the beautiful young lady's fiery hair and lush figure. "Goods heavens, he must be old enough to be her father."

"His latest mistress, I believe," her husband said coolly as they edged through the crowd. "I'm sure they are here at the opera together simply to annoy his wife. Discretion has never been Farrington's strong suit."

The note of disapproval in her husband's voice did not escape her, but at least it wasn't directed at her. That is, not yet. Colton Northfield, the fifth Duke of Rolthven, did not believe in public displays of one's private life. She had learned that much in three months of marriage.

If he had a mistress, he certainly would not bring her out and flaunt the affair in front of all fashionable London society. Neither would he purposely hurt or humiliate his wife. Brianna simply prayed he *didn't* have a mistress, nor did she ever want him to feel he required one.

His touch on her arm was light as he guided her toward the carpeted stairs that led up to the elegant box overlooking center stage. Heads turned as they passed, other friends giving greetings, and Brianna noticed more than one gentlemen allowed his gaze to linger on her, and several ladies raised their brows.

Fine. After all, she wished to make an impression. If the length of the masculine stares was a good measure, she was certainly succeeding.

She felt the moment when Colton first noticed her gown. They were halfway up the stairs and he faltered, his fingers tightening. One foot on the next step, he stopped cold, his gaze riveted suddenly on her décolletage. "Good God, what are you wearing?"

"Should you really halt on the stairs and stare so pointedly at my bosom?" she asked with a calm she didn't particularly feel, taking another determined step past him. "This is Madame Ellen's latest creation and the neckline is a little daring, yes, but I am assured I have the proper figure to carry it off."

Her husband didn't move for a moment, his glittering gaze still intent on the ivory flesh that swelled above the material of her bodice, the entire upper curves exposed. He bit out in a low tone, "You certainly can carry it off, but perhaps you should have asked yourself if you *should* carry it off. Or better yet, have asked me."

Ask him about fashion? As if he normally cared. He dressed impeccably but he never commented on her clothing at all.

Perhaps that would change. It would be a nice beginning to know he actually looked at her.

Brianna murmured, "People are staring, Colton, wondering if we are actually arguing in public."

"We might be," he muttered. "Have you lost your mind?"

The Duke of Rolthven in an altercation with his wife on the stairs at the opera? Never. She had chosen this venue because she was confident of his ingrained sense of politesse. He would be horrified of making a scene. Brianna summoned a serene smile—utterly false, for she could feel the warmth in her cheeks and the beat of her pulse in her throat. "Not at all. Shall we take our seats?"

Uttering a low curse, he responded by almost dragging her up the rest of the way, his long fingers locked around her wrist as he ushered her down the gallery and into the balcony with their private seats. His expression was hard to read, but his mouth formed a tight line as he seated her and took the adjacent chair.

The theater was packed as always, the huge chandeliers glittering, the gilt boxes holding the buzz of hundreds of conversations. People attended not so much to see the performance but to be seen themselves and to observe others, something her husband knew full well.

"I suppose since we are already here, wrapping you up in your cloak and carrying you outside might be remarked upon," he said sardonically, extending his long legs. "I wondered why we garnered so much attention as we went through the lobby, but now I understand perfectly. I imagine more opera glasses will be directed toward your lavishly displayed breasts this evening than at the stage. Whatever possessed you, madam, to choose such an outrageous gown?"

Because I want to seduce you, she thought, gazing at him. He looked as devastatingly attractive as ever this evening, even with a frown on his handsome face and the sensual line of his mouth compressed in reproof. He was tall, with thick chestnut hair and a lean, athletic build, and on one of those rare occasions when Colton smiled, every woman in the room felt a little flushed. High cheekbones gave his face an arrogant cast, his nose was straight, the line of his jaw and chin nicely chiseled. The first time Brianna had seen him she'd been dazzled by his flagrant good looks, and when he actually began to show some interest in her, she had tumbled head over heels in love like some maiden in a romantic fable.

But there were some aspects to her marriage she hadn't anticipated. As a mythical prince, Colton had a few flaws. And he had not married the meek little ingénue she suspected he thought he was going to get.

With as much composure as possible, Brianna answered, "There are many ladies in attendance this evening attired in gowns every bit as fashionably low-cut as mine. I thought you would like it."

"*Like* having every man in London ogle my wife's bare bosom?" His brow lifted, but his gaze strayed downward again. "Think again, my dear."

"Actually," she answered, a flicker of hope stirring because, though he sounded annoyed, he couldn't seem to stop staring, "I thought *you* might like the way I look in this gown."

For a moment he seemed surprised, his eyes, a vivid azure shade, narrowing a fraction. "You are stunningly beautiful, Brianna, and I always admire the way you look. Why do you think I married you?"

That wasn't what she wanted to hear. It was exactly what she *didn't* want to hear. Shaking out her fan, Brianna said furiously, "I hope you didn't wed me, Your Grace, simply to have as an ornament on your arm at functions like this. I am a person, and a woman, and your wife."

Her retort caused an uncharacteristically disconcerted look to cross his face. "Perhaps that wasn't well put. I meant you are always attractive to me. You do not have to be half naked for me to think so."

"Then prove it."

"I beg your pardon?" His arched eyebrows shot up and he stared at her, obviously mystified.

Good. She truly had his attention. All too often he seemed only absently aware of her presence. He was a busy man and she understood and accepted that the responsibilities of title and fortune consumed a great deal of his time. But when they were together, she wanted to know her husband enjoyed her company. They were both still adjusting to marriage—or at least she was, for she didn't notice his changing much about his routine now that he had a wife. He still worked most of the day, still went to his club, still spent more time in the gaming rooms at balls and soirees than with her. Many society couples lived very separate lives. But it wasn't what she wanted for herself, and to change his attitude about it, she was determined to make him truly *notice* her.

The orchestra began to stir. Raising her voice so he could hear her words, not caring about the inhabitants of the boxes all around them, Brianna said clearly, "Tonight I want you to prove to me that you find me attractive."

"What the devil are you talking about?"

Brianna gazed at her husband and gave a small sigh. "I worried you might say something exactly like that."

Women were such unpredictable, irrational, and emotional creatures, Colton Northfield pondered darkly, only half listening to Herr Mozart's creation, his gaze idly resting on the stage, where a brightly clad troupe danced to the same lively melodies he had heard so many times before. Next to him, his lovely wife sat in rapt audience, her fan waving in languid sweeps against the closeness of the huge room. Tendrils of silky pale gold hair brushed her slender neck, and her delicate face was slightly flushed from the heat.

He hadn't lied; she was one of the most beautiful women he had ever seen, and from the first moment of their introduction, nearly a year ago, he had wanted her intensely. Courtship, the necessary engagement, and wedded life had not changed that one bit. Even now, the quiver of her opulent flesh as it swelled above the bodice of an ivory gown that—no matter what she said—bordered on scandalous, made his erection swell uncomfortably against the confinement of his fitted breeches.

What exactly was percolating through her pretty head? If asked before this evening, Colton would have said that Brianna was the last young woman of his acquaintance he would expect to wear something so outrageous. Usually she was a proper young lady. Sometimes too proper, but then again, she was innocent and inexperienced still. He had curbed his lust as much as possible and kept lovemaking between them a subdued experience, trying to familiarize her with the intimacy of the act and loosen her understandable inhibitions.

There was certainly nothing inhibited about her tonight.

She leaned forward and lifted the gold opera glasses in her hand to get a better look at the stage. The mounded flesh barely contained by the bodice of her dress severely tested the material, and he could swear he saw the edge of one pink, perfect nipple.

Maybe he'd been going about things in the wrong way, he mused. Not that he approved in any way of her appearing in public half naked, but he did admire the view. She certainly had lovely breasts, full and pliant, and the virginal color of the gown offset by the sinfully low neckline did some interesting things to the area below his waist.

Very interesting things.

"The soprano is spectacular, isn't she?" The glasses lowered and his wife smiled, her dark blue eyes, framed by long lashes, still focused on the performance.

Since he wasn't really paying attention, it was hard for him to comment.

You are spectacular.

In a noncommittal tone, he mumbled a less than brilliant response, "Yes. Very talented."

"That last aria was breathtaking."

What was breathtaking was the graceful curve of Brianna's bared shoulder and the flawless perfection of her skin. Not to mention the alluring soft rose of her mouth, and the contrast of the darker color of her eyebrows to the golden luster of her hair.

Good God, Colton thought with amused self-disgust. What was he doing? Poetic comparisons and lascivious thoughts while sitting in his private box at the opera were not at all in his character.

He forced his attention to the stage. Or at least he tried.

It seemed like forever before the music ended, the applause ceased, and the chaotic exodus from the theater began. Taking advantage of his superior height to spot the appropriate opening, Colton escorted his wife outside as fast as possible to avoid both gossip over her attire and—if he were honest with himself—any other males having the chance to feel similar appreciation for her undeniable charms. The usual after-performance pleasantries to friends they did encounter were administered as expediently as possible, and he waited impatiently to retrieve her cloak. He swirled it around her shoulders with a deep sense of relief.

"My carriage, please," he said in a clipped tone to a footman who bowed and apparently caught the urgency in his voice, for the young man practically ran to order it.

"Are you in a hurry?" Brianna asked.

Her question sounded innocent enough, he thought warily as he stood waiting for the vehicle to be brought around, but he wasn't sure it was. "I don't care to wait in an endless queue," he lied.

"It does get tedious," she agreed, slipping the wrap from her shoulders just enough to expose the view he wanted covered. "My, it is a warm evening, isn't it?"

He was certainly sweating, and he wasn't completely sure it was the temperature outside causing the discomfort.

Once their carriage arrived, Colton helped Brianna in and then settled himself on the opposite seat, rapping sharply on the roof to signal the driver.

In the shadowed interior of the coach, with her cloak open so the sumptuous flesh that nearly spilled from the front of her gown glimmered pale, Brianna looked more tempting than ever. Clearing his throat, he said, "Did you enjoy the production, my dear?"

"Yes." Her voice was hushed and she gazed at him from under her long lashes in a provocative way he'd never seen before. With every breath she took, her breasts threatened to burst free from the inadequate confines of her gown. "Did you like it?"

He had been riveted. Was still riveted. Oh, hell, hadn't she just asked him a question?

It was only polite to answer it.

"The view was glorious," he said dryly, giving up any attempt to hide his salacious interest. "And, yes, I thought the opera itself diverting."

She smiled, looking nothing like the young ingénue he had married, but instead every inch an alluring, sensual woman. "If *I* can divert you in any way, please, fell free to indulge yourself. *Now* would be fine."

In some deep part of his mind it was irksome that she knew how she had unsettled him, but that part was not in control at the moment. Another part of his body was now in charge.

He didn't intend to move. After all, engaging in an indiscretion in a carriage was most undignified, but suddenly Colton did not care in the least. He reached over and scooped Brianna into his arms, settling back into his seat with her body draped across his lap. Lowering his head, he kissed her hungrily, his tongue exploring her mouth, tasting every sweet corner. She responded with equal abandon, her arms wrapping around his neck, her slender, voluptuous body pressing against him. Not releasing her mouth, he eased the cloth from one shapely shoulder and her bared breast filled his hand with a soft, supple weight.

Perfect.

Everything faded. The clattering of the wheels of the vehicle as it rolled along the cobbled street, the warm evening . . . everything except the hard throbbing of his cock. He could hear her erratic breathing when he finally broke the kiss and slid his mouth down the graceful length of her neck, his lips lingering for a moment at the point where her pulse beat fast and light. Brianna made a small sound as his thumb circled the luscious crest of her pink nipple, her head falling back against his shoulder. "Colton . . . oh, yes."

Her skin was soft, smooth, and infinitely female. His fingers deftly found the fastenings at the back of her gown, and it was around her waist in moments. Licking the enticing valley between her breasts, kissing her mounded flesh, sucking on her nipples until they were erect and tight, he could feel his lovely wife's arousal in the way she clung to him and whispered his name.

The ducal carriage had nice wide seats, something he hadn't particularly appreciated before. "I cannot believe I am doing this but God help me, Brianna, I have to have you now," he said raggedly, laying her down on the seat.

"I want you too." Her hair had loosened and it framed her face in a silken tumble, her shoulders ivory in the dim light, her naked breasts tight and quivering with the motion of the vehicle. He thought he would cease to breathe when she reached down to pull up her skirts above her waist, baring long, lovely legs in their silk stockings and garters. Her pubic hair was a small golden triangle between her white thighs, and as he discarded his coat and unfastened his breeches, she parted her legs in graphic erotic invitation.

So hot with urgent need that he felt like he might combust at any moment, Colton accepted gladly, jerking at the fastenings of his breeches. Freeing his pulsing erection, he lowered himself over his wife's sprawled, half-dressed body, adjusting himself between her open thighs. One hand braced on the upholstered seat, he guided his rigid cock to her entrance, finding her wet and accommodating to his penetration. Brianna clutched his shoulders as he thrust inside her body, a low moan coming from her throat.

It was so good, he thought in feverish pleasure, not even bothering to caution her to be quiet. The idea of his driver overhearing them make love would normally have appalled him, but at that moment, he just didn't care. Withdrawing, he pushed back inside her tight passage with long strokes, the pumping of his lower body matching the swaying motion of the carriage.

Brianna arched to meet him, her hips lifting for each penetration, her eyes shut, long lashes dark against her flushed cheeks. The sharp bite of her fingernails through the fine lawn of his shirt increased as the rhythm escalated, and Colton was startled to realize she was going to climax so quickly, without any other stimulation. A muffled scream rang out as she arched frantically and her inner muscles began to ripple and tighten.

It sent him right over the edge. Pushing deep, he erupted with such intensity that his body shook even though he held himself still, the rapture taking him prisoner, holding him as he flooded her with his seed and groaned her name.

When he could finally breathe again, he registered two things: The first was that his gorgeous wife smiled up at him in a way that could be described only as triumphant. The second was that the vehicle they occupied in a state of scandalous near-undress was coming to a halt.

"Damnation," Colton muttered in disbelief. Had he actually just ravished his wife in a moving carriage like some randy adolescent?